THANK YOU FOR READING:

Looking for all of J.R. Wilson's novels? Scan the QR code bellow!

Or Check out:
https://www.amazon.com/stores/J.R.-Wilson/author/B0DHLN777K

To stay updated on the release of future books in the series and more books by J.R. Wilson, follow his Amazon author page.

BLOOD AT BLACK SPUR

A NEW MEXICO WESTERN

J.R. WILSON

Blood At Black Spur

CHAPTER 1

New Mexico Territory, 1880

The familiar clink of spurs echoed from the boardwalk not twenty feet from me. The bootfalls of the two men were shuffling and uneven, either from too much drink or from trying to avoid the more rickety planks.

This mountain town must've risen and fallen faster than most around here. Only three solid buildings had managed to go up, but the townsfolk had been confident enough in the surrounding mines to lay twice as much boardwalk as they ended up needing. Now there wasn't a soul left here, but there were still several ragged tents dotted around the area. All of them were dusty, half-buried in dirt, and badly faded from the relentless, high desert sun.

I squinted against the fading light of it now. The big orange sun cast a warm glow over the remains of this deserted town, even as it promised a break from the heat at last. Dust blew in from the valley below, and every now and then, a deep black raven cawed and took off toward the setting sun.

My focus was on the two men, though. I was hunkered down behind an overturned barrel at the back of the ruined saloon. The front windows and doors were all busted out, so getting in here was easy enough, but there was plenty of broken glass and wood scattered around to make it difficult to stay quiet about it. The cast of the light blaring right into the place didn't help out, but I'd timed things perfectly enough to know that wouldn't be an issue when the time came to strike.

I'd been closing in on the Hobbs brothers for three weeks now, ever since they left Magdalena. I'd thought I had them out near Cañada Alamosa, but they'd lit out of there fast after robbing the shabby mercantile.

This time, I'd spent all of yesterday up in the cactus-infested hills behind this town just to be sure I'd finally cornered the pair and knew their setup.

It was them alright. Dirty Neal had a crooked right leg, so his boot turned in at a jarring angle on that side. Skeet was just about as wiry as a man could be, but he was taller than most, with a scraggly black beard and no pinky on his left hand.

I shifted and looked between the planks of the broken barrel as the clanking of their spurs drew closer and closer.

Their shadows shuffled into the ruined saloon with heavy sighs and juicy spits.

They cut a pretty pathetic silhouette against the fading sun, but I'd learned long ago not to let a man's appearance sway me. Just about everyone way out in the wilder parts of the country was mostly skin and bones, but these two were more than just a pair of drifters down on their luck.

They were wanted for over a dozen murders.

There were a handful of stagecoach robberies and petty crimes thrown in over the last few years, too, but their main line of business involved murdering decent, hardworking men while they were out tending to their stock. Then holing up at their ranches and using their women up as long as they pleased.

I steadied my hold on my chambered 1873 Winchester

as the Hobbs brothers started bickering about the state of the saloon.

"Them five bottles won't hold for long," the tallest brother, Skeet, said before hacking a few times and washing it down with what looked like a battered bottle of whiskey.

"We'll move on in a day or two," the older brother, Dirty Neal, said.

He shuffled almost out of my line of sight, but I could hear the scraping and his grunt of effort as he sat down against a wall. Then he hissed as I watched him pull his boot from the foot on his crooked leg, prop the leg up on a bedroll, and let out a long sigh.

"Should only be a day's ride from here." Skeet spat again and wiped his lips on his dirty sleeve.

"Yeah, well, it's not goin' nowhere," Dirty Neal said.

"Never said it was," Skeet shot back before he scowled and made his way over to pass his lame brother the bottle of whiskey.

Any minute now, they'd set their gun belts aside and turn in for the night. I wasn't going to risk making a move until I was sure they couldn't draw too quick. That was why I hadn't picked them off yesterday, or the moment they walked in.

Five dead bounty hunters had all tried and failed to bring the Hobbs brothers in. Their sad tales were littered across Texas and most of the eastern half of New Mexico Territory. I wouldn't be joining them anytime soon, though.

The Hobbs brothers certainly looked like a pair of washed-up shadows, with hollows under their eyes, and long, gaunt faces. But they were quicker than they had any right to be. Quick and ruthless.

Men like this didn't have souls left. They had rotted minds, ragged bodies, and the kind of drive only a starved and beaten beast usually musters. Their deadened eyes and careless gaits spoke of years and years of pilfering and killing as they pleased, and their reaction times were too well-honed.

But they'd also gotten too comfortable out here.

I'd been tailing them long enough to know they'd rather chew tobacco than eat, and they'd rather drink than sleep all night. That much was clear from the state of the camp-sites they'd moved on from. They were tired, and they'd worn themselves ragged trying to get through Emory Pass before the Apache could get them. Now, they were drying out in the high desert sun, and they didn't think anyone would follow them way out here.

They never figured a man like me was after them.

I'd been tracking filth like them for the better part of the last five years, and the ten before that had been more of the same, just on a simpler track. Any bounty was a good one when the West needed so much cleaning up, but most places could scrape together enough men to see to the lower crowd these days.

It was evil like that of the Hobbs brothers that I wanted to cleanse from this earth. I didn't mind taking the long way around, or going without for days if necessary. I didn't mind the long stretches of solitude that some men just couldn't abide, and I certainly didn't mind biding my time through the heat of the day or the frigid cold of the night.

If another soul was saved from having to come face to face with wretches like these, then it was well worth the effort.

And tonight, I'd see to it that the Hobbs brothers left this world alone at last.

A loud scuffing sound broke clear as day through the building as Skeet rooted around behind the bartop. He must've come up dry, because he cursed and kicked an over-turned table halfway across the room.

"Not a damn thing left here," he growled.

"Sit down and clam up," the older brother spat. "You been nothing but ornery for the last month, and I'm just about done listening to it."

"Should've been to Silver City a month ago," the taller

man grumbled before I heard him drop his long body down on the floor.

"Oh, you'll last just fine," his brother sighed. His next gulp of whiskey squelched through the air as the sun finally dipped beneath the horizon. "Besides... you got all those memories of that sweet widow up in San Juan to keep you plenty occupied."

Two filthy snickers broke out as I clenched my jaw tight.

"Yeah," Skeet drawled. "She was a lovely bit of flesh, wasn't she? Soft and white all over. Well, 'til she started goin' red."

"Yeah, it's too bad she was spent so soon." Dirty Neal shifted, and I heard the bottle changing over to his brother's callused hand. "You gotta go easier, you wasted the last three having all your fun. I wasn't done with my share, that's for sure."

The smacking of lips on a bottle was joined with another caw from a raven somewhere in the gathering night.

"They got testy." Skeet's already gravelly voice took on a husky tone that brought the taste of bile to my tongue. "Women like that don't have no right to get testy. Ought to just keep still and..."

He let out a hideous, mocking moan that sent his brother into howling laughter. Several ravens startled and took flight out back, but the sudden rush of movement didn't make me flinch.

I kept drawing steady breaths in and out as the men laughed lewdly and recounted their hideous ventures to one another like old war stories.

Not that these men knew anything of war. They'd been preying on innocent wives from the moment I, and thousands of men just like me, took up our muskets and rode forth.

The now empty bottle of whiskey was suddenly sent flying toward the wall. The shattering was joined by the blessed sound of the men's gun belts finally unbuckling and clunking to the floorboards.

Good. I was worn out on listening to the vile pair cackle and spit all over the place. I waited just another moment until Dirty Neal started whining again about his brother hogging their spoils, but then I moved.

I'd cleared the glass around me as best I could in the short time I had to settle into my spot behind the barrel, but that gave me exactly two steps of silence.

The heel of my boot ground down on a shard of glass as I made it around the corner, and I pulled the trigger on the Winchester a split second later.

That one crunch of glass was enough notice. I managed to bury a bullet in Skeet's chest while his hand was already reaching toward his pistol, but Dirty Neal was up and running. I do mean running, too, no matter how bad his crooked leg was. The man took three quick strides and flung himself out a broken window while my next bullet struck the wall just a few inches behind his heel.

Skeet was twitching and gasping. His wiry body had slumped sideways, away from his gun belt, but I sent a swift second bullet into his heart before I ran for the front of the saloon.

Outside, the blue dusk had gathered fast, but I knew where they'd stowed their horses, so I didn't break stride. I tore off down the boardwalk and to the side of the saloon. I stopped short just in time to avoid a bullet. Then I ducked as I slid around the corner.

Dirty Neal was halfway onto his saddle when he saw me and pulled the trigger again. His shot would've struck me, too, if his horse wasn't huffy about the rough job he was doing at mounting up.

I fired the Winchester, and he screamed like a wailing cat as his forearm tore open. He dropped with a heavy thud to the dirt, but his horse wasn't between us for long.

It reared up and brayed as it took off galloping down the street, and the second horse took to stomping wildly around the wailing man by its hooves. I lunged to the side and ducked behind a gnarled juniper shrub, and I snaked the muzzle of my rifle through the branches as another rogue bullet screamed past me and into the wooden siding of the saloon.

Dirty Neal was on his socked feet again and wrestling with the last horse. Its reins were loose, and its patience was worn thin. Meanwhile, the man was trying to scramble onto it with only one good arm, a handful of pistol, and not a chance in the world.

The moment his head cleared the saddle, I took aim, pulled the trigger, and tore open the meat of his neck.

The horse took off as quick as the last. He left a plume of dust behind him as he went, and he left the man splayed in the dirt with blood quickly rushing from the holes I'd given him.

I came out from behind the shrub to see his pistol had landed several feet away from his jolting body.

I took my time strolling over to him.

The air in this dusty, old, abandoned place suddenly felt cleaner. Fresher. I took a deep breath of the evening breeze as I cocked the lever on my Winchester. Then I came to a slow stop and looked down on Dirty Neal Hobbs.

His bulging eyes found me, and they were already glassing over. He was clutching wildly at his bloody throat, but the dirt beneath him was drenched with the stuff already. He had only a handful of breaths left to him on this earth.

"Who- who ar–" he gurgled, but his throat couldn't quite form the rest.

I grinned down at the man, knowing every wicked thing he'd ever done had brought him right here, to this moment, laying in the dirt at my boots.

"The name's Jesse Callahan," I said as I brought the muzzle of my rifle up and aimed straight for his heart. "Now, don't get testy. You just stay still while I send you straight to Hell."

My finger clenched, and the crack of the Winchester split the violet dusk. The last of the ravens in the trees took off and scattered in every direction, and a nice cool breeze blew in from the plains to ease the sweat on my neck.

I smiled a little to myself.

Yes. The world felt much cleaner now.

I couldn't undo all the sinful, hateful acts these two men had inflicted on others, but they were certainly done now. And that was something at least.

I left the bodies where they lay once I'd checked that the wiry Skeet Hobbs was good and dead. Then I went around the back of the saloon, climbed up into the hills, and wound my way to my own campsite.

Birdy was waiting for me, just as quiet as she always was when I went to work. She tossed her mane at the sight of me and let out a low, affectionate nicker. I came over to the tree I'd tied her to and stroked her chestnut neck.

"Told you I'd be back before nightfall," I said in a soothing tone.

She nickered again, and I thought it was a little more pointed this time.

I chuckled. "It's twilight, Birdy. That doesn't count as late. Where are your brothers, hmm?"

I looked around and found the two mules lolling not fifteen feet away. I'd only had the pair for the few weeks I'd been tracking the Hobbs brothers, but I'd already learned that they didn't need any tying up at times like this. As long as Birdy stayed put, they stayed put. Which sure bothered Birdy to no end.

My old mare made no secret of the way she felt about the boys. She'd tried taking a bite out of both of them more times than I could count. They were growing on me, though. They were a docile and steadfast set, and they required even less than old Birdy did. They also put up with her attitude better than most would. I was considering keeping them even after they helped me haul my most recent bounties to Silver City.

I clicked my tongue twice, and the two mules turned and slowly picked their way through the shrubs and ocotillo cactus to join me. Birdy protested in earnest now, letting out a sharp whinny of warning, but they didn't pay her any mind.

"See that?" I said and stroked her neck a few more times. "You might as well make a friend or two, Birdy. No sense being the snippy one of the group. It don't look good on you."

My campsite had been packed and ready well before I'd hunkered down behind the busted barrel, so I stowed my Winchester in its saddle ring, untied the mare, and grabbed the leads of the two mules. Then the four of us slowly headed down the hill and back into the deserted town. It was almost dark by the time I pulled Dirty Neal's body onto the boardwalk alongside his brother, but I could see well enough.

I set to seeing what kind of weapons these two had to offer.

Each brother had a camp knife on him, and they each came with a pair of pistols. Dirty Neal's 1851 Colt Navys were pretty well cleaned and came with forty-two .36 caliber rounds. He also had an 1861 Springfield that had seen better days and was fresh out of ammunition. Skeet's pair of 1858 Remingtons were in much worse condition than my own, and he was just about out of .44 cap and balls for them. This didn't surprise me much. His Barlow was almost rusted beyond use, too, so I left it in his pocket.

Other than that, the brothers had nothing but a grimy pack of playing cards, a few small plugs of tobacco, and about nine dollars between them. I never warmed up much to tobacco, so I left that and the playing cards where I'd found them.

I stowed the men's weapons, ammo, and money in the spare pack I kept on one of my mules. Then I slung Dirty Neal over the back of him, and Skeet was folded over the other like a long, loose blanket.

"Might as well get some miles under us before we turn in," I told the trio. "I'd rather not sleep where the swine have."

I took the two leads of the mules and held them loosely in my left hand while I mounted up. Then I let Birdy take us out of town. About five miles later, we stopped and bedded down for the night beside the river. We were outside San Lorenzo, but I knew the area wasn't the sort that could provide the payment I needed, so the next morning, we continued winding our way down through the rugged mountains and toward the west.

I thought about what my next conquest might be now that I'd finally caught up with the Hobbs brothers, and as usual, wondered whether I should finally retire my gun and get another farm going. Maybe somewhere way out here. But mostly I watched the dense, tall pines slowly give way to scraggly juniper as the craggy mountain cliffs eased into rolling, rounded mounds. I watched the magpies swooping in and out on dark blue and white wings, and the lizards skittering out of our way for mile after mile.

I really never minded solitude like this. The long hours in the saddle and the few rests here and there flew by as natural as anything to me. Even before we'd gotten out of Emory Pass, when every turn brought us to the edge of sheer cliffs with the wild river racing below, I never minded the work. The challenges of the Black Range had only renewed my vigor and refreshed my bones after the longer desert stretches I'd endured further north. And that's how it always seemed to go. No matter where my travels took me, there was an ebb and flow to the dangers of the different regions in the West.

The mules particularly didn't seem to mind the lifestyle at all. They were some of the sturdiest beasts I'd ever had along with me, and twice as strong as the first few I'd bought for various jobs over the years.

Old Birdy was a different story. She was getting up in years, and while she didn't seem to mind the longer rides, I could tell they were taking their toll on her. Especially this last trek through the more rugged corners of the Black Mountains, when the rocky descents really tested her legs.

I didn't like to think about leaving her behind somewhere, even in a nice pasture. Not yet. We'd been together nine years, and I was hoping for a full ten at the very least. She was the closest thing to a friend or family I had way out here.

By sunset, we were passing the abandoned Chino mines, so I figured we were maybe ten miles from Silver City. I'd never been out this way before, but the men I'd spoken to in Magdalena recommended resting up just east of the city in Fort Bayard if I needed another stop. This would be better than risking any run-ins with the Apache after dark.

I'd already passed a few other mines and some ranches along this track, though, and the area hadn't posed a threat thus far. I also preferred to get Birdy bedded down in Silver City and really put her hoofs up for a few days at last, instead of hunkering down for one night and keeping moving the next morning.

When night fully fell, I was coming along the rolling fields and ridges of the upper foothills and making my way toward the mountain pass that would take me south to Silver City. That's when I saw the flames.

They were just starting to build, but they stuck out like a struck match in a closet.

I kicked Birdy into a trot, but it wasn't long before we were close enough to hear the screaming.

CHAPTER 2

We were as close to a gallop as we could get with the mules loaded down when we came to the large iron gate of a ranch I couldn't make out the name of. I only stopped long enough to tie the mules off at the gate, and then Birdy and I went racing up the dirt lane toward the growing flames and screams.

It was a woman screaming. The kind of scream that speaks of wrenching fear and sorrow.

I could see horses running wild all over the lane up ahead. Then I could make out that the fire had started in a large wooden stable that must have housed over a dozen of the beasts. The woman's shape became clear to me next as I neared the burning structure. She was scrambling to hold two children back from the fire, and it was as if none of the three even noticed the dozens of hooves racing around them.

The sight made my stomach drop and my heart bang as loud as the thrumming flames in my ears.

Birdy and I came to a pounding stop near the woman and children, who barely startled at our sudden arrival.

"Frank!" she screamed so loud that her throat sounded torn open from it.

"Ma'am, step back!" I urged as I leapt from my saddle and tried to keep Birdy still, but it was no use.

However many horses and foals had been in that stable had gone mad breaking their way out and through the fire. Birdy took right off with them, and I let her go. The flames were billowing into the night now, but there was a man in there. I tore my hat off and started pulling my gun belt off as I steeled myself for what needed to be done.

"Where was your husband when the flames started?" I yelled above the stampede.

The woman screamed the name 'Frank' again, and I took her arm to shake her a bit and get her attention.

"Where was he when the flames–"

"Behind the house!" she screamed without taking her teary eyes off the stable. "I heard arguing, and horses running back there. Then I saw the flames…"

She broke off as a strangled wail took over her body, and she clung to her frightened children as the fear wracked her body.

My mind was clear as day. The man had been behind the house, and an argument broke out. The house was at least three hundred feet away. There was a good chance her husband wasn't anywhere near this stable when the fire kicked up.

My hands rebuckled my gun belt as I started scanning the area. I caught sight of three men sprinting out of the darkness and straight into the wild, churning mass of panicked horses. Their eyes were blown wide open in worry and fear, and two of them went straight to work trying to direct the horses to an open pasture gate. They yelled in Spanish, and several horses immediately took notice.

"Mrs. Helena!" a third man yelled. He was dark-skinned and not quite fully dressed for work, but he clearly knew this family well. He caught the crying woman the moment she turned to him, and he let her bury her face against his chest as she screamed her husband's name once more.

Then his dark eyes landed on me and turned as hard as gunmetal.

"What happened?" he demanded.

"She says there was an argument out back behind the house," I told him. "I was on my way to Silver City when–"

I nearly bit my tongue from stopping so fast. I heard something. Far beyond the hammering flames and the horses who were gradually being funneled into the pasture.

There it was again.

Laughter, of all things. Wicked laughter.

I flipped around and whistled loud, and good old Birdy kept her head on straight. She peeled off from the panicked herd and thundered straight to me, and she wasn't even standing still when I lunged up onto her saddle.

"The stable can't be saved," I told the dark-skinned man as I grappled for my reins. "Get the horses under control and keep the woman back from the flames. I'll be back."

With that, I kicked Birdy into a full gallop and tore off past the stables. I rounded toward the side the house was on, and then I rode straight into the open ranchlands beyond.

That laugh was one I knew all too well. It was the howling, gleeful laugh of an evil man. A victory song of sorts, and it sent fire through my veins like nothing else in this world.

Once I was far enough from the glaring of the fire, my eyes began to adjust quickly. I made out three silhouettes first. Riders, and fast ones at that. Then three more spread out along the horizon, and the six men didn't slow down for anything. They were headed toward the mountains at a speed I couldn't hope to make up for, especially on old Birdy, and I narrowed my eyes as I let her ease up and slow down to a trot.

I found the body not twenty feet ahead.

Well, some of it.

A severed leg was the first bit I came across. It had a knotted rope tied around the ankle, and I swallowed back some bile as I realized what I was about to witness. I braced my mind and my stomach as I halted Birdy and dismounted. Then I slowly picked my way forward.

Sure enough, the torso of a man was strewn in a pile of brush. The other leg had managed to stay connected, but both arms had been wrenched off.

Six riders. Four ropes. That probably meant the other two riders were in charge of setting fire to the stables.

But why?

I'd seen plenty of horrors in the war, and plenty more in the fifteen years since. Especially out in areas like this where the Apache and Comanche warred fervently with any folks who settled near their lands.

This was something else entirely. I drew a deep breath before I squatted down to take a closer look at the man. He had a thick beard and a strong-looking face. Blood had dripped down heavily from his unruly hair line. It was clear he'd been struck hard near the temple, but he'd been brought out here on his back.

That could only mean they'd knocked the man unconscious before tying him up and delivering this sick and twisted punishment.

I stood back up and returned to Birdy.

Men didn't kill like this for no reason. This looked personal. This looked like a message.

I steered my mare back toward the flames. The structure of the stables had fully collapsed in by now, and all the horses were contained. The three men, who I now assumed must be the hired ranch hands here, were standing with the wife.

The widow.

The words made my heart clench as I slowed down and took in the sight of them.

The young boy, probably only eleven or twelve, covered in dirt and streaked in tears while he glared at the fire. The little girl, even younger than him, clinging as tight as possible to her mother's leg. The mother, face puffy with grief and eyes constantly streaming, but quietly now. She stood tall as she kept her arms around her children.

Behind them, the three men stood with their hats in their hands and their heads bowed.

I didn't want to join them. I didn't want to bring the news that would be worse– much, much worse– than what they already feared.

The dark-skinned man heard my approach before the others. His head snapped up, and he replaced his hat as he strode purposefully in my direction.

I dismounted a good distance from the family so our conversation could be a private one. He met me with that gun-metal stare and waited for me to speak first.

"Six riders," I told him as I busied myself pulling Birdy's reins up over her head. "They headed straight toward those mountains beyond the stable."

"Six?" His stare broke as the shock took over. "What would six men want with burning the Sanduskys' stables?"

"Wouldn't know," I told him, and I met his gaze head-on as I prepared to break the news. "The husband… did he have a beard? Kind of unkempt hair?"

He understood. The man removed his hat and let out a strong enough curse to make most folks gasp and turn the other way. He was fighting tears now, I could tell, and I looked away to give him his privacy.

His language had drawn the attention of the others. The wife struggled at first to remove her daughter from her leg, but she managed to hoist her into one of the ranch hands' arms before cutting a direct line toward us. The third ranch hand was right behind her.

The pair made it to us by the time the dark-skinned man had rearranged his expression to an unreadable one.

"What is it?" the woman demanded before turning to the man I'd been speaking with. "What's he say, Amos?"

"Where?" Amos asked me instead of responding to her.

"About two hundred yards that way." I gestured in the direction I'd found the husband's body.

"We'll go look to confirm it's him," Amos said with a motion for the other ranch hand to follow him toward the horses.

"I'll look." The wife's voice was as hard as slate as she turned on her heel.

I swiftly stepped forward to stop her.

"Ma'am," I tried. "With all due respect, it's not a sight–"

"Don't all due respect me," she snapped. Her tear-stained face was fierce as she turned on me, and even in her grief, I could tell she was a truly beautiful woman. And a stubborn one. "I will see my husband. No matter what state he's in, he's... he's my husband. Mine..."

Her voice broke at these last words, and her face pinched as a fresh flood of tears spilled down her cheeks.

Neither the two ranch hands nor I found any words of protest. The woman would clearly have her way, and she was right. It wasn't our place to tell her otherwise. In the eyes of God, those two belonged to one another, and she wouldn't leave him out there without looking at him one last time.

I just wished she wouldn't.

I stepped back to let her by. The ranch hands were quick to pull three horses from the pasture, and they didn't bother tacking them up. They assisted the woman in mounting bareback, and the three rode off with ease into the darkness beyond the flames.

The third man was still holding the little girl tight in his arms, with the young boy beside him and watching everything that had just transpired. The boy's eyes were sharp and still glaring against his grief. I sent him a short nod before turning toward the lane with Birdy's reins in hand.

I didn't want to think about the state of the new widow when she saw what I'd seen out in that field. Just looking her in the eye cut me clear in half. I knew her grief too well. Me and that grief had been far too familiar for too many years for me to open my arms back up to it. I'd managed it well for a while now, but I'd learned it was best with things like this to just keep moving. Keep looking forward. Don't dwell longer than the heart can stand it.

I found the mules right where I'd tied them. They looked shaken for once. I gave them a couple clicks so they'd know it was me coming, and they each let out a braying sort of whimper in recognition.

"It's alright, boys," I soothed and stroked them down for a moment. "We'll get you up to the house now. See what we can do about some water."

Birdy actually restrained herself from biting the boys upon greeting. She just let me quietly lead the three of them as I took my time returning up the lane. The fire flashed in my eyes the whole way, and I did what I always did. I kept moving. Kept looking forward.

The dark lands around me seemed deadly quiet, like every creature knew what had taken place here. The moon was only just now coming up over the hills to my right, and the cool air smelled charred with smoke.

They'd found the body, and there was no need to ask if it was the husband. The sorrow on the ranch hands' faces said all I needed to know. The wife had already gone into the house with her children. Only a single window glowed with light.

The two Spanish-speaking ranch hands were watching over the fire and pouring buckets of water over the surrounding grasses. The flames looked content to feast on the remains of the stables, but I tied my group off and quickly set to helping out. We spent over an hour filling buckets and dumping them out.

Amos met me near the pasture gate once he called us off. The other two took up their posts watching over the flames for the night, but the black man eyed the dead bodies slung over my mules with interest.

"They're my bounty." I jutted a thumb toward the Hobbs brothers. "Like I said, I was heading to Pinos Altos. That far from here?"

"Not quite three miles," Amos replied. "But you can bunk here tonight."

"I wouldn't impose," I said. "Not at a time like this. If I could just get some water for my–"

"It's no imposition." He looked at me more openly now. "We're grateful you rode out here, and sorry for what you witnessed. Come this way. We've got some troughs of water near the bunkhouse, too."

I nodded my thanks and led my mare and mules into the moonlit darkness to the right of the house. The bunkhouse was farther than I'd expect it to be, but it was nice and quiet, and tucked among a few tall pines. I realized the ample shade they provided was probably the reason for the positioning of the structure. It was a kindness for the man of this ranch to have considered, and in a quiet way, it spoke well of him.

Amos helped me relieve my beasts of their burdens. Then I set them loose in the small paddock beside the bunkhouse. Once I'd settled my things in the back corner of the loft, I called down to Amos. He was moving a few of his own belongings out of the way of the ladder for the night.

"How far is Silver City from here?" I asked.

"Depending on your trail, seven miles or so," he replied.

"I'll go there in the morning," I said as I shifted back and got more comfortable. "It's probably better I stopped for the night, anyhow. Heard there was a lot of strife out here with the Indians."

"There was," Amos said. "Still is down south, but Fort Bayard keeps the peace alright to the east of us, and of course we've got the cross doing so from the north now."

"Cross?"

"Managed to reach a truce with the Apache over those mountains to the northeast," Amos explained. "As long as that cross is up on the peak, the truce with Pinos Altos holds. Has so far, at least."

"Huh." I shrugged to myself. "That's a way to go about things."

Silence stretched between us for a few minutes, but as I replayed the sight of those six men riding and laughing with glee into the night, I cleared my throat.

"If I was to ride straight out beyond… behind the stables," I said.

Amos' tone was harder when he responded, so I knew he was thinking of the six men, too.

"If they rode straight that way, they'd hit Pinos Altos," he said quietly.

"I thought so." I nodded to myself. "Pinos Altos it is, then."

CHAPTER 3

The sun had climbed just above the horizon when I finished saddling Birdy and gathered the boys and their loads. The day had dawned bright blue, and the ranchlands that sprawled out from the bunkhouse were a lively green and dusty orange that pleased the eye.

This was one of the finest plots of land I'd ever seen.

The dirt here had a few sections with a strong red hue that sprawled like ribbons through the hills, and the prickly pears were in bloom, so splashes of pink and yellow dotted the landscape all around. Everywhere I looked, mountains rose up in layers on the distant horizon, with rolling and rugged lands all in between.

As for the ranch itself, things were well-kept right down to the fence posts. The house was two stories and solidly built, with white siding and a large, covered porch out front. Two great chimneys jutted up from either end of the roof, and a proper kitchen garden looked about ready to swallow up the left side of the house any day now.

It looked like a genuine home, especially with the young boy sitting on the front steps and watching the horses in one of the pastures.

The smoldering remains of the stables were like a black stain on the picturesque place.

I led my group across the grassy stretch toward the house. The day was already heating up this morning, and the stench of smoke still hung thick in the air. The breeze was promising, though, so I reckoned it'd clear out by this evening if they were lucky.

As I neared the lane, I saw one of the Spanish-speaking ranch hands raking through the charred remains of the stables. Another was hauling hay to the feeding troughs in the pastures. I didn't see Amos anywhere, but I assumed he too was busy working already.

I moved to tie Birdy at the post near the front of the house and was hoping to speak with the wife before taking my leave, but the boy shot to his feet the moment he saw me coming.

Now, he stood on the top step with his thumbs hooked in the waist of his pants, and his scrawny frame drawn up as tall as he could manage.

"Hold there, mister," he said in what must have sounded like a voice of authority to him. He raised a hand to keep me where I was. Then he eyed the bodies slung over the mules. "What you got there?"

"Couple of bandits," I said and forced back a smile. "Why?"

The boy looked deeply intrigued. However, he kept his 'man of the house' act up pretty well, considering.

"You a bad man?" he asked without preamble.

I looked down and let the brim of my hat conceal the grin that broke out while I finished tying Birdy off.

"Would I tell you if I was?" I countered. When I looked back up, the boy's bravado was a little deflated.

"No, I s'pose not," he called back. "I s'pose you'd lie straight through your teeth… Or not. Maybe you'd be so bad, you'd tell me outright how evil you are."

His small brow crinkled in confusion. He shifted his

weight and looked like he was warring with the biggest questions in the world right now.

"Well, where's that leave us, then?" I asked.

"I'm thinkin' on it," he said and crossed his arms. "Give me a minute."

"I can do that," I chuckled lightly.

So the two of us took to standing just like that-- far apart, silent, with our arms crossed, and stuck in a stalemate. Luckily, the lady of the house came out and freed us both from the predicament. She had the little girl propped on one hip, and she looked between us with some confusion.

"Russel, are you bothering this man?" she asked her son.

"No, ma'am." He uncrossed his arms and fixed his posture again. "I was just as-ascer... ass..."

"Ascertaining?" she asked patiently.

"Yeah, ascertaining if this man was a no-good criminal," he replied.

The mother let out a sigh and stroked his cheek. "Thank you, now please get to your chores."

"But he's got dead bodies over there," the boy scoffed.

"He... what?" The wife looked my way. The daughter looked my way.

I removed my hat and offered her a polite nod by way of greeting.

"Good morning, ma'am," I said. "My name is Jesse Callahan. Your ranch hands were kind enough to–"

"Put you up for the night, yes, I know, I told them to do it," she cut in. "Why do you have dead bodies on my property?"

"I'm a bounty hunter," I said.

Her eyes narrowed. It looked like she hadn't slept well at all, but nevertheless, her strawberry-blonde hair was swept up into a loose, neat bun. Her dark gray dress didn't dull her blue eyes at all, and the darkness hadn't been fooling me last night. She was a very beautiful woman who'd clearly spent years working hard in the sun and still managed to have plenty of health and vitality about her. I figured she was about my age, maybe a little younger at thirty or so.

But the grief was like a veil around her, I could see it, even as she held herself tall and got right to business.

"Bounty hunter," she repeated with skepticism. "And you just happened to come upon our ranch last night?"

I blinked as I realized what she was starting to get at. I replaced my hat, held up a hand, and slowly reached into one of my saddlebags. It only took a little digging around to find the papers on the Hobbs brothers.

"May I?" I asked and gestured toward the papers.

The woman nodded curtly and took the few steps down from the porch. Her son was right on her heels, and he hovered close as I handed her the wanted papers.

I waited with my hands folded at my front while she read. Trouble was, her son's prying eyes were devouring the papers, too, and they suddenly bulged when he got to the list of known crimes.

The mother noticed. She sent him a sidelong glance, pursed her lips, and shifted so he couldn't see any more.

"Those the Hobbs brothers, then?" she asked when she'd finished.

"Yes, ma'am," I said. "I was on my way to Silver city with them. That's when I came across your ranch, I was trying to make it before the night got too far long."

"I see." She handed the papers back. "Well, good riddance to them. And thank you for your assistance, Mr. Callahan. I fear I can't properly express my gratitude to the full extent, but I am deeply, deeply grateful that you rushed up here when you did."

"It was no trouble at all, ma'am," I said.

"Mrs. Sandusky," she supplied. "Helena Sandusky."

I nodded. "I'll be on my way, I just wanted to ask if you'd like me to report all this to the local officials for you while I'm in town. I'm actually heading to Pinos Altos just now."

"Oh…" She looked toward the smoldering stables. "Yes. Yes, that would be a great help to me. The men are quite busy with the horses and the mess and… and the grave of course. Amos found a nice spot out back that he's fixing up for… for my husband."

Her blue eyes welled with fresh tears, but she didn't let them spill over. She blinked rapidly and cleared her throat as she hoisted the small girl higher on her hip. I couldn't see the little girl's face, she had it buried against her mama's neck, but the son dropped his eyes for the first time since I'd walked up. He was glaring at the toes of his boots now.

"You only have the three men working here?" I asked.

"Yes, sir," she replied as she straightened up a bit. "Amos, Abel, and Mateo. They're good men. Might as well be family. Amos has been with us for about eleven years now. The two brothers for maybe eight or nine. Hardworking men. Real friendly with my husband, too. He admired those boys quite a lot. They've done good work for us training the horses as my husband likes. He was particular about their handling."

"I see," I said with a nod. "I don't suppose you can think of anyone who might've wanted to do… what happened last night?"

Every muscle in her beautiful face tensed, and her blue eyes became distant. I hated to know she was recalling what she'd witnessed out in that field, but I had to ask. The violence was just too much to be a chance encounter with some rogue banditos.

Mrs. Sandusky didn't seem able to form words. She gave a tight shake of her head and said nothing more.

"I'm truly sorry," I told her. "I'll be on my way."

I turned to go, but then she called me back.

"Mr. Callahan, may I impose on your kindness just a moment longer?" she asked. "You see, my husband's sister is up in Colorado Territory at the moment. Leadville. Although, it's just Colorado now, isn't it?"

"I believe so," I replied.

The woman nodded. "Would you mind sending a telegram to her while you're in town?"

"Not at all," I said. "I've got plenty of time."

She hurried into the house to write her letter. I was left alone again with the boy, who'd stopped glaring at his toes. Now, he was eyeing the bodies on my mules, and even when I took a small step to the side, he just bent his neck to look right around me at them.

"They shoot at you at all?" he asked me.

I nodded. "Yes, they did."

"You shot 'em back, though, huh?" he asked.

"Yes," I said with a grin. "That's about how that went."

Russel let out a whistle and shook his head. "Well, good riddance to them."

He sounded so much like his mother that I had to bite back a laugh. He had her same blue eyes, but his hair was dark and unruly like his father's. I hoped he found a way to deal with his grief properly, but for now, I was glad to see he was able to let other thoughts occupy his young mind.

"I'm wicked fast with a revolver," he informed me.

He met my eyes and nodded proudly, and I nodded right back.

"That's an important skill to have," I said. "How old are you?"

"Twelve, how old are you?"

"Thirty-five," I chuckled.

"Huh…" He chewed on this for a bit. "You might be faster than me, then. But I'm pretty fast. I don't shoot nobody for no reason, that's what bad men do, but I could if the situation ar-arised? Ar…"

"Arose," I offered.

"That's right, arose." He shrugged. "Mama makes me learn reading and spelling. She says a good man knows how to speak well and command respect through words instead of violence. I guess. But it's real tiresome after a while. I'm better with a revolver."

I smiled. "Me, too. Though I wouldn't use one to command any kind of respect."

"No, sir," he agreed. "That's what fools and banditos do. We Sandusky men stand for more than that."

"I'm sure you do," I said.

Russel started glaring at his boots again. He let out a loud sniff and wiped his nose on his dirty arm, and his voice wavered a little when he spoke again without looking up.

"That's a mighty fine rifle you got over there, too," he told the dirt. "Lever-action, huh?"

"Yes, it's the 73 model, but it's as good as the day I bought it," I said as I glanced at the Winchester in Birdy's saddle ring. "I've got a 76 model that's better at a longer range, but I find the '73 suits me just fine in most cases."

He looked up now and was a little more composed. "I think I'll have me a real nice one when I'm older. I hear Smith & Wesson makes a real handsome lever-action. Ain't too easy to find down here, though."

"I hear the same." I smiled a bit, and I had to admit, I was impressed with the young man's intelligence, but then his mother returned then with a small piece of paper in hand.

She'd folded the letter neatly in half, and I took it and pocketed it without compromising her privacy.

"Thank you, again," she said, a little out of breath.

"As I said, it's no trouble at all, Mrs. Sandusky," I told her.

She shifted the little girl to her other hip and held out the fee I'd need to send the telegram, but I waved her away.

"That's not at all necessary," I assured her.

"But–"

"I'll be making plenty on my bounty," I said. "One telegram won't inconvenience me at all."

She looked unsure, but she pocketed the money all the same.

"Well… May God bless you during your travels, Mr. Callahan." She held out a hand to shake mine, and I was impressed by her sturdy grip.

I offered a hand to Russel as well, and his eyes lit up as he vigorously shook it.

Then I took my leave of the family and mounted up on Birdy. We led the boys back down the lane and toward the large iron gate. It was an impressive structure that must have cost a small fortune to have made. The lettering at the top said 'Black Spur Ranch' without any fancy details or anything like that. Just a modest, well-made nod to the work that went on here.

I turned toward the northwest and rode into the mountains for an hour or so at a slow and steady pace. Birdy seemed positively chipper, and I couldn't blame her. Either Abel or Mateo, I wasn't sure which, had started brushing her out before I'd even woken up. They'd complimented her coat in a thick accent before heading to do their work, and they weren't wrong. She looked almost fancy with the wind rippling through her chestnut mane and tail.

"Well, don't you look nice, Birdy," I told her after we'd passed several miles with her holding her head up high. "Boys, tell your sister she looks nice today…"

I turned in my saddle, but the mules only looked at me and carried on walking without a grunt.

"See that?" I sighed as I gave her a few affectionate pats. "Mules don't forgive and forget too easy, Birdy. I tried to tell you that."

The old mare nickered without much concern.

"That right there is not a gracious attitude," I said. "One day, you're gonna wish you were nicer to your brothers, you mark me on that."

The four of us carried on like this until we started passing more homes dotted around the ridges and valleys with goats, cows, and all manner of livestock penned in. Soon, we were passing roads lined with dense, tall pines and leading up to mines with dozens of men coming and going with wagons. Another half a mile brought us to a long line of barbed fencing that held back plenty of burros and oxen for hauling.

The end of this fencing brought us straight into the main thoroughfare of Pinos Altos, and I was impressed by the size of the place. I'd heard it sprang up when the big mining boom started, and there was no denying it had profited very well in the last couple of decades.

The boardwalks lined buildings made primarily of wood, but some of stone, and the wide lane was packed with freight wagons and burro trains getting ready to haul. Dust kicked up all over the place under the hooves and wheels of the busy mining town, and men and their ladies strolled in and out of the many shops and saloons without seeming to mind the constant bustle around them.

I drew the usual stares as I rode on. I didn't doubt these people had seen their fair share of bodies being brought into town, but I'd learned it didn't much matter how large or rough a place was. People always turned and eyed the wares of a man like me.

Most of the women then eyed me up like they wanted to know just what kind of man did work like this. Their appraising eyes never seemed too disappointed by what they found, and their men were equally impressed. Hats tended to tip in my direction wherever I went, and I returned the gesture in kind.

Of course, I did make a point of trying not to appear too rough around the edges, and this helped. It had been weeks since I'd passed through an honest-to-God town, though. My shirt was badly torn near the elbows from my day spent up in the cactus-infested hill behind the abandoned town, and my pants had seen much better days about a month or so before.

Still, the townsfolk here were made up of quite a lot of

miners and their families, so I looked put together enough. Especially compared to several men around here.

I reined Birdy in as I came to a group of such dirt-covered men smoking cigars outside the general store.

"Pardon me," I said. "Could you point me toward the Sheriff's office?"

"About eight miles south," a mostly toothless man said in a friendly tone. "The seat of Grant County is down in Silver City nowadays, friend. But we got ourselves a deputy. Down that end of the street."

He gestured with his cigar, and I thanked the man before continuing down the way I'd been headed.

I tied Birdy and the two mules outside the deputy's office, just in case they startled with all the wagons rattling by. Then I pulled my saddlebag off her, hefted it over one shoulder, and headed inside the small wooden building.

I found a man not much older than myself seated behind a desk with his boots up. He had a newspaper open in his hands, and he sat up and dropped his boots to the floor when I walked in.

"Can I help you?" he asked.

"Yes, my name's Jesse Callahan," I replied. "I assume you're the deputy around here?"

"Yes, sir," he said. "Deputy Wallace. What can I do for you, Mr. Callahan?"

"Well, Deputy Wallace, my first line of business is to report a murder and a fire."

The deputy sat up further now and promptly put his newspaper side.

"The murder of who?" he asked.

"A Mr. Sandusky," I answered. "Frank Sandusky. He lives about—"

"I know where he lives alright." The deputy had gone pale. "You must be mistaken, though. Frank Sandusky is a highly respected man around here. Are you sure that's the man you're reporting?"

"Yes, I am," I said. "I came here from the Black Spur Ranch by favor of Mrs. Helena Sandusky. A fire struck up in their stables last night, and Mr. Sandusky was found out in their field. Six men were fleeing the area at the time. They... used rather violent means of handling the man."

The Deputy slumped back in his chair with his jaw slack. He stared at me for nearly half a minute before licking his dry lips and shaking his head.

"Who in the world would murder Mr. Sandusky?" he said more to himself than to me. "And they burned the stables? You're sure?"

I nodded. "The six men I saw riding away were headed this direction. By my estimate, they would've gotten into town around about half past ten. Maybe eleven. Did any suspicious riders come around here near that time?"

The details seemed to snap him out of his daze. The deputy sat forward again, and he rubbed the sweat from his brow as he thought.

"Not that anyone's reported," he said. "This is a busy area, Mr. Callahan. Folks come and go quite often between here and Silver City, or the mines, or their homes. A lot of riders, a lot of strangers."

"I see." I scratched the back of my neck. "Well, that's what I've come to report. If anything can be done about this, I'm sure Mrs. Sandusky would be very grateful. She's quite upset about the situation."

"I'm sure she is," he said in his most professional tone yet.

Before he could fully gather himself, I continued on.

"My second line of business is that I've got a couple of wanted men outside." I slid my saddlebag off and found him the battered wanted papers.

"Bounty hunter, huh?" he asked.

"Yes, sir," I replied and handed the papers over.

He nodded and looked down, and for the second time since my arrival, his jaw went slack.

"The Hobbs brothers?" he blurted out. "You sure?"

I resisted the urge to be short with the man. But it did seem I was doing a lot of repeating myself in here.

"Yes."

He read the papers twice over without closing his mouth once. Then he folded them up and got up with some urgency.

"Well, let's see 'em, then." He grabbed his hat from the rack near the door and went outside.

I followed the man out, and the quickness in his step drew the attention of quite a few folks strolling down the street and standing on the boardwalks. I felt more than a dozen pairs of eyes on me as I led the deputy to my mules and brought him around to get a good look at both men. I'd taken care not to shoot them in the heads for this very reason. I wanted to be absolutely sure they were identifiable.

"Well, I'll be…" Deputy Wallace hunkered down close to each man, and he shook his head. "That's the Hobbs brothers, alright. Where'd you find them?"

"About a mile or so south of Emory Pass, holed up in a washed-up town in the mountains," I answered. "Said they were heading toward Silver City."

"That's a bit too close for my liking," he decided as he straightened up.

"Yes, but you don't have to worry about them now."

"Thanks to you." He smiled and stuck his hand out. "Pardon my manners, but I'd like to shake your hand, sir."

"No apology needed," I chuckled. "I've been after these two for some time, it feels good to finally turn them over."

"I bet it does," he said with a laugh of his own. "Come on into the office, we'll get the bounty handled right now."

"I'd like that."

The deputy was downright friendly now that he had the honor of settling the bounty for the famous Hobbs brothers.

He had a bounce in his step all the way to his desk. He spent a minute or so rifling through papers and muttering to himself, and then he returned to his desk with a wide smile on his face.

"Well, this sure is a new one for me," he chuckled. "Are you fine to stay around the area for another day or two?"

I furrowed my brow. "I suppose so. Why do you ask?"

"Well, those papers you brought in are out of date, I'm afraid." He didn't look at all apologetic about this. "Truth is, with a bounty as high as this, I won't be able to pay you all of it today."

My heart started to pound faster. I'd been excited to collect so much, but if there was more owed now, that'd make this the highest bounty I'd ever collected in fifteen years.

"Last I checked, six hundred and fifty was the total bounty on those two," I said slowly.

"Sure was," Deputy Wallace agreed. "And now, it's a whole eight hundred and fifty."

CHAPTER 4

I couldn't help the easy smile on my face as the deputy set himself to counting greenbacks.

Eight hundred and fifty dollars.

A man like me had absolutely no need of so much, but I'd always known that. Truth was, there was good money in my line of work. That's why I'd opened accounts in a few banks around Texas, New Mexico Territory, and even up in Colorado. Anywhere I'd returned to more than a couple times, really. I'd been fortunate enough to save up quite a lot to my name, and it had amounted to more than I truly needed for some time now.

But that didn't make this any less momentous.

Three weeks and sending those reckless, no-good, sinful men to where they belonged was certainly worth the price to me.

"So that's four hundred dollars there," the deputy said as he slid the first portion of my pay over to me. "And as per our agreement, the other four hundred and fifty dollars will be ready in two days' time."

"That sounds good to me," I said and stowed the money in my saddlebag. "I'll return in two days."

"It sure is an honor to pay it out," Deputy Wallace said in

earnest. "And if you please, you'll have to pardon my unprofessional behavior earlier, it's only… Mr. Sandusky is a very well-respected man around here. It's something of an honor having him so close to Pinos Altos."

"Is he involved with some of these mines, then?" I asked.

"No, sir, it's those horses." He seemed surprised I didn't know this. "Can't find a finer horse within a hundred-fifty miles of here. Maybe more. That herd he's got is all prime stock, and real well-trained, too. You can't buy yourself a Sandusky horse for less than two hundred dollars, and that's if he knows you personally. He doesn't know many people personally, either. He settled here some time ago, but he keeps to himself out there. That's why I just can't believe he'd be murdered. I'll have to take your official statement on that, by the way."

"I can do that." I nodded and hitched my saddlebag over one knee.

I gave the deputy every detail I could recount, and he took down every word. He looked sick to his stomach by the time we finished, and he slumped back in his seat as he shook his head sadly.

"That's just not right," he said. "Mr. Sandusky was a private man, but a good one by all accounts. I can't imagine someone would…"

He shook his head again.

"His wife didn't have any ideas as to who might have done this, either," I told him.

"Poor woman." He drew a deep breath and braced his elbows on the desk. "That's the worry now, I suppose. That herd is worth more than most cattlemen can claim around here. Now, horse rustlers would have to be pretty darn stupid to try and sell a stolen Sandusky horse. The branding on them is one of the most well-known in three counties. But criminals are rarely on the smart side."

"That is true," I said. "Do those three men who work for the Sanduskys guard the ranch as well?"

"Not to my knowledge," he said. "His three ranch hands come through town often. They seem like honest men, but they're not killers. They got a way with horses, and they're good at heart, but the truth is, the best thing they had to secure that ranch was Mr. Sandusky himself. Maybe that's changed in recent years, and he's gone and hired some more men. But I just can't think of anyone who'd want to harm him, not with how well-known he was, certainly."

"I see." I nodded with some concern.

The more I heard, the more suspicious I was.

For how respected this Mr. Sandusky was, it didn't sound like many people knew him. I'd have to ask around more to be sure. Either way, relying on a reputation was one thing, but I'd rarely heard of something like that keeping the peace altogether. It was more likely the man was a skilled gunman. Maybe he'd even fought in the war.

I was always one to hope for the best with things like this, but it was my job to consider much more than hearsay alone. And in my line of work, when violence like this took place, I had to ask the question: Did this man deserve the death he got, like so many people I hunted? Or was it the killers who were guilty?

"Well, I hope there's something that can be done," I said as I rose to my feet with my bag in hand.

"As do I." He stood too and came around the desk to walk me out. "Unfortunately, I don't have much jurisdiction out in the ranchlands, let alone beyond the town borders, but I'll be in touch with the sheriff down in Silver City, and I'll look into what I can."

"That's good to hear," I said as I stepped out. "Oh, and I've got a telegram to send. Could you point me in the right direction?"

"Post Office is about eight doors down that way, other side of the street," he replied.

"Thank you."

"No, thank you," he said and offered his hand. "I'm gonna need one more good handshake from the man who got those Hobbs boys, though."

"That I can do," I laughed and shook his hand.

A large crowd had gathered around my mules by the time we made our way over to haul the brothers into the office. Word had spread fast. Everywhere I looked, there was some bright-eyed woman with flushed cheeks and an admiring look for me. Then there were the men who thrust their hands out to shake mine, or pat my back, or just smile and stare like they were witnessing a true rarity.

Which they were. Plenty of criminals could be found all over the West, but desperados like these were thankfully few and far between.

Once I'd unloaded the pair of men and secured my saddlebag, I mounted Birdy and set off toward the Post Office. I would've left her and the boys tied where they were and walked instead, but I thought maybe the crowd would thin out if my group weren't sitting right where the Hobbs brothers had been just moments before.

I hitched the trio outside the post office and went inside. The head postman was a gray-haired man with a prominent belly who was seated at a small desk near the front window. He was sorting through letters while a kind-looking counter clerk chattered at him from her post at the center of the back wall. She wasn't an old woman by any means, but she'd earned a few wisps of silvery hair around her temples. She looked over as soon as I walked in, but she didn't stop talking to the older man until I reached her counter.

"Good morning, sir," she said with a bright smile. "How can I help you today?"

"I've got a telegram from Mrs. Helena Sandusky that she'd

like sent," I replied and pulled the letter from my pocket. "All the information you need should be in there."

The woman took the folded slip of paper, opened it, and smiled even brighter.

"Oh, Lucy!" she exclaimed. "My, I do miss her. Lucy Kimber, that's right, I heard she goes by a stage name now. I guess they just love her out in San Francisco. I wonder where she's performing up in Leadville. You don't suppose she's gotten in at the Tabor, do you? You know, they love her in San Francisco, and I hear that crowd is just about the fanciest you can find west of the Mississippi."

"Lucy who, darling?" the head postman asked and looked up from his sorting.

"Lucy Kimber," she said with a cluck of her tongue. "You remember her, don't you? She was a Sandusky when she lived here, but she's a Kimber now. Got herself a stage name and everything!"

The old postman's eyes were blank for a long moment until recognition suddenly washed over his face.

"Ohhhh, that little Sandusky girl..." He nodded a few times. "Saloon girl, right?"

"Oh, I don't know, she's a singer, though."

"She must've married, then," the old man said. "Kimber, you said?"

"That's her stage name," the woman said nice and loud so the man wouldn't miss it this time.

"Who invents a new name for themselves?" he scoffed. "If the woman's got a new name, she probably got married, Bonnie."

The woman looked taken aback at the thought. "Well, if she is married, I certainly wasn't informed. I think I'd know a thing like that..."

"Why in the world should you know everything?" the postman chuckled and went back to his letters.

The counter clerk ignored him as she met my eyes and smiled from ear to ear.

"Hold on now, are you her fella?" she asked.

"No, ma'am." I smiled politely. "I'm not acquainted with the woman, I'm just helping Mrs. Sandusky by making sure this telegram gets sent."

Bonnie didn't miss a beat. "Oh, she is a fine woman, you'd like that Lucy Kimber. She's just about as pretty as they come, but Mrs. Sandusky sure is a rare beauty. Almost too beautiful, except that her husband looks nice, too. I saw that husband of hers once, and he was a mighty handsome man. All those Sanduskys are pleasing to the eye, I think, but you're probably more handsome by my estimation. I think if you cleaned that beard up, you'd be more handsome than Mr. Sandusky. A beard just makes a man look too rough and tumble. I like a man who cleans himself up well."

"Well, then, I will make sure to do that before stopping in to see you again," I chuckled and gave her a charming grin.

The older woman's cheeks bloomed with a shade of pink that made her look much younger, and she swatted my arm lightly.

"Don't let my husband hear you, he's one of those jealous men, aren't you, Earl?" She craned her neck to look at the postman, who was busy sorting his letters again.

"What's that, darling?" he asked without looking up.

She waved him off and turned back to me.

"I don't think Lucy was here for long," Bonnie said and tilted her head in thought. "But she sure was a lively one. She's come through town just a few times since she left, but I do hope she comes back soon. She's just such a pretty thing, and always in the most modern fashions. Do you think she's coming back soon?"

"I'm not sure," I replied.

The counter clerk looked down at the letter as if this would provide a better answer, but as she read, her sunny disposition abruptly changed. Her thin hand flew up to her lips, and her fingers quivered.

"Oh, my," she whispered. "Oh... Oh, goodness. Is the family alright?"

"Yes, ma'am," I said. "The children and their mother are safe."

"Such a sadness," she said and blinked back a few tears. "And him such a handsome man, too. I'll get this sent straight away, sir."

"I appreciate that," I replied.

Flustered, the woman handled the payment quickly and got straight to work. I bid her and her husband farewell before heading out into the street, and I was pleased to see Birdy and the boys weren't drawing as much attention anymore. There were still a noticeable number of people who lingered closer than was normal, and they all looked over as I left the post office, but I paid them no mind beyond a nod or a smile here and there.

With Mrs. Sandusky's business settled, I set my focus to handling my own affairs.

Three weeks in the saddle had done a number on more than just my beard. I looked around for some fresh clothes first, and I found Pinos Altos offered a couple clothing stores exclusively for men's attire. After purchasing a fresh pair of cotton trousers and two new shirts, I headed for the barber.

The man in there cleaned me up well and almost had me looking like I did before the war. I couldn't do much about the lines on my face that I'd earned over the years, but I got rid of the beard I'd grown since I set out after the Hobbs brothers– not only on account of the counter clerk's preferences. I just wanted to feel like myself again.

With a clean shave and an eight hundred and fifty dollar payday on my ledger, I was feeling plenty refreshed.

I spent the next while getting some sizzling hot huevos rancheros in a small, one-room saloon called the Twisted

Saddle, and then buying a new bar of soap, leather polish for the cracks in my boots, and some essential foods for my travels. Finally, I sold off the poorly tended-to Remingtons Skeet Hobbs had carried. I sold Dirty Neal's Colt Navys as well because I preferred my own pistols, and I was pleased to find the .36 calibers fetched a decent price here. Then I restocked my personal supply of .44s for my Winchester.

Once I'd tended to everything I could here, I returned to where I'd tied my mounts up.

Birdy wasn't too fond of the smell of my aftershave, but the boys perked up at the sight of me. It seemed they didn't enjoy the bustling noise of the people here or the constant rattling of the freight wagons passing by. Unfortunately, I had to stick around the area for a couple of days to await the last of my bounty.

I took a moment to consider my options.

I'd glanced at the hotel I passed while strolling through the town, but the nearby livery had been full near to bursting. I preferred camping out in the surrounding lands to trying to squeeze into a place here, and my boys seemed to be of the same mind.

Then there was the issue of the Black Spur Ranch. I hadn't been able to shake my thoughts of the place all day.

If the Sanduskys' horses were as valuable as Deputy Wallace made them out to be, then I didn't feel right leaving Mrs. Sandusky and her kids out there without some proper protection. Especially considering the violent upheaval they'd gone through the night before. There was also the question of whether something bigger was going on, in which case, whoever attacked their ranch might not be finished just yet.

The image of Helena Sandusky screaming for her husband as tears poured down her face came into my mind like a sudden flash of lightning. Then I remembered how small the family had looked when I returned from the field. How Russel had tried so hard to put all his feelings into glaring, and how the little girl clung to her mama and hadn't seemed able to let go since.

I thought again of the three ranch hands, too, who'd stood solemnly behind the family with their hats in their hands.

I'd have to see how skilled the woman's ranch hands were with firearms to truly settle my mind, but for now, I got my mules' leads together, saddled up, and slowly made my way back out of town and toward the Black Spur Ranch.

By the time I finished winding my way south through the mountain pass and back out into the upper foothills, the sun was over in the western sky. The wind tore in from the same direction and sent walls of orange and brown dust up with it. The brush and large juniper trees bowed under the mighty strength of it, but luckily my back was to the wind all the way to the ranch.

I came up the Sanduskys' lane as the sun started quickening its fall toward the horizon, and my eyes found the horses in the front pasture first.

I slowed Birdy to a stop and took a good long look at the herd this time.

This pasture looked to be mostly for stock horses with a few lively pintos here and there. I didn't know a whole lot about this sort of thing, but I could recognize the Mustang and Thoroughbred influences in some of the beasts. Mostly, I just marveled at how well kept they all were. Every horse was brushed out from front to back, and all of them looked well-worked. There wasn't a scrawny one among them, but I imagined even the terrain here helped to keep them in good health, too.

Each large pasture rose and fell with grassy ridges and winding arroyos, and a few streams split their way through the land as well.

I looked at the branding the horses all wore next. Deputy Wallace had said it was the most well-known branding within three counties, and it struck me as subtle.

The branding was a simple horseshoe shape, but the left side of the shoe was a little elongated, and it flicked outward ever so slightly at the top tip. It was one of the cleaner brandings I'd seen in a while. Every horse within sight had one in the exact same spot with no deviation, and I knew it was what truly made these horses worth their price. Without that branding, they'd be beautiful and well-bred horses, sure. But with that branding, they were certified bred and trained to Sandusky standards, and apparently that held all the important merits around here.

I continued on up the lane and found the ranch hands just riding in from one of the further pastures. The three men were covered in dirt, both from their work and the high winds. I couldn't help but notice how tense they all looked riding in a line like that. Under the brims of their hats, their expressions were just as tense, and I imagined they'd been troubled about the implications of everything that happened last night.

Looking around, they'd clearly kept things running smoothly just fine here, but the future could hold anything for them at this point.

As they saw me tying Birdy off, they headed my way. The three men relaxed a little as they reached the hitching post and dismounted.

"Mr. Callahan," Amos greeted me as he tied his buckskin stallion off.

"Amos." I touched the brim of my hat.

"This is Abel and Mateo," he introduced the other men.

Abel tapped his hat's brim and sent me a quick nod as he tended to his saddle. He looked like the older of the two brothers, probably in his forties, with tan skin, brown eyes, and long hair that fell past his ears.

Mateo was the same height as him, but didn't have a tired hunch in his back just yet, and his shorter hair and lighter brown eyes helped him look less worn down from the passing years. He sent me a smile in greeting and immediately started stroking Birdy's neck.

I realized now that Mateo was the man who'd brushed the mare out early this morning. He'd also held the little girl for Mrs. Sandusky last night when she'd insisted on going out to the field to see her husband.

"How did it go in town?" Amos asked. "Were you able to turn your men in?"

"I was, but the deputy needs a couple days to sort out the rest of the payment."

Mateo's eyebrows shot up. "That much?"

"They were very bad men," I assured him.

"We are in the wrong work," the man sighed, and his brother snorted.

"You should stay here until your payment is ready," Amos told me. "Mrs. Helena won't mind."

"I thought I might ask her if that would be alright," I agreed. "My mare needs a good rest, and my mules aren't too fond of the close quarters in town."

"No?" Mateo smiled and moved over to get acquainted with the boys. He began speaking to them in Spanish with a steady tone they liked, and Birdy looked affronted about it.

She nickered and firmly nudged the man's elbow with her nose, and Mateo laughed as he gave the old girl her fair share of attention as well.

"Were you able to report the fire?" Amos asked.

"Yes, Deputy Wallace was very displeased to hear about the situation," I said. "Shocked, too. He can't think of anyone who'd want to do a thing like that to Mr. Sandusky."

"Neither can we," the black man said with a glance at the others.

"Only good sales," Mateo agreed. "No complaints."

"It does sound like he's got a good reputation around here," I agreed. "Unfortunately, the deputy thinks it isn't likely anyone noticed the six riders specifically. He's gonna ask around and see what the sheriff has to say about all this, but he's mostly concerned about security here, given everything that's happened. He mentioned the branding y'all use is a distinct one, and that might keep anyone from deciding to come around stealing horses, but..."

"That's our main concern." Amos grimaced. "There are plenty of people who wouldn't mind having a Sandusky horse for half the price, no matter how it was gotten. Word will spread quickly about Frank's death. There's nothing we can do about that."

Abel started speaking in Spanish, and Amos nodded in agreement with him before he translated for me.

"Without the stables to lock up even the foals or the finest broodmares at night, we're worried things will get bad here real quick," he explained. "I can shoot, but Abel's eyes aren't too good at night, and Mateo doesn't know much about shooting."

"I can shoot," Mateo said with some annoyance. "I shoot the post okay."

"You want to hit your target on the first shot," Amos told him. "Not the fifth."

"Is still hit." Mateo shrugged.

Abel shook his head and started in on his brother. I recognized a few words here and there, but his large gestures helped me realize he was mostly explaining the difference between a wooden post and a moving man in the night. By the time he finished, I got the sense Mateo had been ignoring him for a while now.

"I shoot okay," he told Birdy. "But not too good maybe."

Birdy gave a cheerful nicker and nipped the young man's shoulder.

"Mateo's skills lie in horse training and flirting," Amos chuckled. "He's too sweet for killing."

This time, Mateo was the one ranting while Abel just laughed and reached over to pinch his cheek. The younger brother smacked his arm away, and when it became clear an honest-to-God argument was about to break out between the two, Amos stepped in between them and brought the focus back to the real issue.

"Security is a concern," he concluded. "Those men last night seem to have kept a close watch on this place. They left through the only path without fencing. We've been getting the whole perimeter closed off with barbed wire for a while now, but it's a lot of land to secure. That slim pass to the northwest is the last that's left open. Only one line of wooden fencing beyond the barn was damaged. It's repaired now."

"I see." I looked out at the distant lands. "How many horses have you got here?"

Amos looked to Abel for this, and the man was quick to reply.

"Two new foals this week," the older man said. "Makes seventy-two."

"But there is a sale tomorrow," Mateo added.

"That's the other problem," Amos sighed and removed his hat to swipe his sleeve over his sweaty brow. "Frank set up this sale of four horses to a man named Mr. Dubois. It was arranged over a month ago, and the man is traveling from Louisiana for the purchase."

I let out a low whistle. "That's quite a journey for some horses."

"Not just any horses," Amos reminded me. "We get folks from all over coming out here."

I nodded as I began to really understand the scope of this ranch's reputation.

"Mrs. Helena could do the sale, I suppose, but she's having a burial this evening for her husband," Amos continued. "I don't think she's ready for business and worrying about pricing and all that comes with sales like this. It ain't even right that she should have to do so, what with being in mourning."

"Can any of you men handle the sale yourselves?" I asked.

I noticed that Mateo glanced at Amos out of the corner of his eye and shifted a little uncomfortably as he focused on my mules for a bit.

"Mateo and Amos don't run sales on account of their English not being so good," the black man explained. Then he cleared his throat and stood up a little straighter. "I can handle sales, but… this particular man isn't quite the sorts I'm too good with. I'd prefer to mind my own."

"I can understand that," I muttered.

I'd been raised in western Texas, where just about everyone I knew thought it was just unnatural for one person to own another. I'd grown up understanding that anyone worth their salt was worth paying for the work they did, and I was certain this Louisiana man was probably of another mind.

Before I could think on it any further, the young boy of the ranch came around the side of the house with a wheelbarrow piled high with weeds. The moment he saw me, he dropped the handles and ran straight over.

He came to a dusty stop after shoving his way between Abel and Amos.

"You shaved," he informed me. "And you're all clean."

"Yeah, I cleaned up while I was in town," I said with a grin.

"What are you doing back here?" he asked.

I opened my mouth to respond, but Amos spoke up first.

"Russel, please let your mama know Mr. Callahan is here," he told the boy.

The boy turned at the hip and cupped his hands around his mouth. "Mama, the bounty hunter's back and all cleaned up!"

He turned back to me like he'd done a sufficient enough job, and the ranch hands and I chuckled a bit.

"So, who are you huntin' next?" he asked.

"I haven't decided quite yet," I said.

"You make a lot of money on those Hobbs brothers?"

"Yes, I made plenty," I replied.

"Men like that worth a whole lot?"

"You could say so, yes."

The boy bit his lip and stared me straight in the eye. He looked painfully set on getting better answers out of me, but before he could figure out how to go about it, his mother appeared on the porch. She had her daughter still propped on her hip, and her face was still buried against her mother's neck.

I began to wonder if the little girl ever did much walking of her own, or if this was a new development for her.

The pair came down the steps and met us near the post.

"Russel, the bounty hunter's name is Jesse Callahan, and you may call him Mr. Callahan from now on," she said with slight exasperation.

"May I call him Jesse instead?" Russel asked.

Mrs. Sandusky raised an eyebrow. "No, you may not. Now, have you finished your chores?"

"No, ma'am." The boy simply shook his head.

There was a long, quiet moment where his mother calmly held his gaze. Finally, Abel nudged the boy in the shoulder.

Russel huffed, turned on his heel, and got back to work.

"I'm sorry about that," the woman sighed and faced me. "How can I help you, Mr. Callahan?"

I let the woman know her telegram was on its way, and I told her what Deputy Wallace had told me. The three ranch hands put in their own two cents here and there. Then they mentioned the sale tomorrow, but Amos didn't confide his own feelings on the situation.

He had guessed correctly, however, that Mrs. Sandusky didn't feel up to running a sale of horses. She said as much herself.

"Of course, I should do it, so I will," she said in a way that made me think she was scolding herself.

"Mrs. Helena, that ain't necessary," Amos stepped in. "You're in mourning now, and–"

"No," she said sharply, but then her tone quickly softened as she sent the man an apologetic look. "Don't fuss over me like that, Amos, you know I don't like fussing."

"It is true, though," Mateo gently put in.

"Frank didn't like anyone who stopped getting up and going about their lives when heartache came along," the woman said. "And I don't, either. I'll honor my husband of course, but I will also carry on as I should. The Lord knows I don't even have as many black dresses or veils as some folks would like me to sit around wearing."

"No one among us expects you to sit around ever," Amos chuckled.

"Good," she said with a smile. "Because I'd like to carry on as I usually do. The pigs certainly don't care how I look, at least."

Abel said something in Spanish, and the woman reached over to squeeze his arm.

"He would be upset," she agreed. "He hated me in black. All the same, I will do my best, and that includes this sale coming up. I should do it. I imagine I'll have to do all sorts of sales for a while, at least until the last of them are sold off."

All three ranch hands' heads swiveled toward her.

Abel looked like he had many opinions he was not going to share, but Mateo looked prepared to argue with the lady of the house. It only took one hard look from his older brother to keep him from speaking up, though.

Amos, on the other hand, looked somewhat unsurprised. I was sure he knew the woman well enough to expect she'd take this stance, but he didn't look at all resigned to accepting it. He just studied her expression for a moment before tactfully changing the subject.

"Mr. Callahan is also in need of a place to stay for a couple days," he told the woman. "Deputy Wallace will have the last of his payment by that time."

"Oh…" Her eyes met mine.

"I'd be happy to help out with anything you need if it suits you," I assured her. "If there are any security concerns in particular, I can certainly offer my services as well."

Amos, Abel, and Mateo all began nodding at this. Helena looked at the three of them before turning back to me. Her blue eyes narrowed, like she was working through something. I was about to assure her I could find other accommodations when she seemed to make up her mind.

"Actually, I have a proposition for you, Mr. Callahan. If you don't mind."

"I'm sure I don't," I said with some confusion.

"Firstly, can I request your presence at the sale tomorrow?" she asked. "A tall man with a polite disposition might do me a great deal of service during the ordeal. And I'm sure Amos would be very happy to not be there, he's just too polite to mention it when he knows there is so much on our minds."

Amos looked so relieved, I knew I'd better accept the job quickly.

"I can certainly do that." I nodded. "I've never sold a horse, but I've had plenty of experience in making sure the right money is handed over when needed."

"Excellent, then I have only one other condition," she said with a sterner look in her eye.

I was almost nervous to hear what it was. Something about a beautiful woman with that look in her eyes was enough to make a man feel as though all his own freewill was about to be tested to the fullest extent. Still, I motioned for her to continue.

"You're more than welcome to stay here with us," she said. "If you'll agree to guard this ranch as if it were your own, at least until my husband's sister arrives. What do you say to that?"

I grinned. "I'd say you can consider every gun I own at your disposal, ma'am."

CHAPTER 5

The next morning, I found myself buttoning up one of my new shirts and slipping on what I called my 'city vest.' I'd bought it out in Austin and took care to only wear it when I wanted to go out among the ritzier crowds.

I'd passed the previous evening in the bunkhouse polishing my boots and cleaning up my Winchester from the long, dusty days. Then I'd taken out all three of my Remingtons and my Schofield for quick wipe-downs and reloading before I reorganized my saddle rigging and gun belt for the work ahead.

The residents of the ranch had all gathered in the field beyond the house for the burial of Frank Sandusky. A single priest rode in for the occasion, but the widow had declined to have any others attend from town.

I certainly didn't feel right imposing, either, so I just focused on making sure I'd be ready to guard the ranch for the next while. Then Birdy and I walked the property to get familiar with it.

Amos had told me the land spanned about a thousand acres, and I took the time to see just about all I could of it. An impressive amount of the perimeter had been fitted with barbed wire over the last couple of years to mark the San-duskys' property lines.

I saw the area the six men must've used to access the place, too, and I agreed with Amos' thoughts on the matter. This land was so large, the murderers had to have spent some time looking around to figure out their clearest route to the house.

A decent-sized red barn was nestled between the back of the house and the wooded area beyond. Chickens, a milking cow, and five pigs shared the area with all the hay and feed for the rest of the ranch. I figured Mr. Sandusky had been crossing between here and the stable beyond the house when the six men cornered him. Then they lit out to the northwest, through the one wooden fence line, and straight to open lands.

For the rest of the property, there were two more barbed wire fences within the exterior one to block out a couple larger pastures, but the three main front pastures were older and fenced in with wood.

All the horses were being kept in three of the main pastures at night now that the stables were gone. They were about forty acres apiece, but I intended to help with the rebuild while I was here, to see their best breeders and foals were closed up safe again at night.

But for now, I had a sale of four horses to conduct.

Very, very fine horses.

Amos, Abel, and Mateo brought the horses in question out to the lane in front of the house at about half past ten. Mr. Dubois was expected to arrive within the next half hour, so I had enough time to learn the details of this particular sale.

The Louisiana man had entrusted Mr. Sandusky to make the selections himself after detailing his needs through a series of several telegrams. They'd settled on this pair of geldings and two mares. The geldings were each a cross of American Trotters and Thoroughbreds, which apparently made them perfect for the harness racing Mr. Dubois intended to train them further for. They were each sleek and colored the deepest black, with corded muscles from head to toe. They stood perfectly even with one another at sixteen and a half hands.

The mares were Tennessee Walkers that stood fifteen hands each and were wanted as saddle horses for the man's daughters. One was a pretty bay with one of the finest kept manes and tails I'd ever seen. She was good enough to show, and her companion was her equal in beauty, but pure white and with a shorter cut to her.

The lot of them were three years old and thoroughly saddle trained. The pair of geldings were also accustomed to the rigging the racing would require, all they needed was a few months of work on the track. So with all things considered, I could see clear enough that Mr. Dubois was coming out of this deal a lucky man.

Why he'd chosen to come all the way to New Mexico Territory for these horses, I couldn't decide. I'd heard plenty of talk about Mr. Sandusky's reputation, but horses of quality could be found all over, and certainly closer to Louisiana than western country.

"My understanding is that Mr. Dubois' father and mother both rode Sandusky horses near the end of their lives," Amos explained. "How that came about, I don't know. Best horses they'd ever owned, though. The son is interested in carrying on the family custom for his daughters. When he heard we had Trotter crosses here, his interest in harness racing led him to expand the sale to the geldings as well."

I nodded. "That all sounds tidy enough."

"It should be," Amos agreed. "Down to the hand, these horses are precisely what was agreed upon. We have the telegrams to prove it."

I noticed the tension in the ranch hand's voice and expression as he handed the necessary papers over. They were luckily already signed and certified by the deceased because Frank Sandusky was a punctual man.

"I'll see the deal goes through alright," I assured him.

"As will I," Mrs. Sandusky put in.

The four of us men turned to find her descending the steps to the house. She wore an older style of black dress that must have been her only mourning attire, but it suited her very well all the same. Her strawberry-blonde hair was swept up nice and neat with a few ringlets framing her face, and true to her word, she bore no heavy black veil of mourning.

Still, anyone with eyes could see how tired she was. How much that grief was trailing after her like its own heavy veil.

She still had her daughter fixed to her hip, but she murmured something to the girl as she met us in the lane.

"Amos, could you?" she asked the man. "Russel is doing his chores in the garden if you'd like to join him?"

"Of course, come here, Honey," he cooed to the little girl, who didn't fuss at all about being passed from her mother's arms to the ranch hand.

He smiled warmly at her and plopped his own hat on her head. It fell all the way down to the bridge of her small nose, but even with a curtain of blonde curls hiding most of the rest of her face, I could see he'd managed to win a tiny smile from the girl.

Then the smile dropped again as she buried her face against his neck.

Amos exchanged a quick glance with the worried mother.

"Come on, Honey, let's go pick some flowers," Amos murmured to the little girl, and the pair headed toward the kitchen garden beside the house.

"Is she okay?" Mateo asked quietly.

"No, she's stopped talking," Mrs. Sandusky confided in the man. "Not one word since…"

Abel looked particularly sad about this, and Mateo patted the mother's shoulder gently.

Mrs. Sandusky didn't let herself dwell any longer than that on the sorrow. She quickly adjusted her expression and focused instead on the task ahead.

"Amos told you everything you need to know, Mr. Callahan?" she asked.

"He did," I said. "All the papers are ready, too."

"Well, that's good," she sighed and straightened her shoulders. "Because our guests have arrived."

I followed her line of sight all the way down to the end of the lane.

My eyebrows popped up at the procession headed our way.

Three stagecoaches swayed their way up the dirt road. They were all pulled by stout draft horses and driven by dark-skinned gentlemen.

As they drew closer, I could see the first of the coaches was the nicest, with curtained windows that were tied back so the passengers could look out on the beautiful ranch. The next two coaches were the standard fare, and I wondered briefly if they were even needed today, or if they were merely for show.

Abel let out a long sigh near my right flank. I glanced his way, and I'd never seen a man less impressed.

I chuckled despite myself. I had a feeling we'd both come to similar conclusions about this Mr. Dubois already.

The three coaches followed one another into a wide turn as they reached us, and they settled in a crescent shape in the broad stretch of dirt in front of the house. Then the first coach's door opened, and a portly man in an all-white linen suit stepped out. His thick mustache curved up a little at the edges, and he checked the time on his pocket watch before smiling and walking forward.

He was followed by a black man who held a black buckled bag and stationed himself right beside the coach door without a word.

No one emerged from the other two coaches, so I

began to think my suspicions had been correct about this showy display.

"This must be the famous Frank Sandusky," the portly man said as he held his arms out wide. "My, but you are a difficult man to locate. I must say, I am pleased as punch I was able to track you down at last."

"Actually, Frank isn't with us today," Mrs. Sandusky said in a tight voice. Her face was a tense attempt at a polite smile. "My dear husband passed away only two days ago, sir."

Mr. Dubois stopped on the spot and let his arms drop. His mouth slackened a bit as his smile faded.

"Dead?" he asked. "Just two days ago?"

"Yes, sir." She nodded. "But this is my–"

"Well, ain't that just the shame of the century," he huffed, but the sorrow didn't seem to come naturally to him. "Shoot, I was looking forward to shaking that man's hand. And him only gone a couple of days? Why, I sure wish that train could've run me here faster now. May he rest in peace, of course."

"Yes." Mrs. Sandusky cleared her throat and gestured my way. "Mr. Dubois, this is my husband's partner, Mr.... Hayford. He'll be conducting our business here in my husband's absence."

I looked at her with some confusion for a second before offering the man my hand to shake.

"Pleasure to meet you, Mr. Hayford," Mr. Dubois said with a suddenly wide smile and a rather limp shake.

"The pleasure's mine," I assured him. "I hope your journey was a swift and comfortable one."

"Oh, always is, always, is," he said and rocked on his feet. "By train or by coach, I make sure to account for all. We've already arranged the transport for these four fine specimens as well, don't you worry. They'll be living the life of the monarchs from now on, yes sir."

"I'm glad to hear it." Mrs. Sandusky smiled. "I recall my husband mentioned you own a rather large plantation."

"Larger than most, yes, ma'am." He waggled his head at this and looked as pleased as a puppy about it. "Had ourselves some trials and tribulations over the years, of course, but the Dubois Plantation is still standing and preserving the spirit of the South, I'd say."

"How lovely," the woman said. "I believe the papers you need are all in order–"

"But tell me, how are you doing, sugar?" he butted in and took the woman's hand without it being offered. He patted it a few times and brought himself what I considered to be too close, but Mrs. Sandusky made no show of being uncomfortable. "A pretty woman like you is far too young to lose her husband, especially such a reputable man as Mr. Frank Sandusky."

"Y-yes, it's been a shock to us all," she said, and her voice wavered a little. "He's with God now, though, and I take comfort in that. We'll be getting on just fine, I'm sure–"

"Oh, I'm sure you will, I'm sure you will." He patted her hand some more. "You got many years ahead of you yet, don't you fret at all. Why, I think I love my third wife more than I ever did my first."

Mrs. Sandusky seemed to go a little rigid at this, and despite her efforts, I could see how taken off guard she was. She managed a shaky smile as she wriggled her hand free of Mr. Dubois' grip, and she took a step back.

"Yes, I'll be sure not to fret," she said.

I realized all at once how tense my stance had become, and I worked to relax. It was hard to stand by and not put this newcomer in his place for taking those small liberties with the woman, but this wasn't my ranch, and this man wasn't my guest.

I was only here to make sure everything with the sale went as planned.

J.R. WILSON

And I was more determined than ever to see it did.

"Now," Mrs. Sandusky said more brightly. "I believe Mr. Hayford has the necessary papers all drawn up–"

"Well, now, hold on there just a moment," Mr. Dubois said with that same waggle of his head. His expression became grave, and he looked between us as he clasped his hands around his large belly. "Now, I had my worries about this deal before, being so clumsily drawn up and all. But I fear they have not been put to rest. Not at all. Not now that I've heard about this… this sorry situation with the late Mr. Sandusky. May his soul rest in peace, of course."

"Worries, sir?" the woman asked.

"Yes, ma'am," he said with a solemn nod. "As far as business dictates, I just can't be sure what I'm buying here. Not without Mr. Sandusky around. Truth be told, them horses could be for anything and trained by anyone."

"I see…" She tried to regain her composure. "Well, I can assure you, sir, that my husband took the greatest care–"

"Ohhhh, yes, I'm sure you could assure me all day long, sweetie, and I've got half a mind to let you," he said with a smile that reminded me of sour milk. "Why, you're certainly beautiful enough to change my mind, I won't lie about that. But business is business, and I am a businessman first and foremost, you see."

Mrs. Sandusky was lost for words. She could only knead her hands for a moment, but our guest hadn't even begun to rattle me.

I nodded calmly when he looked at me for a response. "I can see that clear as day."

His sour smile widened even further.

"Good, good, then you'll understand if I can no longer offer the same price for these here horses," he said with a lazy gesture toward the gorgeous beasts behind me. "There's just no sense in it, of course."

"I do understand." I turned ever so slightly to address the

64

ranch hands. "Boys, you can set these four out to pasture, they won't be leaving today after all."

I caught a glimpse of Mateo's blank and confused expression. Abel, on the other hand, turned quickly to keep his smile hidden.

"Sí, señor," he said at once.

"Well, now, hold on there a moment," Mr. Dubois huffed, and his voice rose a bit. "I did not... I did not say I don't want to purchase these horses. Don't go putting words into my mouth now, it ain't polite. I can see that they're adequate horses, of course. It's only–"

"It's only that you believe these certified papers here are not legitimate," I finished for him. "You believe this lady and myself are swindling you."

Even the draft horses and the drivers of the coaches didn't make a sound. Silence rang as loud as a gunshot as Mr. Dubois and I looked at one another.

"I... I did not say–" he tried.

"You don't have to," I assured him in my kindest voice. "I can see you've traveled a long way, only to be met with the unfortunate news that the breeder and trainer of these horses is no longer with us. It is a shame, I can see that. Especially given the understanding the two of you had come to."

"Yes, precisely," Mr. Dubois pushed, and he squared himself as if he'd just gotten his feet firmly set again. "I have an understanding that states those horses are to be sold to me. Those papers say as much, do they not?"

"Yes they do," I agreed. "But as you've mentioned, there are concerns now that Mr. Sandusky is unfortunately unable to make the sale himself. You see, it's myself and Mrs. Sandusky making the sale, so by law... these papers don't have to mean anything if I don't want them to. I could tear them up right here and rid the both of us of this awkwardness altogether. And in truth, given the implications you've made against this woman's word of honor, as well as the reputation of this ranch at large, I don't see how you and I can come to any sort of understanding now."

The words came out as smooth as honey, no matter how false some of them were.

I knew I had no right to go against a sale Mr. Sandusky had approved, but I also knew the woman beside me didn't deserve to be taken advantage of in her grief, and that the hardworking men behind me alone were enough to vouch for the quality of the beasts.

Most importantly, Mrs. Sandusky looked perfectly content to let me say and do as I pleased now.

She stood calmly with her head held high, and her beautiful features gave absolutely nothing away. All the natural sweetness and kindness she'd shared with the man before had dried up. She just looked at him as if he were as uninteresting as a stick in the grass now that I'd said my piece.

Her faith in my handling of this made it easier for me to forgive the lies.

I waited for the Louisiana man to grapple with the situation he'd gotten himself into. He was sweating in the dry, high desert heat and looking anxiously between me and the horses at my back.

I let him sweat a few seconds longer before I sighed as if I was troubled by all this.

"Again, my apologies for the sad news," I told him. "It has inconvenienced us all, I can promise you that. Safe travels."

"Hold on," he said firmly before I could even turn my back. "I… I feel as if we've gotten ahead of ourselves here. Let's all calm down. Now, if you say those horses there are certified Sandusky stock, then I believe I can trust your word, and the word of this honorable woman here, of course. And seeing as the three of us are all good and honest folk, I agree to pay the agreed upon eight hundred and seventy dollars. How's that?"

Mrs. Sandusky started to nod, but she caught herself as she noticed me shaking my head.

"I'm sorry, sir, that deal is no longer on offer," I told him.

This time, I turned swiftly and gestured for Mrs. Sandusky to lead the way. She only hesitated a second or two before dipping her head to the Louisiana man and heading back to the house. Abel, Mateo, and the four horses followed after her. I tailed the group without another glance in Mr. Dubois' direction.

"Well, now, hold on!" Mr. Dubois finally found his voice before we could fully desert him in the lane. "Hold on there just a moment!"

I only slowed my gait. I didn't turn around until he'd dogged after me for quite a few paces. Then I turned so abruptly, he bumped into my chest and startled himself.

He was flustered and twice as sweaty now, and I looked down at him with an air of irritation.

"If you please, Mr. Hayford," he said in his most civil tone. "I believe we have gotten sorely ahead of ourselves. Now, I have traveled very far to obtain these mighty fine horses of yours, and truth be told, I am not a man who wants for much. Money is certainly no object. I'm sure the two of us can come to some kind of understanding."

I shifted my weight and crossed my arms. "I don't believe we can. With all due respect, you don't seem to understand the situation we've unfortunately found ourselves in here. See, these horses are some of the last horses Mr. Sandusky himself trained."

This could not be all true. I'd learned enough of the ranch hands to know the Black Spur Ranch was a democratic operation, but any training done by Amos, Abel, and Mateo was clearly good enough for Mr. Sandusky.

And I was good and mad now. I'd been pleased to see Mrs. Sandusky looking proper and confident in herself before this slimy 'businessman' arrived, and if he wanted those horses now, he was going to have to make up for the way he'd treated her.

"Truth is, men have already been sending inquiries from all over trying to get their hands on the last of the Sandusky stock," I said. "We've got more interested parties than we know what to do with, and with so many people in need of quality horses–"

"Oh, I certainly understand all that," Mr. Dubois anxiously cut in. "I am a businessman first and foremost, always have been, and Lord do I understand and respect your predicament. Leeches, that's you've got to deal with now. Vultures. You've got to be careful, Mr. Hayford. The missus as well. People will try to swindle you any which way they can with so much on the line."

He leaned forward now, as if we were conspiring together.

"The important thing is to not lose sight of how much is at stake," he said and looked around at the vast ranch. "This land, those horses… This is a legacy, Mr. Hayford. Why, my daddy rode a Sandusky horse 'til the day he died. You know why?"

"Why?"

"Because the very first time he sat on one, he knew he'd never truly ridden a horse worth their price before that moment." Mr. Dubois' eyes were theatrically wide, and he waved his hands across the landscape like I could picture his father along with him. "The smoothest ride, the most steadfast composition, and the most glorious proof of God's great hand he'd ever known. That's what he said. He wouldn't trust another horse in all this world after that. That's why he arranged for my mama to have just the same. The pair of them used to ride all over the plantation together looking finer than anyone you ever saw on those two horses."

I smiled. "I bet they did."

"Lord, they cut a pretty picture together," he sighed. "That's what drove me to travel so far, of course. The love of my family. My girls loved their granddaddy and nana so much. Admired them with all their hearts. So when they came to me and said, 'Daddy, could we ever ride as beautiful a horse as Granddaddy did?' do you know what I did?"

"What did you do?"

"I tracked down the very same man who'd bred those fine horses after two months of tryin'," he laughed. "And it was some endeavor, let me tell you. But I have no regrets whatsoever about it. None at all. Because this here, this legacy you're looking after, is worth all the trials in the world. Don't you lose sight of that. Don't let no swindlers come through here and insult the memory of such a rare man. May he rest in peace, of course."

I nodded slowly as I looked out across the ranchland.

I didn't think I'd ever heard a rich man try so hard to get a thing he wanted. That sour milk smile was back on his face, too, but I didn't mind this time. I'd only been waiting to get him to this very moment before I made the deal I'd been looking for.

I stared at the horizon for what felt like the appropriate amount of time before giving a resigned sigh and turning back to Mr. Dubois.

"I'm glad you can appreciate all we have here," I said. "Very few folks understand what they're asking when they come around here looking to buy up the last of what Mr. Sandusky gave this world."

"Oh, I don't doubt it," he assured me with a waggle of his head. "Folks will take all they can get these days, you mark me on that."

"They sure will," I agreed. "But seeing as you understand the legacy we've got to uphold here, I suppose we could reach an agreement between us."

"I knew you were a good and smart man." He clapped his hand on my shoulder. "How much would you like?"

"For a man like yourself?" I said with a charming grin, "I

suppose I could part with the four for just one thousand and four hundred dollars."

Mr. Dubois turned a color I'd never quite seen on a man. It was something between cloud-white and moldy-green, and he cleared his throat in a way that reminded me of a frog.

"Fourteen hundred?" he clarified. "Uhhh... Well, Mr. Hayford, I ain't gonna lie, that's quite a bit more than I intended on spending."

"I'm sure it's more than most can afford," I acknowledged, "so you can understand my misgivings with all this. But business is business, as you pointed out, and I've got the legacy of the Sanduskys to uphold here."

"Yes, of course," he said with a twitchy smile. "That's true, that's true."

He let out an uncomfortable laugh, and I placed a friendly hand on his linen-clad shoulder.

"All the best, Mr. Dubois," I said with a smile. "It sure was nice talking to you today."

"Uhh..." He stared at me and wetted his parched lips. "Yes... Well, now hold on. If you say the price is fourteen hundred on those horses, then I suppose... I ought to take that deal. Given how rare these horses are, especially now, may he rest in peace..."

"Safe in the arms of the angels," I said with a solemn nod. "Thank God."

"Thank God," he said blankly.

"Did you come equipped for such a purchase, though?" I forced myself not to smile.

"Yes!" he blurted out suddenly. "Yes, of course! I plan for all, Mr. Hayford, never you mind!"

Mr. Dubois turned on his heel and motioned for the man beside the first coach to join us.

The man in question jolted to attention and scurried forward with the black bag held out like it was a silver tray. After a short, hushed conversation with Mr. Dubois, the helpful man sprinted back to the coach and returned with a less showy brown leather bag that apparently held more funds.

I turned and glanced at Abel and Mateo while Mr. Dubois busied himself with the money he'd brought. Both ranch hands' eyes were stuck wide open, but they managed to keep their lips from curling up into smiles. It was a strange attempt at looking professional, but I couldn't blame the pair of them.

I was just about ready to do a darn jig.

Still, I kept my expression calm and unaffected as Mr. Dubois came my way with that same huge smile on his face. He happily counted out the one thousand four hundred dollars, holding the bills high between us like he wanted us to both admire the view to the fullest. When he'd finished counting, he had his man wrap the bills together in brown paper with some twine tying it all together. It was the oddest way I'd ever been handed money in my life, but I just nodded my thanks.

Then the Louisiana man signed the papers with a flourish, let out a whistle, and brought the drivers of the last two coaches over to retrieve the horses.

Abel and Mateo helped them secure the racers and the Tennessee Walkers to the back of the last two coaches. Then they stepped back as the whole procession prepared to depart.

"Pleasure doing business with you both!" Mr. Dubois hollered as he backed into his fancy coach. "May God bless you and this prosperous land of yours!"

I smiled and tapped the brim of my hat as the man with the buckle bag climbed in with his boss and closed the door. Then the trio of coaches swayed their way back down the lane.

It was at this point that Abel said something in Spanish that I knew the meaning of well enough, but certainly wouldn't repeat here. The exclamation sent Mateo snickering into his hands, and he had to turn away to hide his laughter from the group still leaving the property.

Abel grabbed my hand and shook it ten times as well as Mr. Dubois had, and he had tears in his eyes from the laughter he'd been holding back.

"Good," he managed between his hearty chuckles. "Very good."

"Yeah, I'd say that deal went about as well as it could have," I laughed.

Mateo burst out laughing in earnest, but I knew Mr. Dubois was too far away to hear him now. I just shook my head at the ranch hands and let them clap me on the back and have their celebrations. Then the two carried on chuckling their way over to the house and disappeared into the garden. I supposed they were going to fill Amos in on how the sale went.

I met Mrs. Sandusky on the steps of the front porch.

"I couldn't hear everything you were saying at the end there," she said with an anxious look in her eye.

"The sale went through nicely," I assured her and handed her the paper wrapping with the twine around it. "That's one thousand and four hundred dollars for the four horses. Congratulations on your first sale."

"One... what?" she gasped. She tore the paper open, and her blue eyes went wide at the sight of the neat stack of greenbacks inside. "One thousand four hundred... That's nearly twice what my husband agreed to. And more than Mr. Dubois ever wanted to pay. How in this world did you manage it?"

I smiled and shrugged. "That man came out here all the way from Louisiana. He didn't want to leave without those horses, no matter what the price. I just wanted him to see he'd made a mistake questioning your honor first, is all. That price there is what struck me as fair, all things considered."

This made the woman laugh nearly as hard as Mateo had, and her smile was one of the prettiest things I'd ever seen. Especially after how much sadness she'd endured since

I'd arrived, I was pleased to see I'd helped cheer her up a little today.

"I don't know what to say," she admitted as her laughs settled down. Then she looked out at the lane where the coaches were just passing under the ironwork, and a worried look crinkled her brow. "I couldn't have done any of this without your help, Mr. Callahan."

"I'm sure you could have," I said.

Mrs. Sandusky shook her head and pressed her hands to her flushed cheeks. She dabbed at her neck and began fanning herself.

"Are you alright, ma'am?" I asked gently.

"Yes," she said, but she was out of breath. "Yes, Mr. Callahan, I'm fine, I'm sorry. It's only… Goodness, I don't feel like myself. I'm afraid I'm a bit embarrassed about all of this, to tell you the truth."

I furrowed my brow. "I can't see anything to be embarrassed about. You've made a very handsome sum from those horses. I think you handled a difficult man as well as can be expected."

She huffed. "No, I know myself well enough, sir. This…"

She gestured at her discomposure and pinched the bridge of her delicate nose.

"This is not me," she confided. "That man… Well, he just about walked all over me, and I would've let him if not for you. I forgot every good word I have in my mind, and I… I clammed right up."

I considered this and gave the woman time to collect herself.

"That goes away eventually," I finally said, but I looked out across the sun-drenched pasture ahead of us instead of meeting her gaze. "For a while, words just don't come to mind when people like that want to push you around. The harshness of people rubs a bit coarser than it used to when you're struggling to find sense in the sorrows. You feel raw all over. Not up to the fight. But with time, you'll feel like yourself again. You'll push back harder, find your tongue as sharp as a whip. Sharper than it was before, that's for sure."

I met her blue eyes now, and I found her studying me more closely than I'd let anyone do in a long, long time. Her gaze was steady and searching, but it didn't make me uncomfortable. Not after what she'd been through. I just let her look and looked right back at the woman while she came to her own conclusions.

"It'll make you stronger than you ever thought you could be," I told her. "As long as you don't get too hard on yourself before that happens."

"Yes." She nodded lightly and sent me a small smile. "Thank you, Mr. Callahan. I needed to hear that from a person like you."

"Glad to be of any help, Mrs. Sandusky." I tapped the brim of my hat and turned to make my way back down the steps.

I was a few feet away when she called out to me again.

"You can call me Helena, by the way," she said. "We're not so formal around here."

I turned and grinned a little. "Should I expect you to be calling me Mr. Hayford from now on?"

"Oh, that," she laughed. "I'm sorry, I wasn't sure what you're accustomed to, given your line of work. I don't know any bounty hunters. I suppose I got it in my mind that you might not like using your real name. Unless Mr. Callahan isn't your real name? Russel has a lot of opinions on that point."

"I'm sure he does," I chuckled. "It's my name alright. And I'm no outlaw looking to hide my identity from anyone. Just an honest man who does honest work. So you may call me Jesse."

"As you like it," she said with a smile.

The two of us parted ways after that, and I went to the bunkhouse to remove my city vest and new shirt. It was only midday, and I intended to pull my weight around here until it was time to move on, so I put on something more suitable for a day's work.

Then I returned to the lane, but Russel came sprinting out from the garden before I made it too far.

"That was a mighty fine sale," he panted as dust billowed up around his slim shoulders.

It was clear as day that the boy had found some means of spying on the whole exchange.

"Thank you," I chuckled.

"Mama probably admires you," he told me. "All that fancy talking… It's just what she's always telling me I need to work on. A man ought to speak real well and command respect with words and whatnot."

I smiled. "I've personally found it serves me well, especially when money is involved."

"Why?" He cocked his head to the side.

"Well, a lot of men want to buy up whatever they can these days."

"Why?"

"Because there's a lot worth buying," I said with a shrug. "Having a lot of money doesn't make them smarter than you, though. If you learn to speak real clear and hold to your word, you'll find a lot of things start to go your way."

Russel smiled wide as he nodded at this.

"Of course, being a man of your word comes first," I told him. "You done your chores?"

"No, sir," he said with a shake of his head. "I been watching the work going on out here and thinkin' on how I might do the same when I come of age and take over the running of this ranch."

I sighed a little. "Well, then, I'd say you'd best get to it."

"Yes, sir." He nodded and sprinted back to the garden, and I laughed lightly as I headed off to meet with Amos and the other men.

The little girl must have been back in her mother's arms by now, but Amos had a bundle of wildflowers tucked in the band of his hat that he'd apparently promised to keep there forever. The combination of the flowers and the big smile on his face made him look like the happiest man alive.

He spent several minutes thanking me on both his and Helena's behalf, but then he sobered a bit as we headed toward the burned remains of the stable.

"Maybe seeing how much can be done around here will help Mrs. Helena understand that selling all the stock ain't the right choice," Amos sighed.

"She can't give up on the ranch," Mateo said and kicked a stone straight into the charred heap. "We can do work. Frank knows our work, he likes our work. We can do good work for her also."

"I'm sure she knows that," I said as we all took up shovels. "I don't think it's the work that worries her."

Mateo nodded. "It's the shooting. But I can shoot! Jesse shoots! It's nothing!"

Abel and I laughed and shook our heads.

"It's more than that," Amos muttered mostly to himself. "I suppose if she wants to wash her hands of all this, there's not much to do about it. She's the sort of woman who makes up her mind all in a whirlwind. And she's usually right to do so."

"Is that right?" I asked with a half-grin.

"Yeah, I'd say so." He grinned back. "Frank said he asked her eight times to marry him. Then one day, just like that, she decided she loved him with her whole heart and said yes."

I chuckled. "She's got spirit, that's for sure."

"I'm sure she just needs some time to think on it, is all," Amos said. "Especially after today, she has to see this place is worth running. Jesse, you just keep making sales like that."

"No thank you," I laughed. "I'd rather deal in my kind of business than entertain men like that every day."

"Can't say I blame you," Amos snorted.

The four of us spent the rest of the day cleaning away the remains of the rubble and setting plans in place for the new stables we'd be starting on tomorrow. Then I helped with the few tasks that needed doing around the ranch, and once Mateo started with his daily training, I assisted with rotating horses in and out of the paddock for him.

At suppertime, I got a fire going outside the bunkhouse, and I sat and ate pork and beans with Amos, Abel, and Mateo. They were some of the most honest and hardworking men I'd met in a long time. Abel seemed like an older brother to both the other ranch hands, and Mateo seemed to take up the role of being Amos' little brother, too.

It was clear Amos was in charge of the brothers, but he was respectful about it and worked just as hard in just as dirty of jobs as the others.

I learned a lot about the running of this ranch that evening. Like the fact that Abel did the bulk of the farrier work and brought in a man named Gilly once in while to help out with it. Amos had a way with real stubborn stallions and tended the most to the ranchlands themselves, and Mateo had been a sort of protege to Frank. That was why he did so much training himself these days, but it was Frank who had really understood the horses inside and out.

The men told me stories about difficult wild ponies he'd tamed and brought in over the years, and even horses he'd bought straight from the Apache and lived to tell the tale. It was clear he'd been one of those rare sorts who understood beasts as if they were humans who could talk, and I couldn't help but feel more strongly how big a loss his death had been.

Still, for all the stories the men told, none of them knew much of Mr. Sandusky before he'd settled in New Mexico Territory. The man hadn't ever talked about his past, and the three ranch hands never pried.

As for the men, Amos was an open book. He'd escaped a sugar plantation in western Louisiana the year the war broke out. He and the two men he escaped with got lost up in Indian Territory trying to head north. They doubled back, but both his companions were killed by some Kiowa before they could reach Texas. From there, Amos had spent a long time hiding out and camping as he slowly made his way west. Once he reached New Mexico Territory, he took up work of just about every kind he could as he kept on moving. He was a miner here before settling in with the ranchers, and when Frank saw him working to tame a young and wild mustang stallion for a neighbor, he offered him a job right there. Bought the mustang for Amos to bring along with him, too.

Abel and Mateo were born and raised near Albuquerque, and while Abel spoke very little English, he could understand what he heard pretty well. He'd worked as a farrier all his life, but he knew plenty of ranching to help out all over the property. Mateo was better with English due to his time working for a whiskey merchant up near Santa Fe, but neither man ever ran the horse sales. That task was always on Frank or Amos' plates, and most sales only required one or two of the ranch hands to be present helping out.

As the twilight settled in, the wind picked up, and I mounted up on Birdy and headed out into the first of the main pastures to start my watch for the evening. We took it nice and easy following the wooden fencelines and watching bats dart around overhead. It was one of those restless nights when broad patches of clouds raced across the night sky, leaving quick glimpses of the stars here and there. The wind whooshed past my ears, but the crickets chirped loudly enough to be heard, and distant coyotes broke out into the frenzied yipping of the chase.

The moon was beginning to climb into the sky as I crossed into the next pasture, and I started to think on how long it had been since I'd been among a family like this one. I stayed put once in a while, but even when I spent a few days enjoying the finer things the cities had to offer, I didn't speak to much of anyone.

The people I saw most were either lawmen, bankers, or outlaws.

Now, I'd met people I felt I could consider friends. Even Helena and I had begun to get to know one another, but once her sister-in-law arrived, I'd be on my way again.

Even as I thought the words, my mind argued right back.

The thought of those six men riding off and leaving the ruins of this place behind them wasn't something I could forget. Fire lit in my veins just thinking about it, especially now that I knew the people of the Black Spur Ranch better.

"Birdy, I think we ought to look into a few things while we're here," I told my mare as we turned along the far fence and started making our way north.

She nickered softly as if she knew I'd come to this decision eventually.

I was about to tease the old girl about it, but then I came to the western gate between this pasture and the larger one beyond.

It was swung wide open.

I got closer, and in the patchy moonlight, I could see the latch wasn't too good, but I didn't think Mr. Sandusky seemed like a man who'd let a thing like that sit if he was risking the wind blowing his gates around.

I pushed Birdy into a trot and decided to take a quick look around the next pasture, in case some of the horses had ambled over there since the sun went down.

As far as I could see, all was perfectly still over here, aside from the cool breeze rustling the tall grass. I crossed the whole pasture, looking left to right all the way, and I didn't see a single horse. Then I turned along the fenceline for a ways, but I slowed Birdy down as I saw a break in the fence up ahead.

The barbed wire had been cut.

I narrowed my eyes as I turned and saw this gap was directly across from the open gate I'd come from.

A horse let out a long, warning bray far off in the pasture beyond. Several others took up the call within seconds, and before I knew it, hooves were pounding the dirt as the horses scattered.

I thought I heard a few men's voices drifting on the wind, and as I pulled my Schofield from its holster, the racing clouds shifted.

A beam of moonlight struck on three riders galloping after the herd.

Rustlers.

CHAPTER 6

I didn't doubt the final line of wire at the edge of the property would be cut like this one. These men thought they could run the horses straight out through the western gate and into the lands beyond.

That meant they'd be coming this way once they were done rounding up what they could.

And I'd be waiting.

I reined Birdy in at the open gate. Then I jumped down to the ground, closed it securely, and got back into the saddle. I stayed right where I was, too. I didn't want to risk the horses being so riled up that they'd try and make the jump, and I knew having me right there in front of them was my best chance at forcing them to turn away.

The three rustlers had managed to separate ten horses from the herd by now.

Even at the standard price, that was over twenty-five hundred dollars' worth of stock right there, and probably much more now that Frank was gone.

There was no way I'd allow a loss like that for the ranch.

The men started running them this way, with one man at the back, and two on the sides near the flank of the group. The shadows of the racing clouds ran right along with them, and the herd was cast in moonlight and then thrust into shadow over and over.

Still, the horses at the front would see me at the gate clear as day. I couldn't be sure the rustlers would with so many horses ahead of them, but either way, I knew my plan.

I had the wind blowing straight at my back, and this was the best position I could be in.

I kept Birdy steady with her reins in one hand while I leveled my Schofield on the right-side rustler as soon as he was within range. Then I fired.

Every horse except my old mare startled badly from the report and the flash. They frantically peeled off in either direction as they reached me, just as planned.

Through the passing horses, I could see my bullet had struck the right-side rustler straight in the chest. He tumbled from his saddle and hit the ground like a sack of potatoes, and before I could blink, three horses trampled him as easy as a bit of shrub.

His body rolled twice before his mangled form laid sprawled in the dirt.

The other two rustlers had tried to rein their mounts in, but they'd both reared up as the herd broke apart. They still managed to keep their seats, and they'd kicked their horses and taken off with the fleeing herd.

I kept Birdy steady where she was and considered my options.

I'd have to be careful not to accidentally shoot one of the Sanduskys' horses now that the rustlers were among them, and the strong winds wouldn't help my trajectory. I was a good shot, but at this range any bullet could be cast off an inch or even feet in the wrong direction.

Just as I thought this, one of the thieves aimed wildly in my direction and shot without hesitation, and I realized I'd need to hurry up and end this. Otherwise, one of these lowlifes was likely to take out a horse themselves.

Birdy took off as I sent a warning shot into the air.

We were in the southernmost pasture with the wind flying in hard from the west. The rustlers were just rounding the northern edge of the fence and trying to double back. They probably hoped to get that gate open again and make a break for it, but I couldn't stay sitting here and waiting for them to close me in.

Instead, I took us east and cut all the way across to the other side of the pasture. The flashes of moonlight gave me glimpses here and there of the men or their silhouettes, and they were panicking. They'd riled the herd up too much, and their own mounts weren't taking direction.

They zigged when they needed to zag, and twice, one of them almost crashed into a passing horse at least five hands taller than his own. Their curses were only somewhat lost in the wind, and the furious braying of their mounts only urged the herd on.

I'd reached the eastern fence and was galloping north now. When the time was right, I turned swiftly so I could cut them off on their way to the western gate.

They'd barely made it halfway there now, but I was almost in position. I had clear open pasture at my back instead of a line of fence closing me in. I could get my shots off facing into the wind instead of dealing with a crosswind, too, and neither of the men seemed to have realized where I'd gone.

That wouldn't last long, but I could work with this.

I urged Birdy onward as I steadied my aim as best I could. The frontmost rider would only be about twenty feet ahead of me when he darted across my path, but the moment he did, his head whipped around and he saw me.

He raised his pistol, but I'd just pulled the trigger.

My shot struck him in the gut, and he folded forward as his own bullet flew wide of me. His mount brayed and changed direction, and I let them go as four more horses thundered after them.

I turned my aim on the next rider as quick as I could, but he fired first on his way past us.

The bullet grazed my left shoulder, and I cursed and gritted my teeth against the biting sting.

Then Birdy jolted as half the darn herd came barreling at us, but she kept her head on straight and seamlessly took us into their ranks.

We rode along with the frantic group as I squinted against the flashing moonlight.

Both of the men had gotten shoved off course. The one with a bullet in his gut was barely staying on his mount, but he fired two more blind shots in our general direction. He missed us all, luckily, but I knew I had to separate myself from the herd.

Unfortunately, I was blocked into the center of the group, so I waited until they peeled off at the next fence to push Birdy safely to the outer line. Finally, the horses took off ahead of us. I got Birdy turned around and spotted the uninjured man galloping along the eastern fence.

Then a shot cracked off, and he swerved in a panic.

"What in the...?" My eyes darted all over to find where the rogue bullet had come from, and in a brief pocket of moonlight, I saw Mateo and Amos running along the lane in opposite directions. Both had a pistol in hand, and Mateo headed north while Amos made his way south toward me.

"On your left!" he hollered.

I whipped my head around in time to see the injured rider coming straight for me.

My bullet would never strike true from this angle, but none of the Sandusky stock were in range, so I fired all the same to keep the rustler frazzled. Then I kicked Birdy onward while the rider tried to correct his mount's direction.

I'd have to circle back around to really be sure I had a good aim on him, but my back would be left wide open in the meantime.

I cursed under my breath as I urged Birdy to hurry up, but then a crack behind me sent a bullet whistling right past my head.

A split second later, another shot fired, and Amos whooped in victory.

I craned my neck around to see my pursuer was no longer in the saddle. He was just a lump beneath the racing clouds, and I chuckled at Amos' wild celebration. The dark-skinned man had thrown his head back and was howling toward the sky, and I couldn't help chuckling.

His camaraderie and mettle brought me back to the war, when just the sweat and grit of the man next to you could steel your strength and revive your spirit for the fight ahead.

I'd have to thank Amos later for the backup, but for now, I had one more rustler to deal with.

He was ahead of me and trying to turn toward the western gate yet again.

I sharply shifted Birdy, cut off his course, and forced him east, but I couldn't fire with half the herd right beyond him, so I just hauled after him for now. I figured our arrival would send the horses scattering again, and I'd be able to crack a shot off real quick with the wind still at my back. I only had two bullets left, so unless I wanted to pull out my Winchester, I had to make this count.

But Mateo had other plans.

The young ranch hand shot from his spot on the fence, and while he missed his target, he managed to startle every horse in the area.

That's when everything went to Hell in a handbasket.

Nearly thirty horses scattered at once, and as I wrenched on Birdy's reins to avoid a collision, the final rustler galloped straight into a big black stallion.

The clash brought painful bellows from both beasts, and I thought I heard Mateo yell out in shock just before the rustler's horse reared back all the way and crashed to the ground.

Now, it was the rustler who was yelling. His leg was briefly pinned beneath his beast, but not for long. By the time my path to the man was clear, his horse was up and taking off without him, and he was raggedly running for the northern fence.

Mateo tried to fire again, but his target was already over the fence and hobbling through the next pasture.

The thief seemed to fear the larger beasts kept in there, though, most likely because all seven of them were draft horses. If I squinted, I could see the man trying to make it back to the eastern fence and into the lane beyond. Which would take him straight up toward the house.

My gut clenched, but just a second later, I heard a sharp whistle to my right.

"Jesse!" Amos hollered.

I found him holding the gate to the lane wide open for me and frantically waving his arm.

I didn't hesitate.

Birdy and I galloped straight through the open gate and rounded our way up along the lane by the time the last rustler made it over the fence. Mateo stumbled into the center of the lane ahead of me with both hands clutching a pistol. He fired after the fleeing thief, but the bullet shattered a fence post on the left instead.

He was causing more damage than good at this point.

"Mateo!" I yelled as Birdy quickly closed the gap between us and him. "Put the pistol down!"

"Yes! Yes, okay!" he yelped as we thundered past him.

My heart hammered in my throat as I tried to keep the rustler in my line of sight, but the constant shift between pitch dark and pale moonlight only made things trickier as he neared the large house. I certainly wouldn't risk firing in that direction with a crosswind, but I'd be caught up to him once he was clear of the place.

I lost sight of him briefly after he crested the hill near the garden, but Birdy was only ten feet behind when we found him sprinting toward the shadowy side of the barn.

I raised my pistol and tried to steady my aim as Birdy barreled down the hill, but just as the man reached the back corner of the barn, he was suddenly stopped in his tracks.

He flailed and dropped to the ground, and I barely reined my mare in before we could trample him. Birdy's hoofs shot up and stamped back to the ground just a couple feet from the man's head.

I stared down in confusion as he wheezed, clutched his chest, and rolled to the side.

Then Abel stepped out from behind the barn with a bent shovel in hand.

"Did you…" I gaped at the older ranch hand.

"Shovel," he said with a nod. "Work good for everything."

I couldn't help but burst out laughing.

The man on the ground was still fighting for breath when I climbed down from my saddle and sobered up enough to glare down at the captive. He was scrawny in build, with three missing teeth and a pair of tattered overalls trying their best to stay on his shoulders.

"You got some rope?" I asked Abel.

"Sí." He nodded, passed me his shovel, and slipped into the barn.

I flipped the shovel over and planted the head into the ground beside the final rustler, and he flinched violently.

I chuckled a bit. "Yeah, well, what did you think would happen coming into the Black Spur Ranch?"

The man let out a gurgling wheeze.

"Not your brightest idea, was it?" I continued, and he managed a slow shake of his head. "That's what I thought."

Mateo and Amos joined up with us just as Abel finished tying the rustler's hands behind his back. He'd mostly stopped wheezing by now, but that also meant he could run his mouth more than we'd like, so Amos took his bandana from his pocket and tied it tight around the man's mouth.

"Phew!" Mateo sighed and raked his fingers through his hair. "That was wild, no?"

"Yes, sir!" Amos chuckled and clapped a firm hand on my back. "Jesse, you sure know how to ride, I'll give you that. There was about ten times I thought you were about to get thrown, but that mare of yours moves like you're one and the same."

"She does," I agreed with a grin. "Although, I owe you my thanks. I don't think I'd have made it if you hadn't shot that one rustler down at last. You're pretty sharp with a pistol."

"Not if I was up on a horse like that," he laughed. "I can hold my own, but you hold just about everyone else at your mercy once you got a pistol in hand."

I shook my head. "I do best with the tools I'm used to working with, same as anyone else."

"Yes, we all shot good tonight, I think," Mateo said and nudged me in the side.

I cast a glance at the younger ranch hand. I was trying to decide how to word my opinions on his own shooting, but Abel got there first. The older brother launched into a rant that made Mateo jump back, and he didn't let up for several minutes except to draw a breath.

Amos and I just chuckled, hauled our captive to his feet, and headed toward the lane. The black man knew of a good spot to tie him off for the night, and he quickly hurried ahead to make sure he had enough rope there. I carried on dragging the bound-up man across the yard, but then a sudden shift in the clouds illuminated Helena standing on the front porch.

She had a blanket wrapped around her and a scattergun clutched across her front. Her long, strawberry-blonde hair was braided over one shoulder and rippling in the wind, but she didn't look at all rumpled by sleep. Quite the contrary.

She somehow managed to look regal despite her intimate attire as she glared down at the tied-up rustler. The expert grip on her firearm probably had something to do with that.

I brought us to a stop at the base of the stairs and gestured toward the dark pastures.

"I suppose you heard the commotion."

"I heard alright," she said stiffly. "How many were there?"

"Just three," I said. "Two of them will be seeing the undertaker. This one I'll drag into the deputy tomorrow. I'm sure this lot have been causing trouble for more than just you around here."

"Probably so. A few of the ladies I know say their husbands' cattle have been picked over the last couple of months." She pursed her lips. "How are the horses? Did any get out?"

"They're shaken up, but none of them were harmed or set loose," I assured her. "Amos is gonna fix the two fences they damaged tomorrow."

"The old wooden ones?"

"No, some barbed wire was cut," I said. "Nothing that'll cause you too much trouble."

"Well, that is a relief." Her expression softened a little, and she lowered her scattergun to a neutral position.

It struck me then that she looked like some fabled warrior or battle-savvy queen from tales of times long past. It wasn't just her natural, feminine beauty that made me think so, either. It was the steady look in her eye, her sure posture, the way her mind went quickly to the important things rather than getting caught up in emotions.

I started to wonder if she'd be able to defend this ranch herself one day. She was struggling with grief just now, but one day, she'd probably gain the courage to do so with a little encouragement.

The stubborn breeze blew a few loose strands of hair across the woman's moonlit face, and she raised a slender hand to brush it away as she sent me a grateful smile. I found myself smiling back without thinking much about it.

Then the man in my hold shook violently, as if he thought I'd grown too distracted to keep him in place.

I hadn't. I gave him an even firmer shake, and after a few curses, he grunted and gave up for the time being.

"Thank you," Helena said. "You've been— Your arm!"

I frowned but then realized I'd forgotten all about the bullet that grazed my shoulder. The woman had already descended the steps and shifted to get a look at the bloody left sleeve of my jacket.

"It's no trouble," I told her. "Barely feel it now."

"Are you sure?" She bit down on her lower lip as she looked more closely, and she carefully pulled back the torn fabric to look at the wound. "It's not too deep."

"As I said." I smiled. "No trouble at all, don't worry."

"I suppose if you're certain—"

"That sounded like a whole lotta shootin' out there, Mr. Callahan!" Russel suddenly hollered from an upstairs window. "You sure do know how to run some rustlers outta a place, that's for sure!"

"Thank you, Russel," I laughed.

The boy's mother gave that same exasperated sigh her son seemed to inspire a lot.

"I'll be just fine," I assured her.

"Well… Thank you, Jesse," she said softly. "I am very grateful for your help, once again."

"My pleasure." I grinned, shunted the tied man ahead of me, and carried on prodding him toward the bunkhouse.

When we got there, Amos was ready to hog-tie him and secure him to a post out back. Then he stood guard while I met with Abel and Mateo to drag the two dead rustlers out of the pasture and over to one of the Sanduskys' wagons.

We gathered a total of three dollars, twenty-three cents, and two golden eagles from the pair, as well as a pair of rusty old wire cutters. We'd have to search for their lost guns once the sun came up, but for now, we loaded them up into the wagon. Then Amos and I took turns standing watch the rest of the night. Aside from the many furious curses our tied-up friend let out, all stayed quiet on the ranch, and the horses settled down easily enough once peace was restored.

The next morning, the ranch hands helped me load up the foul-mouthed rustler beside his dead companions. We hitched my two mules up to do the hauling and give them some work, and once I slid my Winchester under the seat, Mateo and I headed down the lane.

Birdy was out pasturing with a calm-looking set of horses this morning, but I found her hugging the fence line and not looking too pleased about it.

I reined the boys in and hopped down to give her a pat or two.

"Still not making friends, huh?" I asked the old mare.

"She nipped at our boss girl, Bonita, over there," Mateo called down. "One of our best broodmares."

I looked in the direction he pointed and found a stunning Morgan mare with about ten other horses gathered near her. Her belly was swollen with a foal.

"Ah." I smiled at old Birdy. "You know, there's plenty of pasture out here. Why don't you take a walk, huh? You've sure earned a calm and pleasant day in the field, and this fence will hold itself up alright…"

Birdy let out a fierce neigh right in my face, and she tossed her head as she looked at the two mules.

"Hoooold on, now," I chuckled and held my hands up in surrender. "You hate wagon pulling, don't forget that. These boys don't mind at all, and they didn't have to run all over protecting this ranch last night. They're doing you a favor here, Birdy. It's a kindness."

She pushed her face against mine, and I smiled as I gave her a hug.

"I'll be right back," I assured her. "Think about that walk, alright? Look at all those fine grasses out there, just waiting to be eaten."

"Here, give her this," Mateo said.

I turned and saw him holding out a dirt-covered carrot.

"Do you carry these around with you everywhere?" I grinned and passed the carrot to old Birdy.

"Of course." Mateo smiled. "Is why all the horses like me."

I laughed as I left Birdy with a few more gentle pats, and then Mateo, me, and the boys headed toward Pinos Altos together.

We intended to gather supplies for the new stables once we finished speaking with the deputy. He should have the last of my bounty for the Hobbs brothers ready by now, but I'd also been instructed to check in at the post office to see what Helena's sister-in-law had to say about the telegram. Then we'd be set to get to work on building for the next while.

Once we made it to the main thoroughfare, the folks in town were even more curious about our wares than they had been during my first visit, but we carried on down the road all the same. Several passersby seemed to recognize me and took to pointing and murmuring to their neighbors about 'that fella who got those Hobbs boys.'

Mateo looked pleased with the stir we were causing, but I kept my eyes forward and just nodded or offered a brief greeting to those who came up to us.

We got the wagon settled outside Deputy Wallace's office, and the lawman was as friendly as he had been during our first meeting, although considerably disappointed by the news of rustlers out at the Black Spur Ranch.

"That's been my concern," he sighed as he crossed his arms and considered the three lumps in the wagon. "Thank God you stuck around to keep an eye on the place."

The bound-up rustler was trying to say something

through the spit-drenched bandana in his mouth, and the deputy walked over to pull it out.

"We weren't doin' nothin'!" he insisted at once. "We were just—"

"Oh, pipe down, Bart," Deputy Wallace spat and shoved the bandana back into place. "You three have been rustling half the ranches out here for months now that Jim joined up with you. And always cutting the wires the same. Let me guess, you found an old gate and then laid your little path out, didn't you?"

Bart looked stupefied, but said nothing.

"Uh-huh." The deputy nodded. "That's what I thought. You're lucky these fine folks around here didn't catch you and string you up themselves for all the trouble you've caused. They're hanging horse thieves down in Silver City, I'll have you know."

This caused the scrawny rustler to start arguing more than ever, but the lawman ignored his muffled words as he gestured for us to head back into the office. He hauled Bart off the wagon before he followed, and he chucked him into the jail in back before meeting Mateo and I at his desk.

"Alrighty!" he said with a clap of his hands. "Let's see what we've got for you boys."

CHAPTER 7

It only took a minute for the deputy to find the information he was after.

"Okay, we've got Bart Pritcher, Hank Hart, and the new fella, Mississippi Jim," he read off. "These three have been costing people around here quite a lot lately, but Bart and Hank tend to stick to the cattle, I hear. They have fifty dollars apiece on their heads. Mississippi Jim out there is the one with the scars all over his cheek. He's been dabbling a lot longer in these sorts of things, and he wasn't above leaving a man stranded without a horse in sight, so he's gonna bring you another hundred and twenty. How's that sound?"

Mateo laughed in surprise at this, and he removed his hat to fan himself as he nudged me in the arm.

"That's very good for three ladrones, no?" he asked with a wide grin.

"Sure is," I chuckled and turned back to the deputy. "Where do we stand on the last of my bounty for the Hobbs brothers?"

"Got that all set for you!" Deputy Wallace hopped up and opened a small square safe in the back corner of the room. "I gave you four hundred when you first came in, so that's four hundred and fifty I owe, correct?"

Mateo stopped fanning himself. His smile went slack as he gawked in my direction.

"That's correct," I said and took a seat at the lawman's desk.

Mateo stayed right where he was, and I got the sense he'd forgotten how to blink.

Once the deputy finished counting out the last of my pay, he counted out a separate stack of bills to cover the rustlers we'd brought in. I slid this pile over to Mateo, who shook his head and refused to take it.

"You guard the ranch, not me," he said. "I can't even shoot the post good."

"I know," I chuckled lightly. "I saw as much last night. You just make sure Amos and Abel get their share. Amos took out that Mississippi Jim himself."

"Abel won't take all that's left," Mateo said and counted out fifty dollars. "Here, you have your share. Abel won't take it all."

"Fair enough." I took the fifty.

The deputy smiled as he watched the two of us stow our earnings in the inner pockets of our vests.

"You ever consider becoming a lawman?" Deputy Wallace asked me. "Sure could use a fella like you out here. Seems you work fast and thorough, no matter the class of criminal. And you could find a worse place to settle down than Pinos Altos."

I smiled at this, but settling down anywhere was the last thing on my mind. I'd settled down just once in my life, and that had gone just about as bad as it could have.

"I don't think the life of a lawman would suit me too well," I said. "Besides, I make good money in the work I'm in."

"Sure do," the deputy agreed. "You're making more than me, no doubt about that. Probably work less hours, too. If you're looking after the ranch, though, do me a favor and let me know if those six men show back up. This town's always growing, and it's not unheard of for folks to stick around once they're here. Pinos Altos has a lot to offer. And if they killed Frank Sandusky to get at that herd, they're bound to show up eventually."

"I'm not sure that was their aim," I said. "Not with how violent the crime was. Seems personal. Maybe due to a sale gone bad, but the men out there can't recall any instance of the sort. Have you found anything out on your end?"

Deputy Wallace leaned forward and braced his arms on the desk as he frowned in thought.

"Not a thing," he said. "Not looking likely that I will, either, but the sheriff is willing to place a steep bounty on all their heads if we find out who they are. He rides a Sandusky horse himself."

I wasn't much surprised to hear it. If I lived in these parts, I'd see to it that I had one of those fine horses, too.

"I think I'll do some digging of my own while I'm here," I told the man. "Mrs. Sandusky has asked me to help with security concerns until her sister-in-law arrives, and I won't be able to rest until I know something about this whole ordeal."

"Well, I'd sure appreciate you letting me know if you find anything," he said in a serious tone. "With a man like you looking into things, I feel a lot better about those men being found."

"Any advice on where I might start?" I asked as Mateo and I headed for the door.

"I've been through most of the saloons and the hotel," he said. "Haven't met with anyone who could give me information. But some of the folks over at La Casa Dorada seemed to know Frank personally. A lot of the longstanding locals go there. They could know more about what the man's been up to as of late, if that's a help."

I nodded. "I'll start there, then. Thank you."

"Anytime." The deputy smiled, shook mine and Mateo's hands, and bid us farewell.

Mateo and I strolled down the boardwalk, and a few

families we passed offered us smiles and greetings. Two men even thanked me personally for clearing out the rustlers, so word had clearly spread fast.

"You been to La Casa Dorada?" I asked Mateo once the men went on their way.

"All of the time," he said. "Good people there. Good food and drinks, too. Many neighbors of the Sanduskys go in there when they come to town."

"Sounds promising," I decided.

"Do I help with this part?" He looked eager at the prospect.

"You could help me. If you see anyone around who you're sure knew Mr. Sandusky personally, let me know who they are, alright?"

"I can do that," he assured me.

The two of us stopped in at the post office on our way to the saloon. Bonnie and Earl were as cordial as they had been during my last visit. The counter clerk positively lit up when she passed me the telegram Lucy Kimber had sent the day before in reply to Helena's.

Mateo and I read the slip of paper:

THE WESTERN UNION TRANSIT COMPANY
INCORPORATED
21,000 OFFICES IN AMERICA.   CABLE SERVICE TO THE WORLD

THOS. T. ECKERET, President and General Manager.

| NUMBER | SENT BY | REC'D BY | CHECK | |
| 51 de | Cr | Al | Paid | 23 Collected |

RECIEVED at _Pinos Altos,_
Dated _September 19th 1880_
To _Helena Sandusky_

Currently contracted. Show finishing September 23rd.
Traveling to you then. Hug the children.
Sleep with a gun.

Lucy Kimber

Received at Pinos Altos
Dated September 19th, 1880
To Helena Sandusky
Currently contracted. Show finishing September 23rd. Traveling to you then. Hug the children. Sleep with a gun.
Lucy Kimber

I raised my eyebrows a bit at this last bit.

Then again, after seeing Helena with her scattergun last night, I supposed it was likely her sister-in-law simply knew her to be a capable woman in that regard.

Or she suspected the ranch and their residents were in more danger.

The question was whether this was on account of Frank's death alone, or instead based on some private knowledge she had. I couldn't be sure, but I was eager to speak with the woman when she arrived.

Mateo and I headed to La Casa Dorada next, and I gestured for him to push through the batwing doors ahead of me when we arrived.

Inside, the saloon was one of the cleaner establishments I'd seen so far west. The floors weren't covered in sawdust, and a man played an upbeat tune I actually recognized from a tinny piano in the corner. The wooden fixtures all matched everywhere I looked, and I did a double take when I realized there were real gold embellishments inlaid into the beams on the ceiling. They formed mosaic designs that caught the glow of the sunlight bouncing off the floorboards, and the effect seemed to make the room a warmer hue.

The place had more than a couple large rooms to offer quieter eating quarters for the guests who preferred it, and while it wasn't the sort of overdone, two-story setup I'd seen in the cities, there were no soiled doves or comfort girls trying to entertain the guests, either.

Right away, I liked it for that.

It looked like a lot of people around here had my same

taste. The saloon was fuller than I'd expected so early in the day, and the delicious smell of their food was probably part of the reason. My mouth started watering as soon as I walked in.

The folks behind the counter smiled kindly at us when they saw us. One was an older Spanish man who was deeply tan, with a black mustache and neatly combed hair to match. He seemed to be doing three things at once as he swiftly moved from one customer to another, and his rolled-up sleeves were stained from the day's work already.

A woman who looked to be around the same age as him worked at his side, and her pale, milky-white skin was proof enough of how many hours she spent here. She kept her soft brown hair pinned up nicely away from her face, and her dress and apron were crisp and clean. She reminded me a little of Helena, except her eyes were a light shade of brown that was almost gold.

"Mateo," the woman said with a warm smile. "It's good to see you again."

"It is a pleasure to see you, Mrs. Vallejos." Mateo met her at the counter before nodding at the older man. "Mr. Vallejos."

The mustached man quickly finished pouring the drink he'd been working on, handed it to a patron, and promptly came over with a deep frown on his face.

"We heard about Frank," he said with concern. "Are you doing alright out there?"

Mateo waved his hand in a so-so manner and began speaking rapidly in Spanish. I could tell he was going into great detail about everything that had taken place in the last few days, and Mr. and Mrs. Vallejos listened intently to his every word.

"This is him," Mateo suddenly said and placed a hand on my shoulder. "Jesse Callahan. Very, very good shooter. Even on horseback."

"It's good to meet you, Mr. Callahan," Mr. Vallejos said

and shook my hand. "You can call me Diego. This is my wife, Shasta."

"Good to meet you," I told the man.

"It's a relief to know you're helping out at the ranch," he said.

"Poor Helena must be..." Mrs. Vallejos started, but she seemed lost for words.

"Such good people, the Sanduskys," her husband sighed. "You are planning to stay with them for a while, I hope?"

"I've offered to help out, yes." I intentionally kept my response vague in case anyone in the saloon was listening to our conversation. As far as I was concerned, I was working now, and I never took careless strides when I got to work.

Diego Vallejos was keen enough to pick up on this.

"Good, good." The man nodded and motioned for us to move down the counter to the deserted end. "Many patrons of mine are worried at the news of what's happened."

"Murder is such a sinful thing," Mrs. Vallejos murmured. "Who on Earth could do such a thing to such a kind man?"

"That's what I'd like to sort out," I said in a low tone. "The six men who did it rode off in this direction that night. You wouldn't happen to recall a band that size passing through, would you? This would be around ten-thirty in the evening. Possibly later."

Mrs. Vallejos frowned and looked at her husband. "I retire early, I'm afraid."

"I couldn't say," he admitted. "I work alone at the counter in the late evenings with just my daughter to help sometimes. But I will see what she has to say. She was working that night."

"I'd appreciate that," I said. "The deputy doesn't have much to go on, and I'd like to help out where I can."

"Then anything you like is on the house," Diego said. "Sit down, we'll bring you anything you like."

Mateo tried to decline the kind offer, but he didn't get far once Mrs. Vallejos started insisting. So the pair of us took our seats at a table in the corner, and I cast a glance around the saloon while we waited on a pair of beers.

"That man over in the far corner," Mateo said. "He lives two miles from the ranch. He knew Frank I think. His wife brings pies to Mrs. Helena sometimes."

I nodded and took note of the tall, scrappy gentleman at the corner table. He had a gentleness to the way he moved, and he laughed heartily with the young man he sat with. Judging by their attire, I assumed the younger man worked at a mine, and the older one spent a lot of time working around coal.

Our beers arrived then with a couple bowls of posole and a plate of piping-hot tamales. Mateo and I drank slowly while he pointed out the patrons he could recognize as having any personal acquaintance with his boss. Most of them were older folks who had lived here for longer than Mateo himself, and none of them struck me as the sorts who'd hire a killing like the one I'd witnessed.

I'd expected as much, but more importantly, none of them were what Mateo would consider to be friends of the deceased. They'd bought from him, tipped their hat at the man once years ago, or their wives were friendly with Helena. As far as personal friends of Frank Sandusky, it appeared none could be found here.

"The two men near the counter were soldiers," Mateo said as he started running out of people to point out. "Very old now, and old when they fought, too. Good men. They both buy horses from us years ago."

The two veterans were weather-worn and stooped from age, which I took as a testament to how much they'd muscled through and managed to survive over the years. Now, both of them sat in silence together with their floppy hats side by side on the tabletop. They ate at a slow pace, and they looked mildly bored about it.

Until a young woman came in from the back of the saloon

JR. WILSON

and checked how their meals were going. Then the pair of old-timers perked right up, and their eyes crinkled at the sides as they nodded and smiled and talked with the girl.

She was the only woman I'd seen around here who wore her hair down in the daytime, aside from a turquoise and silver clip that held part of it back from her face. The rest tumbled down her back in soft, dark brown waves the color of a good strong cup of coffee, and her skirt was embroidered around the waist with small flowers that matched the color.

Mateo visibly straightened up at the sight of her, and he whipped his hat off his head faster than a rattler could bite.

"That is Rosa," he practically whispered. "She is the most beautiful woman."

I grinned and shot him a look. He dug his elbow into my side and insisted I remove my hat as well. I chuckled at that, but obliged the man just in time for the woman to turn and make her way through the other tables.

I quickly understood Mateo's reaction.

Rosa only wore a loose white top tucked into her skirt, but she held herself like some of the finest dressed women I'd seen. The steady sway of her skirt as she walked spoke of a steady confidence, and there was an almost rhythmic quality to it that reminded me of slow dancing.

She spoke easily with all the patrons she passed, and not one of them took liberties with the beautiful woman. Just about everyone suddenly remembered how to sit properly, and for every word they shared with the woman, their smiles grew wider. Then she'd pass on to another table or fetch a fresh drink for someone, and it wasn't long before she reached our table in the corner.

Up close, I could see that her warm bronze skin was unmarred by years of strife. Her smile was calm, and her rich brown eyes caught every bit of sun from the front windows to make them glow almost as much as the gold on the ceiling.

102

"Buenos dias," she said in a low tone and gave Mateo that same calm smile.

Mateo smiled back and began conversing in Spanish with the young woman as she tidied up our table, and I started to see what Amos was talking about. This boy knew how to flirt like no one's business, but he was charming about it. He talked and talked, and the more he did, the more Rosa's smile grew. She had a knowing look on her face that made me think she was used to him going on like this.

She said very little back. Besides a nod or a word here and there, Rosa continued quietly making sure every bit of dirt or food was brushed away from the tabletop, and her hands moved gracefully while Mateo tried to charm her still.

He just about forgot I was next to him, too.

I worked through most of my posole and had just finished my beer when the young woman suddenly turned that smile of hers my way.

"Can I get you another?" she asked.

"No thank–" I started to say, but Mateo cut in.

"Always, Rosa, gracias," he said with another charming smile. "Jesse, this is Rosa, the most wonderful woman you will ever meet. And this is my good friend, Jesse Callahan. He is the best shooter you will ever meet."

"Really?" Rosa asked.

"I wouldn't claim as much," I chuckled.

"Oh, but Mateo would never speak too highly of someone for effect," she said smoothly.

Then the clever woman took our tankards and made her way back to the bar with her skirts slowly swaying behind her.

It was the longest sentence I'd heard her speak to either of us.

"That woman's got your number," I snorted and shook my head at Mateo.

"All of the numbers," he sighed and watched her go. "I do not care. She is Rosa, and I am a mosquito who gets to talk to her sometimes. She smells like flowers. She smiles like the sun. Her voice is like music…"

I laughed heartily at this. Then I watched the young lady converse with Mr. and Mrs. Vallejos behind the bar as she refilled my beer.

The older gentleman leaned in close to speak with her, and her smooth brow furrowed intently. Her expression betrayed only a flicker of concern before her calm demeanor returned. Then she helped Mrs. Vallejos with a few plates as if nothing had happened.

With the three of them all standing together, I realized Rosa must be their daughter. She shared some of Diego's features, and her hair was a perfect mixture between his black hair and his wife's lighter brown.

Her striking eyes must have come entirely from the kind woman behind the counter. They were a deeper, richer shade, but they glowed with pure amber in the centers.

I was surprised with myself at noticing such a detail, but I shook it off.

It was when Rosa returned that my interest truly piqued.

"Here you are, señor," she murmured kindly.

Mateo received a new beer as well, and he was about to launch into another charming conversation with the woman when she abruptly shot him a pointed look.

Mateo's smile faltered as she busied herself with collecting our bowls and plates. Her eyes didn't meet mine at all, but her movements were calm and natural as she kept busy and spoke barely above a whisper.

"The six men came here that night," she said. "They moved on to the Buckhorn down the street."

CHAPTER 8

Mateo and I strolled side by side down the boardwalk five minutes later. We'd only stayed at La Casa Dorada long enough to finish our drinks and converse very briefly and discreetly with Rosa, then made our way toward the Buckhorn.

The calm, unassuming woman had been incredibly helpful in those few stolen moments.

The night of Frank Sandusky's murder, six men had come into her family's saloon with red dirt smattered on their boots and chaps.

This was of note because I knew well enough that ribbons of red dirt ran all throughout the Black Spur Ranch, and I'd seen none like it all the way into Pinos Altos.

Rosa knew as much, too, it seemed. This was why she'd mentioned it. She then said the six men arrived right around the same time I'd suspected they'd make it here, but after inquiring after some sporting girls, they'd departed and made their way to the Buckhorn as per her suggestion.

I was deeply appreciative of the young woman's keen eye and memory. She'd even given me a loose but promising description of the men, which was a lot more than I'd thought I'd find today.

Rosa had been a Godsend, but this didn't explain why

her rich, brown-and-amber eyes and soft features wouldn't leave my mind.

I drew a deep breath as I suddenly realized why.

She'd caught me off guard because she reminded me a bit of my own wife, and very few women ever did.

My wife was also the rare sort of woman who said very little but somehow made a man feel entirely at ease. Every little smile or glance from her spoke clear enough what was on her mind, and I could've spent a whole day quietly watching her thoughts flit across her pretty face.

I shook away the painful memory before it could settle too much in my mind and focused on the street ahead.

"What will we do next?" Mateo asked me with his same eagerness.

"Take a look around the Buckhorn and see if any of the men in there match the descriptions Rosa gave us," I said.

"She is so wonderful," he sighed.

"When has she been out to the ranch?" I asked. I'd been curious from the moment she mentioned the red dirt.

"Many years ago now. I am surprised she remembers the way it looks."

"It's a very beautiful slice of land out there," I put in. "Not easy to forget."

"I suppose that is true." He nodded. "Her father bought a donkey that wouldn't stop biting. Brought him to Frank, and we straightened him out in a few days. He had a bad tooth."

I raised an eyebrow. "How'd you figure that out?"

"He only tried to bite me if I came near the right side of his face." Mateo shrugged. "Obvious."

"Hmm." I smirked. "Not bad."

"Rosa looked beautiful on the ranch that day," he continued. "Did I tell you she is a… what is the word for it? I say 'partera.'"

"Midwife," I supplied.

"Yes! She is midwife as well, which makes me happy to

think of. Such a woman as her, helping mothers to bring good, strong children into these lands. She is like a mother goddess. Or… something pretty like that."

I glanced sidelong at the man. "Well, she seems keen on you."

"I see what you are thinking," the young man chuckled. "But no man gets to have Rosa. They all ask, and she says no to everyone."

"I don't know about that, I saw the way she smiled when you talked to her," I said.

"She smiled at you the same!" Mateo scoffed. Then he clutched his heart like some poor Shakespearean actor. "And that is the problem. Her smile is torture. She's so kind all the time, and so she gives that smile to everyone."

"You intimidated by a little competition?" I asked.

"Not at all, I ask her to be mine every month. Just in case," he said with a grin. "She always says no, and I don't mind. Women like Rosa are too beautiful for men like me. I would get no work done with her around."

I laughed at this and shook my head. "I can tell you from experience that you make a very good point."

The two of us came to a stop outside The Buckhorn. It was a large, adobe-style building with a substantial amount of ruckus coming from inside. Apparently it was the first saloon established here, but once they started dabbling in the bordello business, the other saloons saw a rise in their patronage. Although, this place clearly wasn't hurting for the decision.

"You been here before?" I asked Mateo.

"Many years ago." He shrugged. "I like La Casa Dorada or the Twisted Saddle. It's very wild in this place. A lot of people passing through enjoy this. Men heading south to the smelters, that sort of thing."

"Well, I'd say there's a small chance some of the men we're after might be here," I said.

"Still?" Mateo asked.

"Deputy Wallace said folks tend to stay around the area on account of all there is to offer, and in my experience, men who frequent establishments like this don't mind sticking around to… get their fill of all that's available."

Mateo made a face at this. "None of the women in there will be half as beautiful as Rosa."

"I don't doubt you're right," I said. "Keep your eyes sharp, though. If we don't see any of the six, I may ask a few questions of the barkeep, depending what kind of man he is."

Mateo bobbed his head in understanding, and we headed inside.

We were met with a hammering piano that seemed determined to be heard over the ruckus right away. Under the thick, wooden beams of the ceiling, men packed the place from one corner to another for drinks or gambling or both. The crowd here was rowdier than at La Casa Dorada, but most of them seemed to be hardworking folks coming and going for a quick bite to eat.

If I craned my neck, I could see the next room was where the bulk of the gambling took place. Some men over there looked like longstanding guests who'd made themselves at home at the faro and poker tables, but others were scrappy and hungry-looking as they hovered between different tables, anxious to try their luck.

The two bearded men behind the front counter wore gruff glowers and kept busy without much of a word for anyone, but I could understand why. This place seemed like a constant, churning room of boisterous voices and thirsty men.

And of many strangers. Not a soul turned to look our way out of curiosity. Much of the conversations I picked up were about nearby towns, faraway cities, and the long trails men had taken to get here.

It was the perfect place to ask questions without rousing too much suspicion.

Mateo and I took two beers and wove our way through the patrons into the gambling and dining room beyond. I kept a casual but sharp eye on the men I passed all the way, and when a painted woman with a high-pitched giggle stumbled rather purposefully into my arm, I merely shifted aside and kept on walking.

My young companion was discreet enough, even if he did seem squirrelly whenever a woman came by. All the smooth charm I'd seen him use with Rosa was gone now, and I chuckled a little at the way his eyes went wide at every soiled dove we passed.

"So much painted on their faces," he murmured when we paused to get the lay of the gambling room. "My mother would not like me to be here, God rest her soul."

"Remember the faces you're supposed to be looking for," I said.

Mateo nodded and sipped his beer. "Right. Yes. I am looking."

We took up a spot in the corner again, but I stayed standing along with just about half the room. The bustle of places like the Buckhorn was something I was accustomed to during my travels, and I never tired of getting the feel of a new place.

Pinos Altos certainly drew a colorful array of people from all over. One group of men had come down from Utah Territory looking to get into the silver business but ended up buying three of the shops on the main thoroughfare instead. They were well-liked by those who knew them in here, and the one who'd cut my hair over at the barber shop had apparently fallen in love with a lady who entertained the patrons.

I shook my head and silently wished him well.

Another man near us was a decorated General who'd got himself ten thousand acres north of Santa Fe and now supplied most of the lumber for the stretch of track they were laying across his land. He came to Pinos Altos every couple of months simply because there was a faro dealer here who he figured was his lucky charm.

None of the intriguing men I saw around me matched the descriptions Rosa gave us, though. I was about to head back to the counter and try my luck speaking with the barkeep when a man pushed through the crowd hollering Mateo's name.

He was considerably shorter than either of us, but sturdily built with broad shoulders and corded forearms covered in veins. His face was creased and bore a resemblance to leather, and his stubble and short hair was peppered with gray.

Mateo beckoned the man over with a broad smile. The two met as only good friends would, and I shifted over to make room for the fellow to join us.

"This is Gilly," Mateo told me. "He is a farrier who comes to help Abel. His bits are the very best you can find here, the horses never fuss with his work."

I recalled Amos mentioning Gilly, and I introduced myself before the man started asking about Frank.

"What in Sam Hill is going on out there?" he asked.

"We are working to find this out," Mateo sighed. "Everything is hard right now. But Jesse is guarding the ranch now, he ran some men out just last night."

"The men who got Frank?" Gilly asked as his eyes bored into mine.

"No, some local rustlers," I said. "Bart, Hank, and some—"

"Mississippi Jim?" He gawked at me. "Well, hell, it's about time someone snatched those fools up. There ain't a ranch out here that hasn't had some trouble from them lately."

"Jesse has fixed it all, don't worry." Mateo grinned proudly. "And he will find the men who killed Frank. He is working hard on it."

I didn't correct the man to remind him that I would only be staying until Helena's sister-in-law arrived. I saw no reason to. I did intend to learn as much as possible in that time.

"Who you reckon it was?" Gilly turned to me again.

"Don't have a lot to go on just now. We've got a description, and word is the six men came in here that night."

"Six?" Gilly gasped. "What they need six men for?"

"It would be best not to say," Mateo said, and his voice sounded tight. Then he drained the rest of his beer in one gulp, and Gilly frowned at the floor.

"I'll get you another," I said, took the man's tankard, and started weaving my way back to the outer room.

I found the two barkeeps just as bearded and surly as before, and when I asked after the six men, the man I spoke to only shrugged, shook his head, and sloppily plunked two beers on the counter.

"Thank you," I muttered and took my leave.

I was making my way back to Gilly and Mateo when my eyes caught on a peculiar face.

In the far back corner to my left, a man with a protruding browline and a crooked nose sat at the last faro table. He was joined by a few others of little note, except for one man with the brightest blond hair I'd ever seen, and eyebrows to match.

The blond man and the one with the crooked nose fit perfectly with some of the descriptions Rosa had given.

I slowed my step and circled a little closer to be sure. Rosa had said the man with the crooked nose had a brow so large it was hard to see his eyes, and there was no mistaking the likeness now. The blond man was tall and built like a rail, which she hadn't mentioned, but the starkness of his eyebrows and hair were unmistakable, especially with the other man as his companion.

I made my way over to Mateo and Gilly now that I was satisfied.

The pair had noticed me changing directions, and they both had their necks craned trying to make me out through the crowd.

"What is it?" Mateo asked the moment I returned.

I handed him his beer. "Two of the men are here."

"Here now?" Gilly's eyebrows shot up toward his hairline and crinkled his leathery forehead. "You sure it's them?"

"Sure as I can be with what I'm going off of." I settled myself against the wall, but I shifted two feet to the left so I had a clear view of the faro table in question.

"What do we do?" Mateo hissed.

"Keep on talking," I said and cast a casual glance around the place. "I'll keep an eye on them for now."

Gilly nodded fervently and swiped a hand over his head. Then he stared at Mateo and waited for him to strike up a conversation.

"The... horses are doing... good," Mateo said in an almost natural tone. "Very good, really. So good."

"Good, good." Gilly nodded vigorously again.

"Easy," I chuckled. "No one's getting shot today. You just carry on as you normally would."

"Speaking of, I shot a cougar out at the Farris' place last week," Gilly suddenly supplied.

"Really?" Mateo was genuinely intrigued now.

The men settled a little after that, and Mateo and Gilly carried a less odd conversation from there. I occasionally gave my two cents, but I mostly kept checking on the two men at the faro table.

Now that I had two of them in my line of sight, the question was what to do about it.

I'd been honest about not looking to shoot anyone today. Truth was, I had no cause for attacking the two murderers right here. I'd be deemed a murderer myself and end up locked up as quick as a blink.

No, I had to take my time with these two. Now that I had them here, I needed to learn their names. If I could just get that information, the whole game changed. No matter where they went, I'd track them down.

Hopefully it wouldn't come to that, though. I'd bring the

names to the deputy and have him look into the pair. If they already had bounties on them, then it'd probably be a simple matter of increasing that amount and doing as I saw fit.

If they had no bounties yet, things became trickier. I'd have to get to proving without a doubt that they were some of the six who took out Frank Sandusky.

I hoped to avoid the annoyance, but I also suspected these two were wanted somewhere for something. Men didn't kill the way they had without having done wrong in plenty of other ways first.

The longer I watched them, the simpler the situation became. It wasn't long before I noticed the two already seemed familiar with the dealer at their table. They also had wolfish eyes for the ladies passing between the tables, so if the dealer didn't know their names, some of the women might.

In the end, luck was on my side today.

The moment the two men started rising from their chairs, I started in their direction. They each settled their ledgers with the dealer, gathered their drinks, and moved into the crowd.

I came up on the faro table a few seconds later, and as the dealer busied himself resetting the table, I leaned down to be heard beneath the throng of folks.

"You happen to know the name of the two fellas who just left?" I asked.

"Sure do." He nodded and continued working without another word.

I pursed my lips a little and slid a few dollars onto the table for him.

"Jeb Osiah and Petey McCaw," he said at once. "Blond man's Petey."

"They from around here?"

"No sir." He shook his head as a few new men sat down to try their luck. "Come up from Silver City. On their way there now, I believe."

"When did they get here?"

"First saw 'em three days past."

"Thank you kindly," I said and walked away.

A few minutes later, Mateo, Gilly, and I were on the board-walk outside the Buckhorn.

"Where are they?" Mateo hissed as his eyes darted around the street.

"On their way to Silver City," I replied and gestured toward the deputy's end of the street. "I'll drop their names off with Deputy Wallace, let him know about it. Whatever turns up, we'll proceed from there."

"Shoot, you done this before?" Gilly asked as he dogged along with us down the street.

"Yes."

"Jesse is a bounty hunter," Mateo supplied. "He kills many bad men. He came here to make hundreds off some brothers."

"Now, hold on!" Gilly caught up finally and smacked my arm. "You the man who got them Hobbs brothers? Why, the whole town's been talking about that! I didn't know I was talking to the very man who done it."

I slowed to a stop as we reached Deputy Wallace's door.

"Yes, I brought the Hobbs brothers in," I said.

Gilly grabbed my hand and shook it with both of his as he let out a loud, throaty laugh.

"Well, hell, you coulda started with that! And Helena's up and hired you, huh? Don't blame her at all. You sure did a bang-up job with those brothers. Heard you blew their heads clean off their shoulders!"

I furrowed my brow. "No. That's not how that went."

"That's what folks are saying!" Gilly laughed and shrugged. "Just as well, they were some filthy desperados, those two. Hate to think what would've happened out here if they'd made it this far."

"Yes, Jesse has handled those fools," Mateo assured him as

he stepped forward and hooked his thumbs in his belt. "He's the best shooter you will meet, probably."

"That's not… never mind," I sighed, and I left the men on the boardwalk as I entered the dim quarters of the deputy's office.

The lawman was stunned I'd come up with a lead so soon. I explained where I'd found the names, and what I'd both heard and suspected of their stay here in town.

"The dealer says they arrived three days ago," I finished. "That lines up real tidy, timing wise."

"I'll check in with the Sheriff, see what these two have been up to," he said with a nod. "This was at the Buckhorn?"

"That's right, they went in there looking for some sporting girls," I answered.

"Haven't made it there yet, but I'll see what the girls there have to say," he decided. "They've been cooperative in a few past instances. I'll send you word when I hear something from Silver City. Might be a few days before we know where we stand."

"I suppose I might come into town by then, but if not, you know a farrier named Gilly?"

"I know him, you want me to send him out to the ranch?" he asked.

"I'd appreciate it," I replied.

"Can do," he assured me.

"Much obliged." I tapped my hat and headed out.

Gilly and Mateo were talking with a few miners who'd apparently come around looking to hear about the rustlers. Mateo was in the middle of a very vibrant rendition of the occasion, while Gilly supplied plenty more details as if he'd been there himself.

Neither noticed my arrival, so I posted myself against the wooden siding of the office and crossed my arms as I listened to what must've been the most fantastical way of telling a thing that I'd heard in a long time.

Round about the part where I fired two pistols at once from atop a galloping horse, I cleared my throat and interrupted.

"We best be on our way," I said with a nod toward the wagon.

"This is him!" Mateo smiled from ear to ear. "Jesse Callahan, these men already heard about your work at the ranch. They came to meet you."

"Pleasure." I nodded at the three miners, and I spent a few minutes talking with them about the last several criminals this town had seen.

They were good men, and eager to hear all I had to say about my recent jobs, but I didn't linger too long. The midday heat was on now, and we still had lumber to gather and the building to start, so I got Mateo back to the wagon.

Gilly offered to ride along with us to the sawmill and help load our lumber. The work went fast with the three of us sharing the duties, and I got to know the broad-shouldered farrier better as we passed planks onto the wagon.

He'd been a blacksmith out near Cimarron until he took up a few farrier jobs to help a cousin of his. The work brought in what he considered to be easier pay at that time, so he stuck with it and got himself a job as the personal farrier for a big-name freighter. The job took him to and from Grant County so many times that he got to know some of the folks here in the Pinos Altos area, and after seeing the sizable ranches around here, he decided to settle in and work freelance.

"I try to get all the work I can with the Sanduskys," Gilly said as he hefted another few boards into the wagon. "Best-kept horses out here, I'll tell you that much. Abel is good at what he does, though. Frank only brings me in if there's a lot of shoeing to do in a day, but he likes my bits most of all. I custom fit them when needed, anything for Frank."

"You know how Frank ended up out here?" I asked in a casual tone.

"No, never asked," he said. "He wasn't a very talkative guy, but hell, he had a way with horses. And women. Got himself just about the finest wife he could have found out here, I reckon. How is Mrs. Sandusky doing?"

"She's keeping busy," I said and chose to keep the woman's private struggles to myself.

I wasn't surprised to hear that Gilly didn't know about Frank's past. At this point, I'd come to understand that no one around here seemed to. I hadn't found an appropriate time to bring it up with Helena, either, but in the last few hours, I'd decided it didn't much matter to me what Mr. Sandusky had been up to lately.

Based on all I'd heard, he sounded like an upstanding man who worked hard, provided amply for his family, and lived up to his reputation. His wife clearly loved him deeply, his workers respected him entirely, and even at above-asking price, folks seemed more than happy with their purchases.

As far as I could see, the world had lost a downright decent man the day Frank Sandusky was murdered.

So, now that I had two names out of the six men who'd killed him, I shifted my focus to handling them in kind.

Mateo sorted out the charge with one of the sawyers before we took our leave of Gilly and Pinos Altos. We took it nice and slow through the mountain pass and down to the foothills, and Mateo told me his stories of running coyotes off the ranch and trying to trap the mountain lions to pass the time.

We saw a few small groups of deer along the way, as well as two stately elk, and I could tell the hunting would be just as good out here as it had been further north in the Black Range. The tall pines and cool beds of needles beneath them spanned most of the mountainsides, and along with the long, winding rivers, this area was ideal for all manner of game.

I decided I'd try my hand at some hunting in these parts if I stayed out here long enough.

We made it back to the iron gate of the ranch with several

hours of daylight left to us. Birdy was now grazing around the pasture, albeit without any company. All looked quiet and peaceful under the glaring sunlight, and I eyed the cheerful blooms of the cacti among the swaying grasses all around us.

Amos and Abel were nowhere in sight, and I was about to ask where we might find them to help out with the lumber.

Then the peace was shattered as a shot cracked off and echoed clear across the land.

CHAPTER 9

Mateo yelped at the sound, and I flicked the reins to urge the boys to a faster pace.

Another shot split the air as we came to a dusty stop near the ruined stables.

I only paused long enough to pull my Winchester out from under the bench. Then the pair of us leapt from the wagon and ran for the house. This time, I was sure the sound had come from out back. My legs pumped harder as I crested the small hill near the garden, and I barreled around the short picket fence just in time to almost flatten Helena.

"Jesse!" she screeched and clambered to shield her daughter from all six foot three inches of me about to run straight through them.

I stumbled just in time to catch the woman and her daughter and slide them sideways out of my trajectory. Mateo slammed into my backend in the process, and I was launched straight onto my hands and knees as my rifle skidded ahead of me. Then the young man tumbled over my back and splatted himself across the dirt, and the woman burst out laughing.

I hastily righted myself and snatched my rifle up.

"We heard gunfire," I said, though my voice had more of a croak to it than usual.

"Yes, I gathered as much," she managed from behind her hand.

A fresh bout of giggles overtook her, so she just settled for gesturing toward the barn.

I whipped around and saw Russel with a revolver in hand standing by the far side of the barn and turned partially toward the trees beyond. He had a big, goofy grin on his face as he watched Mateo struggle his way to his feet.

"Ah." I drew a deep breath and dusted the dirt off my shirt. "That's… not so alarming."

"Mm-hmm," Helena chortled, and I sent her a grin.

Her cheeks were a lively pink, and her blue eyes were damp from laughing so hard. Mateo was laughing, too, and I couldn't help but join them.

"We thought, uh… Well, we thought there might be something amiss," I chuckled. "My apologies."

"Don't you ever apologize for running like mad to assist me or my family," Helena said and swiped her eyes. "I count myself lucky to be almost run over by you, given your heart was in the right place."

"You're mighty fast, Mr. Callahan!" Russel hollered out. "You best check that rifle of yours isn't packed with dirt, mind!"

I waved in his direction. "He practicing?"

"Yes, he likes to practice back here," the boy's mother said as she finally settled her giggles. "I think all that business with the rustlers has him concerned about the ranch."

I nodded in understanding.

Mateo came to my side and handed me my dusty hat that must've rolled down the hill when I hit the dirt. The two of us exchanged a grin at the state we were in, and then he clapped me on the shoulder, tipped his own hat to Helena, and quickly headed back to the wagon.

"How's this little one doing?" I asked as the little girl in Helena's arms snuggled her face away again.

"She's alright," the mother said softly. She stroked her daughter's curls. "This is Honey, by the way. Her name is really Adelaide, but no one calls her that. Do they, Honey?"

The little girl only snuggled tighter against her mother, and the woman smiled and hugged her back.

"Perhaps you should speak to him for a bit," Helena told me and nodded toward her son. "Just to settle his mind. I don't want him fearing for our safety here, and I don't see any reason he should have to with you around."

"I can do that," I said and made my way over to the boy.

He seemed to have a nice arrangement over here, with a long log to rest his guns on, and a cut-off stump beside it that was flat enough to keep his cartridges from rolling around. There was a rifle with a mahogany stock laying on the log already, but he held a revolver in his hand.

I watched him finish off the last three rounds, and he did better than any other boys I'd met around his age.

"That a Colt?" I asked.

"Yes sir, got me the '73 Peacemaker," he said. "You need any .44s you let me know, those are chambered for this revolver and your Winchester as well. Mighty convenient. You got a Colt?"

I grinned at this. "No, I used to have a pair, though. You're right, it was convenient back when I didn't want to lug all kinds of ammo with me."

"But you luggin' now?" he asked.

"Yes," I chuckled. "Over the years, I've developed my particular taste in weapons, and truth is, I like shooting what I've got. I travel enough that locating special ammunition isn't too inconvenient for me, either."

"That sounds real fancy." He pressed his lips together and narrowed his eyes in thought. "I might do that one day. Right now, I gotta stretch my cartridges much as I can, seeing as I'm not really supposed to go buying things like that."

"Understandable." I smiled.

"I'd still like to get me a nice '73 Winchester first. Lots of folks around here have one, and I like the idea of being able to use my .44s on more than one firearm. Sounds nice and simple."

"What have you got there?" I gestured to the rifle laying on a log.

The boy perked up, placed the Colt down, and brought over the rifle with a wide grin on his face.

"This here's all the way from Europe," he said proudly. "Martini-Henry."

My eyebrows popped up. "Is that right? Let me see that…"

Russel promptly passed it over for me to admire, and I let out a low whistle as I ran my thumb over the smooth, mahogany stock.

I'd heard of the Martini-Henry, but only really knew it was used by the British Army. It was a breech-loading, single-shot with lever action, and it was both heavier and longer than my '73. The whole thing must've been nearly fifty inches long, and weighed about eight pounds.

It looked practically brand new, with only a few scratches on the buttstock, and I noted the checkered pattern that was carved into the buttplate. I eyed the crown and 'V.R.' stamped into the action body, right above the word 'Einfeld' and the date 1873.

"Is this a thumb rest up on top?" I muttered under my breath.

"Sure is!" Russel gushed. "You gotta put your thumb there because if you wrap it over the top like usual, you'll smash your thumb into your face. And that ain't good."

"Huh." I frowned. "That's something, I guess."

"It can shoot a whole four hundred yards!" Russel added. "I never shot anything that far away before. Have you?"

"I have," I said. "This is a beautiful weapon right here. Mind if I try?"

"Sure!" He jumped aside to grab me a .45 cartridge from the stump behind me.

I loaded it, cocked the lever, and then took care to place my thumb on the proper rest. It felt odd, but I could get comfortable with it.

I aimed into the trees ahead of us, and I kept my eye on a particular trunk I gauged to be about three hundred and fifty yards away.

"Here goes," I said, and I pulled the trigger.

The report must've echoed for a mile around, and Russel cheered with both fists up in the air.

I grinned and admired the weapon again before letting Russel go check if I'd hit my mark. Sure enough, I'd struck true. Russel cheered all over again as he came bolting back to me.

"That was amazing," he panted.

"Quite the specialty," I agreed.

"Yeah, it needs that special kind of ammunition, too," he said as his shoulders sagged a little. "So I can't be using it much, I suppose. It's kinda hard to hold anyway, but it sure is beautiful."

"Sure is. Where'd your pa find a piece like this?"

The boy shrugged without much concern. "Dunno. It's his favorite, though. We liked to come back here shooting sometimes. All those holes over there are Pa's, from his revolver."

He pointed to a line of posts to the right. I strolled over and noticed the shattered wood was centralized in just one area on each of them. Not even a stray shot here and there. He'd had killer aim, that was for sure.

"Not bad at all," I said as I made my way back to Russel.

"I do some mighty fine shooting myself," he said.

"That you do," I agreed. "Glad to see you keeping two eyes

open when you aim, but try and let out a long, steady breath before you pull that trigger."

"I can do that," he said eagerly.

I motioned for him to give it a try, and once he'd reloaded, the boy took direction better than some of the men I'd fought beside in the war. He shot better than some of them, too.

With a few more tries, he managed to strike the post within an inch of his last shot every time. Then he took up the old Martini-Henry next to him and tried the same approach, but it was so heavy that the shot fired straight into the ground not thirty feet away.

"Better give that one a couple years to work up to," I decided as he set the rifle down beside his pistol. "Shouldn't be needing it any time soon."

I studied the boy's reaction to this, and he nodded as he started glaring at his toes. It was clear something was on his mind, so I waited patiently for him to decide if he wanted to talk about it.

"What if I do need it?" he asked in a quieter voice. "Anything could happen, Mr. Callahan. A man's got to be prepared."

"He does," I agreed. "But as far as I can see, you are. How long you been working with these guns?"

"The Peacemaker I've had since Pa gave it to me for my tenth birthday," he said. "Never want to need a pistol and find yourself without one, that's what he said. The rifle... well, that one's his, of course. Mama said I could have it, as long as I only shoot toward the trees over yonder. She said Pa would want me to have it."

The boy kept on glaring as he kicked some dirt, but then he straightened up and managed to keep a tone that was a little too firm.

"I figure one day soon, it'll be my job to run this ranch, so I gotta keep in practice," he said.

"I can't argue with that."

"Pa taught me to clean 'em up real nice, too, don't worry." Russel gave me a serious look. "A man's skill ain't nothing if he's slanging a grubby firearm, neither."

I smiled a little as I realized these must be his father's words.

"Sounds like your pa really knew a thing or two about shooting," I said.

"Sure did." He nodded and started counting a few lessons off on his fingers. "Never go at a man who's up to no good from straight ahead if you can catch him off guard from the side. No-good men don't live by the same rules as honest folks. Never fire a gun if there's a chance of someone else getting in the way of it, and never let Honey near the weapons until she's good and big enough to learn how to use them proper. Always reload with a clear mind and use that time to settle your nerves. Never get yourself in a pickle where you're outgunned and outmanned. Nothing wrong with retreating and getting your bearings if it'll save your life and bring a victory in the end."

This last lesson caught my attention the most.

"He learn that in the war?" I asked.

"No, sir, my Pa never wanted nothing to do with that sorta thing," Russel said. "That's why he come south after the war. He said it was a good thing that truce was found with the Apache 'cause this land out here didn't need more wars. Course, he's got friends among the Apaches, that's why. And people he knows in town, so that'd be real hard."

"You said he came here right after the war?" I kept my face expressionless.

"I dunno." Russel shrugged and started reloading his Colt. "I think that's what he said."

"Hmm." I crossed my arms. "Well, either way… I can tell you right now, you got some good aim on you, boy. Good sense, too. You just keep practicing, but for now, I don't want you to worry about the ranch, alright? Your daddy kept it running real smooth, and the ranch hands aren't gonna let him down any time soon. As for protecting the place, that's what I'm working on."

"And what if Mama don't keep the horses?" he asked anxiously. "What if it's too much trouble? She been talking like it's too much trouble, and she don't want any of us being in danger over some beasts."

"Well, there's a chance of that, I suppose," I said. "But even so, you might still get these lands one day. And the nice thing about owning so much land is you can do what you want with it when the time comes, can't you?"

This cheered the boy up. His eyes lit up at the prospect.

"I'm gonna raise horses," he said with complete conviction. "And shoot guns. That's just about all a man needs to be happy. I don't think I even need a wife, and that'll save money on the food, too!"

With that, he promptly went back to practicing with his Peacemaker.

I laughed lightly and watched for a bit before taking my leave, but I couldn't stop thinking over some of the things Russel had said.

From what I could tell, his father had done well with schooling him on the important things where firearms were concerned. He'd gone a little more in-depth than I'd expected, but Russel was a smart boy and seemed to have a level head about this sort of thing.

I didn't mind the man's position on war, either. I'd fought with pride and always would if I was called on to do so, but I'd seen enough death to know I'd prefer if a solution could be found by less violent means.

As far as Mr. Sandusky went, I could see there was certainly a lot of good that horses like his could do for people out in wild country like this, and I could understand sticking to your line of work and minding your own. Especially if you had folks on either side of a squabble who'd look to you for assistance. That was a tricky spot to be in.

No, the only fact that caused me to pause was that I just couldn't be sure how true all this was. A man only confided what he considered to be appropriate with his children, after all. And it sounded to me that despite the firm opinions he'd shared, Frank Sandusky would've made a natural soldier.

Who happened to come down here after the war, claiming not to have fought for either side.

And kept a British soldier's weapon as his favorite rifle.

I'd call that peculiar.

I left Russel to his practice and returned to the lane. Mateo had found Amos and Abel, and I joined in hauling the lumber down before we set to work.

After that, the days became a wash of laying out the groundwork on the stables, raising the first walls, and improving the few issues there'd been with the original in terms of how the stalls were laid out. I spent the next five days working all day in the sun with the ranch hands, and then I shared the night watch with Amos every evening.

We had two mountain lions roam through the property in that time, but only one foal was lost. I got my first glimpse of the wolves out here after the third night, and I had to admire the way they prowled in an orderly way and never took risks as a pack that they couldn't handle.

Amos said they never shot the wolves unless they truly started trying to pick away at some of the herd, and I respected his decision. The herds were large enough that they didn't try and find a meal among them. A few warning shots in the dirt near the pack was enough to send them on their way, and wolf urine helped keep the number of mountain lions and coyotes down.

No rustlers tried their luck again in those five days, and they were my main concern, so I was pleased with the way things had turned out.

The children of the ranch were kept busy with their usual chores, and it looked like their mother maintained her own routine quite strictly as well. Every single day saw Helena up by daybreak and working, and whether she wore black or settled for her simple ranching attire that day, she didn't make too much fanfare of her grief.

Several different ladies from the area came along to offer their condolences here and there, but aside from that, the new widow seemed determined to stay busy every moment of the day.

We all were.

By the end of that week, the bones of the first level of the stables were standing firm. We'd need more lumber in a day or two, but we had enough left to close in the space.

Helena was happy with the progress. She'd also approved two more sales Amos had lined up with some visitors in town, and they went off without a hitch. I only assisted with one of them and left Amos and Abel to handle the other. When Mateo needed assistance in the paddock, I readily lent him a hand, too.

I came to like the business of the ranch, both the labor and the training. I learned more about horses in that week than I had in all my life. I came to like the routine out here as well. The folks of the Black Spur Ranch had a way of balancing the rugged demands of the land here with steady, methodical ways that made even the harshest circumstances manageable. Even when a storm blew in wild enough to rattle every wall of the bunkhouse, the four of us men repaired the damage the flooding caused within just a handful of hours and kept on stepping.

It made me miss my own farm back in Texas. My parents had worked hard to build what we had there, and I'd taken up the work myself at only fifteen when scarlet fever took them from this earthly plain. I'd caught it as well, but God had seen fit to let me live and carry on my family's legacy.

I'd thrived in the grit and grind of those years running the farm on my own, starting a family at eighteen, and taking up arms when war called me forth.

Until it was all lost in one fell swoop.

Then I'd taken to life in a saddle, and I'd never regretted the decision.

I sighed a bit at the thought as I came to the wooden fence of the front pasture where Birdy had been spending her days as of late.

My old mare was my family now, and I'd made sure to give her plenty of affection between tasks while I worked to help improve the ranch. She'd been settling in here, too, now that Mateo had come up with the idea of sending my mules out to pasture with her.

It had become clear early on that she'd made not a single friend among this portion of the herd after sullying her chance with Bonita. The Morgan wanted not a thing to do with her, and I couldn't help disliking her for it. Birdy had a certain way about her, and beautiful as Bonita was, she clearly didn't have my keen eye for quality horses.

Then the unthinkable happened.

The moment my mules were let out, they made their way straight for Birdy, and against all my expectations, the old girl had been downright happy to have the boys back.

She tossed her chestnut mane and led them all over those forty acres after that, and I was proud of my boys for keeping their loyalty, despite the way she'd treated them on the trail.

Now, I found the trio grazing happily among the others without any butting of heads.

They made a pretty picture out there with the freshly risen sun warming their backs, and the dew in the grass staining their legs a darker hue. All was quiet this morning, even the wind, and I watched Russel trudge his way to and from the barn with Amos and a few bales of hay while I brushed Birdy and the boys out.

Then a clomping of hooves drew my eyes to the lane. I

watched a lone rider kick up a line of dust as he made his way up toward the house.

Once he drew closer, I recognized the broad shoulders of Gilly on the mount, and I waved him down. We met at the wooden fence line, and the man hopped down with some urgency.

"Everything alright?" I asked.

"Deputy Wallace sent me," he said and thrust a piece of paper my way. "He said to give you this. The sheriff got back to him about those two men we saw at the Buckhorn."

I quickly unfolded the paper and found just one name written on it:

Captain Charles Sellick

"Who's this?" I frowned.

"That's the man those two work for," Gilly told me with wide eyes. "He's one of the wealthiest prospectors down in Silver City."

CHAPTER 10

I climbed over the fence to join Gilly as he gave me a rundown of what the Sheriff said.

"The girls at the Buckhorn knew who that Jeb and Petey were alright," he told me. "Said Petey was runnin' his mouth about 'swinging by a real nice ranch' on his way into town. Said he only 'rustled up a small bit of mess for some folks.'"

I ground my teeth. "That's a real lazy way to put it."

"Don't I know it," he agreed. "Deputy wasn't pleased to hear it. Sent their names down to the sheriff, and low and behold, he comes to find they've been working for this Sellick."

"You know anything about the man?" I asked.

"Same as everyone else, I suppose," he said. "He's a Union man, come down here after the war. Struck silver down south and made a mighty nice way for himself down there. His operation's real big now, I hear."

I frowned as I considered this.

"Did the deputy mention whether the sheriff is going to bring the two men in?" I asked.

"No, sir." He shook his head. "All he said was this ain't an easy thing now that they work for Captain Sellick."

"I see." I pushed the paper into my pocket.

'Not an easy thing' was the sort of phrase most lawmen

used when they weren't about to take action. I'd come to learn that years ago, and it always chafed on my mind, but it wasn't much of an obstacle.

It just meant I had to move ahead on my own until they had no choice but to take action.

I certainly didn't mind the prospect.

"Silver City's about eight miles from here?" I asked Gilly.

"Closer to nine from the ranch." He eyed me carefully. "You goin' down to see the sheriff?"

"I think I'll take a look around the city," I said. "Would you let the deputy know?"

"I can do that," he assured me and climbed back into his saddle. "Good luck down there, Jesse."

"Thanks," I said and turned toward the house, but then I paused and called out to Gilly. "You keep in mind that message is for the deputy only. I can't have anyone else knowing my business on this one."

"Don't you worry, Jesse, I've got your back!" he hollered as he trotted down the lane.

I ran into Amos on my way to find Helena, and once the woman sent her young daughter off with Russel, I explained to the pair of them what the sheriff's findings were.

"Do either of you know anything about this Union man?" I asked.

"Not a thing," Amos said with a shake of his head. "First time I've heard the name."

"I've heard of him alright, from the neighbors, I think," Helena said. "He's well known down in Silver City."

"Well, he's also in charge of this Jeb Osiah and Petey McCaw," I said. "So I reckon I should head down there and see what I can find out."

"I think that's a wise decision," Amos said as his eyes took on that gunmetal cast I'd seen before. "Can't have those men getting away with none of this. I don't care how well known their boss is. Murder is murder."

"I'm of the same mind," I assured him. "I should be able to make it down to Silver City in an hour or so, if I keep my pace quick. My plan is to make it back before nightfall."

"Take one of our horses," Helena said at once and gestured for Amos to handle the job. The man quickly turned and got to work. "The land's a bit rugged between here and there, and I recall Birdy's on the older side."

"She is," I replied. "I don't doubt she can make the trip, but it'd go quicker on a younger horse."

"Then it's settled." She nodded. "Amos will find you just the thing."

Amos had gotten my saddle sorted in the lane by the time I finished deciding on bringing my trusty Winchester and one of my Remingtons with me. I'd have to look for more ammunition for my Schofield down in Silver City, since the general store in Pinos Altos hadn't kept what I needed in stock. For now, I left the bunkhouse with plenty of ammunition for the day's work, and I met Helena beside a gray-dappled stallion that looked to stand about seventeen hands high.

"The men call him Flint," Helena said. "He's half Thoroughbred and real smooth in the saddle, and he needs to stretch his legs. He'll keep a good pace for you."

"That sounds good to me." I slid my Winchester into the saddle ring, and the woman eyed the weapon for a moment. Then her blue eyes met mine.

"What are you gonna do down there, Jesse?" she asked in a low tone.

Her features were tense, and the weight of the world seemed to be on her shoulders just now.

I didn't see a reason to lie to her. Of anyone involved in this mess, Helena deserved the truth at every turn.

"First line of business is finding out who sent those men here," I said. "That's the tricky part, and might not be a one-day job. This Captain Sellick might be their boss, but that doesn't necessarily mean he hired them for this. I'll see what sort of man he is all the same, just in case, but I'd like to try my hand at finding how this all connects."

"And if you find the two the sheriff looked into?" she asked.

I removed my hat and swiped some sweat off my brow. I was careful to consider her question fully before responding.

"Deputy Wallace has good enough proof they came by here that night," I said as I settled my hat back on my head. "For myself, I don't need more proof than that. I'll handle the situation carefully, but with four more men still to track down… If the chance to thin out the pack comes along, I'll deliver the proper justice to the both of them."

The woman took my meaning. A grim determination came over her face, and she didn't look tense any longer. Her blue eyes cleared, and she gave a single nod of agreement.

"You know, I believe God sent you here that night," she confided in me. "He sent you to us like a guardian angel, to be sure none of those evil men could escape their punishment for what they've done."

I held her gaze. "With all due respect, I'm no angel."

"Sure you are." She smiled a little, and it lit her face up beautifully in the bright morning sun. "Plenty of angels have dirt on their hands and an iron will in their hearts. I've seen the way you are around here. You always do the right thing, and if anyone needs help, you're the first to offer it. You're a man of honor, Jesse Callahan, that's clear as day. And this work you do is something that helps everyone, no matter where you go."

"I suppose that's true," I said. "It's why I do it. Men like the ones who came here don't ever get enough of sin and strife. Nothing stops them until justice finally catches up to them. One way or another, I intend to make sure it catches up to as many criminals as possible before my own time comes."

"Well, may God see to it that that time remains far off," she said as her face softened. "It'd be a loss indeed if a man like you left this world too soon."

Helena reached out to place her hand on my arm, and I placed mine over hers as she dipped her head to say a quiet prayer for my safe return.

Then I saddled up on the dappled stallion and bid the woman farewell.

Russel and the little girl were strolling hand in hand through the grass alongside the lane. I slowed the stallion when I came up beside them, and for the first time ever, I found myself looking straight into the face of the little girl who'd been clinging to her mama ever since my arrival.

She was exactly her mother's likeness, but with blonder hair that fell in little ringlets around her round-cheeked face. She couldn't have been any older than four or five.

"Where you headed to, Mr. Callahan?" Russel asked me as he eyed the horse I was riding.

"Silver City," I replied.

At that, the little girl clung more tightly to her brother's hand and wedged herself right up against his leg.

"You... you're coming back, ain'tcha?" Russel asked uneasily.

"Sure am." I nodded. "Don't you worry. I aim to be back by nightfall, I just have some business to tend to down south."

Russel straightened up at this. "Well then don't you worry. I'll watch the ranch while you're gone. I'm a steed-- stead? Stead... fast?"

"Steadfast." I nodded in confirmation.

"Yeah, I'm steadfast." He nodded back, but then settled for a shrug. "I'll get my gun."

"Thank you," I said and fought back a grin. "I appreciate that."

I tipped my hat at the little girl and her brother as I nudged the stallion onward, but I stole a glance over my shoulder before I left the lane. The little boy and girl were right where I'd left them, and Russel waved wildly at me when he saw me looking back.

Their mother was still in the lane near the house, too. She held one hand against her chest while the other shielded the sun from her eyes, and she was looking all the way out to where I was riding toward the gate.

My chest clenched a little at the sight of the three of them there, all watching me carefully and anxious for my return.

"Let's get up." I gave Flint a firm nudge and got him cantering out into the foothills.

That clenching in my heart didn't want to ease up, though.

I'd always intended to be the sort of man who had a family like this to turn and wave at whenever business called me away. But that was before my business became hunting bad men down and oftentimes killing them if the situation called for that kind of deliverance. That was before the war escalated and turned uglier than ever, and long before I turned my back on the ruin of my family's land and rode toward the horizon for good.

Somehow, all that riding had brought me here, and maybe Helena was right. Maybe God did want me right where I was, protecting these good people and hunting down the vermin who'd shown up in their honest, hardworking lives to destroy their happiness.

A white-hot sense of vengeance and duty settled in my gut. I made up my mind right then that I wasn't leaving this family until I'd tracked down every last man who'd dragged Frank Sandusky into that field and set his whole stable alight.

I wasn't leaving until justice had been served.

This sense of duty settled my mind to a quiet calm as the gray-dappled stallion carried me east until we reached the mouth of the mountain pass. Then we turned our backs to Pinos Altos and rode due south.

The rugged foothills spanned for miles in this direction, with rolling hills covered in junipers and sage as far as the eye could see. The track was crowded with both peddlers and freight wagons, one of them pulled by over forty burros, and drovers dotted the way here and there off to the sides.

After staying in one place for a while, I was in need of some trackless lands, so I chose to tarry a ways into the rugged country I was more accustomed to traveling over.

Each rise and fall brought a fresh view of this expansive, untamed stretch of land, and we careened down rocky ridges and through winding arroyos with as much haste as we could manage.

Which, for a horse like Flint, was quite a lot.

The stallion was all muscle and the drive to keep moving, but without that stubborn, headstrong energy so many stallions I'd ridden before had. He was quick to take direction and quick to take the lead when the terrain became challenging. Even when a short burst of desert rain blew over us, he didn't pay it any mind. He just kept on working his way up to the next ridge while his gray and white fur turned a bluish color from the rain.

The brief burst of weather lasted just long enough to brighten the stark orange dirt amid the dark evergreens and ocotillo cacti. It cooled the heat on my back and washed the last of the dust off my hat, too, so I had a grin on my face as Flint took us through the next valley at a smooth gallop.

If this was what riding a Sandusky horse was like, then I sure as heck wanted one for my own someday.

We started veering back toward the main track once the city came into view ahead, and we slid in among a group of cowhands who looked to be bringing nearly a hundred head of cattle to market somewhere. The group filtered off to the side as we passed into the mouth of a broad valley basin. Some adobe-style smelters dotted the plains here, and a large grain mill was being erected just outside of town, right before the livery.

Then we came into Silver City.

I'd heard plenty about the town way back in Magdalena.

It had only sprung up about ten years back, but word was the place would be triple its original size come next summer. I'd doubted the assumption at the time, but now that I was riding down the main street, I could see why folks would think as much.

Several buildings were being converted from wood structures to brick, and I overheard some folks talking about a new ordinance that had been put in place on account of the frequent fires they'd experienced lately. There also appeared to be plenty of flooding to contend with down here. The main thoroughfare ran north to south right in the lowest point of the valley, so the street was several feet lower than the boardwalks to account for any rise in water.

I saw no less than five freight wagons heading north, loaded down with silver, gold, and barrels of whiskey. Two young and peppy men who must've just gotten into town were selling sacks full of piñon nuts from up north. Stagecoach drivers and express riders wove their way through the crowded thoroughfare, and a little further along, a large pile of bricks supplied the material for a group of about twenty men all hurrying to rebuild yet another shop.

But in all of this, the question was where to start looking for some information on Captain Charles Sellick.

I slowed Flint to a stop as a big, freshly painted sign that read *Sellick Mercantile* came into view. Three doors down was the *Sellick Distillery*, and way down at the end of the street, I could just about make out the *Sellick Gambling Hall*.

I sighed and ground my teeth a bit.

Deputy Wallace may have had a point about things not being so easy now that this Sellick man was involved.

CHAPTER 11

A cheery bell jangled as I pushed through the door and into the Sellick Mercantile.

I'd gotten Flint a stall at the livery before heading this way on account of not knowing how long I might be looking into things today. He was the most expensive horse I'd ever sat on, and he was only a loan, so I wouldn't risk losing him to anyone with light fingers around here.

The man running the livery had actually recognized his branding. He immediately gave me a stall tucked near the back of the livery where no one but himself went, and I felt better knowing the impressive stallion would have plenty of water, shade, and fresh hay while I settled my business here.

Starting with looking into Sellick's general store.

It was cleaner than most general stores I'd been in, with long shelves of candles, cutlery, lanterns, coffee, and all else stretching from front to back. The back wall even had a nice selection of coffins propped up, right beside sacks of chicken feed and brown sugar.

A short, cheerful man came bustling out from the back of the shop to greet me, and he brushed some dust from his jacket sleeves as he settled in behind the counter.

"Welcome, welcome!" he boomed. "What can I do for you on this fine day?"

He spoke loud enough to be heard in every corner of the shop, but we appeared to be alone at present.

"Just got into town," I told him as I joined him at the counter. "I'm looking for some ammunition for a Schofield of mine. Model 3."

"Ahhh, that's a nice little Smith & Wesson," he said with a large nod. "You a Union man?"

I sighed a little at the assumption. "Nope. Tools are tools. It's a good gun."

"Sure is, sure is!" he agreed and started fussing with a few boxes beneath the counter. "Don't mind a Union man at all, don't you worry. Why, the owner of this very mercantile is a decorated Union man. War's long past now, and I'm of a similar mind. Tools are tools, no matter who's making them."

He popped back up and plunked a box on the countertop.

"Here we are." He gave me a pinched smile. ".44 S&W if I'm not mistaken?"

"Those are them," I said. "I'll take four boxes."

"That suits me just fine," he said and started placing a few small boxes to the side.

A thought occurred to me, and I figured I'd check just in case.

"You wouldn't happen to carry any ammunition for a Martini-Henry?" I asked. "1973? It's a military weapon, but a foreign one. Takes a special .45."

The man looked up at the ceiling for a moment before shaking his head.

"No, sir, never heard of it, I'm afraid," he said. "What kinda military is using that?"

"British, I think," I said and eased into a conversational tone. "You said the man who owns this shop is a decorated soldier?"

"Yes, sir, Captain Charles Sellick," he said with obvious

pride. "Won't find a better man around these parts. He's going to change this city for the better, I'll tell you that much. He's setting up a real nice collection of businesses out here, and all of them reputable and well managed. This here mercantile was his very first business venture once his mines were established, and we keep it stocked with some of the finest variety you could imagine. Why, the ladies' soaps along that left wall come all the way from France. Every one of them smells prettier than anything you'll find most places. And those teas you see on the stand right there are of the oriental variety."

"That does sound nice," I said with a smile, although I'd realized this man could not help me with my own needs.

He was a salesman through and through– so much so that he felt he had to sell me on his own boss. His words may have been true, but I'd have better luck speaking with a less biased party on the matter of the captain.

With that in mind, I settled my payment with the man and took my leave.

I strolled past the Sellick Distillery, and the clanging of machinery poured out into the street. I eyed the many men in overalls hauling wooden crates out to a wagon out front. The bottles therein said "Sellick Rye," which I'd never personally seen on any shelves, but my curiosity was piqued. Not that you could tell the quality of a man by his rye. I just wondered if Charles Sellick kept as high of standards in his distillery as the mercantile worker attributed to his own fare.

As I watched the men, I caught the eye of a fellow inside the shop who was a blistered sort of red at the cheeks. He had a bottle of what I could only assume was the rye in one hand, and a smaller, sweaty man with a pile of paper in his hands was trying to get his attention.

He just spit on the floor of the shop and kept on eyeballing me with a bleary eye, and I decided to walk on.

Clearly, Charles Sellick wasn't always so careful about

the men he employed in his businesses. Granted, it was a distillery that likely only relied on the drunken man in the workings of the shop itself, but I noted the observation all the same.

It was the gambling hall I intended to investigate, though. Men in those types of establishments tended to speak with more truth and less bias. Whether ample liquor was the cause of this or not didn't much matter. I had limited time today and wanted answers quick.

The Sellick Gambling hall had two stately, carved wooden columns out front, and the windows were drawn with green velvet curtains. I took this to mean there were more unsavory things occurring inside than was strictly advertised, but I was quickly proven wrong.

Two men in full dress jackets, vests, and pressed pants stood within the double doors and welcomed me to the establishment. From there, an ornate rug led into a wide room with matching polished-wood game tables dotted throughout. There was a large, circular bar in the middle of the room, and a sizable chandelier made from iron and wood cast the room in a warm yellow light.

The drawn curtains and expensive lighting made it easy to forget it was mid-day, and I understood the decision. It would be easy to get caught up in gambling in here and simply stay put, especially with so many amenities around.

A fast-footed waiter was even carrying a fancy dessert dish to someone in the room.

In short, it was surprisingly swanky for a hall inhabited primarily by miners and teamsters.

Still, plenty of the patrons looked like well-to-do businessmen. I gathered Charles Sellick hoped his dressed-up gambling hall would draw the interest of prosperous men like them, but I was glad to see he wasn't too picky.

A rowdy group of dirt-covered, bony men had taken over a third of the tables at the front of the hall, and from the sounds of it, luck was on most of their sides today. In the back corner, a more docile set of men in black vests and starched white shirts were quietly frowning at their cards, and some jovial young husbands and their wives were enjoying a lively game of roulette together. I saw folks who looked down on their luck and men who couldn't possibly want for more all sitting side by side at the various tables.

Then there were three men firmly berating a three-card monte dealer in Spanish, but in the end, the men I'd met at the door escorted all three from the premise with an admirable amount of discretion.

I made my way to the circular bar, and I greeted the red-headed barkeep who looked very young and eager to perform his duties well.

"Welcome to the Sellick Gambling Hall," he said as he made fast work of shining up the counter in front of me. "Can I interest you in a cocktail? We've got juleps, sours, you name it. We also have our signature Sellick Rye, and the new Sellick Bourbon is only available here at present."

I smirked a little at the business-savvy approach.

"I'll take the Sellick Bourbon," I decided. "Neat."

The redheaded man got to it just as a second barkeep came in through a dim hallway toward the back with a big crate of liquor in his meaty arms. He was a rotund man, with a thick black beard and full cheeks, and he had to shift sideways to fit through the split in the counter that led to the circular workspace.

He must have outranked the young barkeep, because the scrawny man stood up straighter and focused extra hard on his work as soon as the man joined him.

The rotund man sent me a nod by way of greeting as he placed the crate down and started pulling fresh bottles out.

"How do, sir?" he asked.

"Just fine," I said with an easy grin. "Heard this was an

upstanding place and thought I'd come by and take a look. I'm passing through from Pinos Altos."

I'd already confirmed with a few glances that none of the six men were in here, but I partially hoped someone in here might know them. This was their boss' business after all. At this point, mentioning the situation I'd come from as much as possible could only help me find out if anyone knew about the task the six had undertaken recently.

"I've got cousins up that way." The bearded man came closer and rested a heavy arm on the counter. "You in Silver City for long?"

"I'll head back today," I said as the redheaded young man slid my bourbon over. "This man here sold me on your signature bourbon."

"It goes down real smooth," the larger man chuckled proudly. "I like it better than the rye, but don't tell anyone I told you that."

I laughed lightly as I swirled the whiskey around my glass. "I can understand that. Isn't your boss' name on that rye?"

"Sure is," he sighed. "And truth be told, he wouldn't give a lick about my opinion on the matter."

"I take it he's a cut above the rest," I said with some sarcasm and took a sip.

The barman hadn't been lying, it went down fifty times smoother than the usual rotgut, but it was more than that. The spice on the bourbon wasn't too harsh, and the burn left a pleasant ghost of itself that made me want another sip.

"He's not too high and mighty, as a matter of fact," the large man chortled. "I could probably walk right up to the captain myself and tell him outright his rye just wasn't to my liking, and he'd simply thank me for my input."

The man laughed heartily at this, and his redheaded companion joined in on the joke.

"Mind you, he's not much like other bluebellies I've

met," the man sighed and went back to pulling bottles from the crate.

"You telling me a bluebelly came up with this here spirit?" I cocked an eyebrow.

"Sure as shit," he snickered. "I was thinking the very same thing when I heard old Sellick was starting his own distillery, but low and behold, I can't name a better option. Not one that's come from around here, anyhow. Give him another few years to age what he's started with, and I'd say he's in the money. Again."

I nodded and took another swig. This barkeep sounded more to my liking in terms of gaining information, and I continued to sip on the bourbon as I looked around the hall some more.

"Sellick…" I said. "So the man who owns this place is the same prospector I've heard of?"

"Sure is." The redhead nodded as he perked up and joined the conversation. "Captain Charles Sellick."

"A Captain of the Union," I mused. Then I shook my head and chuckled a bit. "The West sure has changed."

"Always, I'm afraid," the larger man said and straightened up. "Although, I can vouch for this one. Blue he may be, but he's an honest man. Busy, too. He doesn't come in too often, but when he does, he takes particular care about what the customers think of the place, what us workers think… He's a fair-minded man. Doesn't frequent the bordellos or even stop into the saloons. Real close with his family. Folks reckon he'll change this whole city for the better."

"My granddaddy don't think so," the redhead put in. "Says he's a rotten carpetbagger no matter what he's like. He settled out in Texas before he came here, and my granddaddy thinks he ought to stop pushing his way into the West and just pack up and go back where he belongs."

The larger man sighed and sent the younger barkeep a pointed look.

"I ain't gonna argue with your granddaddy, on account of him being a good and honorable man," he muttered in a low voice. "But you best watch your tongue in here. That's all I'll say."

The redhead paled and shot a quick look around him.

"Sellick came south from Missouri and broke into the milling business out in Texas," the larger man explained as he turned to me. "Got it in mind he'd come out here when the silver rush started since he missed the gold rush by a bit, and his hunch paid off."

"Seems like it," I agreed.

"What kind of work you do up in Pinos Altos?" he asked.

I made sure my voice was just loud enough to be heard by the nearest patrons.

"I work at the Black Spur Ranch," I said, and before I could elaborate, both of the barkeeps jolted a little.

"Did you say Black Spur?" the larger of the pair asked. "That Sandusky place?"

"The very same," I agreed. "You know it?"

The redhead laughed at this statement like I'd made a joke, and his companion let out a heavy snort.

"You'd have to be pretty dim to not know the name of Sandusky," he chuckled. "Best damn horses in five hundred miles."

I raised my glass to that, but as I finished it off, I couldn't help marveling at how grand Frank Sandusky's reputation was. I was only a small matter of miles outside of Pinos Altos, and already things had gone from 'the best horses in five counties' to 'the best horses in five hundred miles.'

I decided I'd share this compliment with Helena as soon as I returned. It might cheer her up to hear her husband's legacy was ever-growing.

"You do any training of those horses?" the larger man asked.

"No, my services have more to do with protecting the ranch," I replied.

He let out a whistle and shook his head. "Brave man. I imagine all kinds of folks get it in their mind they could make a pretty penny off of those horses if they tried."

"They do," I agreed. "Mostly, it's paying customers who come by, though. Well-off men... like your Captain Sellick, that sort."

"I believe it." He stroked his black beard in thought. "Sellick does strike me as a man who'd appreciate a Sandusky horse, but as far as I've seen, he don't have the time for riding. All I see is him coming and going in his coach, and those horses aren't anything showy. Just your basic stock horses, you know."

The redheaded man opened his mouth as if to say something, but then the double doors of the establishment parted and drew his eye.

I glanced the same direction, and I just managed to conceal my surprise as a pair of men I recognized strolled in.

Jeb Osiah and Petey McCaw.

CHAPTER 12

Jeb Osiah's protruding browline cast a shadow over his close-set eyes as he shuffled over to the bartop. His hair was ragged and black under his old hat, and his thin mustache sprawled over his top lip like twisted wires. He had dirt packed into the creases on his sweaty face, but his much taller and lankier companion was a little more cleaned up overall.

Even still, Petey McCaw struck me as an odd and murky sorta fellow. His eyes were a pale brown that reminded me of mucked-up river water. He seemed about half-focused on the world around him, and the skin beneath his eyes was a greenish yellow that looked sickly beside his bright blond hair and eyebrows. Without any facial hair on his long, thin face, it was easy to see his mouth was stuck hanging open like a guppy, too.

Both of the men reeked of drink at only high noon, but they plunked their elbows on the bartop all the same and lazily ordered the cheapest rotgut on offer.

The redheaded barkeep hopped to. He drew up their orders in seconds flat and swiped their coins off the counter without a word. Then Jeb silently cast his beady eyes around the hall before nudging his companion in the arm.

The pair of them nodded to a man he'd seen about five or six tables away, and they joined him at a game of faro.

"Can I get you another?" the larger barkeep asked and gestured toward my empty glass.

I had no intention of imbibing more, but I nodded all the same.

It was time to settle in and get a feel for the situation, so once my drink was poured, I thanked the two men at the counter and made my way to a table for a few rounds of five-card draw.

I made sure to choose a seat that gave me a clear view of the pair of killers but didn't place me too suspiciously. Especially because the man they'd nodded at must have overheard my conversation easily at the bar. He was eyeing me every few seconds while his friends got started gambling.

I anted up, but by the time my opponents had done likewise and started their draws, the man at the faro table was muttering in Jeb Osiah's ear.

The dirt-creased murderer only tilted his head slightly to listen. Then he spared me just about half a glance before snorting and shaking his head.

After that, none of them bothered looking in my direction, and a brief smile hitched on my lips as I drew two.

Yep. They didn't have a worry in the world about being caught.

That friend of theirs knew well enough that I worked at the Black Spur Ranch, and that I'd come down from Pinos Altos for just a day, but it appeared this was all coincidence to the trio. My being here meant next to nothing to the ragged, drunken men now gambling their day away without a care in the world.

Which meant I might've just become the luckiest man in this gambling hall.

So far, of the six, at least these two men were confirmed to work for Charles Sellick, so they were settled in this area. I had to assume the other four were likewise, but whether the captain was their boss or not, he didn't sound like the sort to send filth like this after a man like Mr. Sandusky. Frankly speaking, Sellick had established himself too well here to risk a stain like that on his ledger.

Then there was the fact that I'd found these two ruthless banditos easily enough, and they just happened to be drunk enough to make some bad choices.

So all things considered, picking these two off real quick– in their own town, miles from the ranch– shouldn't spook any of the remaining men into fleeing. Especially if I swayed it all to look rather circumstantial.

The question was whether to proceed today, right now, or sit on things a couple days longer until I sorted out more answers.

I checked, same as my two opponents had done, and added another ante to the pot as I thought briefly of Helena, Russel, and Honey.

I thought of the young boy shooting post after post just to ease his mind, and Honey going quiet and clinging to her mama at all hours of the day. Then I thought of Helena losing sleep in her grief and worrying daily whether she was welcoming trouble into her children's lives just by keeping the ranch running.

Finally, I thought of the hammering flames of their stables that night, and the wicked laughter out in the fields, and the weight on the ranch hands' shoulders now that Frank Sandusky was torn from this earth.

No, I wouldn't let this opportunity pass me by. Too many people needed to see some kind of justice being served. Myself included.

It was the perfect time to start thinning out the pack.

If I could learn any other names from the two killers before I put them down, then I would. But if not, I'd keep on hunting down the others as I had been.

As long as I made sure that fellow at the faro table didn't know it was me who ended them, it shouldn't be any harder than it already had been.

I carried on with another two rounds. I was seven dollars down, but I pulled an ace of spades on the next hand, and thirty minutes later I was ten dollars up. The man across from me sweated profusely as he gestured for another card.

I did as well, and I managed to put together a quick four-of-a-kind to win the table again.

I exchanged a few words here and there with my opponents, one of whom handled the bookkeeping of Charles Sellick's mines. He was one of the starched-shirt types, and he didn't sweat nearly as much as the other man. Once he started talking about his boss, though, he didn't seem able to stop, and it was more of the same.

How Captain Charles Sellick was going to change this town for the better, how respectable he was, and that he ought to run for mayor. The more he spoke, the more certain I became that Sellick wouldn't tarnish any of his chances out here by dabbling in a crime of this nature, but more than that, he certainly didn't sound like the type.

All the while, I kept half an eye on Jeb and Petey.

I tallied four drinks going down Jeb Osiah's rotten gullet since he'd entered the gambling hall. Petey drank the same and had long since taken to hunching over the other man's shoulder with his jaw slack and a doggish look on his face. The pair were clearly set on raking in as much as they could real quick, and they seemed to be faring well, but the friend they'd joined was packing up.

He stayed for one more draw, finished his beer, and headed out into the street with the kind of haste that made me think he wasn't supposed to be wasting his time here mid-day.

It was about this time that Petey started urging Jeb to back out while they were ahead. I eyed their table and saw they only had about half a deck left in this round. This suited me just fine.

I laid out a flush and closed out my hand. I was fifty-three dollars up, and the dealer paid me accordingly before shaking my hand and politely bidding me a good afternoon. The two men at the table with me looked pleased to see me go.

I made sure to share a word or two with the barkeeps on my way out, but then I headed for the door. I glanced up and down the street and quickly spotted the friend who'd recently left the hall. He was nearly all the way to the end of the road, and he broke into a run in time to catch a wagon before it headed further into town.

I nodded to myself, crossed the street, and entered a clothing store with large front windows looking out at the gambling hall.

Helena had insisted on tending to my jacket from where the rustler's bullet had torn the fabric open, and she'd done a much better job of patching it than I would have. Still, I used the recently patched sleeve as an excuse to look around at the jackets on offer, which put me close enough to the windows to keep an eye on the entrance of the Sellick Gambling Hall.

Just as I expected, Jeb Osiah and Petey McCaw shuffled their way out the doors only a few minutes later. They were greedily dividing up their winnings as they crossed the street, and I waited until they'd passed the door of the clothing shop before quickly taking my leave.

I was about fifteen paces behind them now, but the reek of them still seemed too strong.

Petey had a jaunty gait to him at this clipped pace, like his legs were too long for his body to keep track of in his drunken state. But Jeb took long, purposeful strides while his arms swung wide at his sides, and it was unsettling how little he swayed with so much drink in him.

I noted they each had a pistol holstered on their right hips, but I had one of my Remingtons as well.

Ideally, I would've liked to get the pair of them off the street and force some information out of them, but I wasn't sure the opportunity would arise with so many folks out and about. By the few words I caught in their conversation, they were headed straight for a bordello on this side of town, so I supposed I could set myself up at a nearby shop and keep biding my time.

I saw the bright, red-painted sign of the bordello coming up that said 'Lady Luck' in a gaudy print, and was about to cross over toward a diner when Jeb let out a lewd chuckle that sent my hackles rising.

There was a pretty woman coming our way, with a fine-looking dress and gloves, and a soft smile on her face. She seemed preoccupied with her thoughts, but then she must've seen the way Jeb and Petey were looking at her.

The young lady's cheeks reddened as her gaze dropped to the ground. She quickened her steps to pass them and be done with it, but Jeb had other ideas.

He caught her skirt between his grubby fingers the moment she was close enough, and he growled out a disgusting remark about 'women like her belonging in the bordello where they could be enjoyed.'

I broke into a run, and I noticed two men on the other side of the road doing the same. They'd both seen Jeb grab the lady, and all three of us were watching when she bravely pulled her hand back and slapped the filthy rat right across his sweaty face.

I was only three steps away when he growled and brought his own hand back to strike her.

Then my fingers closed on the bastard's wrist.

CHAPTER 13

Everything was over in a matter of seconds.

Jeb reeled and tried to swing his free fist into my ribs, but I blocked him and twisted to bring his wrist around behind his back.

Then I wrenched upward and got him rooted in place for the time being.

The woman was in the arms of one of the onlookers who'd rushed over with me. The man was now fanning her and attempting to find out if she was alright. Meanwhile, the other helpful man who'd run this way was dodging a punch thrown by a belligerent Petey McCaw.

The next attempt landed smack in the center of the innocent man's face.

I managed to shift slightly and plant my elbow into Petey's gut as he finished lunging for his target.

Jeb wrenched himself out of my hold in that very same instant, but I ducked his right fist and countered just in time to clock him hard on his jaw.

The crunch of bone meeting knuckles sent a shock up through my wrist as my hand started to burn, but it didn't feel broken. More importantly, I'd sent Jeb toppling sideways toward the street. He flailed as he tried not to drop from the raised boardwalk.

That's when I heard the cocking of a hammer behind me.

I ripped my pistol out of its holster and spun on my heel just in time to let Petey McCaw's bullet slip past my left hip. I saw the look on his gaunt, greenish face as he thought he had me. Then my own bullet struck him square in the chest, and the smug sneer on his face dropped.

The stumbling sound of Jeb Osiah trying to rip his own gun out turned my head.

He'd managed to stay on the boardwalk, but he hadn't gotten his weapon out just yet.

I had just enough time to draw a steadying breath, level the barrel of my Remington on his chest, and look him straight in his dark, probing eyes. I held his gaze with the blank sort of vengeance I often felt in my expression when looking evil straight in the eye. And for a scrap of a moment, I saw recognition in Jeb's eyes.

He knew me from the gambling hall. He knew what his friend had tried to warn him of.

Then there was the briefest flash of fear before I pulled the trigger and ended him.

His pistol was in his hand as he swayed backward and dropped the several feet from the sidewalk to the muddy street below. He landed with a squelch and a thud, and three women across the way let out piercing screams.

I sighed, holstered my Remington, and turned to check on Petey McCaw.

The blond string bean still had his mouth hanging slack the very same way, even in death, and his murky eyes stared blankly at the sky above Silver City.

"Mister, that was some fast shooting," the man who still held the woman upright said with wide eyes. "Your hand alright?"

"It's fine." I glanced at the two splits in my knuckles, and I flexed my hand easily enough. "Is she alright?"

I gestured toward the woman who'd been the unfortunate victim of Jeb Osiah's belligerence. She flushed red all the way to the roots of her hair as she nodded, and her assistant frantically started fanning her when he saw how overwhelmed she looked.

"Y-yes sir," she breathed. "Thank you so very much. I never… I didn't mean for any of this…"

"Shhh, don't you go blaming yourself, now," her assistant said.

The other man, the one who'd taken a fist to the face from Petey McCaw, was clutching a bandana to his bloody nose. He sent me a harried nod when I asked if he was alright, and then he pointed his bloody bandana down the road.

"Sheriff's coming, don't worry," he said. "He'll take care of this. We saw how it all happened."

I nodded and eyed the four men charging down the street from a building not eight doors down. They cut a scornful picture, with each of their faces bunched up in a mean scowl, and their fists either on their guns or clenched at their sides.

"Oh, boy," I muttered to myself as I glanced down at the two dead men.

The two murderers.

The reek of liquor wafted up from their bodies, along with the smell of freshly spilled blood and gunpowder. Both had their pistols right beside their lifeless hands, and a grim sort of satisfaction settled in my chest as I thought of Helena Sandusky and her ranch.

Whatever came next, I'd made sure this could only go my way.

And I wouldn't stop now. Having taken out even just two of the six men who'd spilled blood at the Black Spur Ranch that night sent a fresh sense of righteousness through my veins.

Justice was officially let loose in these mountains, and God willing, it was coming for every last one of the six who'd murdered Frank Sandusky.

The Sheriff of Grant County and three of his deputies joined us beside the dead, and the two men who'd also come to the woman's aid were quick to say their piece. The woman herself was adamant about the violent and inappropriate nature of the pair on the ground, and she insisted I was a hero who didn't hesitate to defend her and the other men here. She even said that the dead men had been first to break the local ordinance by pulling a gun and meaning to fire it within the city streets.

I hadn't been aware that Silver City's marshal had a no-shooting law around here, but I even lucked out there, it appeared.

In fact, all went as smooth as I could've asked for, up until it was my turn to speak.

"I'd like to know about any bounty these two here have on them," I told the sheriff, but it was a deputy with a short-cropped stache who answered.

"Slow down, fella," he drawled. "There's a lot to be done about this, we haven't even identified these two yet."

"This one here is Petey McCaw," I said with a point at the slack-jawed man at my feet. I jutted my thumb toward the street next. "That one is Jeb Osiah. They're wanted for murder."

All the witnesses suddenly looked twice as concerned about the ordeal, and the woman gasped as she clutched the man who held her.

As for the sheriff, his white-streaked eyebrows jumped slightly when I listed the names, and his eyes darted to the bodies as if he was seeing them in a new light now.

"That's a mighty tall accusation," the deputy scoffed.

"Especially if these men are who you say," another put in and stepped between me and Petey's corpse. He was slightly shorter than me, and his stout black mustache concealed both his lips. "Jeb and Petey work for Captain Charles Sellick. Have for ages now. And a man of his stature don't hire no murderers. Which you'd know if you was from around here, but I don't recall ever seeing your face in these streets, stranger."

"I know who they work for," I said. "And I know they're wanted men. Ask your sheriff."

The deputies looked insulted by my words, but they caused the Sheriff's calculating eyes to snap to mine. He stepped forward, but he didn't respond to my inquiry.

"Who are you?" he demanded.

"Name's Jesse Callahan," I supplied.

"Callahan?" The Sheriff looked closer at me now. "You that fella from up north? Brought the Hobbs brothers into Pinos Altos?"

I nodded. "The very same."

The deputy with the short-cropped stache dropped his jaw at this, but the one directly in front of me was determined to dislike me all the same. The third deputy just exchanged a look with the sheriff, who then sucked his teeth and gave me a good, long glare.

"We'll finish this conversation in my office," the sheriff told me. "Boys, get the statements of these fine folks out here. And drag these two fools out of the street, will ya?"

"Yes, sir," the deputies replied.

"Follow me," he gritted out as he brushed past the bodies, and I followed in kind.

A few minutes later saw me sitting at a desk with the name 'Sheriff Harvey Whitehill' burned into a plank of wood in the center. The sheriff himself sat behind the desk and dismissed the deputy who'd just finished handing over a few slips of paper.

"Whitehill?" I asked as the deputy left us alone. "Are you

the same Whitehill who got that Bonney kid for stealing laundry years back?"

A muscle twitched in the sheriff's jaw. "That's me."

He'd removed his hat to reveal a head of crisp white hair that was generally kept well, and he stroked his white mustache as he looked down his large nose at me.

"I was out in White Oaks recently," I said. "Heard he got his hands dirty in quite the war there in Lincoln County."

"I hear the same," I said. "Boy's been on a dark path, but he's a loyal sort. Started out a good kid. We all fall on hard times."

"Anyone making headway on bringing him in?"

"Man named Pat Garret's been known to have his eye on him," Sheriff Whitehill said stiffly. "He ain't pursuing him just yet, but no doubt he will soon enough."

I nodded, but decided to drop the subject. The notorious Billy the Kid had been doing a number in the last few years, but based on what I'd heard, he wasn't the sort I normally hunted. He'd gone bad, but not evil. I'd looked into him plenty, which was how I'd known he was only seventeen when Sheriff Whitehill arrested him for his first petty theft, and at that time, he'd recently been orphaned.

Word was he hadn't even committed one of the thefts they'd gotten him for, but he'd escaped Whitehill's clutches all the same.

I could understand the sheriff's reluctance to discuss the matter. He was right. Hard times came for us all eventually, and I wasn't one to judge a man for how he proceeded. Especially when I'd heard that business in Lincoln County was a messy ordeal. It sounded like the Kid was on the right side of things there, too, so to speak.

But killing was killing, and stealing was stealing, and someone would bring the Bonney kid in one day. I didn't reckon it'd be me, though. Not unless he twisted himself up and became a real ruthless sorta man.

"So you're the bounty hunter Wallace has been talking to," Sheriff Whitehill said and sat back in his chair with his papers in hand.

"Yes, sir."

He nodded slowly. "I won't lie, I'm grateful to you for handling those Hobbs boys the way you did. I wasn't sure anyone was going to catch up to those two. Surprised you managed it on your own, especially tracking them down Emory Pass. That's a rough spot."

"Everyone can be caught," I said. "Some just take more patience than others."

"I'm inclined to agree," the sheriff said but then narrowed his eyes. "But you and I are in a predicament now."

"How do you figure?"

"Well, trouble is, I only sent word to Wallace not a full day ago that those men you just shot were employed by Captain Charles Sellick. Now... I did not place a bounty on either of their heads just yet, and I certainly did not intend to have no bounty hunters coming here looking to haul them in, either. I was handling this matter with a bit of patience, as a matter of fact."

"Wallace didn't send me, if that's what you're implying," I said.

"That widow hire you to come down here?"

"No, sir," I said.

"Then how's about you explain to me why I've got you in my office, and two dead Sellick workers to deal with," he snapped.

"I thought I'd come have a look around the city and happened to get into an altercation," I said in a calm tone. "As the people on the street said, those men had both over-imbibed and pulled their firearms on me, after assaulting a young woman, nonetheless."

The man's glower deepened, but I continued.

"As far as the Sanduskys go, I've offered to help look after the ranch until family arrives. Nothing more."

"Uh-huh, well then, you do just that." He tossed the papers onto the desk and steepled his fingers in front of him. "You keep to that ranch, and let the law handle those six men from now on. You understand?"

"As long as you do mean to handle them." I held his gaze. "Your reputation precedes you, sir, and I believe you know as well as I that it'd be a shame if those men got by on account of their boss' station down here. Friends and family of the ranch wouldn't take too kindly to knowing Frank Sandusky's murderers went unpunished for the horrible crimes they've committed. Might make them question whether your duty is to that badge or to the Sellicks these days."

"I ride a Sandusky horse," he said through clenched teeth. "And my duty has been more than upheld for seven years now. I've cleaned up more filth in this town than any one man has ever managed in this valley, and I won't have some rambler of a bounty hunter come into my town acting like he's the law here."

"I don't pretend to be the law," I assured him. "Just a man who thinks justice ought to be upheld. One way or another."

The sheriff snorted and offered a nod of agreement.

"Can't fault you for acting as such," he sighed and sat back again. "But Sellick is a big name out here, and while that don't mean we're looking the other way, it does mean there's an order to handling this. Fact is, my information tells me those men you killed were wanted out east for three murders and two robberies. Now, you tack on the killing they did up at Black Spur, and you're looking at about five hundred dollars' bounty for the pair."

I nodded, but the man leveled me with a stern point of a finger.

"That doesn't mean we suspect Sellick has any involvement in this mess with the Sanduskys," he informed me.

"I'm inclined to agree," I replied. "So far, I haven't seen any clear connection."

"You can stop looking for one," he said.

"I won't pretend I'm blind if the facts start to line up," I said with half a shrug. "I take my work seriously, Sheriff, and I know firsthand the violence that was inflicted that night. It isn't something anyone will forget anytime soon."

"That don't change the fact that no one has formally hired you to handle this matter, and the jurisdiction of this county is telling you to keep your hands off it," Sheriff Whitehill said with a steely stare. "So you let my deputies and I handle the rest of this. Understood?"

"Understood." I nodded. "I'll be sure to pass any more helpful information your way, though, just as soon as I've gathered more names for you."

The sheriff sucked his teeth again and pointed toward the door. "You can grab your bounty from Deputy Shelley on the way out, boy."

"Thank you, kindly," I said, got to my feet, and left without another word.

Deputy Shelley looked just about as pleased to pay me as the men at the gambling hall had been about forfeiting their earnings. He shoved the five hundred dollars over with a tight-lipped grimace, and I tipped my hat before heading out into the street.

I offered a nod of greeting to the pair of deputies now hauling the bodies of Jeb Osiah and Petey McCaw to the undertaker, and they did not return the gesture.

I didn't mind. I was used to staunch lawmen getting their hackles up over my presence in their towns. Men like me didn't wait for orders like these deputies did, and I could always tell when this chafed on their minds. They took it personal sometimes, when I cleaned their streets up for them. That kind of reception just came with the territory.

But I'd never been formally told to keep my hands off my gun by a sheriff before.

That part, I did mind.

I found Flint in the livery and paid the master for his attentions to the horse.

"That's one heck of a fine horse you've got there," the man said with an appraising glance. "Black Spur, huh?"

"That's right."

"Shoooo-y," he whistled. "Love to get my hands on one of them myself one day, but I hear old Sandusky bit the big one."

I ground my teeth. "Something like that."

I stowed the five hundred dollar bounty, as well as the fifty-three dollars I'd won at the gambling hall and the ammunition for my Schofield, in my saddlebag before tacking up and riding out.

Then I left Silver City behind me just as the sun's rays took on the strong, golden hues of late afternoon. We cantered through the wide valley basin to the north and then branched off onto the smaller, less-used tracks all the way back to the rugged foothills near Pinos Altos.

Somewhere along the way, a warm haze settled on the rolling land that promised the cool air of the coming evening as the stallion carried me over each rise and into the winding canyons. He rode with a sense of purpose and assuredness to each hoof-fall, and I couldn't help but feel I was meant to ride this horse after ending the lives of Jeb and Petey.

He was the kind of beast that perfectly defined what it meant to be of the Black Spur stock, and tonight, the Sanduskys would go to bed in a world that was less stained with the sins of men.

Still, I wasn't wholly settled in my mind.

Sheriff Whitehill's words stuck with me all the way to the ranch, and by the time I trotted beneath the ironwork of the gate, I still hadn't resigned myself to minding my own. I wouldn't risk getting caught out and hauled in over the mess, but I certainly wouldn't sit by and wait for Silver City to decide where they stood.

For now, I pushed those thoughts away and instead set my sights on letting Helena know how things had gone down south.

Amos, Abel, Mateo, and Russel were all off handling the usual tasks of the ranch before nightfall as I tended to my gear and the stallion. I made thorough work of getting Flint settled, and as I set him loose to pasture, he tossed his great head as if he was exhilarated from the day's trip. Then he trotted off to join his usual herd, and I found Helena out in the barn behind the house, tending to the pigs.

I came to a stop on the hillside as I admired the way the orange sun made her strawberry-blonde hair glow like a halo around her. She dusted her hands off on a well-worn apron that hugged her small waist, and then she carried two empty buckets out from the pigs' stall. She sent a smile over her shoulder as she stored the buckets with the others.

I followed her gaze to where Honey sat cross-legged in a wheelbarrow. The little girl's round face was fixed in a pout as she squinted against the sun, and she clutched a dead bundle of wildflowers in one hand.

Helena's smile faded as she looked at her daughter, and I could understand why. The little girl sat as stiff as a pole, and her little hands clung to the flowers and the edge of the wheelbarrow as if her life depended on it. As a matter of fact, it looked like the very same flowers she'd been gathering when I left this morning, and I wondered if the small girl had really been clinging to them ever since.

But then Honey caught sight of me on the sloping hill.

The flowers dropped all over her lap, and she let out a whine as she pointed my way.

Helena's beautiful face shone with pure relief when she saw it was me there.

She hurried over to grab Honey, and I made my way to the

barn. We met just outside the red doors, and I realized the little girl was looking at me more intently than she ever had.

"How you doing, Honey?" I smiled.

Her eyes suddenly filled with tears, and I frowned in confusion as she buried her face against her mother's neck.

"Just a second," Helena breathed. "I'll meet you by the garden, I'm not sure where Russel got off to."

I nodded as the woman went to find her son, but it seemed she ended up settling for handing Honey off to Mateo for the time being. I watched her hurry back across the pasture to meet me near the garden, and a prickle of anticipation scattered down my spine.

I hadn't known it until now, but I'd been wanting to deliver some good news to this woman since the moment I found her screaming at the blazing fire that night.

Even now, her soft features were tense as worry creased her brow. Every step she took was sturdy and filled with determination, and I was relieved luck had been on my side in Silver City today. I would've hated to disappoint Helena after she'd probably spent all day wringing her hands.

I removed my hat as she brushed the dust from her cheeks and came to a stop in front of me. Her blue eyes darted all over my midsection, and she leaned to get a look at my arms, too.

"No new bullet holes?" she asked with a slight curl to her lips.

I smirked. "Don't worry, I didn't give them the chance."

Her lips popped open in surprise, and her blue eyes sparkled with hope as she met my gaze.

"You found 'em?" she gasped.

"Two of them," I said. "That Jeb Osiah and Petey McCaw were down in their boss' gambling hall."

Helena's shaking fingers flew to her lips, and tears threatened to spill from her lashes, but she blinked stubbornly as she barreled on with the important parts.

"So you found them," she said in a tight voice. "Then what?"

"They got into a bit of trouble on their way out of the hall," I said with a vague wave of my hand. "Turned out I was in the right place at the right time to help another woman out. Everything was handled real clean. And that's two of Frank's murderers you don't have to worry about ever again."

Helena's face crumpled as the tears finally broke free. A small heave of relief broke from her lips. She looked ready to collapse right where she stood, but I stepped forward in time to keep her steady.

Then she buried her face against the center of my chest, and I held her quietly as she wept. Her slender body shook violently, but her tears were silent, and I didn't release her until I was sure she was ready.

Finally, she pulled back and patted her strawberry-blonde hair, as if it must've become a mess in the last few minutes. It hadn't, but her eyes were swollen and her nose was pink. Despite this, she looked happier, and she let out a shaky laugh as she swiped the tears from her face.

"I can't believe it," she managed. "I was so worried something would go wrong, and you would... But you're here, and they're gone from this earth, and I just... I can't thank you enough, Jesse."

"You don't have to thank me," I assured her.

"Then I'll thank God," she laughed and clutched my arm. "I'll thank him every single day for the rest of my life that you found us. I know it's only two of the men who... who came here that night... but it's something. It's a breath of relief to me, it truly is."

I smiled as she needlessly fussed with her hair some more, and just seeing her laugh through her tears brought a warmth to my chest and a sense of rightness to my bones.

I didn't often see the relief on folks' faces when I wiped their assailants from this earth. I delivered the kind of justice that oftentimes went unknown by the poor people my bounties had hurt. But seeing Helena's hope and joy and pure gratitude was one of the sweetest victories I'd ever known.

"The bounty on those two came to five hundred dollars," I told her. "I've got it in my saddlebag, I figured it's only right that you and the kids–"

"No." She fervently shook her head. "Keep it. Keep all of it."

"Ma'am, I didn't do this for the bounty, and I'm sure your husband would want–"

"You pulled that trigger not me," she said with a firm tone, and I could recognize that I wasn't going to win this one. "I'm just so pleased you're alright and that everything went well down there. I'm so relieved! Did you speak to the sheriff about the others?"

"Yes." I grimaced at the not-so-good news I had to share. "Sounds like they're looking to take things slow, on account of this Captain Sellick's standing in the city."

"Slow?" Her blue eyes flared with fury. "And what? Just let the whole lot of them scurry off like the vermin they are so they can feast on some other poor family's happiness? Just let them carry on killing and hurting all manner of folks without ever paying for the sins they've committed? For the homes they've broken?"

Her words bit with venom, and I was once again reminded of how fierce she looked the night those rustlers had the audacity to try and rob her ranch. Sweet and beautiful as she was, Helena Sandusky was a strong and loyal woman, and part of me feared for anyone who crossed her from this day forward.

I could tell she'd always had this fire in her, but I could also recognize how loss had honed the edges of her blade already. She didn't want to settle for 'slow' on this, and I didn't blame her.

"I'm in agreement with you," I said and held up my hands. "Now, the way I handled things down there, I don't believe the other four will get it in their minds that anyone is on their tail. But if those deputies down there make a mess of looking into things, they'll catch wind of it. It happens often enough."

Helena pursed her lips and cast a stone-cold glare at the mountains on the horizon for a moment.

I gave her time to process her feelings on the matter, but she only settled on a disappointed shake of her head.

"It ain't fair," she murmured. "Frank gave so much to the people here. He wasn't a talkative sort, but he gave the very best he could to folks. Always. He always, always gave what he could to those who needed it. The least they could do is…"

She trailed off and shook her head as angry tears sprang to her eyes.

"I know," I said gently. "But two of the men have paid. In full. I've made sure of that. And as for the others, I've got time to see they answer for what they've done, don't you worry. If that's what you want…"

Helena's face softened as her eyes met mine again. I was about to explain my own feelings on the matter, and how determined I truly was to see this thing through, if that's how she wanted it.

"Is it strange that I feel guilty?" she asked as she searched my gaze. "Those men down there are dead because of me."

I turned to make sure I was looking her square in the eye as I held her shoulders. "Don't for one second think like that. What I do is between me and the criminals I hunt, and it has nothing to do with the innocent folks who got caught up in their mess. Those were evil men, and all they got today was exactly what's been coming their way since the moment they chose to turn their back on a righteous path."

Helena nodded a little, but I could see her mind wasn't settled.

"If it makes you feel better, even the sheriff of Silver City knows you had no hand in this," I said. "So don't worry about what these men have coming their way. They've earned it."

"I suppose," she murmured. "But what's this about the sheriff?"

I was about to explain his opinions on how and where I did my work, but then the rattling of spokes echoed from the lane.

"You got another sale lined up?" I asked as I glanced in confusion at the fading daylight.

Helena furrowed her eyebrows. "No, not that I'm aware..."

I narrowed my eyes, turned on my heel, and made my way around the garden's fence. Helena hurried to keep step with me, and the pair of us came to the front of the house side by side to find a stagecoach settled in the wide clearing ahead.

Beside it stood a young woman in a full bustle ensemble made of rich black silk, with her dark auburn curls piled high in an elaborate do and then cascading down the back of her head. Her skin was as pale and as unmarred as white silk, and her bow-shaped lips probably looked quite appealing, when they weren't pinched tight in disapproval.

Her eyes were bright green and seemed to burn straight through my head as she stared me down.

"Lucy!" Helena gasped.

The new arrival spared the briefest glance for Helena before she crossed her arms over her perfectly tailored front and shot that green-eyed glare my way again.

"You got about three seconds to explain who in the Hell you are," she informed me.

Sorry.

CHAPTER 14

"Peas?" The green-eyed woman held the steaming dish aloft over the long dining table, but her expression just about dared me to try and take the peas from her.

"No, thank you, ma'am," I said politely.

With that, Lucy skirted her way over to where Russel sat across from me and started shoveling the peas onto his plate.

I shifted a little uncomfortably in my seat as I glanced around.

I'd had every intention of declining the offer to join the Sanduskys in their family home for dinner. I'd almost gone blue trying to excuse myself from the occasion, but Helena wouldn't hear a word about it.

So, instead of enjoying the crackling fire and a simple supper under the stars with the men out at the bunkhouse tonight, I was wedged into a corner seat at the dining table with Russel, Honey, Helena, and Lucy Kimber.

The arrival of Helena's sister-in-law couldn't have come at a better time for them. Honey had actually squealed at the sight of her auntie, and I was pretty sure Russel used up all his biggest words in the first five minutes of her being here.

Helena had made quick work of introducing me as "the man I wrote about," but had left it at that. Now, she was pink-cheeked and bustling around to ready the dinner for everyone, and every time she looked at Lucy, a smile naturally sprang to her face.

Lucy, on the other hand, seemed rather standoffish. She gave her niece and nephew all the hugs and kisses in the world, but I didn't miss the loaded look she'd given her sister-in-law after they hugged. She'd relaxed a little now that we were all settling in around the dinner table, but I hadn't received a single kind word from the woman yet.

I didn't want one, either. I just wanted to go rest up before I started my nightly watch, but here I was, stuck between a wall and a dolled-up singer who clearly wanted me removed from her sight.

"Would you like some peas, Jesse?" Helena offered.

I looked over to see she'd refilled the dish with piping-hot and buttered peas that really did look delicious. The smell wafted over me and made my stomach growl, and I cleared my throat with some embarrassment.

"Uhh, yes please," I replied. "Thank you kindly."

"Of course." Helena smiled brightly and scooped a couple helpings onto my plate, and she nestled them between the pork chops and buttered rolls she'd already delivered.

The moment she turned away, I was met with Lucy's cocked eyebrow sitting behind her. She kept on eyeing me, too, as Helena finally took her seat at the head of the table. Then we all bowed our heads as Russel said Grace.

As soon as he was done, Lucy's eyes were sizing me up again.

I raised my brow, scooped up a spoonful of peas, and ate them.

"Hmm." The woman pursed her lips and turned to her own plate.

I did all I could not to snicker, but I wasn't sure what this woman expected me to do. The lady of the house insisted I join them for dinner, and that was that.

And the peas did smell much more delicious when Helena offered them up with a smile versus when her sister-in-law offered them with a sour attitude.

"So, tell me Mr. Callahan," Lucy suddenly said. "Where are you from?"

"Texas."

"Whereabouts?"

"West Texas."

"Hmm." She chewed on some pork chop, and Helena looked ready to speak, but Lucy cut in just in time. "Got a family back in… West Texas?"

"No, ma'am," I said.

"None?"

I shook my head and took a sip of water.

"Well, it's mighty nice that you found your way allllll the way out here to this one," Lucy said in a tone that was anything but light.

"Jesse's been a real help to us," Helena said and shot a look at her sister-in-law. "He's been guarding the ranch. Ran a few rustlers outta here just last week."

"He's a real sharp shooter," Russel butted in. "You should've heard all those shots firing that night. And some of the men were wailin' in pain, and–"

"Thank you, Russel, that's enough," his mother said. "Jesse's been helping Amos and the boys with rebuilding the stables as well, and fetching things we need from town."

"You just do it all, don't you, Mr. Callahan?" Lucy's green eyes danced as they met mine, but I saw the challenge in them.

"I do what I can," I replied.

"I bet you do," she said under her breath.

Helena and the kids missed it, but I sure didn't.

I chose to ignore her pointed remarks, though. I knew why I was here and where my interests lied, and so did Helena. That was all that mattered to me. Even though having someone who didn't know the first thing about me deciding I was up to no good did grate on my nerves a bit.

But then I saw the way Honey giggled as her auntie made a silly face in her direction, and the way Russel did his best to come up with a better one, and I decided my nerves were just fine.

The family felt more full suddenly, and I knew they needed this. They needed their auntie with the silk dress and the perfectly coiffed hair to show up and shake things up for them, so I settled for biting my tongue and enjoying a home-cooked meal.

"How was the Tabor?" Helena asked the other woman with an eager smile. "Was it everything they say it is?"

Lucy smiled mischievously. "It's so much more, Lena."

"What's a ta-bore?" Russel asked around a mouthful of bread.

"The Tabor is one of the most respectable opera houses this side of the Sierra Nevadas," Lucy told him before turning a lively smile toward Helena. "It's a whole three stories high, with a great, rounded balcony of extra seats. My, I've never seen such velvet curtains in all my life, Lena. They're as good as new, even with it having been open almost a whole year now. Lord, I could've sang another three weeks there. I wish you could've seen it, the folks up there threw flowers and silk handkerchiefs on my last night, can you believe it?"

"I can," Helena said with a warm smile.

"What you need a bunch of silk handkerchiefs for?" Russel scoffed. "That just sounds like a waste of expensive materials. And it can't help your singing, so I can't see no reason for it…"

Helena and Lucy laughed at this, and I chuckled as well. Until Lucy shot me a sidelong glance, then I went back to my peas.

"Well, next time you're up in Leadville, we'll all come

watch you sing," Helena said. "I can't remember the last time I saw you perform."

"I am sorry about that," Lucy said as her tone became less playful. She looked around the table at the others, and I noticed the soft, white skin of her long neck starting to turn a little pink. "I know I've been traveling all over the place the last few years, and I should've come back more often–"

"Not at all!" Helena reached over and clutched her hand. "Lucy, we are so, so proud of you. All of us. And Frank especially. He knew this place wasn't for you, and that you were made for bigger things. And he always loved your letters. You... made him proud."

"Oh, we don't have to talk about it," Lucy croaked as she shook her head, and she batted her hand through the air as if that alone would change the subject. "I just miss y'all so much."

"We miss you, Auntie Lucy." Honey's sweet voice took me so much by surprise that I dropped my spoon.

It clanked to the table, and I scrambled to catch it before it could hit the floor. By the time I straightened up, Lucy was on her way to the other side of the table, and she scooped Honey up in her arms.

"You did?" the woman gasped. "You really missed me? Because I'm pretty sure you're much too busy picking flowers to even think of me at all!"

"Nu-uh!" Honey giggled, and her aunt spun her around.

"Ohhhh, well, good!" Lucy laughed. "Because I think about you every day. And every night. And every week. And every–"

"Alright, that's enough spinning!" Helena chuckled. "She's still eating, Lucy."

I grinned as the pair stopped spinning, and they both wore big, bright smiles on their pretty faces. Of course, one of them had dirt-smudged cheeks and kept rubbing her eyes

from how tired she was, and the other shone so bright, she practically seemed to light the whole room up herself.

The rest of dinner was filled with more shenanigans between the children and their aunt, and Helena watched it all go by with a small smile on her face. She caught my eye a few times, and the pair of us shared privately in the joy of the moment now that family had finally arrived to help cope with Frank's death.

I joined in the conversations once in a while, but mostly I just minded my own. Helena seemed determined to thank me any way she could for the work I'd done that day, and while she didn't mention a word of it to anyone else, I found my plate was constantly being refilled, and an extra-large helping of peach pie ended up in front of me for desert, along with a hot cup of coffee.

And yet, I couldn't help but feel maybe it really was time I moved on.

Helena had gotten some sense of justice, and I knew part of her wanted more, but the idea of killing didn't sit well with her. Now that she was surrounded by the laughter of her children and the charming banter of her sister-in-law, perhaps she'd like to move forward without spilling any more blood.

This thought stayed with me as I thanked the kind woman for the best meal I'd had in a long, long time. I helped clean up the table while Lucy got the children into bed, and then I strolled out into the moonlight and made my way toward the bunkhouse.

On my way, I heard soft singing coming from one of the upper rooms of the house, and my boots came to a stop of their own accord.

It was only a lullaby, but I'd never heard such a beautiful sound in all my life. Every line eased me into a deeper sense of calm, and the wind and all the grasses around me seemed to go still so they could listen as well.

That Lucy Kimber might've had a sharp enough stare to

make a grown man feel like a scolded boy, but she could've sung the cap off a nun.

I could only imagine what the woman's voice was like when she was standing on a stage in an opera house with hundreds of patrons hanging on her every note.

That was probably where some of her spunk came from. I didn't know many women bold enough to make a perfect stranger feel untrusted and unwanted in someone else's home, but the kind of audience she usually commanded might have made her feel I was beneath her notice.

Maybe not, though. Something about her seemed genuine and made of tougher stuff– beneath all the ruffled skirts and painted lips.

I walked a little slower as I tried to enjoy all I could of her singing, but soon, I was in the shadows near the bunkhouse with only the distant coyotes' songs around me. The ranch hands had turned in for the night, and they snored like only hardworking men could after a long day in the heat.

I found my saddle all prepared and Birdy already waiting for me in the paddock. I smiled as I imagined Mateo sweet-talking her and brushing her out real nice before heading to bed. I'd have to thank the man tomorrow for taking the extra time to see that my mare was well looked after.

That night, as I loaded up my firearms and set out to take my watch, I thought a lot about Silver City.

I seemed to have hit a barrier with Captain Charles Sellick, and with Sheriff Whitehill. Nothing seemed clearly connected, and sometimes that's just how things went. Mostly, it wasn't my job to worry about that sort of thing. By the time I went after a man, I knew well and full what he'd been up to, and the hows and whys of it didn't matter.

But what those six men did was too sick and twisted to be borne. And entirely out of the blue, it would seem.

The bounty hunter in me wasn't ready to quit, and the

honorable man in me, the one who'd been brutally wronged in the past as well, needed to know how all this had come about.

I'd leave it up to Helena, though. I didn't like the idea of stowing my gun on this just because the sheriff had his own way of doing things, but if Helena truly wanted me to let it lie as it was, then I would. If it came to that, at least I'd feel better about leaving now that the sister-in-law was here.

That wouldn't cover security, but I'd already made up my mind that I would spend part of tomorrow making sure the ranch hands were better equipped to defend this place without me. I'd buy them all the firearms I could find in Pinos Altos if necessary.

The rest of my watch went by without issue, and when there was only a few hours left before sunup, I shook Amos awake, crawled into my quarters, and fell into a heavy sleep.

I woke about half past seven, and I washed up quickly before I got dressed and headed out to lend a hand anywhere I could. I caught sight of Lucy and Helena near the barn with Honey, and Russel was way out in a pasture helping Mateo with one of the draft horses.

Amos and Abel were getting ready to move one of the herds to a new pasture, but they hopped down from their saddles the moment they saw me coming. Both men looked like something was on their minds, and I hurried to meet them near the pasture gate.

"Something happen?" I asked.

Amos shook his head. "Yesterday, while you were gone, I mentioned Captain Sellick to Mateo. He hadn't heard of him, but I guess later on he told Abel."

"Alright." I crossed my arms and eyed the older Spaniard beside me. "I'm listening."

"Abel says he helped Frank with a sale a little over a month ago," Amos said. "The buyer was named Charles Sellick."

CHAPTER 15

"You're sure it was the same Charles Sellick?" I asked as I turned to Abel.

He nodded as he removed his hat and scruffed his long black hair that looked like it hadn't seen a comb in a few weeks.

"Captain from the North," he confirmed.

"What was he like with Frank?" I asked. "Did anything seem off about the sale?"

Abel switched to speaking Spanish, and his rapid-fire words seemed to mostly land with Amos. The dark-skinned man nodded here and there, paused him a couple times, but then turned to me to translate.

"Sounds like Sellick was real respectful," he said. "No haggling, no strange business on the side. He seemed real pleased with the purchase, too. I guess he heard a lot about Frank down south and finally found time to take a look himself. He bought two horses for himself and three for some men who have worked with him since he got here. He said he wanted the best of the best."

"Huh." I thought on this for a moment.

Nothing about the sale sounded suspicious, but there was a connection now.

Abel's information put the sale just one month before Frank Sandusky was murdered, but by all accounts, it didn't answer any of my bigger questions.

"Well, I'll let Deputy Wallace know," I decided. "Maybe this will move their work along faster down south, but in the meantime, I thought it'd be best if we tighten up security here. Starting with y'all's shooting."

"No shooting," Abel said with a shake of his head. "Bad eyes."

"That's alright, you never know when you may need it anyway," I told him. "Just in case, I'd like you to feel comfortable shooting if you have to. If you get used to a certain stance and hold, it'll ensure your bullets go pretty much where you want them, even if your eyesight isn't quite right."

"I agree." Amos nodded.

"Si, señor," Abel relented.

Amos turned to me. "We have three groups to rotate to fresh pastures, but then we can start on that. Before we begin, though, Helena told us about Silver City this morning…"

"Good," I said. "Things went real well down there, all things considered."

"Better than well," Amos said, and his gunmetal eyes burned with sincerity as he stepped closer. "'Thanks' isn't the right word, Jesse. I've never known a man who up and handles a thing like this as quick and thorough as you, and I'm not sure you even understand how much you've done for us all here, but—"

"It's no trouble," I assured him, but the man would be heard.

"But," he continued with a grin, "I owe you, alright? I don't mean money, either, I mean as men… I owe you for all this. And I intend to repay you as best I can. You mark me on that."

I didn't particularly feel he owed me anything, but I understood his need to repay me in some way. He and Frank had been friends, and his own livelihood was wrapped up in all the mess that had happened as of late. As much as Helena had needed a taste of justice, the men of the ranch needed the same, and I was pleased to know I'd given them that. Especially after they'd run out into the dark to give me a hand when those rustlers were stirring up trouble.

That only reminded me of how sorely they needed some training.

"We'll worry about all that another time," I told Amos. "For now, let's move these horses and get to shooting."

"Fine by me," the man said with a nod. "How's about you ride Flint for this one, seeing as Birdy worked last night."

"I'd like that," I agreed.

Abel headed off to bring the dappled stallion out from the pasture, and Amos and I discussed further plans for the stables while I got my tack together and saddled up. I also grabbed my three Remingtons, holstered my Schofield on my hip, and slid my Winchester into the saddle ring for later. Then the three of us trotted to the western pasture, and we made our way in amongst the herd before getting the gate open wide.

The pasture beyond was the same one the rustlers had hoped to use to get their haul out of here, and it was a beautiful stretch of about a hundred acres. A rushing stream from deep in the mountains wove its way through the slopes down here, and stout junipers and ocotillo dotted the grassy ridges.

It was a horse's paradise, but it was a man's paradise, too. From the highest rise, there was a clear view of the mountains layering the horizon in all directions. A stormy haze clung to the many peaks, and the promise of rain blew in on the warm breeze.

I reckoned we had until about midday before the clouds reached us, but that left plenty of time for the work that needed doing.

"Why don't you take the left," Amos said and gestured to the grazing herd. "I'll drive them from the rear, and Abel will steer the right side. Shouldn't be much trouble, there's only forty-three out here right now. The rest we'll run to the north pasture next. Gonna put the draft horses in the front pasture to the east for a few days, too. They can stay there overnight."

I nodded. "Let's get it done."

I'd helped with rotating the horses a couple times now, and I found I was looking forward to it. There was nothing quite like the thrill of running the herd, and even Abel wore a rare smile on his weathered face as he circled his bay mare around to the right side of the group. He worked his way slowly inward to get the stragglers walking, and I brought Flint along the left to do the same.

Amos hung back a ways on his buckskin mustang while we finished tidying up the herd. Then Abel and I nodded at the man, and he gave a few sharp whistles.

That got all forty-three horses moving.

A few pealing whinnies and forceful snorts mingled with the thundering of hooves, while ravens scattered in the wake of the oncoming horses. They moved like a sea of dusty manes as they gathered speed, and from there, it was all finesse and a bit of keep-up to steer the herd over the final rise in their pasture, through the broad gate, and out into the rolling hills beyond. Then Abel and I eased outward and let the herd scatter across the grassy hillsides and down toward the rushing stream.

My mount seemed content to hang back as I reined him in, and I gave him a few sturdy pats as Amos and Abel cantered over. The three of us looked out across the foothills as the horses settled, and then we turned our mounts, secured the gate, and did it all over again.

By the time the draft horses were let out to the east, the storm had slid down the mountainsides. Walls of rain covered the horizon now, but the wind had stalled a bit to buy us some time.

The three of us met Mateo and Russel in the lane, and Mateo looked surprised to find me riding the gray-dappled stallion.

"Ohhh, you are trying out Flint now?" Mateo flashed all his teeth in a wide smile. "Brave man."

I frowned. "How do you figure?"

"He's a clever horse," the man said.

"That's how he got his name," Russel put in as he hopped up to sit on the fence.

Mateo nodded. "He's a tricky one. He might go strong and steady for you… Or you might strike a nerve and end up sky high. He must like you."

I turned in my saddle to eye Amos, the man who'd saddled him up for me yesterday without a mention of all this.

"What?" He held his hands up and grinned. "He's been ornery in the past, but I knew he'd like you. I have a way with this sorta thing. Like Mateo with women too beautiful for him."

Abel began snickering to himself as Mateo thwacked the black man hard in the leg.

"How's a woman gonna be too beautiful?" Russel asked as his brow bunched in confusion. "I always thought you were supposed to pick the most beautiful one there was."

"You pick the right one," Amos corrected him. "There's a difference."

"Yes, and your father was spoiled," Mateo chuckled. "The rest of us are not good enough for such beauty as he had for himself."

"I dunno, Mama's not *that* pretty," the boy said with a shrug.

"The heck you say?" Amos scoffed.

Abel sighed and started muttering to himself in Spanish.

"She always says she's no beauty!" Russel insisted. "She says people put too much stock in the looks of a person, and she's just getting along with what God saw fit to give her."

This made the ranch hands laugh, and I couldn't help joining in. It was just the sort of thing Helena would say.

"Got a couple hours before that storm hits us." Amos jutted his chin toward the indigo haze in the distance. "Jesse, you reckon you can teach these fools how to shoot alright by then?"

"I can try," I chuckled. "What kind of firearms you boys keep? I can lend you some for the day and then buy a few more if needed another time, but you'd do well to keep a few options on hand. All of you."

Abel cleared his throat and seemed to be focusing extra hard on the horn of his saddle suddenly. Mateo started fidgeting with the dirt under his fingernails, and Amos shifted in his saddle as he eyed the men.

"We can get by for today with what we've got," Amos said. "Russel, go see what your mama needs help with, alright?"

"Why?" Russel screwed his face up. "She told me to help y'all with the horses."

"And you done a good job of it," the ranch hand said. "Now, go on and get to the rest of your chores before she's gotta ask you ten times."

"But I wanna go shootin' with—"

"Go on," Amos cut in.

Russel groaned, hopped down from the fence, and dragged his lanky legs all the way to the house in just about the grumpiest fashion possible.

"Alright, what am I missing?" I asked the moment he was out of earshot, and I glanced between the three men.

"Nothing really," Amos said. "It's only... Well, we don't particularly keep a whole lot of firearms ourselves. I got the one pistol, and Mateo is the same. But... we might have some more options."

I cocked an eyebrow. "How you figure?"

"Mateo, you're gonna need to ride with one of us," Amos said with a wry grin.

"Stop by the north gate on the way," Mateo said as he hurried over to his brother.

The bay mare Abel rode seemed used to Mateo clambering up behind his brother when needed, but she let out a short whinny of annoyance. Abel talked her down easily enough, and then Amos led us onward toward the house.

I trailed the group with some intrigue, and we all tipped our hats to Helena and Honey in the garden on our way.

Honey surprised me by waving and smiling at me, and I returned the gesture. The little girl giggled over this, and her mother sent me a glowing smile from beneath her sunhat.

Then Amos made sure to let the lady of the house know we'd be practicing some shooting on the property before we turned into the first pasture, headed through the far gate, and stopped long enough for Mateo to choose a horse.

From my eyes, he picked one at complete random. The all-white mare he strolled up to nickered affectionately at the sight of the young ranch hand, and it only took a few cooing words from him before he climbed up and rode her out of there bareback.

Then we crossed through the final gate and out into the open ranchlands beyond.

This was close to the same route the six murderers had ridden the night they killed Frank, and the thought put a bad taste in my mouth. Still, the ranch hands stayed the course, and we rode at a steady gallop for several minutes.

It felt good to get out in open land with the other men and really let the horses go. Amos had a rugged style of riding that suited his tamed mustang well, and as the pair ripped across the land, I could easily imagine the buckskin stallion in his wild days. Meanwhile, his rider sat tall and relaxed, and he led the way as if he knew every cactus and blade of grass out here.

Abel was just about as opposite as he could be to the dark-skinned man, with his hunched posture and blank-faced frown. His bay mare's gait reminded me of Birdy a bit, and her black mane whipped through the air as much as Abel's long, black hair did.

Mateo was the show-off, though. The young man made bareback look as easy as breathing, and he moved with the white mare as if they were one being out in these hills. His broad smile was a little cocky, but his joy was earnest, and I couldn't help chuckling whenever I caught sight of him between the large shrubs.

As for me and the gray-dappled stallion, I eased into the ride without a second thought, and he took to our partnership as well as he had done yesterday. There was an extra bit of eagerness in him today that made me think he'd had a lot of fun going down to Silver City, but with other horses around him, he seemed to really shine. His surefootedness didn't miss a single boulder, and the three rattlers we passed didn't faze him for a second.

The land became overgrown with trees on this northern side as the terrain became steep, so we finally slowed down when they grew too thick for the horses to gallop safely. Another few minutes of walking brought us to a rocky outcropping tucked among the tall pines. The air was cooler here, and we'd gained plenty of elevation on the trip.

"This is it..." Amos nodded as we came around the craggy rocks and stopped ahead of a pair of solid steel cellar doors.

They were set into the base of the mountain, and grasses had grown up over the edges, so I figured no one came back here much.

"What's this?" I asked.

"It's Frank's," the black man said. "Only, no one really knows about it except us."

I furrowed my brow. "Helena doesn't know this is here?"

"No, sir." Amos shook his head. Then he dug into his vest pocket and pulled out a key. "Here. Take a look."

I eyed the man for a moment before I took the key and got

down from the saddle. The men dismounted and tied their horses to the pines around us. I did likewise while Mateo used the rope on his hip to secure the white mare, then I squatted down by the cellar doors.

The heavy lock protested, but a bit of jimmying got it open alright. Mateo helped me haul the doors open, and the four of us stood looking down into a cold, dark stairwell.

"Lantern's on the right," Amos said.

I glanced at the three men around me. They all looked somewhat solemn, but there was a glint of excitement in their eyes.

I shrugged to myself, took a few steps down into the darkness, and grabbed the rusty oil lantern hanging on the wall. There was a stale matchbook wedged into the wooden planks beside it.

Once the lantern was lit, I continued down the steps, and I heard the men following after me. The walls of the stairwell were lined with wooden planks, but the steps seemed to be made of any suitable stones that were on hand at the time it was built. The ceiling quickly became too low for my hat, so I removed it as I started hunkering down at the knees a bit.

Abel grunted with the effort somewhere behind me.

Then we came to a cellar that was just barely tall enough for me to stand upright in, and my boots scuffed to an abrupt stop. "What in the…" I raised the lantern as my jaw slowly unhinged.

Ahead of us was a stone room about ten feet squared. And every wall was lined with guns and blades.

CHAPTER 16

I'd never seen such a stash in all my life.

My eyes weren't even sure where they wanted to look first. The right wall was lined with no less than twenty muskets, carbines, and shotguns, and the left wall displayed over thirty pistols. Some were cap and ball, some were centerfire, but all of them were neatly mounted above case after case of various styles of ammo.

The furthest wall was nothing but bladed weapons. Bowies, camps, machetes, you name it.

This was no regular horseman's cellar.

This looked more like a soldier's stash.

"Y'all got something you've been keeping from me?" I asked as I eyed what looked like a collection of Indian-made tomahawks in the far corner.

"No, sir," Amos snorted. "Except that we've got all this that we can shoot with if we need it."

I turned and eyed the ranch hands. All of them wore honest expressions, and I raked my hand through my sweaty hair as I drew a deep breath.

"This ain't a regular thing," I muttered.

"It's not much." Mateo shrugged, and when he caught the

look I gave him, he grinned. "Oh, it is a lot, I know. But… it's Frank. He's had all this since I've known him."

"Longer," Amos said. "He told me once that he built this before he even met Mrs. Helena. He takes care of it all, too. Keeps it oiled and cleaned up. He gave me a key to it and said if anything ever happened to him, all this was mine, but that Russel could have his pick of it all, too, once he turned sixteen. I figure we can outfit ourselves for now, but I'll give it all to him when the time comes. Boy should have it since it was his daddy's."

"Shoot," I chuckled and shook my head. "That boy's gonna faint when that day comes…"

My eyes roved over it all in a respectful sort of silence for a long moment. A collection like this must've taken most of Frank's life to build up.

Unless he was up to something in recent years.

Nothing about this went in line with what I'd learned about the man, and I started wondering if I should bite the bullet and ask Helena outright about her husband. I hadn't pried because the woman was grieving, and I didn't want to insult her or her husband's memory by sharing my concerns with her.

Maybe the sister would be a better option.

The singer's sharp and calculating green eyes made me think she'd have a less biased ear on the matter, but that could wait.

For now, my gaze suddenly caught on a particular weapon.

"Hold on, is that an 1842 Springfield?" I closed the gap between me and the smoothbore musket.

I'd had one when I first went to war. In fact, that old '42 and the clothes on my back were all I brought with me, and while it put me in a hard spot more than a few times on account of its shorter range, I'd grown attached to the musket. About six months into fighting, I'd traded it out for the 1855 most everyone else was using. I ended up with the 1861 by the end of everything, and all that saved me plenty of time reloading, but looking at the '42 now brought a strong memory over me.

I remembered being just eighteen, newlywed, and scared shitless as my regiment, the 14th Texas Infantry, moved out and joined in with Walker's Greyhounds. The war was already a couple years on by then, but I was determined to see it through now that I felt sure my family was settled enough to get by without me until I returned.

That's what I'd thought, at least.

I took the musket in my hands, and the weight was still familiar. I probably knew that gun better than any I'd ever held, and I briefly regretted trading mine out. It was a rugged weapon, and I'd been young and in need of a more suitable firearm at the time, but now I appreciated all my '42 had done for me. It was the start of a new life that made me a man real quick.

"This one I like," Mateo said, and I turned to find him brushing his fingertip over the engraved cylinder of what looked like a Colt Paterson.

"That is nice," I agreed, placed the musket back in its bracket, and came over.

It turned out to be very, very nice.

The Paterson looked like one of the earliest models, with a short muzzle, a bluish tint to the steel, and a well-worn walnut handle. It was well-kept, though, and the engraved cylinder depicted an intricate scene that brought half a grin to my face.

I took it down to admire it more closely.

"What is that thing?" Mateo pointed to the engraving.

"It's called a centaur," I chuckled. "Half man, half horse. Looks like he's using his own Colt to take down these horsemen on the other side."

Mateo looked affronted. "Why is it on the gun?"

"I heard it was a selling point at the time," I said. "My

father told me about them. Some of these had scenes of stagecoach robberies engraved on them, all sorts of things. They got more intricate over the years."

"Hmm..." The young man let his eyes wander over the other pistols, and he gasped as he reached for the one Abel had just taken down.

The ivory handle must've caught both their eyes, but I didn't recognize the revolver.

"This one is beautiful," Mateo said, and his brother swatted his grabbing hand away.

Abel scolded him, but then he handed the revolver over to me without any issue, and Mateo rolled his eyes.

"It's a Smith & Wesson," I muttered as I eyed the stamp on the barrel. "But I don't recognize the model. Could be custom, I suppose, but that'd make it pretty steep in pricing. Very steep, in fact."

I turned the pistol over and saw it was stamped 'July 1865.'

I raised my eyebrows at that, seeing as I didn't personally know anyone who could afford a piece like this back then.

My interest was certainly piqued, but then my eyes hitched on something I didn't think I'd ever see again.

"Ohh..." I loosened the top button on my shirt as sweat broke out on my neck. "Ohhh, you've got to be raggin' me. He's got three LeMats?"

"What is LeMat?" Mateo asked as he craned his neck over my shoulder.

I grinned. "Ten-shooter."

"No shit?" Amos hurried over from where he'd been studying the cavalry swords on the back wall.

The engravings along the tops of the barrels all read 'Col. LeMat' in various scripts, so there was no mistaking them.

Each one was recently oiled and cleaned up, but there was a bit of a variance between them. One had the loading lever along the right side with a brown checked handle, and it looked like an earlier rendition. The other two had the loading lever along the left and sported blacker checking on the handles. Regardless, each had the unmistakable 18 gauge shotgun bore beneath the main barrel that made the LeMat stand out.

"Heck of a weapon," I murmured and trailed my thumb over the checkered pad of the hammer.

"You ever had one of them?" Amos asked.

"No, never." I shook my head. "A few higher-ranking officers I fought beside had one, but I never even got close enough to shoot one."

"Well, I'd say today's the day, then." Amos grinned and clapped a hand on my shoulder. "Let's bring out a few options for everyone, and we'll get started."

"Fine by me," I chuckled.

We got my own pistols laid out on a fallen tree trunk, along with my rifle, and then I selected an array of options for the men to try out based on the skills they already had. Amos was a fine shot, I'd learned as much when he saved my life. But Mateo and Abel would take some work, so I focused on them while Amos tested out a few different rifles.

He and I had already agreed that each of the ranch hands should have at least two pistols with belt holsters, and one good rifle apiece.

Mateo ended up cleaning up his aim pretty fast once I got his grip sorted out, stiffened his arm up, and made him focus on keeping it all steady when he drew back the trigger. He was also prone to pinching one eye shut no matter how many times I told him not to, but he didn't stop trying to correct the habit.

Abel, it turned out, had good eyesight in the daytime, but we got him more comfortable with anchoring his aim the same way over and over so he'd stand a good chance at night if he knew generally where his target was.

Amos never really had time to sit and shoot posts all day,

but an hour in the woods brought a smile to his face as he started hitting the same mark several times in a row.

Then it was time to test out the LeMat. I left the men to their target practice while I returned to the cellar and dug out the proper ammunition for both bores. I'd seen a ten-shooter loaded enough times to know I had to raise the loading lever and half-cock the barrel to get easier access to the cylinder. Once the nine rounds were set, I pulled out the end of the ramrod to pack the shotgun barrel before I headed back up to the fresh air and joined the men in the woods.

"Everyone be quiet so Jesse can have his fun now," Mateo laughed as he saw me. "This is historical moment for him."

"This I've got to see," Amos said and rubbed his hands together.

I chuckled as I lined up next to him and decided on a knotted branch as my target.

There was nothing quite like trying my hand at a new gun, and each shot sent a thrill through my veins. When it came time to give the shotgun a try, I cocked the hammer, flicked the lever to pivot the hammer face down, and pulled the trigger one last time.

The shot cracked like thunder through the forest as it split a final branch, and wood chips blasted out in every direction. Mateo whooped and threw his hat in the air, and Amos and Abel laughed as they applauded the finale.

"I gotta try that myself," Amos chuckled.

Once Amos had his fun, we pulled out a few of the prettier pieces Frank had collected. We spent another hour trying them out and growing more and more eager for Russel to finally get a look at his inheritance. Amos could hardly wait to share a day just like this with the boy when the time came.

Soon the clouds were too close to be ignored, so we packed everything away as it had been and made our picks.

Abel settled for an 1865 Spencer Carbine, even though it took custom cartridges. It looked like there was plenty of ammo for it in the cellar to last him quite a while, and his aim was sharpest with the sturdy rifle, so that was the final decider.

Pistols weren't his forte by any means, partly because his hands weren't as reliable as they used to be after all his farrier work, so he'd need more practice before he felt it was worth carrying a pair.

Mateo wanted that ivory-handled pistol so bad, he was just about drooling over it, but Amos wouldn't allow it. He knew Russel would want the custom piece in its best condition one day, and the young ranch hand couldn't argue with that. He already had one Colt Navy, but for his second pistol, he happily took a Remington like mine instead. For a rifle, he liked my '73 Winchester best, too, so we'd pick one up in Pinos Altos tomorrow.

Amos found a Peacemaker to match the one he already had, and he chose a very nice Henry rifle to complete his set because he liked the classy look of it and the larger magazine it offered.

He helped me close up the cellar and get her locked again, but as I turned toward the gray dappled stallion, the man caught my arm.

"Don't forget this," he said and held out the LeMat.

"I couldn't," I told him in earnest. "That there's a real nice weapon, and not easy to come by."

"And Russel is set to inherit two more," Amos chuckled as he grabbed my hand and plunked the ten-shooter into it. "That boy admires you, and as I told you before, I owe you. So please, take the LeMat. You're the sort of man who should have one on him."

I held the man's gunmetal gaze, and I could see he wouldn't be turned down.

"Well, alright," I relented. "Thank you. Sincerely."

"Anytime." He clapped me on the shoulder. "If you wanna

use it to kill some of those murderin' fools, you be my guest. Frank would like it that way."

I grinned and admired the weapon one more time before stowing it in my saddlebag with the ammunition he'd brought out for it.

Lightning and thunder were threatening to bring the sky down on us by the time we saddled up and rode south again. The wind whipped in a frenzy beyond the trees as we spurred our mounts into a gallop once more, and we managed to make it back to the ranch just as the first cold drops started striking the brims of our hats.

I felt better about the defenses at the ranch now that I'd gotten a good feel for the men's skills. They'd have to keep in practice, but I knew they'd improve in no time. More importantly, they were more sure of themselves and their abilities to defend the Black Spur with or without me.

The storm blew through the ranchlands like a freight train before settling within only half an hour. The clouds remained, and a few more scatterings of rain came and went throughout the rest of the day, but it didn't hinder the work that needed doing.

We managed to get another six hours of work done on the stables before it came time to round up the horses again. Amos considered leaving them out in the pastures like they used to, but in the end, we decided things were too unsure around here still.

The notion prodded at the back of my mind.

The Black Spur couldn't stay in this state of uncertainty forever. If I was gonna get to the bottom of Mr. Sandusky's murder, I needed to make bigger strides, and soon. Which meant I needed to talk to Helena.

The sun had just gone down, and the rainy evening glowed with cool, blue light as I made my way toward the house. I was just knocking some mud off my britches and

straightening my hat when I looked up to see Lucy standing on the porch with her arms crossed and a subtle smirk
on her face.

There were no silk ruffles or perfectly coiffed hairdos this
evening, but she still managed to look the most well-tailored
among us. Her black blouse made her auburn hair a more
noticeable dark red, and she'd gathered all of her curls into
a matching black ribbon at the nape of her neck. She still
wore red paint on her lips, though the shade was much less
showy today.

All in all, she looked more the part of a rancher's sister as
she looked down at me from her perch on the porch.

"Evening, ma'am," I said as I came to a stop at the bottom
of the steps. "I was just hoping to–"

"I've got a question for you first," she informed me.

The sharp look in her green eyes made me uneasy, but I
nodded all the same.

The woman took three steps forward and planted her
hands on her small waist. "How much to hire your services,
Mr. Callahan?"

CHAPTER 17

"My services?" I blinked in surprise.

"That's right," Lucy said with a nod.

"Well… I don't charge Helena anything to guard the ranch," I explained. "It's something I feel is simply the right thing to do, so–"

"Yes, and you do it well," Lucy assured me. "But that is not where my interests lie. I'm talking about your… other areas of expertise. You see, Russel had quite a lot to say about you last night. Things that my sister-in-law happened to keep out of her introductions. Including an interesting story about you, Silver City, and two of the men who murdered my brother ending up dead in the street."

My eyebrows popped up, and the woman nodded slowly as if this alone confirmed the boy's stories.

"I can assure you I never told Russel a word about Silver City," I said.

Lucy scoffed at this. "You think that boy minds his business around here?"

"No, ma'am, I don't suppose he does."

"Good, then let's not pretend we're dim-witted individuals," she said. "How much do you charge?"

I shifted my boots in the mud as I tried to decide how to

proceed with this one. Plain and simple was probably best with a woman as direct as Lucy Kimber.

"Ma'am, I'm not a hired assassin," I said. "I'm a bounty hunter."

"As I said, let's not pretend either of us are dim-witted," she said and sent me a pointed look. "I am aware of how your job works. But the fact is, this town is rather short on hired killers. You see, I've grown used to the bigger cities, where folks hire what they need when they need it. I know that there are plenty of options out there for a girl in my predicament."

I nodded in agreement. "I'll tell you what. Why don't you explain your predicament, from your side of it, and I'll decide if there's anything I can do to help."

Lucy cocked an eyebrow, but the bold woman finally smiled and agreed to my terms.

"Very well," she said. "I've recently found myself torn straight in half because the most honest and hardworking man I've known in all my life was murdered in what I'm told was a brutal and horrific fashion."

She'd lost her smile now, and even in the blue dusk, I could tell her long, white neck had flushed pink as emotion got the better of her.

"To tell you the truth, I'm mad enough that I think I could twist the heads off of those murderers with my bare hands," she continued. "I've thought about doing it more times than I'd care to share. Sometimes, I tie 'em up first and scream at 'em until I'm satisfied. Other times, I just take their big, ugly heads in my hands and bash them open on anything I find nearest to me."

I swallowed hard as I realized how honest the woman was being. Her green eyes were hard and entirely earnest, and I could understand her fury. I'd felt the very same way at times in my life, but I'd never heard a woman explain that kind of anger so clearly before. I'd certainly never expected such a fashionable woman like Lucy to say such things, either.

"But when I calm down, and I really think on it," she continued, "I know I'd generally like to keep my hands, and the hands of my lovely sister-in-law, clean. That's what my brother would want, anyway. He was the kind of man who believed women shouldn't have to think such thoughts. He believed all good men wouldn't hesitate to help a woman out if she was in need. And I assure you, I am in need."

"Of?" I asked.

"A righteous hand and a swift deliverance," she said, and her hard expression left no room for misinterpretation.

I nodded and scuffed my boot around as I thought on the woman's predicament.

"Does Helena know what you're asking of me?"

"She knows how I'd like to handle the situation," she replied. "But she's Lena."

"Meaning?"

"Meaning she's too good a soul to think about such things," Lucy sighed. "She seems relieved about the work you've done, but she doesn't feel right asking more of you. Or taking matters into her own hands, as she sees it. I've known her half my life, though, and more than anything, she doesn't abide holding onto anger. Thinks it shows weakness of character. But she's angry, Mr. Callahan. More angry than I've ever seen her, and she just doesn't know what to do about it."

"I figured as much," I said. "It's a hard spot to find yourself in."

"It is, but may I be blunt?" she asked, and I nodded. "I spoke to Lena about you. And the men this morning. And Honey, of course, she's your biggest supporter."

I cocked an eyebrow. "You sure about that?"

"Yes, she calls you the 'brave man with the pretty horsey,'" she giggled. "Makes you sound quite intimidating."

I laughed heartily at this, and the young woman joined in. Then she looked around and leaned closer, as if she had a secret to tell.

"She picked you flowers yesterday but got too shy to hand them over," Lucy confided.

A slow grin spread on my face as I recalled the bundle of flowers the little girl was still clutching when I got back to the ranch. A small lump formed in my throat, too, because I'd been worried about Honey. It was hard not to be.

I had no idea I'd made the sweet girl feel safe.

"From what I've heard," Lucy continued, "you're made of the same sorta stuff as my brother. You act on that same sense of duty that he always did. So I owe you an apology."

"That's not necessary," I assured her.

"Yes it is," she insisted as she came down the steps to stand on the same level as me.

She was close enough now that I noticed her perfume smelled of some sort of exotic flowers. She was also quite petite, probably no taller than five feet. I supposed I hadn't realized before because her strong personality made her seem larger than life.

Now, she was just a lovely woman standing in the mud and tilting her head back to look me in the eye.

"I'm sorry, Mr. Callahan, for assuming some things about you at first," she said. "I know I was hostile and a little... pointed. Maybe even impolite, I can't quite recall."

"No?" I grinned.

"Nope." She smiled back, and her eyes danced with amusement. "Can't say I'm one to behave rashly, either, so I'm sure I wasn't so rude as to really warrant using the word 'impolite.'"

"Huh." I chewed on this for a moment, but I couldn't resist the beautiful woman's charm. "S'pose I can't recall any particular instance, either."

"Good." She smiled. "Then we agree that I owe you an

apology, but I haven't wholly embarrassed myself in all this. Correct?"

"Agreed," I chuckled.

The woman laughed lightly, too, but then she sobered as she studied me more closely.

"I only worried for Lena," she said quietly.

I nodded in understanding. "Apology accepted, miss."

This was all the woman seemed to need, and she smiled again, but it was sadder this time.

"You know, my brother loved Lena for her pure heart just as much as her beauty," she said. "He could've been a blind man, and he'd have loved every little thing about her all the same. And as for me, ever since we were little, he told me to go on and sing as much as I could anywhere I wanted, and to never, ever let people push me off that path if it's what I dreamed for myself. He didn't care what anyone had to say about me, even after Mama and Daddy died. Plenty of folks back home expected him to marry me off as soon as he could. But he just kept our ranch running, and kept on shooing me out the door whenever I tried to help because I 'belong on a stage, not in a stable.'"

Her voice had gotten strained now, and a couple tears slid down her cheeks. It occurred to me that her skin looked as smooth as porcelain in the bluish light, but then she straightened her shoulders and leveled those green eyes on me again.

"So what I need, Mr. Callahan, is an honorable man with some real good aim who's no stranger to killing," she said. "Keep in mind, I listened carefully to my brother, too, so I make quite a decent living nowadays. There's a fairly good chance I'd pay whatever price a man with those qualifications asked. Just as long as every last one of the filthy bastards who killed my brother are buried six feet under as soon as possible."

She certainly knew how to make a speech.

In fact, I didn't take issue with her inquiry at all. Especially when I thought about Sheriff Whitehill, and his firm opinions on how I conduct myself on this matter.

Frank's own sister hiring me made it a lot easier to proceed as I saw fit.

But that only reminded me of how strange all this business had been from the beginning.

"Ma'am, before we come to any kind of agreement, I have to be honest with you," I said, and she gestured for me to continue. "I'm not exactly clear on why anyone would want to murder your brother, and the thought's been irking me from the start. It's been hard enough finding out who did it, sure. But the 'why' isn't becoming easier to understand at all. From all I hear, and what you say, he was a good and honest man."

"Lena and the boys said the same," she admitted as her forehead crinkled with worry. "I wish I had any kind of help on that, but I truly don't. Lena always wrote the letters in the house, and all I heard about was how many foals they were expecting this season, any particularly nice horses he'd been training..."

"You did advise your sister-in-law to sleep with a gun, though," I pointed out. "I thought maybe you had reason to believe more trouble was coming. Someone who might be after the Black Spur..."

"Oh, that." She waved a dismissive hand. "That was just for Lena. She's got aim almost as sharp as my brother did. He taught her well, and I know it gives her peace of mind to be so capable. But I've reckoned from the start that if this was about getting my brother's ranch, they'd have done more the night they killed him."

"I'm of the same mind," I said. "Just wanted to be sure I'm not missing anything."

"Not to my knowledge. Although, that does bring me to something I could use your advice on."

"Alright," I said.

"A man came by the house yesterday while you were... delivering justice down south," she confided, and my eyebrows furrowed. "He apparently came all the way up here from Silver City to inquire about buying this here ranch. All of it. The land, the horses, the men working in those fields right now."

"Yesterday?" I repeated. "Helena didn't say a word about it to me."

"Nor to those hardworking men," she muttered and glanced around. "I just about had to drag it out of her, too."

"Who was it who came?" I asked.

"Some man who works for a fella named Wicket," Lucy said. "He's a rancher in Silver City, I guess. And he's interested enough in this property that he sent his lawyer up to inquire about it. She said he was very respectful, but as word has spread real quick about Frank, he thought it pertinent to put himself forward in case Lena was interested in making a very nice sum for herself. As security, you know."

I'd expected as much since the moment I understood the Black Spur's reputation, so I wasn't too surprised people were starting to make inquiries. Still, it worried me a bit that I hadn't known about the visitor, but in truth, it wasn't really my place to put my oar in. Same as my opinions on what Helena did with her husband's ranch.

"Well, I won't lie, I don't like the sound of that," I admitted. "But if she wants to sell the place, it's her own choice to make."

Lucy's eye flashed as she crossed her arms over her blouse.

"It certainly is not," she informed me. "This isn't just any old ranch, Mr. Callahan."

"Okay," I said with some confusion. "Then what is it you'd like my advice on?"

"How to shake some sense into her!" Lucy huffed. "Those men out there were very carefully selected by my brother, they have a way with horses, and they know the standard he expected. Why, they're worth more than anyone could pay to hire them off us! And that's not even talking about the horses!"

"I can see that, but–"

"And Lena could easily keep this ranch running with the help of those three men alone!" the woman barreled on. "Russel's a big help, and he'll be ready to run horses himself here in another year. But she didn't exactly turn this lawyer down outright, so I don't doubt for a moment that he will return, and Lord, I don't even want to think on what I'll say if he convinces her to sell..."

I removed my hat and rubbed at the back of my sweaty neck. "Ma'am, I don't know what kind of sway you think I hold here, but let me tell you, it ain't much. I just point and shoot."

Lucy clicked her tongue and cast a disgruntled look at the dimming lane. She sulked for a brief moment, but then she fixed her face and sent me a mischievous look.

"Fine," she said. "Then are you willing to point and shoot for me?"

"Well, I suppose if you're certain about all this, then I'd be willing to offer my assistance."

"Not just assistance," she said and held up a stern finger. "I want results, and I mean that."

"Big city results," I said with a grin. "Understood."

"Good," she laughed. "Then how much do you charge?"

I eyed the woman, but I knew the answer before she'd even asked.

"How about one dollar?" I deadpanned.

"Per day?" she asked.

"Total sum."

Lucy's smile went flat. "A dollar? You mocking me?"

"No, ma'am," I said in earnest. "I got a real strong feeling I'm gonna make quite the bounty getting involved in all this. And while I didn't know Frank Sandusky, I can respect the sort of man he seemed to be. Truth be told, I wouldn't feel right taking pay from his family for this, so one dollar is all I'll agree to from you."

Lucy let out a laugh. Then she saw I wasn't kidding around, and she bit her lip to try and settle her smile down as she narrowed her eyes. She looked determined to make me budge on this, and I realized all at once that she looked exactly like Russel did whenever he started asking about my work.

"Might as well give in," I chuckled. "I'm not one to change my mind on matters like this."

"Hmm…" Lucy quirked her lips to the side but then shrugged. "We'll see about that. For now, one dollar it is, Mr. Callahan."

She stuck her pale hand out, and it felt as soft as downy feathers when I grasped it in my own to shake on our agreement.

"Please, call me Jesse," I said.

"Lucy," she returned with a curt nod. "I am looking forward to this endeavor with you, Jesse. And while you work on hunting down those men for me, I'll work on bringing Lena to her senses."

With that, the elegant woman turned on her heel and headed back onto the porch and into the house. I was left in a violet twilight, staring at the closed door with my hat in hand and my mind churning.

I supposed there wasn't much reason to try and speak with Helena now, so I headed instead toward the bunkhouse. I managed to get a good supper down before it came time for me and Birdy to start our watch, and despite the rain that kept rolling through every now and then, we passed a peaceful night on the ranch.

The next morning, I rose early and got the wagon ready to go to Pinos Altos for another load of lumber. The stables wouldn't need much more now, and I hoped we'd have it complete in a couple more days.

I'd expected Mateo to join me on the trip, but I found a

much prettier passenger climbing up onto the bench beside me instead.

"Fine day for a trip into town, isn't it?" Lucy said brightly as she got her skirts situated.

She wore a nice, black ensemble with a woven sun hat, but she still managed to look like the fanciest thing in the Black Mountains.

"I'd say so," I replied. "You gonna help me load lumber, then?"

Lucy pursed her lips at me, and I grinned as I got the mules moving.

"I will actually be picking up a few things for Lena while we're there," she told me. "I admire her frugality, but I reckon she could do with a few of the finer things for once. Lord knows my brother stored up the money for it."

"Ahhh, so that's your angle," I said.

"It is not an angle," she huffed. "I simply think a woman as pretty as her should have some pretty things, that's all. Why, the only outfits she has that are fit for mourning are over a decade old. Not that she cares, and nor should she. My brother would've been furious to see either of us in such a color out in this heat. But she should have something nicer. And if she comes to understand how very comfortable her life could be, living on the money those horses fetch all year round, well then… that's just how that'll go."

I snorted out a laugh.

"Helena doesn't strike me as the sort of woman to be won over by pretty things," I said.

"She isn't," Lucy sighed. "That's why I am also buying some essentials she's been putting off. Like a butter churn that doesn't get stuck every third crank, and a new pair of overalls for Russel that don't leave half his legs showing at the bottoms."

I nodded. "It's a nice thought."

"Thank you." She sent me a smile as the wagon passed

under the iron gate. "Now, since we have a while to sit here together, what would you like to talk about?"

"How about you tell me where you're from," I said. "Since you know where I'm from already."

I sent her a sidelong glance, and she giggled at the memory of our dinner together.

"I live in San Francisco nowadays," she told me. "Got me a nice little house there, by the sea. It's not much, but it suits me. Better than this rugged country down here does, anyway."

"You don't like it?" I asked.

Lucy pinched her lips in thought, then shrugged. "I didn't when we first came down here, that's for sure. It's dangerous now, but it was real scary back then, especially for a girl only fifteen years old."

"I'd imagine so."

"Before all that, I grew up in Colorado Territory," she said as the wagon swayed its way toward the main track that'd take us up the mountain pass. "There was a little town in the eastern plains out there called Atwood. It's dried up now, but that's where my mama and daddy kept their ranch before the consumption took them from us."

"I'm sorry," I said.

Lucy nodded. "That was a hard winter. And a hard land, too. The most bitter cold comes blowing in on those plains. That's why my brother up and decided to leave back in '66."

"Is that right?" My interest piqued.

"I guess so," she sighed and glanced up at the tall pines drawing closer. "Frank wasn't much for explaining himself to folks. Not even to me. He just did what he thought he should, and if he wanted to do something else, he up and did it. I always figured it was those cold, hard winters and losing Mama and Daddy that made him want to come south. He'd been running the ranch for a few years by then. I thought he did a real nice job of it, too, but he'd heard about some cattlemen's trail that'd take us through Trinidad and down into New Mexico Territory."

"The Goodnight-Loving Trail?" I asked.

"That's the one," she replied. "Told me about it one Tuesday morning, and just like that, he sold off most of the horses and the land, and we left for good not a month later."

I furrowed my brow at this. "Just like that? Without saying much about the reason?"

"Yes," Lucy chuckled as a wistful look came over her. "That was Frank, though. I didn't mind, I'm about the same. I only ended up in San Francisco because a friend of mine was marrying a jeweler there. A very rich one, too. They paid all my expenses to bring me there from a contract I'd just finished in Chicago, and after the wedding, I just decided I was gonna stay there."

"I hear it's nice country over there," I said.

"You haven't been?" Lucy gasped.

"No, ma'am." I shook my head. "I've been all over, but never crossed over the Sierra Nevadas."

"Oh, you should go," she gushed and clutched my arm. "It's about the prettiest place I've ever been. Of course, that's how I feel about everywhere I go. Like this here…"

She raised a delicate hand and brushed it across the scene ahead of us. We were coming up on the track that would take us north, and the river running alongside the other end of it sparkled in the dappled sunlight. The air was fresh and damp this morning after the various storms that came through over the evening, and the cooing of doves echoed above us as we rode along.

"This was certainly a lovely change after the plains, let me tell you," Lucy laughed. "But even with the house in San Francisco, I still like traveling around too much to stay put."

"That I can understand," I said with a smile.

We fell into a comfortable silence after that, but we chatted now and then about the area, her life here as a girl, and the different places the pair of us had been to.

Then we came into Pinos Altos, and I quickly realized Lucy had quite a lot of admirers here. Most of them were local folks who either knew her all those years ago, or had formed an acquaintance with her the few times she'd returned.

Everyone was eager to offer their condolences about her brother, but I noticed she didn't seem too keen on dwelling on it. She was quick to change the subject, or find some lively compliment to pay the folks around her. That just seemed to be her way, though. No matter how much she was hurting, she wanted to talk about better things, and share a few smiles and laughs.

I helped her down from the wagon outside the general store, and then I went straight to the sawmill. We needed less lumber than we'd been getting, so the loading didn't take long, and I found a nice spot with some good shade around the side of the mill for the boys to wait while I handled some business of my own.

Starting with buying a Winchester for Mateo and a few new belt holsters.

Lucy must've moved on from the general store by now, but the clerk was quick to brag that Miss Lucy Kimber the opera singer was just in there. I smiled and let the man preen a bit before I settled on a well-maintained '73 he had in back. I bought four boxes of ammunition as well, plus five belt holsters and a couple saddle rings, before I headed back out to the street.

I wanted to stop in and speak with Deputy Wallace while I was in town, so I loaded my purchases into the wagon and turned in his direction. I was just passing the barbershop when a soft, husky voice caught my attention.

"Hola, Mr. Callahan," Rosa murmured as she came around the corner.

I stopped in pleasant surprise and tipped my hat. "Hello, Miss Vallejos."

The woman gave me that warm, pleasing smile that Mateo liked to go on about as she strolled to my side. Her brown-and-amber eyes caught the sunlight in a way that left me feeling suddenly hypnotized. She'd been beautiful in the gold-clad room of La Casa Dorada, but out in the daylight, she positively glowed like gold herself.

"Would you be so kind as to escort me back to the saloon?" she asked, and the daze I'd been in suddenly cleared.

"Oh," I said with some surprise. "Yes, I can do that, miss."

I didn't think a woman who was so admired in this town would need me as an escort, but I certainly would never deny a woman in need of escorting. What really confused me, though, was the fact that she boldly looped her arm with mine before we began walking.

A few steps later, I realized why.

Rosa pressed herself closer as she brought her lips up to murmur quietly in my ear.

"One of the men you are looking for is across the street from us now."

CHAPTER 18

Ice shot through my veins as my eyes darted around the main street.

The first thing that caught my attention was the words 'Sellick Distillery' painted on the side of a freight wagon. There were three men unloading crates outside one of the local saloons.

"Red hair?" I guessed as I recognized a man who fit Rosa's initial descriptions.

"Yes, with the bandage on his hand," the young woman confirmed. "He was lively that night when he came in. Seemed drunk and happy."

Rosa's eyes slid my way, and her grim expression said plenty.

The man in question walked like he'd spent too long in the saddle. His bowed legs had a stance that made my own back-end ache just looking, but he wasn't too far along in years by any means. His red hair was as stark as his beard, and his skin was freckled all over as he spit in the dirt and ordered the other two men around.

"I'll take care of it," I murmured as Rosa and I carried on walking arm in arm.

She offered a small nod, and her expression gave nothing

away as we neared La Casa Dorada. I stopped once Rosa had stepped up to the entrance, and her amber eyes flicked briefly to the wagon before they met my gaze.

"You will be safe?" she asked in a husky tone.

"Safe as I can be," I replied, tapped my hat, and took my leave.

I crossed the street right behind a pair of passing riders, and by the time I hopped onto the opposite boardwalk, two of the distillery workers were disappearing into the saloon.

That left the red-haired man alone with his tobacco.

My pulse quickened as I closed in and eyed the street around us. Folks were busy at this hour, and the majority were tired miners trying to wet their whistles before finishing their shifts.

There was a slim alley between the saloon and the Post Office beside it, and the red-haired man moved to bring himself around the wagon, right toward it.

This was my chance.

I quickened my step, caught him by the puppy scruff, and shoved him into the alley in a matter of seconds.

"Hey!" he yelped and almost landed flat on his face.

He struggled to stop his momentum, but I didn't slow my step. The second he was upright, he turned with his gun drawn, but I planted my boot square in his gut first.

"Ungh!" he huffed and was thrown backward into a stack of discarded crates.

His gun went flying, and I kicked it toward the street before dodging the kick he sent my way.

Then I grabbed his leg, yanked him out of the rubble, and kicked him once more in the ribs.

The wheeze he let out assured me I'd broken at least one bone, but the man was a stubborn rat. He rolled, scrambled to his feet, and raised his freckled fists, but he was disoriented now. I only had to dodge one wild punch before I grabbed him again and shoved him backward even harder.

This time, he crashed all the way through the broken crates and slid a few feet deeper into the alley before going still.

He groaned and twitched a bit, but made no attempt at standing.

I reached down and wrenched him to his feet. Then I slammed him into the wooden wall beside us and got him pinned there with the nose of my pistol rooted in his back.

"AH!" he yelled.

"Holler again and it'll be the last thing you do," I growled and pressed my gun more firmly between his ribs.

"Alright!" he wheezed. "Alright! I'm not movin' nowhere, hold on! Who the hell are you?"

"I'm the man the Black Spur hired to hunt your ass down," I told him.

His body went as rigid as the wall ahead of him. His breaths quickened as the panic set in, and I could almost feel the fear jolting through him from head to toe.

I let him stew in it for a moment as the folks of Pinos Altos carried on past the alley without a glance.

"Now, the only thing I wanna hear from you is answers," I said. "Starting with your name."

"Theo!" he answered at once. "Theo K. Lawson, sir!"

"Well, Theo K. Lawson, you wanna tell me why you got the bright idea of killing Frank Sandusky? Or should I just shoot you and call it a day?"

"No!" he yelped and jerked in my hold. "No, don't shoot! I'll tell you anything!"

"Start talkin'."

"It was Sellick!" He gulped and choked on tobacco juice in all his panicked breathing. I sighed and shook some focus into him. "Sellick sent us, I swear! I didn't do nothin'–"

"Nothing?" I snarled, and fury laced my words. "Nothing except dragging an honest man out to be quartered. Nothing except lighting a stable bigger than three of these darn saloons on fire. Nothing but cold, hard murder."

I twisted my gun in his ribs, and the man cried out. Then I smashed his face against the wooden planks to quiet him again.

"I don't abide liars," I said. "Now... You did some killing that night, didn't you?"

"No!" He gulped. "Well... I... I set the fire! Me and Petey set the stables alight and then lit out of there! We was just supposed to kill off the breeders, I swear, that's what Tommy said! He was the boss on that one, not me!"

"Tommy who?" I demanded.

"Tommy Masters! Hardly know the man, too, you can ask anyone. Don't run with him at all, I just–"

"Shut your mouth," I growled. "Did I ask for your life story?"

He shook his head vigorously. "No, sir."

"But you went there to burn those horses up, didn't you?"

"Yes, sir!"

"Tommy Masters was in charge of you lot?"

"Yes, sir!"

"Who else?"

The man let out a whimper as he went limp against the wall, but another firm shake got him talking.

"T-Tommy's cousin," he managed. "Man named Bill Masters. And-and Boone Slim, and Petey McCaw, and Jeb Osiah! Th-they did the killin', me and Petey were only sent after them horses! Boone got the rancher knocked out and then... then that all went down. I swear on God!"

I nodded as a cold, killing calm washed over me.

"And what does Captain Sellick want with the Sanduskys?" I asked. "Why'd he hire you?"

This made the man pause, and while he still spit all over in his attempt to catch his breath, he was confused now.

"C-Captain?" He craned his neck to try and look me in the face. "Wh... What you mean? It was George who hired us."

"George?" I hadn't heard any whispers of the name in all this.

I was just caught off guard enough for Theo to suddenly buck himself backward off the wall, too. He elbowed me straight in the center of my gut in the process, and my breath gave out as I lost my hold on the man.

Next thing I knew, he had a ten-inch camp knife in hand.

He jumped at me, and I stumbled back as my lungs tried and failed to work properly. The blade sang as it passed my ear, then struck out toward my chest.

I ducked, spun, and got my gun up, but Theo was quick. I caught the glint of light on his thick knife as it streaked toward the side of my skull.

Then the pop of a pistol split the alleyway, but it wasn't my gun that fired.

I stared with wide, harried eyes as blood suddenly oozed from the side of Theo K. Lawson's head. The bullet hole was small, but it had struck directly in the man's temple, and it never exited the other side of his head.

He hit the ground as his knife clattered to the dirt. Then he laid still and lifeless, with a plug of soggy tobacco hanging halfway out of his mouth.

I whipped around and found Rosa standing at the entrance to the alley.

She had a smoking pocket pistol still clutched in her hands, and her amber eyes were narrowed on her kill.

"Put that away," I hissed as I hurried to her side.

Meanwhile, screams and shouts broke out in the street behind her. The few men I could see were drawing their weapons with purpose.

I eyed the small silver pistol as Rosa stuffed it into the pocket of her skirts without blinking an eye. The townsfolk descended moments later, and we were blocked in by no less than two dozen angry locals.

More than half of them were armed and furious, and I kept my Remington in hand as I shifted to put Rosa behind me.

"What the hell did you do?" A voice rose up, and I recognized the two other distillery workers shoving their way to the front of the crowd. "Murderer! You murdered Theo!"

A few men managed to keep them back, but they didn't look like they wanted to stop my accusers.

One of them stepped forward and raised his revolver.

"Don't move, mister," the large, burly miner commanded from the other end of his Dragoon.

I recognized the look in his dark eyes. He'd defend this town with everything he had if need be, and I was the man spilling blood in the streets.

I held my hands wide. "I don't want trouble. My name's Jesse Callahan, and I'm just–"

"Wait." The miner squinted at me. "You Gilly's friend? The one who got them Hobbs boys?"

I almost sighed as I realized Gilly's tongue had been working overtime around here.

"That's me," I confirmed. "And the man behind me is one of the group who murdered Frank Sandusky."

That got all their attention.

Murmurs and whispers spread through the townsfolk, and while half of them looked mad about a murderer amongst them, the other half looked positively excited to be involved in the ordeal.

The two distillery workers looked stunned and stupefied by the news. They quickly holstered their weapons, too, and suddenly, they didn't need anyone to be holding them back.

The Deputy showed up right about then.

"Back on up, folks!" he hollered as he pushed through the crowd. "I said back away, now, let me get in here."

When Deputy Wallace made it through, his eyes locked on mine. They darted to the dead man in the alley, the gun in my hand, and the beautiful Spanish woman at my side.

"Miss Rosa!" he gasped and snatched his hat off his head almost as fast as Mateo. "Are you alright, miss?"

"Sí, señor," she said.

The deputy looked my way. "Did she get caught up in this nasty business?"

Rosa's amber eyes flicked toward mine just long enough for me to catch the smallest shake of her head. Then she smiled warmly at the deputy.

"I happened to be passing by when the man in the alley tried to kill Mr. Callahan with his knife," she replied before I could.

"Well, that is a relief," Deputy Wallace sighed, but quickly clarified. "Not the attack of course, only that you're safe, miss. That's all. I didn't mean to imply…"

He offered me an apologetic nod, and I bit my cheek to keep from smirking.

Rosa must've had every man in this town wrapped around her finger.

The same finger that had pulled that trigger and saved my life.

I eyed the woman now, and there was no hint of anything being amiss in her expression. She didn't look anxious or overwhelmed about what had occurred, and while I was impressed to see it, I was equal measures confused.

I hadn't pegged the beautiful girl for a killer.

Regardless, the townsfolk didn't seem to have noticed her with her pistol earlier. Voices rose up all over from folks who were eager to give their recollections, some who swore they saw Theo drag me into the alley themselves. Even the men from the Sellick Distillery joined in, and their confusion seemed earnest.

Deputy Wallace listened patiently before waving them back a ways and pulling me aside.

"I don't suppose I need to ask," he muttered under his breath. "But is that one of the six?"

"Yes, sir." I nodded. "Theo K. Lawson. Got the other names, too."

The deputy's eyes widened before he nodded, replaced his hat, and hitched his britches up a little higher.

"Why don't you come by my office," he said.

"I'll do that," I replied. "Only let me escort this lady to her family, and then I'll be over."

"Of course, of course." He waved us onward, and after a brief farewell between him and the lady in question, Rosa looped her arm in mine and let me turn her down the road.

The deputy's voice rose up over the crowd as he started gathering a couple men to get the body to the undertaker, but my attentions were all on the calm woman who's skirts swayed slow and methodically at my side.

"You alright?" I asked.

"Sí, señor," she murmured.

I eyed her face. "Seems so. You ever kill a man before?"

"Only three before this," she said.

I slowed my step as La Casa Dorada was only a few doors away.

"Three?" I asked. "That deputy know you're the most dangerous woman in town?"

This made Rosa's plump lips curl up at the sides, and she sent me a playful smirk.

"Sí, señor," she replied.

I chuckled. "You gonna make me guess what happened?"

We stopped outside her family's saloon, and the woman came around to face me.

"Two were men who tried to rob my father," she said simply. "He was alone in here, but I was in the back when the men broke the front windows to get to him."

I nodded. "He's lucky he had you there."

"The third man attacked my mother," she said with a little more fire in her tone. "He… was not handled very cleanly, I admit. I was very angry."

Her amber eyes seemed to blaze briefly, and I removed my hat and raked a hand through my hair. It was clear enough what the circumstances had been, and I had to admit, I admired the heck out of Rosa for defending her family without pause.

But I wasn't family.

"Well, it seems I owe you more than thanks on this," I told her in earnest.

"Do not think of it," she said with a small smile.

"Not likely," I replied. "I feel guilty you got caught up in all this, though. You should have stayed here at the saloon, I can certainly handle myself."

"Sí, señor," was all she said.

I couldn't help laughing lightly. She really was so much like my wife, it was uncanny. Especially the way her eyes held all the weight of the words she wasn't saying.

I waited patiently, and she finally let out a soft sigh.

"The people here are like family to me," she said. "To all of us who have been here so long. Just because the town has grown so fast, doesn't change that. Mr. Sandusky was kind to me whenever I did see him. Many of our patrons respect him, in their own way. Particularly Mr. Delgado, and I respect him quite a lot."

"Who?"

"Cattleman," she said. "He, I believe, is close with Mr. Sandusky. I think, anyway, but what do I know?"

I furrowed my brow. "Can I ask what makes you think so?"

"Things I see." She gave a simple shrug. "They spoke out here once, many years ago. I saw them in the window, and they seemed like brothers to me. I could be wrong. Anyway, if I can help at all with this sadness, I will. No one deserves to suffer the sort of loss they have."

I bobbed my head as I worked to process all of this.

This was the first mention of any person around here

having a close connection to Mr. Sandusky. It sounded like a tentative thing, too, except for the woman saying it.

Rosa Vallejos was a very observant young lady, that I'd already come to realize. If she thought someone as quiet and closed-off as Frank Sandusky treated another man like a brother, then she was probably right.

"You have important people waiting for you," Rosa broke me from my thoughts. "Go. Speak with the deputy."

She shooed me away with an amused little laugh, and I grinned as I backed away and did as I was told.

"We're not done talkin' on this," I informed her.

"I should hope not," she said. "I like talking with you. Luckily, you are alive enough to do so."

"Luck," I snorted. "That wasn't luck."

"No?" She smiled and turned for the door.

I sighed and shook my head a bit.

These women out here sure were an interesting lot. In fact, I seemed to have my hands full of capable, clever women suddenly.

One of whom was running down the boardwalk toward me now.

"Jesse!" Lucy hollered as she struggled to keep all her boxes balanced in her arms. The gathered folks in the street seemed even more intrigued to see the famous opera singer hauling toward me, but she didn't pay them a glance. "Jesse! Are you alright? I heard what happened!"

"Slow down," I chuckled as I caught a runaway box. "I'm just fine."

She fanned her flushed face. "My, you sure do go to work when a woman asks. You just out here pointin' and shootin' already, huh?"

I laughed as another two boxes tumbled to the ground.

"I go to work regardless," I assured her and grabbed her things. "Come on, we've got a deputy to see."

"We sure do," she huffed. "I have many things I'd like to say to that man."

"You... what?"

Lucy was already strolling back the other way with all the purpose in the world, and I hurried to catch up with her.

"Ma'am, I'll be leading this conversation, just so you know," I said. "I have things to discuss with the deputy about the very matter you hired me to see to."

"I'm sure you do," she agreed.

"So any impertinent speeches from you in there could hinder my progress," I hinted.

"Fine." Lucy rolled her eyes. "I will behave."

"Thank you," I replied.

"But I will be heard."

"Nope, that's..." I trailed off as we reached the throng of folks near the alley.

Lucy offered polite smiles and nods to the people who called to her or sought to comfort the grieving sister, but she didn't get derailed. The pair of us slipped through the crowd as quickly as we could manage, and we came out a few doors down from the deputy's office.

"I'd appreciate if you'd let me be heard on this one," I finally managed.

"Jesse, my brother's been murdered, and this deputy hasn't lifted a single finger about it," she said. "Now he's got himself in a position where a perfect stranger can come waltzin' into town and handle his work better than he does! I frankly don't see what the point of his position in this town is if he's gonna–"

I caught her arm to rein her in just before she could open the deputy's door. Then I turned her around and planted myself between the hot-headed woman and the entrance.

"Firstly, I do not waltz anywhere, no matter the town," I informed her. "Secondly, that deputy has provided me important information in the past, and given what I now know, can start doing a whole lot more. And thirdly..."

I glanced around to be sure no one was listening in.

Lucy sighed and waited with very little patience.

"Thirdly," I continued more quietly. "I didn't kill that man over there."

"What?" Lucy blinked her big green eyes, and her prissy expression eased by several degrees.

I grinned. "See? That's why you ought to let me handle my business. You would've made a fool of yourself just now."

Her lips popped open with indignation, but I was already reaching for the deputy's door. I did my best to open it swift and get it closed right behind me, but the many boxes I carried for Lucy impeded my progress. The stubborn woman managed to slip inside at just the last moment, and she stuck her tongue out at me before sending the deputy a demure smile.

"Lucy Kimber!" He shot to his feet.

"I haven't had the pleasure," she said and stuck her hand out.

Deputy Wallace's smile wavered. "Oh... uh, we have met, actually. Hugo Wallace, remember? Magdalena's–"

"Brother!" Lucy gasped with sudden realization. "Oh, my, you've gotten so tall and handsome!"

"Thank you, yes, I plumb shot up like a weed," he said with a blush.

I cleared my throat.

"Oh, pardon my manners!" The deputy quickly pulled an extra chair over to the desk for Lucy to join us. "Please, sit, the both of you. And Miss Kimber, please accept my sincerest condolences. Your brother's loss has been felt deeply by all of us here in Grant County. Truly. It's a wretched, wretched business, I can't imagine the pain you and your family are going through at this time."

"Yes," she said, and all the wind went right out of her sails as she read the sincerity in the deputy's face. "Thank you, Deputy. I do appreciate that, and all you've done to help."

"Well, I'm ashamed to say, it hasn't been much," Deputy Wallace replied. "Mr. Callahan has been a big help to us on that, and the sheriff is of course doing all he can to address the matter."

"Yes." Lucy stiffened up again. "I hear."

The woman turned her head rather pointedly toward me, and I read her expression loud and clear.

At least she was gonna let me handle my own business, though.

"Deputy Wallace, about those names," I said. "The man out there said he was Theo K. Lawson. He named the two men we already knew about, Jeb and Petey, but he also mentioned Tommy Wallace, Bill Wallace, and Boone Slim."

The deputy took the names down quickly, and he listened closely as I explained my interaction with the man in the alley. He was just as confused about who this 'George' was, but hearing about the sale with Charles Sellick only a month ago really threw the man.

He promised to send all the information down to Silver City immediately.

"I hope I didn't get you into trouble with the sheriff," I told him with a wry grin. "He didn't seem too pleased about my being down there."

"Yeah, well…" The deputy scratched his stubbly cheek. "What you do in your business is your business, that's how I see it. I just want this area cleaned up and this horrible affair handled once and for all."

"As do I," I agreed. "In fact, Miss Kimber has hired my services."

Deputy Wallace smiled at the woman. "Is that right? Well, you couldn't find a better man to see a thing gets done right, that's for sure."

"I'm realizing that," Lucy said with a brilliant smile.

I cleared my throat. "Anyhow, about Theo…"

"Yes!" The deputy hopped up and headed to his little safe in the corner. "Now, word from Silver City is the deputies down there caught on about this Theo K. Lawson. They were suspicious about Boone Slim, so I'll make sure they know what we know, but those other men, they didn't know a thing about. Theo, I got a telegram about just this morning."

He returned to the desk with his cash box and a stack of telegrams. It only took a few flips through to find the one he needed.

"Here it is." His eyes trailed over the message. "Wanted in Massachusetts and Pennsylvania for six robberies, three of which were minor, three more being violent in nature. Consider the murder charge into that, and the bounty is set at one hundred and seventy-five dollars. Now, that isn't strictly dead or alive, mind you, but given Miss Kimber's right to hire who she sees fit, and given the evidence at hand and all that…"

"Understood," I said with a nod.

In my experience, most murderers could easily be brought in one way or another without folks making much fuss, but an official warrant like that from Grant County would mean the sheriff was taking things a little more firmly.

I would've preferred he did, but it was no matter now.

If Silver City wanted to handle this, they were just gonna have to act quicker than I could.

"So that's another one hundred and seventy-five dollars to one Jesse Callahan," Deputy Wallace confirmed with a proud pat to the paper. "Boy, you sure are a quick one. I only learned this fella's name this morning, and here we are at midday, and you've already handled the fool."

"Incredible," Lucy put in. "The lawmen of Grant County ought to take a few notes."

"Don't I know it," he chuckled and shook his head, and I was glad he was too busy to notice Lucy's pursed lips.

He counted out the bounty, and Lucy watched carefully while managing to bite her tongue from there forward. Then we readied ourselves to leave, and the deputy assured me he'd send word as soon as he heard back from Silver City.

I opened the door for Lucy, but I paused before following her.

"Oh, and Mr. Wallace," I said, and the man looked up. "Be sure to let Sheriff Whitehill know that Frank Sandusky's sister has hired my services. I'd like him to know."

"Sure will!" he assured me.

I tipped my hat, stepped outside, and grinned a bit to myself.

It was good the sheriff would know my current employment.

I didn't want his feathers getting ruffled when I used my gun as I saw fit.

"Are you going to explain yourself now?" Lucy blurted out the moment we were on our way in the direction of the wagon.

"Explain what?" I asked.

She smacked my arm. "You know what! What in the world do you mean you didn't kill him? And how dare you collect a bounty like that without having done the deed! I thought better of you, Jesse Callahan. That is not right, you hear me?"

I chuckled at how easily Lucy could work herself up about any old thing. Her neck was flushed now, and she was clearly determined to be in the loop on this one.

"I accepted the bounty on behalf of someone else," I clarified. "Now, more importantly, Theo K. Lawson admitted he was one of the two men who lit your brother's stables on fire. Seems they had the intention of killing off the best broodmares."

"Bastards," Lucy cursed, and two young women passing us gasped. "Although, shouldn't his bounty be a bit lower for that?"

"He rode with the group to carry out the attack, so he gets the murder charge all the same," I explained in a lower tone. "The other man who helped with that particular task is dead as of my last trip to Silver City, along with one of the four who had a direct hand in your brother's murder. That leaves just three of the same left to find."

Lucy nodded with determination. "So they'll be a dangerous bunch."

"I don't doubt it. One of them was apparently in charge of the whole group, and he'll be my main concern– besides the man who hired them, of course."

"I've never heard of a George Sellick out here," Lucy said.

"Neither have I, but that's what the deputy is useful for." I shot her a look.

"I held my tongue!" she huffed. "Mostly. And he did seem sincere and honest and all that, I suppose… It's not as if I told the man off or anything. I would never."

"No, of course not," I chuckled and motioned for her to cross the street.

She followed my instructions, but when we came to a stop outside La Casa Dorada, she screwed her face up.

"What are we…" she began.

I held up a finger, peered through the window, and caught Rosa's eye. She was talking with the old veterans in the corner again, but I tipped my head toward the street, and she quickly nodded in recognition.

Lucy gasped.

"Are you making eyes at Rosa Vallejos?" she hissed like it was the most scandalous thing she'd ever heard. And yet, a giddy sort of excitement was written all over her face. "The nerve on you, I swear… Of course she is an absolutely gorgeous Spanish rose, and only twenty-five, too. I tell you, I always knew some handsome stranger was gonna ride into this town and finally steal that girl's heart, but is this really the time to–"

"I am not 'makin' eyes,'" I muttered, then offered a nod of greeting as Rosa herself came out to join us. "Afternoon, miss."

"Mr. Callahan." She smiled a little uneasily before turning a proper greeting Lucy's way. "Lucy, it's good to see you back. I'm sorry it's under such sad circumstances."

"Thank you," Lucy replied. "It's good to see you, too."

"Mind if we speak somewhere more private?" I asked, and Rosa obliged by leading the way around the side of the saloon.

Lucy looked all the more scandalized as she hurried along with us. Then the three of us stopped in the shade cast by La Casa Dorada, and I slid the bounty out of my vest and handed it over to Rosa.

Her brown eyes flared, and she shook her head vigorously.

"No, I cannot," she insisted as Lucy stared between us in utter confusion.

"It wasn't my bullet that took that man out," I told the woman. "And I don't take payment for work I haven't done. That means this one hundred and seventy-five dollars is yours, plain and simple."

"But…" Rosa chewed on her bottom lip.

Meanwhile, Lucy had caught up.

"You killed him?" she gasped.

Rosa's bronze cheeks blushed a warm red as she offered a small smile and a nod. "Mr. Callahan was in a… tight spot, and I happened to be–"

Lucy yanked Rosa into a tight embrace as tears sprang to her eyes. The women held one another for a long moment before they finally broke apart, but Lucy cupped the Spanish woman's smiling face in her hands.

"You're an angel," Lucy sniffed. "Truly."

Rosa shook her head, and the women laughed a little as they parted.

I then briefly explained the ordeal that had taken place

in the alley, and Lucy stayed enraptured until the very last sentence. She also insisted Rosa take the bounty for Theo K. Lawson, and the modest woman finally relented.

Rosa insisted we keep the truth of all this between ourselves as well. She didn't like drawing extra attention to herself, and the way she saw it, this town would be better off thinking I'd taken care of the murderer myself, given all she'd heard of me lately.'

"A lot of that is just waggin' tongues," I sighed.

"You did not shoot down an entire pack of wolves without missing a shot?" Rosa's eyebrow lifted in a perfect arch. "I am shocked."

Lucy snorted through her laughter. "The seamstress told me he strung those rustlers up himself in a few pines outside town to make sure the job got done thoroughly."

"I also heard you wrestled a mountain lion at the ranch with your bare hands," Rosa said. "True?"

"That one's obviously true," I deadpanned. "But don't believe everything you hear."

Rosa smiled. "Well, true or not, you have become a hero here."

"There's a whole mess of difference between heroes and bounty hunters," I assured her.

"No, there isn't, Jesse, pipe down," Lucy said curtly, and Rosa giggled behind her hand.

Regardless, we gave our word that we would hold our tongues about all this, aside from letting Helena know. Then Lucy doted on Rosa a bit more for all her help and for coming to my assistance, before it was time we take our leave.

"Come sing for us if you feel like it," Rosa said as she held Lucy's soft white hands in hers. "We could use a true angel in here, with a voice like one, too."

"I will," Lucy promised.

I felt much better about all this now that the proper 'hero' had been rewarded, even if very few would ever know who really killed one of Frank Sandusky's murderers in the middle of Pinos Altos.

I didn't much like Rosa's idea about letting folks think I'd done it, but the mysterious woman had come to my aid without hesitation, and I figured I owed her my allegiance for the rest of my life for doing so.

If privacy was what she wanted most, then I'd give it to her.

"She likes you." Lucy smirked once she was settled on the wagon bench at my side.

"Rosa smiles like that for everyone," I replied. "Just ask Mateo."

"Oh, I'll be telling Mateo everything I have to say on the matter," Lucy giggled. "He's the only one who's any fun to gossip with around here."

I chuckled and flicked the reins, and the boys took us out of Pinos Altos.

We rode the rest of the way in companionable silence, and the doves had stopped their cooing by now. The only birds in the trees at this hour were the deep-black ravens, and they cawed here and there as we made our way to the rugged foothills.

The whole time, my mind turned round and round with all this new information.

One more cruel man had met his gruesome end for his deeds.

But who was George Sellick?

And now that three of his six hired killers were dead, would he realize we were closing in?

CHAPTER 19

The next morning brought howling winds down from the Black Mountains and all across the foothills.

It was the kind of day you would spend hunched in half with one hand holding your hat, and the other blocking the dust from your eyes. But life went right on among the ranch folks.

Lucy had wasted no time in telling everyone about our trip into town the day before. Helena was determined to lavish Rosa with some sort of gift for her help, but the ranch hands only knew another of Frank's murderers had ended up dead.

We'd shared a few swigs of moonshine that Abel apparently bought off Gilly a while ago, and while it bit something fierce going down, it sure tasted like victory.

But we all knew where we were at now.

After everything that took place yesterday, word that the Black Spur had hired their own killing hand would spread like wildfire. Nearly half our targets were taken out, too, so there was no saying whether more danger would be swiftly on its way to snuff out any chance we had at rebuilding.

Or whether the guilty would flee while they still had a chance.

Tensions were high, but we put all that pent-up energy into work all that day.

By the following afternoon, the stables were finished enough to bring the youngest foals and their mamas in out of the still-howling wind. Locks weren't secured just yet, but bedding was being brought over from the barn. We had two broodmares that would be birthing any day now, one of them being Bonita, so we made sure to give their stalls special attention, but mostly we worked on securing the many stall doors and latches.

There were twenty stalls in all, with two extra-wide ones for births. A big oil lantern was mounted near both entryways, and a few others hung here and there near the stall doors. The tack room and feed storage would be our biggest task this afternoon, but all that would be the easier part.

All in all, it was the biggest stable I'd ever personally seen, and it was a beauty, too.

Amos had modeled the place almost exactly after the previous one, but with a wider breezeway between both lines of stalls to allow for some extra horses to be locked up if need be. The back let out directly into the north pasture, in case anything like the fire ever happened again. The front opened up into the lane still, but we classed up the entrance to really make an impression on the buyers who came by.

Abel had asked Gilly to put his blacksmithing skills to work on some iron detailing around the doors and windowpanes, and it made a world of difference. Just like the sign on the gate, the stables looked well-made and of superior design, but without too much nonsense dressing it up.

By the time we were getting the last of the chosen horses secured for the evening, the sun was sinking toward the mountains on the horizon, but the wind hadn't let up at all. All the other horses had been moved to the proper pastures, and they lolled around with coats made of dust. With every twitch of their muscles, plumes of dust sifted into the golden sky like smoke.

It was around this time that the lady of the ranch came out with her sister-in-law to get a look at the new stables, and the pair of them strolled along the breezeway taking in the mighty wooden structure while we got feed and water put out for the foals.

Helena was lost for words at first. She looked proud of the place, and I was glad to see we'd done well. After all, it was her family's money that paid for this mighty stable, and it was no small charge. To know it was worth every penny in her eyes made the long, backbreaking labor in the heat worth it as well.

"It's so beautiful." Helena sent a shining smile in Amos' direction. "You did the beams just the same."

"Sure did." He nodded with pride. "Kept it all just as it was where I could, but I figured with so many horses, we could always do with some extra room. The herd's quite a bit bigger than it once was."

"Certainly is," Lucy said as she patted the fresh timber. "You've all done a very fine job since last I was here. Why, I think this is the largest herd we've had since we left Colorado."

"Really?" Helena smiled. "That's incredible."

"It is, isn't it?" The singer turned with a little too much enthusiasm, and I quickly realized where this was going. "It's really something special. Some would say you can't put a price on all this."

"Lucy," Helena groaned.

Amos snickered a bit, and Mateo looked very pleased to have the sister-in-law boldly taking their side of things. He didn't bother trying to look busy, he just hung over a stall door, ready to watch the two ladies hash it out.

Meanwhile, Abel's eyes were wide as he rubbernecked from a few stalls away.

I carried on hauling bridles and brushes toward the tack room.

"What?" Lucy blinked innocently. "I'm only saying–"

"I know what you're saying," Helena assured her. "And I'm not discussing this with you, what's done is done."

"Done?" Amos stopped snickering. "What's been done?"

Helena went a little pale as she started fussing with the ties on her apron, but Lucy was going full-steam ahead now.

"Go on." Lucy cocked an eyebrow. "Tell them about the 'guest' we'll be having here in a couple days. By invitation."

Helena propped her hands on her hips. "You know, I really would appreciate it if you would refrain from berating me in front of everyone on this ranch, Lucy."

"I'm sure that could be arranged," the singer returned. "Simply refrain from giving me a reason to berate you, Lena."

Mateo buried his mouth against his sleeve before a laugh could burst out, and I focused extra hard on some tack I now realized wasn't hung up quite nice enough.

It was clear this conversation was more of a private, family matter, but Lucy was good and worked up now, so I had a bad feeling about this one. I could see her chest rising and falling with quickened breaths, even from the tack room door, and I didn't think it was just her corset causing such a stir.

Amos, as usual, seemed to have caught up all on his own, too.

"Mrs. Helena," he said in a calm, steady tone. "You find a buyer for the ranch?"

"No!" Helena said hastily. "I only invited the man who sent his lawyer over to discuss his offer. He... well, he says he's interested in keeping the ranch running as it is. All the horses, and... and the workers, too, of course. He doesn't want to put anyone out."

Abel's curse was heard clear as day from his stall, but Amos only nodded once in acknowledgment. Mateo was staring at me as if I could read all his thoughts with one look alone, and I felt for the man. It wasn't his place to put himself into this conversation, no matter how badly he wanted to, but the fact was, it wasn't mine, either.

Lucy, of course, had no trouble voicing her opinion, though.

"Well, I'm sure this prospective buyer would just looooove to make hundreds of thousands of dollars for the rest of his life off the hard work of my family," she said with about as much tact as a drunken donkey.

"Lucy," I muttered as I hung another couple bridles on the wall.

"It's alright, Jesse," Helena said as her cheeks flushed a bit. "She's entitled to her opinion, I suppose."

"Good, because it's true!" Lucy huffed. "My brother worked himself raw for this place. And he would never, ever let anything ruin this ranch, not even his own death."

"You don't know what he'd think of this situation," Helena pointed out.

"Oh, don't I?" Lucy was really worked up now. Her long, slim neck was slowly turning pink, and I decided the tack could look after itself.

I abandoned my post and casually made my way into the breezeway, but my arrival didn't have the intended effect.

The moment Lucy saw me, a spark of mischief came to her eyes, and she strolled toward me like a cat toying with a mouse.

"Now that you mention it," she hummed. "You're right, Lena. I'm not the sort of person who could put myself in my brother's shoes and decide what he'd think of all this. But Jesse is, and he agrees with me."

"Pardon?" I glanced between the two women.

I could feel the eyes of every man in the room on me now, and the silence in the stables rang far too loud, considering the howling wind and how many horses were in here.

It seemed no one was going to speak until I did.

"I don't recall ever saying such a thing," I stated in a firm tone.

"Not in so many words," Lucy agreed. "But you said yourself you didn't like the sound of this buyer."

"Is that true?" Helena asked.

I stared at the young woman, and then I stared at her sister-in-law.

Lucy bulged her green eyes at me, as if that alone would get me talking, and as much as I liked being on her good side, I wasn't about to get caught up in this.

"I'd prefer to stay out of this," I said at last.

"Jesse," Lucy hissed and stomped her foot.

"Nope." I shook my head. "It isn't my place to have an opinion on any of this. Now, if I spoke a little too freely before, then I do apologize, but I know well and full that any decision Helena makes for her and her family should have nothing to do with my say on anything."

I said this all with the utmost finality, but that finality landed on deaf ears.

"Please, have your say anyway," Helena said simply, but her face was what got me.

Her big blue eyes were pinched with worry, and I could see she was terrified to make the wrong choice. She was doing her best without Frank around to steer the ship, but all this mess with the rustlers, the murderers, the buyers, and the rebuild had shaken her.

"I would like to hear your thoughts on the matter," Helena said with some more backbone this time. "You're a logical man, but also an honest one. You've also seen more of the world than I have, and your opinion matters quite a lot more to me at present than… some others I could name."

Her blue eyes flicked toward Lucy, and the opera singer dropped her jaw in indignation.

"How dare–" she started, but I quickly cut in.

"Alright," I relented and cleared my throat. "If you'd like my input, then I'll give it."

"Thank you." The strawberry-blonde woman gestured for me to continue.

It wasn't lost on me that all the ranch hands were as still as death while they waited to hear my take, but I focused on Helena, because the truth was, I'd been wanting to make my opinions clear to her for quite some time now.

"All in all, I'd say this is the finest ranch I've ever come across. In all my travels, mind," I clarified. "I think your stock has been carefully curated for years and years, and while your husband may have been the driving force behind this operation, he's gotten it to a place where it can keep right on sailing without him at the helm, so to speak. These men here work hard, sure, but they work hardest for the Sandusky family specifically. What you've got here is not something a lot of folks come by."

Amos nodded at this, and his gunmetal eyes burned with sincerity on the matter.

"I know it's looking like a whole lot to take on," I continued. "But you're not doing that alone, by any means. Running this large of a ranch can certainly make or break a man, or a family, but I think the fact that it's still standing and earning back more than ever makes it worth the harder days."

I tried to put my meaning into my eyes for the woman without making her uncomfortable about the topic. Her grief wasn't so heavy as it had been at first, but I knew it still clung to her, and I knew how something like that could wear on the spirit day after day if a person let it.

"Now, I can see clear as day that your husband put all he had into this place, but he seemed to care for his family above all," I continued, and Lucy grinned in triumph. Still, I made sure to make my point clear. "His entire family, especially the mother of his children."

Lucy took my meaning, and she dropped her eyes at once as she realized I was right.

"I reckon, if I was him, I'd want my wife to do anything she needed to have some peace and happiness," I said. "If that means staying, then stay. If that means selling this place, going anywhere you see fit, and living off the very handsome sum it'd fetch for the rest of your life, then there ain't nothing wrong with starting anew."

"Russel would be disappointed," Helena murmured.

"He would." I nodded. "But he'll be a man before you know it, and in time, he'll come to understand the choices you've made. In the meantime, well... He'd be cross."

"And I'd be furious," Lucy put in. "But... I'd forgive you. Eventually. Somehow. Your happiness is... important, too."

The stubborn singer glared at her toes just like her nephew, and she sulked for a moment longer, but I was proud of her for easing up even that little bit. She was hotheaded, but she was also goodhearted, and I knew she didn't want to hurt her sister-in-law or make her feel such guilt. She only loved her family and the legacy she'd come from so fiercely, and deep down, she truly believed Helena could look after that legacy for many years to come.

So did I.

"That's just about all I have to say on that," I said as I straightened my belt. "Except that, personally, I happen to believe you could run this ranch and make four times as much as you once did. This is the Black Spur, after all. Best horses in five counties, so I hear."

"I think I heard it's seven counties now," Amos snorted.

Helena chuckled at this, too. Then she lifted her chin and squared her shoulders, and I was glad to see her confidence restored.

"And how about the rest of you?" she asked the ranch hands. "I'd like to hear everyone's say on the matter. This involves all of us, after all."

Lucy started forward. "Well, I think–"

"I know," Helena interrupted, and I carefully tugged Lucy back a few paces by her elbow. "Abel?"

Her blue gaze landed on the older ranch hand, who just shook his head, held up his hands, and started muttering in Spanish. He eventually trailed off as he focused hard on raking some straw around, so Helena turned to Mateo instead.

But Mateo just looked like a stunned deer, and he turned to Amos with wide eyes.

Amos shrugged. "I agree with Jesse. He's right on all counts."

"Me, too," Mateo promptly announced. "Jesse is right."

Helena eyed Abel, and the Spaniard was less shy about it now.

"Si, si," he said with a few nods. "Is… Jesse."

Lucy was positively beaming from ear to ear, and Helena gently cleared her throat as she adjusted her apron.

"Well, thank you for your honesty," she said. "And I'm sorry for not keeping y'all informed. I'd only like to hear what this buyer has to say so that I can make the proper decision. That's all. Nothing's decided, but I will certainly take Jesse's points into consideration."

Amos nodded in understanding, and Mateo offered a smile that reminded me of a dog who's getting pets again after being scolded. Abel didn't say a word, but he had a bit of pep in his step as he worked now.

"Lovely," Lucy sighed as her green eyes roved all over the stables again. "Now I can properly admire this place, since it won't be sold off like some fat pig at market to some greedy–"

"That is not what I said," Helena sighed.

Lucy waved her off. "You'll listen to Jesse. I know you will, you're a woman of sense, and he's… well, he's Jesse. Just look at him, I'm sure not gonna argue with all that."

"Lies," I snorted.

Lucy sent me a glittering smile, and I rolled my eyes as I got back to the tack room.

The ladies continued admiring the stables while the men and I finished tidying things up. They were much more cordial to one another now, and I had to hand it to Lucy. She may have liked pushing folks into uncomfortable conversation, but the effect was generally positive.

We all decided to have a bit of a celebration tomorrow once the stables were fully finished, and then the ranch hands and I started closing up the stables for the night.

Dark was still a few hours off as the six of us strolled out into the lane.

We all stopped as we spotted Deputy Wallace cantering toward us from the front gate.

His face was grave as he came to a stop and tipped his hat to the women, but then he dismounted and turned to me.

"We need to talk."

CHAPTER 20

Lucy was sent to look after the children since she alone could keep Russel too busy to eavesdrop.

Then the ranch hands, Helena, and I gathered in the stables to stay out of the wind.

The deputy removed his hat and smacked the dust off it before he settled it back on his head.

"I just got back from the marshal's office," he announced.

That got our hearts racing.

"The sheriff brought the marshal in on this?" I asked.

"Sure did." Deputy Wallace nodded. "On account of those names you found out for us."

"What's he say?" Amos asked.

"George is a Sellick," the deputy confirmed. "Only not so well-liked as his prospecting brother. He's a bluebelly, too, and only just come down a few weeks ago."

"That's what… two weeks before Frank was murdered?" I checked.

Deputy Wallace nodded. "That'd be about right. He's not so upstanding as the Captain, either. Word is he's more prone to gambling, drinking, and exploiting his newfound riches as his brother's new business partner."

"Business partner?" Helena asked. "He's taking over some of the Sellick mines?"

"No, he took a liking to the distillery. Runs that operation alright, I suppose, but most of Silver City don't even like to acknowledge he's there. He's gotten into a couple scrapes over at one of the bordellos, and just recently, the Captain banned him from his own gambling hall."

I narrowed my eyes as I thought back to my trip down to Silver City.

I'd only walked by the Sellick Distillery, and it had been bustling with plenty of men moving crates of rye. Then there was the one fellow who'd been eyeballing me from inside the shadowy shop.

He'd looked blistered from the sun, and he'd had a bottle of whiskey in hand as he oversaw the workers.

"Son of a gun," I sighed and took my hat off to rake my hands through my hair. "I may have seen him down south."

"Really?" Helena looked worried at the notion.

"Possibly," I said. "There was a larger man over at the distillery who seemed to be letting everyone else do the hard work while he drank the day away."

"Sounds like it could be George," Deputy Wallace said. "Those other men you named– Boone Slim, and Tommy and Bill Masters– they all got hired by the Captain together about a year back when he started distilling. The marshal's working to dig up what he can about them, but no luck yet."

"No doubt he'll find something on them, though," I said.

"I'm of the same mind," he agreed. "They still don't have any idea down there how all this connects to Sandusky, but there that is. Now, to the most important part… George Sellick and the other three men you mentioned are missing as of this morning."

I suddenly found the deputy's eyes boring into mine, and the ranch hands looked to me as well, even though they knew well enough where I'd been all night.

"I didn't kill 'em." I shrugged. "Me and Birdy were on watch last night."

"Just had to check," the deputy chuckled. "The sheriff went over to the Sellick estate this morning to bring George in, and he was gone. Spoke to the Captain about all this mess, and he's right put out about it, it seems. They've spent most of the day hunting for all four of them, but nothing's come up."

Amos let out a long, slow breath as he took to pacing along the breezeway.

"I got a bad feeling about this," I muttered.

"Uh-huh," the black man agreed.

"You reckon they'll come here?" Helena asked me.

"Depends if they're mad or just scared," I said.

"I know a man who could hunt anyone for you, Deputy," Mateo said as he turned an eager look my way. "Jesse can help Silver City, he will find the men for you."

"If I felt more sure they'd fled, then I would," I told the younger ranch hand. "But I certainly don't want to be off chasing shadows with the ranch in danger."

"That's true," Deputy Wallace said. "You got a mighty wealthy man with some kind of grudge on your hands. Best to get this place secured in case more trouble's coming. You ought to talk to the other ranchers out here, too, see what they can do about keeping an eye out."

"I'll do that." I nodded. "I also want to get in contact with a Mr. Delgado. He live around here?"

"Delgado?" Amos stopped his pacing. "What you want with Delgado?"

"Not sure yet," I admitted. "Following a lead."

The ranch hand looked confused by this, which only confused me further. Of the four ranch hands, Amos was closest with Frank, so he'd be the one to know about a connection between them.

"Mr. Delgado's not just some friendly neighborhood

cattleman in these parts," Deputy Wallace said as he eyed me curiously. "He's got his own reputation."

"Go on," I said.

"Well, he's got some rough edges, that's for sure," the deputy laughed lightly. "Doesn't come into town often these days, but last I heard, he just brought about a thousand head of cattle over from Texas. Now he's busy divvying up the three thousand head he's sittin' on."

"That is a lot of work," Mateo mumbled and shook his head. "Horses sound better."

"Where can I find him?" I asked again.

"I know where he's at," Amos said. "I'll ride out with you to speak with the neighbors first thing tomorrow, they know me. And then we'll head on over to Delgado's Pass. His house is southeast of here."

"He's got a whole pass to himself?" I asked.

Amos smirked. "Man's got twenty-five hundred acres to himself."

"Good Lord in Heaven," Helena breathed. Then she looked at me. "You're certain you've got the right man?"

"I'm certain he's the man I want to talk to," I replied. "Whether it'll come to anything is another matter. Do you happen to know him?"

I watched her expression carefully to see if any flicker of secrecy passed over her blue eyes, but the good woman was as honest as I knew her to be.

"I've heard of him, I think he greeted me once at the general store," she said as she frowned in thought. "That's about it. I don't think he's got himself a wife out there or anything."

I nodded. "Well, I'll start with the folks nearby, make sure they know about all this."

"You do that," the deputy agreed as he headed for the door. "I'd best be off before dark falls."

I walked with the man to his horse as the ranch hands

hung back to get the stables closed again, and Helena hurried to the house.

Once he was up in the saddle, he looked down at me with an anxious expression.

"Be careful, Mr. Callahan," he said. "The sheriff was real mad about all this, and when Whitehill gets real mad, it's always something real big going wrong. He's got his men still hunting for those three killers and the Sellick brother, but…"

"I'll keep a sharp eye," I assured him. "Did you happen to mention to Whitehill about my employment?"

"Sent the telegram off the same day you killed Lawson." He nodded, but then his brow bunched up. "He mentioned it while I was down there, actually. Seemed to think it was a fib. Can't imagine why. I made sure he knew it was all true, though, and that Miss Kimber had been in my office to confirm it and everything."

I smiled a little. "What'd he say?"

"Well, Whitehill's a bit colorful sometimes," the deputy chuckled uneasily. "He says some things he don't mean, I'm sure, and I didn't catch all of it. Though he did call you a stubborn upstart. Then he just kinda shrugged and said 'it's just as well.'"

"Good," I said with a genuine grin now. "Glad we see eye to eye."

The deputy cocked a brow. "If you call that seeing eye to eye…"

I chuckled and gave the man's horse a few pats, and once he got him turned around, the deputy took his leave.

That night, Mateo and I stood first watch together, and both of us were on our guard with pistols and rifles close at hand. We took opposite posts and circled our mounts inward toward the lane to update one another every hour, and then Mateo stayed out with Amos for the second watch to keep up the patrol.

That was the first night since I started guarding the ranch that I felt uneasy about security.

The howling wind made it impossible to hear if anyone was riding up, and the moon didn't rise until well past two in the morning. The oil lanterns near the stable entrances were heavy enough to stay steady in the wind, but they didn't provide light beyond the lane and the bit of pasture they illuminated.

The rest of the Sanduskys' thousand acres were washed in shadow for the better part of the night, and the only one of us not bent out of shape about it was Birdy.

True to form, my old mare stayed steadfast and focused on what mattered most, regardless of how on edge I was.

"You want to take this seriously?" I asked her when she stopped to graze for the fifth time.

Birdy snorted and kept on munching.

"You've gotten spoiled out here, you know that?" I said as I nudged her onward. "What am I gonna do with you if you get too fat and happy, huh? You think I'm gonna just let you do as you please? Deliver carrots to you at all hours of the day like Mateo?"

Birdy gave a cheerful nicker, and I couldn't help laughing.

There was a time when Birdy would've been the one nudging me to get back out and get going. She was a spunky one in her youth, but I was glad she still took to the work. Even if she was a bit pointed about her priorities these days, having Birdy under my saddle helped me keep my mind steady and my focus sharp through the tense evening.

We managed to make it through to morning without trouble, and luckily, the wind had worn itself out by then.

Amos and I helped Abel and Russel with the morning work while Mateo slept off his first night on watch, and Lucy came out to help as well. She promised to give Abel a hand with anything he needed while the younger ranch hand rested, and then Amos brought out his mustang and the dappled stallion for myself.

The black man was tense as we got our tack together, and I could tell he didn't like the idea of leaving the ranch for so long.

"They'll be alright until we get back," I said. "In my experience, criminals like this bunch prefer to work in the dark."

"You're probably right," Amos agreed. "Still, I gave Russel a talk this morning. Helena asked me to."

"He know what's going on?"

"Sure does." Amos nodded before he climbed into the saddle. "Boy cares about this ranch as much as his daddy did. He deserves to know. He's got his Peacemaker on him, and I don't know a man alive who watches the goings on around here more than he does."

I smirked. "Well, that is true. How's Honey?"

"Lucy didn't tell her all about it, but she did promise her you'd kill any bad men who ever tried to set foot on this ranch again," Amos chuckled. "So you got your work cut out for you."

"What about you?"

"I just gotta keep my flowers in place." Amos grinned and tapped the dried-out bundle he still had in his hatband from the little girl.

The pair of us shared a laugh as we rode out of the stables and down the lane, and we found Russel sitting on the fence about halfway there.

He had an oversized hat on his head that was so worn out, it could only be his father's, and his Peacemaker was holstered at his hip. He sent the pair of us a firm nod as we passed, and we returned the gesture in kind before heading for the gate.

Then it was time to go to work.

Amos and I pushed our mounts as much as was comfortable as we rode hard to meet with the neighboring folks.

There were three families whose properties abutted the Black Spur Ranch, and we stopped at the Brimbley homestead to the south first, where I learned that Helena was famous in her own right on account of her pies. The wife of the homestead regularly traded goods with Mrs. Sandusky, and the husband I'd seen before in La Casa Dorada when Mateo pointed him out.

He was an older, coal-dusted gentleman who moved in a gentle sort of way, and he thought of Mr. Sandusky as a peculiar sort who kept to himself, but was a good man.

"Sold my boys them two horses out there for just the ten dollars they had on them a couple years back," Mr. Brimbley said and gestured out the window to a pair of pintos.

Amos did a double take as he spotted the horses. I could tell from the look on his face that he recognized them, and they must've been worth well above even the usual price.

"Guess they crossed paths one day by the stream that runs down from your land, and he saw my boys were sharing our old gelding," the neighbor continued. "He parsed those horses out of the herd right then and there for 'em. Told them they should last 'em plenty of years to come, and we haven't had a bit of trouble at all with the pair."

"Oh, they'll be at top performance for another fifteen years at least," Amos said in a strained voice.

"Good, then you boys don't worry," the older man said. "We see any riders headed your way, I'll send my boys. They're faster than lightning on those horses, I'll tell ya what. They take 'em straight across to your ranch, they can probably be there in under five minutes."

"That's all I ask." I stood and shook the man's hand. "And like I said, anything you need, you let the Black Spur know. We owe you."

"Is that right?" Brimbley shared a look of pride with his wife. "Well, alright then. Never thought I'd hear that. Old

Mitchum's gonna be green with envy over this. You haven't headed over his way, have you?"

"We're headed there next," Amos said with a grin.

"Ah, well," he sighed. "Here's hoping it's us who spot those desperados first. Then we'll have something over him at least."

Amos chuckled at this as he shook the man's hand next, and we gathered the five bread loaves the wife pushed on us for Helena before taking our leave.

"So how much are those horses really worth?" I asked as we reached our mounts.

Amos eyed the brown-and-white pintos with a slightly pained expression.

"Well, those there are purebred Paints," he sighed. "So I'd rather not even think on it."

I snickered as we turned from the homestead and headed northwest a ways until we came to a small family farm run by a man named Mitchum.

He, too, had himself a Sandusky horse he'd acquired four years ago. It cost him thirty dollars and one of the nice axes the man smithed himself, and he hadn't heard a word from Mr. Sandusky since. Amos knew about this sale at least, and he apparently did some work on the farm for Mitchum once in a while when hunting was good and he could get some fresh venison in return.

Mitchum was quick to agree on keeping an eye out, and he had a farm boy who lived with him that he could send over with haste.

The final neighbors were directly east of the Black Spur, and I wasn't surprised I'd ridden right past their home without spotting it when I first came down from Emory Pass. It was the modest home of a Chinese couple who spoke decent English, and they mentioned the jam Helena brought them a couple months ago about fifteen times. It seemed the ox they had for tilling their one-acre field had 'wandered onto'

Black Spur land the very month they got settled here, and Frank happened to notice their house over here and brought it to them.

Free of charge.

The horse he offered them was refused on account of them preferring their wagon and burro for transportation, so they had no means of sending word to us if they saw any riders heading our way, but that was fine. Given their location, I doubted they'd need to, but for their own safety, we warned them of the situation.

That's when I learned that the husband had a very nice Martini-Henry on hand that he'd gotten accustomed to using.

I stared at the distinct weapon in the corner as my spine started to tingle with recognition.

It could be no coincidence that two folks within a few miles of one another both had one of the rare firearms.

I asked him if Frank had sold it to him, but the man looked confused by the suggestion.

"Delgado man sell to me," he said as he gestured east. "Right after ox from Sandusky. Very kind man."

I smiled politely, but my mind was running a mile a minute.

That was a connection I never would've dreamed I'd find out here.

Before we left, Amos helped fix the lock on their gate that had been busted for some time now, and then we climbed back up on our mounts.

"Ain't no ox that ever wandered onto our land," Amos snorted and shook his head. "He must've bought the darn thing off a freighter and walked it over here."

The man's amusement went stale as sadness washed over his face, and he was briefly overcome by the thought of his departed boss. I gave him time to collect himself as we steered our horses further east and then to the south, and I thought over our conversations with the neighbors.

All of them had heard about Frank Sandusky's murder,

and they were shaken up about it. Hearing about my presence at the ranch and my involvement in finding the guilty parties so far had eased their minds, though, so we'd arrived at all of their homes already well-liked.

I was relieved to know they all had firearms and would alert us if they could. That still left us with fewer shooters on our own property than I would've liked, but the situation was improving bit by bit.

Now I just had to figure out how in the world a murdered horseman, a bigtime cattleman, and a Martini-Henry were all connected.

We were a few miles south of the Chinese farm when Amos cleared his throat and glanced my way.

"So you gonna tell me before we get to Delgado's why we're going there?" he asked.

I chewed on this as I tried to decide on the proper words.

"Did you recognize that gun back there?" I asked at last.

Amos was quiet for a moment. "Yes, sir."

"That's why," I muttered. "I've said it before, but killings like this one don't happen for no reason. Something strange is going on out here, and Delgado's the first chance I've found at figuring out what that could be."

"How?" He looked over as we came up to a stream and let our horses take a drink.

"Rosa Vallejos said she saw Frank talking with Delgado outside La Casa Dorada a few years back," I said. "Seems she got the impression they were close. Like brothers, she said."

Amos' expression was impossible to read, and his dark eyes roved over the water ahead of us for a long, quiet minute.

"I'd like to say I'm uneasy, not knowing a thing like that about Frank," he finally said. "But I ain't. He was a good friend to me, and he was a good man. You've heard enough of him to know that–"

"I have," I quickly assured him. "That's why I've carried on hunting down his killers. I believe he didn't deserve what he got in the end, but whatever their reason for killing him, we're better off trying to figure out what it was before they come our way."

"That I can't argue with," he said as we led our horses into the stream and over to the opposite bank.

A couple miles later, we came up over a rise to find a large iron gate with one word on it:

Delgado.

We were right where the foothills met the rolling plains now, and Amos explained how Delgado's land was split between a good chunk of foothills to the northeast and a long mess of plains all the way to the south.

I shook my head as I realized my eyes couldn't even see as far as this one cattleman's ranch stretched.

It reminded me of the ranches out in Texas, and my heart ached with joy at the sight. Hundreds of head of cattle were sprawled in a few different masses here and there, all over the sundrenched earth, and there must've been plenty more of the herd in the more rocky regions to our north that I couldn't see.

The swaying grasses of the plains rippled in waves over the open land, and a dozen men on horses rode among the cattle to the south of us, kicking up walls of yellow dust that twisted through the air and then scattered over the fields.

Several other men were walking around near the buildings of the property. I couldn't see all of them, but I figured there were at least ten buildings, probably more. Most of them were short, sturdy, timber buildings that were weatherworn and scorched by the sun.

"Best get to it," I said, and Amos offered a tense nod.

I led us down the rise and toward the gate. We passed five separate wagons either coming or going that were loaded down with all manner of goods, and then we were riding down the long lane. Several workers who saw us passing either ignored us or only offered a quick nod of greeting, so I mostly focused on where we were headed.

The house ahead of us was a stout, one-story timber home made from the long, solid trunks of the tall pines the mountains were covered in here. It was clearly the oldest structure on the lot, but it looked like it was being added onto just now. If my eye was correct, the place would soon be twice its original size.

Which was already much bigger than even the Sanduskys' home.

Amos let out a low whistle as we came up to the impressive house, and I was about to remark on how well this Delgado was doing for himself when two shots were fired, and the dirt just ahead of our horses' hooves blasted apart.

Flint reared up, and Amos' mustang tried to turn tail on him, but we reacted quick enough to settle them.

It didn't matter, though.

The moment we got a look behind us, we knew we weren't going anywhere.

Fifteen of the workers we'd passed without a second glance had followed us to the house, and they stood in a line at our backs with rifles in hand.

CHAPTER 21

"Hands up," the man at the center of the line growled in a thick Mexican accent.

He had the biggest mustache I'd ever seen, and a revolver in his hand.

Amos and I raised our hands up where everyone could see them.

"You boys got ten seconds to state your business or get gone!" a gravelly voice called from the direction of the timber house. "After that, Pedro can have ya!"

The mustached Mexican spit in the dirt before sending me a grimy grin.

"It's Amos Robinson, Mr. Delgado, sir!" Amos hollered as he held his hands even higher. "I work for the Black Sp–"

"I know where you work, boy!" came the gravelly response. "But whoever it is you've got with ya sportin' all them firearms is sure as shit not on the payroll."

I cast my eyes sideways and met Amos' gaze. He gave a harried shrug and raised his voice again.

"Actually, he is," Amos quickly replied. "This here's a bounty hunter by name of Jesse Callahan. He's killed three of Mr. Sandusky's murderers, sir."

There was a tense silence as I eyed the many unchanging

scowls of Delgado's men, but then I heard the scraping of a heavy wooden door opening behind me.

I glanced over my shoulder to see a big and tall man with a broad-brimmed hat, a sandy-blond beard, and a permanent squint come out a few shuffling steps. He had a double-barreled shotgun in hand, with a cigar bitten between his teeth.

"You that bounty hunter everyone's talkin' about?" he asked.

"Yes, sir," I called out as I kept my hands where they were.

"Heard you were runnin' around shootin' two pistols at once from the back of a horse…"

I sighed. "No, sir, that's not how that went."

I could hear the man's gravelly chuckle from here.

"Well, alright then," he said as he gestured with the nose of his rifle. "You boys can get in here. Pedro, stand down."

Without a word, the fifteen armed men holstered their pistols or slung their rifles over their backs, and they dispersed among the buildings to get back to work. Pedro left last, and he squirted another wad of spit between his front teeth before finally dragging his eyes off me.

I had to admit, I was impressed by the cattleman's operation here. It wasn't often someone caught me so off guard.

This man meant business.

Amos and I didn't dismount until all the workers were well gone. Then we walked our horses up to the house and hitched them on the thick post out front.

The big man with the big beard and hat stood in the doorway all the while, and he watched us through the smoke puffing from his mouth.

"Amos Robinson was it?" he asked as we ascended the thick wooden steps.

"Yes, sir."

The cattleman propped his rifle in one arm and stuck out his hand. "Delgado. Good to finally meet you, boy. Get on in out of the sun. You too, Killer. Get in here."

We followed the man into his home, where we were met

with a wide, open living area with a high, heavy-beamed ceiling and an iron chandelier. All of the furnishings were made of the same thick, stout wood as the home itself, and it was clear the man lived here alone. What amenities he had looked well-made and expensive, like the copper and silver fixings that adorned the shelves, but there was no feminine touch about the place. All was sturdy, well-worn, and built to last, with a layer of dust and dirt to it all that showed how long he'd been settled on this land.

Amos and I sat at the stout dining table, and the cattleman dropped himself into a chair with a heavy creak and a puff of smoke.

"I'd apologize about the welcome party, but I ain't sorry," he snorted. "I know Sandusky never wanted a whole bunch of folks prowling all over his land, but it's different for a horseman as reputable as him. Cattle's a mess. People think just because a man's got upwards of three thousand head at any given time, he won't notice a few hundred missing now and again. Then I've got people coming out weekly from God knows where trying to buy up even a parcel of my lands, and don't even get me started on the squatters my men find out there."

He leaned forward and grabbed an intricate copper dish with about two-inches' worth of ash in it, and he tapped his cigar on its edge before sitting back and eyeing us both.

"So," he grunted. "Tell me about this business with Sandusky. What went down out there?"

I'd heard all I needed already to confirm Rosa's suspicions were at least founded in some truth. This man spoke of Frank as if he knew him well, but more than that, he'd shown real respect for Amos before we'd even walked in the door.

Anyone who knew what Amos brought to the ranch understood a whole lot more than an enemy would. But that didn't mean I'd trust him with the whole truth of things outright. Not without being sure of where he stood first.

"I'd like to know what you've been informed of first, if it's all the same to you," I replied smoothly.

Delgado chewed on his cigar. "Whitehill was right about you. You're a bit of an upstart, ain'tcha?"

"I'm a bounty hunter," I said. "Nothing more. Nothing less."

"Huh." He ashed his cigar again. "That 'nothing more,' I don't buy, but I went in to see old Whitehill the day after I heard about Frank. Some of my men saw the smoke on their way to Silver City. Couple others heard more up there in Pinos, but it's a lot of talk, you know. So I go in. Whitehill tells me he can't do a thing yet, and I tell him I'd like to see his badge on someone else's chest for a while."

Amos chuckled, and I grinned.

"He must like you about as much as he does me," I said.

"Oh, Whitehill loves me," Delgado assured us. "He loves to come out here and remind me of the local ordinances, and the approaches he'd prefer to take with the Indians, and even scold me a bit for the messes my men get up to at the dance hall. That's why I figured he owed me some answers on Frank's murder. I been letting that sheriff talk my ear off for years, the least he can do is string up the lowlives I want dead."

"Fair is fair," Amos joked.

"That's right," Delgado chuckled. "Whitehill and me butt heads, but that marshal of his, I like. Dangerous Dan Tucker, they call him. Alleged criminal turned hard-handed marshal. Now that's got a ring to it."

"Hold on," I said in disbelief. "Is that the same Tucker who was out in that Salt War in El Paso?"

"That's him." The cattleman nodded. "He gets the job done, and I don't mind a man choosing a bloody path for himself if it helps some people out. But fact is, I been here longer than both of them, and I don't take too kindly to having a lawman telling me my place on my own damn land."

"That I can understand," I replied.

"So," he sighed and leveled me with a narrow stare. "It seems you're my best chance of learning anything about all this, Killer. Start at the beginning. What'd they do?"

I exchanged a glance with Amos, and the black man nodded for me to continue.

So, I told the cattleman about my arrival at the Black Spur Ranch that night, the fire that blazed through the night and into the next day, and the torn remains of the man providing the best horses to all who needed them in the area.

Delgado didn't flinch, wince, or groan over the gory details. He calmly puffed his cigar, and when I'd finished, he gave a single nod.

"I'm gonna kill that damn sheriff," he muttered.

"Not advised," I said.

He snorted. "Your call, Killer. What's been done about the mess?"

"Both of the men who started the fire have been put down," I replied. "The man who knocked Frank out and helped haul him to pieces in that field is dead, too. That leaves the other three riders, all of whom held a rope. And of course, the man who hired them."

"Name?"

"George Sellick."

Delgado finally stopped puffing. "That drunken ass of a bluebelly? You better be yankin' my chain."

"No, sir," I said. "You know him?"

"I know he's a spineless, muck-headed, rot-gutted, waste of a sack of skin," Delgado scoffed. "That slimy son of a bitch is behind this?"

"He is," Amos replied. "And he's disappeared with the last three murderers as of yesterday."

Delgado sat forward, and he braced his forearms on the table. "Then what in the name of Pete are you boys doing all the way out here? You better lock that ranch down fast."

"We aim to," I said. "But it's hard knowing what kind of

heat we've got coming our way if we have no idea why this group wanted to kill Frank in the first place."

"I see." He puffed his cigar. "That's why you're here, is it?"

"Rosa Vallejos mentioned you knew Frank," I said.

"She's a clever girl," he chuckled as he sat back again. "Not a soul out here knows that. Not even that pretty wife of his."

"Which I find strange," I said outright. "There must be some reason your friendship's stayed so secret all these years."

"I'm of the same mind," Amos agreed as he gave the man a hard once-over. "I'd figure you'd at least come by the ranch, offer condolences, anything of the sort…"

"What for?" He folded his hands over his belly as the cigar smoked between his fingertips. "My condolences ain't gonna help that poor woman feel better. She don't know me from Adam."

"But you'd call yourself Frank's friend?" I asked.

"On God." He nodded with complete conviction. "I wouldn't stick my neck out for many people in this world, but I'd blast a whole damn mountain in half for that man if he needed it. Still, he had his life, and I have mine. Neither of us have minded keeping it that way, either. Hell, I'm gone running cattle half the year, and he's a family man. I ain't no family man."

"That hardly sounds like a reason for secrecy," I pointed out.

Delgado glanced my way with a probing eye. I could tell he didn't like my prodding, but I came here to get some answers once and for all, and I didn't mind grating on his nerves to see that happen.

"You're right," he conceded. "There's a reason I've kept my distance from the Black Spur and the Sanduskys. Frank wanted a new start, and I could respect that because I wanted the same. Our past… it's a tricky one."

"Did you come down here together?" Amos asked.

"No, I came down here right after the war. Picked up a new name somewhere along the way…" He sent us a wink.

"Turned out there was land aplenty for men willing to work for it. Frank was worn out on the ranch up north, after losing his Ma and Pa, so I told him to get his ass down here. We got things put together alright out there, but we both had a lot we were looking to move on from. He started another herd, got some connections in the area, and once he got that pretty wife of his, I saw he was gonna be alright."

"But the pair of you share a troublesome past?" I clarified, and he nodded without responding. "I ask because I've got a feeling Frank's murder is tied up in something bigger. Something that may have followed him here, even."

"I've got the same feeling," Delgado said quietly as he focused on his cigar.

I waited for him to elaborate. Amos' gunmetal eyes seemed just as eager to hear what he had to say, but he sat calmly like he always did when tricky things came up.

Finally, Delgado sighed and looked over.

"I know you," he told Amos with a steady gaze. "Frank respected the hell outta you, boy. Always said so. Never known a harder workin' man with a better head on his shoulders, that's what he said. And as for the Killer here... well, he'd respect the hell outta you, too. So you want answers, I'll give 'em. But just know, Frank was a better man than me. I'm the type who'll bury the pair of you under this here ranch with my own hands if any word of this gets out."

"I don't love that deal," I said with a smirk. "But I'll take it."

"Good. The mess started up in Colorado, back when it was still a territory," he said as he settled in and took a quick puff. "I met Sandusky a couple years before the war broke out. His family had their ranch out in the eastern plains, not far from the Kansas border. Fine horses. Just as fine as what he's got now, only much more of 'em. I settled out there for my own purposes."

I expected the man to elaborate, but he simply continued with his story.

"When the war started up, we looked around and found our country in shambles, torn right down the middle. Men and boys alike were burning with passion and the drive to defend what they stood for. And war is a wicked game. Hard and relentless, and full of folks looking to outsmart the next."

"You serve?" I asked.

"Not quite," he muttered. "We was on the fringe of it out there in Colorado, watching and waiting to see what'd come next. I figured I'd up and serve, but I got bad lungs, so they gave me the boot. Sandusky's Pa just about broke himself trying to keep Frank home, on account of the sister and the hard lands out there."

"But neither of you could keep still about it," I surmised.

"Here's the thing that Frank understood," he sighed. "He come over one night talking about our duty to our country. He said, 'the country's in need, it's our duty to provide.' And he was right. Them men and boys needed horses. Good ones. Steady ones. Warhorses who wouldn't leave them stranded for nothin', wouldn't slow down until the canons stopped firing. He knew he could give that, if anything, and he did. Whether his folks knew about it or not."

"The family never knew?" Amos asked, and I knew he was thinking of Lucy now, same as myself.

"I think the old man knew," he said. "Frank was running the ranch by then, and sales were always good for the Sandusky Ranch, but that herd started out over three hundred strong, and by the end of the war, there might've been eighty left. Of course, it wasn't just his own horses he was moving. Sandusky knew all the breeders in the area, and he got a strong supply train set up for himself. Well... we both did."

Amos furrowed his brow. "You worked together on it?"

"Sure did." He smiled a bit at the memory. "You got two solid supply trains you don't mind crossing, business gets real tidy."

"And what did you provide?" I asked as I eyed the herd out the window.

It sure wasn't horses.

Delgado's squinted eyes shifted between me and Amos, and he leaned forward to ash his cigar before drawing a deep breath.

"I gave what I figured they needed most," he said in a low tone. "The means of stayin' alive. All of 'em. The way I saw it, the right to arm yourself is inherent to being alive on this God-given earth. Folks wanted to start a war, and send their boys off to the muck and the grind of killing, then tell 'em because they picked the wrong side, they're gonna have to do without the right weapons."

I nodded as understanding washed over me.

"Arms dealer?" I asked.

"Dealer, smuggler... call it what you will," Delgado replied. "I've heard several strong words for it over the years. But if the boys down south needed Colts or Sharps, I got 'em. If the boys up north wanted some of those European firearms, I got 'em. See, manufacturers needed to be careful, keep a good look about them, maintain contracts and whatnot. But I didn't give a rat's ass how I looked. Those boys looked scared as all get out and ready to finish that mess, that's all I knew. And I wasn't about to tap dance around about who's right or wrong."

Amos and I raised our eyebrows at that, and I recalled how dangerous the transfer of military weapons had gotten deep in the thralls of the war. For those willing to cross divides and provide to the men in need, rather than the side in need, it must've been doubly so.

"Couldn't have been easy," I pointed out.

"Hardest work I've ever done," he said. "And I run cattle. Frank and I worked ourselves ragged keeping up with demand over those years, and always having to keep half an eye over our shoulders, too. But as the war got more gruesome, the trouble with the Indians got worse out there. We pulled back and were less involved in the final year of the war while folks in our parts were busy defending our own. I lost half my family to war, and the other half to the Indians. Then the war ended, and the Reconstruction began."

I grunted in acknowledgement, but I didn't think the topic needed more remark than that.

"Texan?" he guessed, and I nodded. "I thought as much. Well, you can guess where we had found ourselves by then. For myself, at least, I had about a hundred people I could've named who wanted me dead, same as a lot of arms dealers back then. As for Sandusky, he was tired, alone with his sister to look after, and just wanted to go back to ranching and let the blood stay in the past."

The cattleman got up and headed to the decanter in the corner, and he poured three glasses of red-amber bourbon that must've cost a pretty penny.

"Is that how Frank gathered all them weapons?" Amos asked. "Through your supply?"

Delgado's smile spread wide beneath his sandy-blond beard. "Sure is. He's still got it all, too. We cross paths and go off shootin' sometimes, even still. We did, anyway. You take care of those weapons, you hear?"

"I will," Amos said. "Frank left it all in my care, but it's for his son, Russel. He'll get 'em in a few years."

"Good, good." Delgado nodded as he came to the table and slid our glasses over. "I'd like that. 'Course I've never met the boy. I've ribbed Frank about it, too. Told him 'bring that boy of yours out here, I'll teach him a thing or two about chores,' but he wouldn't budge. Said that boy wouldn't be allowed to meet me until he was at least sixteen."

"Why's that?" I asked as I swirled my glass.

Then the three of us drank, and I groaned as the smooth bourbon slid right down like warm honey.

"He'd like me too much," he snickered. "And Frank didn't

think that pretty wife of his would appreciate a cursin', spittin' son strolling around that ranch like he owns the place."

"I am relieved he hasn't met you, I won't lie," Amos laughed. "But he'll sure want to meet you once he meets them guns."

"Boy sounds just like his daddy." Delgado sighed and puffed his cigar. "I've never known a man more fascinated by the mechanics of weapons. So much was developed and altered and perfected just so during that time, and it's kept on ever since. Boggles the mind, really, the things man has come up with. Frank was just fascinated with it all. He sure appreciated a good weapon when he saw it, and I never could keep my hands out of the business, even down here. I keep my head low, mind, but anything I find that he'd get a kick out of, I send his way."

He smiled a bit, but the lines around his eyes seemed heavier now. He lowered his head in a private moment of prayer, and after a small nod to himself, he lifted his glass.

"He was a singular man," he said.

We raised our glasses as well, and then we drained them in honor of the departed horseman.

Outside, the day was heating up bad under the afternoon sun, and I knew we'd have to leave soon to be rested and ready for our watch this evening. Just the thought brought my mind straight back to the dangers at hand.

"That brings us to all this mess now," I said as I turned to Delgado.

He nodded. "I've got no idea how this Sellick plays into all this, but if anything personal is going on between a Union man and Sandusky, I'd bet money it's got to do with those horses."

"Just because he sold some warhorses?" Amos asked.

"Because he sold horses to anyone," Delgado said with a sober look. "Same as I told it… Boys were in need on both sides, and we provided what they needed. It don't sound like much now, but where I'd say I gave men what they needed to live, another man would say I gave them what they needed to kill. Even with fifteen years between us and the war, there's some folks who are still holding some strong animosities about the things that went down."

"I'd have to agree with you," I said. "Which means the ranch may be in more danger than we thought."

Delgado snuffed out his cigar at last and pushed his chair back from the table. Then he gestured for us to follow him as he headed for the door.

Amos and I watched him with some confusion, and he turned back with an air of impatience.

"Well, come on, then." He shoved the heavy door open. "Like I said, I'd blast a damn mountain apart if need be, but that don't seem necessary just now, so how's about an army instead?"

"I don't take your meaning," I said.

He let out a gravelly chuckle. "How many men you want on patrol out there, Killer? You just say a number, and I'll round 'em up."

CHAPTER 22

The ride back to the Black Spur was a quiet one while Amos and I thought over all we'd learned.

For his part, the black man had a lot to grapple with now that he understood more about the friend he'd worked beside for nine years. He was also returning home with ten times as much to worry about, too, so I left him to his thoughts while I mulled over my own impression of all this.

We'd done what we set out to, and the folks closest to the ranch knew to keep an eye out for trouble. More than that, Delgado was sending ten of his own men up to the ranch for added security in case George Sellick and his band of murderers showed up. They'd be under mine and Amos' command while they were there, and he assured me he'd only send men Frank wouldn't mind having around his family, too.

This I particularly appreciated, seeing as Russel was gonna have about fifty questions for us all once he found out.

The sun battered our backs as we led our mounts further into the foothills and along the ridges, and after a while, I found myself thinking on the things Delgado had confided about his and Frank's work during the war.

There was a lot of truth in Delgado's words.

I knew too well the sort of animosity he'd talked about people hanging on to all these years. It was a hard thing to shake when it really cut a man deep, and I didn't doubt that if this Sellick did take issue with Sandusky over something from wartime, and he'd stewed on it this long, he'd be back soon enough.

And all that boiling anger would be set loose on us all.

I shook my head at the thought.

Then I had to ask myself if I'd do the same.

If I could track down a single soldier or captain– blue or gray– responsible for what happened to my sweet wife and my beautiful little girl, would I murder them in cold blood today?

Would I hire men as bad as these six to do what they did to Sandusky?

Fifteen years ago, I might've said yes.

I'd felt myself crack straight in half the day I found my family farm was rubble and those I loved were ash. I'd spent plenty of time in the throes of grief over it.

But now, without hesitation, I could say my answer would be no.

No victory is won without bloodshed, and some are just the unfortunate few who suffer a little extra without any sense to it. That's what a man signs up for when he decides to fight for big changes.

I still mourned deeply, even to this day, for the loss of my wife and child, but if the weeks I'd spent among the folks at the Black Spur had proven anything to me, it was just how much time had truly passed since that fateful day.

That past was a while gone now.

This George Sellick sounded like a man who hadn't wrapped his head around that line of thinking.

And that was dangerous as Hell for Helena and her family if he decided he wasn't done getting his revenge.

We arrived back at the ranch with a few good hours of

daylight left. Abel, Mateo, and Russel had gotten the last things finished up on the new stables once the younger ranch hand awoke, and they said Helena wanted to have a celebration over it.

"That'll have to wait," Amos said as we exchanged a glance.

"Those bad men you talked about coming?" Russel asked.

"We think they are," I told him. "We've got ten men coming to help guard the ranch, though. Should be here before dark."

Russel nodded. "Good, you sure we shouldn't get more? Maybe thirty or even forty men?"

"Ten ought to do," I said with a smile. "They're hard, ranchin' men, and I don't doubt they'll be some of the best shooters we can get."

"I'll make sure they are," he assured me, and Abel chuckled as he scruffed the kid's mop of unruly black hair.

Then Amos sent Russel off to help Lucy and Honey with chores so we could speak with the ranch hands and Helena about the day's events.

We only shared what was strictly necessary– and wouldn't get either of us buried beneath Delgado's Pass– but the cattleman had agreed the wife should know as much as Frank would be alright with. So, once everyone knew where we stood, Amos and the others headed out to ready some sleeping quarters for Delgado's men, and I sat with Helena to explain a bit about Frank's past.

She wasn't the least bit surprised.

The good woman was as proud as a wife could be, hearing how her husband had risked so much during those dark years to help his fellow countrymen. She also understood at once why he never mentioned a word of it to her.

"My daddy wore the blue," she said with a sad smile. "Decorated Brigadier General. Died in service. But I think even he would be proud. He respected men who managed to stay neutral where they needed to back then. Still… Mr. Delgado may have rubbed him the wrong way."

"I'm sure I would've, too," I chuckled. "I wore the gray."

"Perhaps." Helena puckered her lips in thought as she eyed me up and down. "He always trusted me to judge for myself, though, and in my eyes, you're precisely what a man ought to be. Honest, kind, and willing to go as far as you have to for what's right."

I dipped my head in thanks.

"Please tell Mr. Delgado I'm grateful to him as well for all he's done for my husband, and for us, even if we didn't know about it," she said in earnest.

"I will," I promised as I rose from the little sitting area near the fireplace.

"When those ten men get here, send them up to the house, I'll have food for them," she said. "You ought to head out back, though. There's something that might interest you taking place in our little corral back there."

There was a twinkle in her blue eyes as she said this.

"Well, if that doesn't sound like a trap, I don't know what does," I chuckled as I headed for the door.

"And Jesse?"

I stopped and glanced back to find Helena's beautiful face shining with happy tears. Her eyes were bright, and my chest swelled with pride to know I'd been able to bring her some joy in all this.

I returned to her to pull her into my arms, and I could feel the way her whole body relaxed in my hold.

"Thank you," she said softly. "You didn't have to find all this out for us, but you did, and it's truly made all the difference to me."

"Good." I smiled against her strawberry-blonde hair. "That's all I wanted."

When I pulled away, her cheeks were pink with emotion, and she laughed lightly as I brushed her tears away with the pad of my thumb. Then she shooed me out of the house so she could get to cooking.

I had an easy smile on my face as I went outside, rounded the house, and walked down to the little corral. It was a small, circular area I'd noticed behind the red barn, and the sight waiting for me there only made me smile more.

Lucy looked stunning today in a crisp white blouse that made her stark green eyes seem to glow all the way from over here. Her auburn ringlets were done up nice enough for a night at the opera, but she strolled around the corral with dust splattered halfway up her skirts and a long, worn-out lead in hand.

That wasn't what really caught my eye, though.

What got me was the fact that old Birdy was tethered to the other end of the lead, and Honey was perched in her saddle with a dimpled, giggling smile on her face.

I grinned as I hitched one boot up on the fence and leaned forward.

"Why do I get the sense you two just stole my horse?" I asked. "That's a crime, you know…"

"You gonna place a bounty on our heads, Jesse Callahan?" Lucy asked with a teasing smile. "Wanted: Two beautiful young ladies for the despicable crime of saddling up a man's horse and doing a very fine job of riding it."

Honey giggled as she petted the old mare's neck.

"Despicable," I agreed. "Look at Birdy. She's affronted."

Birdy snorted happily at the sound of her name, and she tossed her mane as she circled toward me. She took her time bringing her young rider over, and she came to a gentle stop before nuzzling her face against mine. Then Lucy asked her for a kiss, and the mare was quick to turn and brush her muzzle against the woman's waiting cheek.

I blinked a few times. "Did you teach her to do that?"

"Sure did." Lucy smiled. "She doesn't seem very affronted about it, either."

Birdy nickered and carried on walking the little girl around the corral with Lucy holding her lead.

"Traitor," I sighed. "After all we've been through, too."

I certainly didn't mind in the least. Birdy looked like a proud mother escorting Honey around nice and slow, and I felt a lump gathering in my throat as I thought over just how long she'd been rambling around with me.

And how much she'd been enjoying her treatment here at the Black spur.

She was as good a horse as I could've asked for, and in my mind, worth more than any of the Sandusky stock. She deserved some slow, sweet days like this.

Honey did, too. The little girl had positively lit up since Lucy's arrival, but up in Birdy's saddle, she looked happier than I'd ever seen her.

When the trio finished their little ride, they gathered over near the gate, and Lucy lifted Honey down as I joined them.

"I love her!" the little girl said and petted Birdy's flank. "She's a good horsey."

"The very best," I assured her. "Although she does seem particularly well-behaved when you're holding her reins."

"Because she loves her back," Lucy decided with a nod. "Don't you, Birdy? You love Honey, huh?"

"She loves me," Honey giggled. "And I love her."

"Is that right?" I chuckled. "Well, that's a serious thing. I'm not sure I feel alright keeping Birdy for my own when the pair of you are so in love."

Lucy's eyes snapped up to mine, and a slow smile spread on her face like she'd already guessed my next words.

"I'll tell you what," I said and crouched down beside Honey. "If you promise to take very, very good care of her, I might be willing to sell you this horse. And she'd be your own from now on."

"Me?" Honey gasped, and she started jumping up and down. "I get my own Birdy?"

"You prepared to make that promise?" I asked.

Honey got real serious as she stopped jumping and nodded fervently. Then she crossed her finger over her heart and spit in her hand before holding it out for me to shake.

"Oh, Honey," Lucy groaned. "Did Russel teach you that?"

The girl nodded but didn't look away from me.

"I promise, Mr. Callahan."

I smiled as I shook her hand. "In that case, I can sell you Birdy for… three flowers. But they've gotta each be a different color, or there's no deal."

Without another word, Honey turned on her heel, ducked under the fence, and ran her little legs toward the garden as fast as she could.

I worked on swallowing that lump down as I watched her go, but then I turned my attention to old Birdy.

"You are inordinately good with children, Mr. Callahan," Lucy said as she narrowed her eyes suspiciously. "You sure you don't have a whole family somewhere waiting for you?"

I smiled and shook my head as I focused on patting my old mare's neck and giving her a kiss or two. That made it easier to keep my expression clear, but I must've given something away, because Lucy wasn't smiling as much when I glanced her way.

She didn't say anything. She just started on Birdy's tack, and I helped her remove the saddle and bridle.

"Well, I think that was just about the sweetest thing I've ever seen a man do," Lucy said lightly. "Hard to believe you murder men for a living."

"I don't," I said. "I kill the murderers, when the need arises. There's a world of difference."

"That is true," she agreed more seriously. "You're the bringer of true justice. One of the few who knows and lives by the meaning of honor. Certainly too honorable to be bought or corrupted like some of these so-called lawmen out here."

I cocked an eyebrow at the tone she took on when she said this last part. She almost sounded scornful, and I realized she was being a bit rough with the rope she was rolling up.

"You say that like you've got some experience with corruptible lawmen," I said.

"A bit," she sighed and glanced my way. "But that's my luck. I am the most unlucky woman you will ever meet."

"That's not the way I've heard it," I said. "I hear all of San Francisco admires your singing."

"Oh, I've worked hard to earn their admiration," she assured me. "That's got nothing to do with luck. I travel more than I stay put in one place, and I sing more than I talk. That's how admiration came my way. No, my bad luck comes around whenever I get the notion I'm in love with a man."

I laughed at this, but she insisted this was no laughing matter.

"It's true!" she huffed. "The first boy I ever loved went off to war and fell in love with a nurse instead."

"Well, that is impolite," I acknowledged. "Weren't you just a young girl, though?"

"It was love," she said in a no-nonsense tone. "And I was so mad, I figured I'd fall in love with his cousin instead, but he was only nice to me because he hoped to get a job working at my family's ranch, so that all came to nothing."

"I'm not too surprised," I chuckled.

"Next time I fell in love was with a proper gentleman who was awfully sweet," she went on. "Though not very smart. Sweet as he was, he went and got himself killed by a passing fire wagon out in Chicago."

I frowned. "I'm sorry to hear it."

"Not as sorry as I was," she said. "He'd just given me his mother's ring the day before, and she was awfully angry at the funeral demanding I give it back. Turns out he was too afraid to even tell her I existed, so I looked like a little thief walking into the church with her ring on my finger."

I chuckled and shook my head, and Lucy laughed with me.

"But that was years ago," she said. "I stopped looking for sweet after that and started looking for a man who really stood for something. The last man I fell in love with was a tall, handsome deputy in San Francisco. He came to hear me sing four times when I was at Wade's Opera House. Sat right in the front and brought me roses for my last performance."

She smiled prettily at the memory, but I narrowed my eyes.

"Alright, and when did your bad luck show up?" I asked.

"That's just exactly what I started to wonder!" She threw her arms up. "I think I said yes when he asked to marry me simply because I couldn't believe nothing bad had happened yet. And wouldn't you know it, two weeks later, I come to find out he's one of those contemptible men who can be swayed to look the other way when horrible things happen just because some scoundrel handed him money to do so."

"Ah." I nodded. "So he's the corruptible lawman."

"Yes, and not so handsome as I thought," she said curtly. "Not so tall, either… It's funny how ugly a man starts to look when you find out he's a spineless bit of nothing after all."

"When did all this happen?" I asked as I led Birdy out of the gate and toward the pasture.

"I gave him his ring back last month, right before I left for Leadville," she said.

"That's not long ago at all." I slowed a little and studied the woman over Birdy's back. "I'm sorry he turned out to be a disappointment. That must've been upsetting."

She shrugged. "I think part of me knew it was so. I never told Frank about him. Usually, I tell Lena and Frank every little thing about what I'm up to and where I'm at and who I think I'm in love with, but I didn't write a word about him. It's just as well."

We let Birdy out to pasture, and my two mules came right over to take their places behind her rear. Then the trio wandered off to graze the evening away, and I smiled as I imagined my old mare passing plenty of happy days here for the rest of her life, with Honey giggling and learning to ride from atop her back.

The little girl in question came sprinting over with much more than three flowers not long after that. She couldn't decide which would be best for buying Birdy, so I picked one white one, one purple, and one yellow flower the color of Honey's hair. I pulled my hat off and slid the flowers into the band inside to keep them safe, and the little girl kissed my cheek before she ran off to tell her mama about her new horse.

Lucy and I watched the herd for a while after that, but when we strolled away from the pretty scene, the singer let out a heavy sigh.

"I suppose we've got trouble coming?" she murmured without looking up.

"Could be," I replied.

"Don't do that," she said and stopped me. "Tell me straight. You think we do, don't you?"

I nodded. "There's very little doubt in my mind."

"What can be done?" she asked.

"Well, all we've—"

I cut myself off as I spotted a line of ten men riding toward the gate, and I gestured toward them for the singer.

"That's our plan," I said. "Ten shooters who've spent plenty of time guarding valuable property. Plus myself, the ranch hands, and God's will."

Lucy cocked her head to the side in a discerning way as she watched the rugged men turn up the lane. Pedro wasn't among them, so I knew Delgado had kept his word about choosing carefully, and it appeared he'd done well.

Every man approaching had straight and strong backs, broad shoulders honed by years of roping, and gun barrels jutting off their packs from various holsters and riggings.

"You think any of them are half as tall and handsome as you?" Lucy asked as she tapped her lip.

"Who said I was tall and handsome?" I snorted.

I glanced over to find her green eyes dancing with their usual amusement.

"Wouldn't you like to know…" she teased.

I gave the young woman a polite shove toward the house.

"Go on, get," I muttered. "You don't need no tall and handsome. With your luck, he'll probably walk right off a mountain while he's busy staring at you."

"True," she sighed. She feigned a woeful look over her shoulder at me, but when I rolled my eyes, she broke into giggles and hurried up to the house to help Helena.

I carried on toward the stables and met up with Amos, Abel, and Mateo.

"What was that about?" Mateo asked with a grin.

"Some silly nonsense that woman's gotten into her head about tall and handsome something or others," I said.

"Ah, you mean how you and Rosa will be married by winter." He nodded. "I agree with this. You would have to be a very, very foolish man to wait longer than that with a woman like her, no matter how handsome you are."

"No." Abel shook his head and tapped his nose. "Is Lucy. She marry Jesse."

"Lucy?" Mateo scoffed. "No, Lucy is too fancy, no man likes that in a wife."

"Speak for yourself," Amos said. "Fancy's nice."

"Not for any of us," the younger ranch hand assured him with the utmost authority. "No, if Jesse marries a Sandusky, it will be Helena. She is…"

He waved his hands through the air, but seemed to be at a loss for words when it came to the beautiful lady of the ranch.

The rest of us nodded in agreement.

"But he should marry Rosa," Mateo decided. "She is… glorious to behold. That is what Jesse wants. Right, Jesse?"

I turned to Amos. "Do I got a sign on my head that says I'm looking for a wife, or something?"

"Hard to tell," he snickered. "All that tall and handsome's in the way."

The men burst out laughing and left me standing there with nothing but my worn-out sense of humor and a long sigh. Then I followed after and joined the new arrivals where they were dismounting and pulling their packs down.

Introductions went quick, and I could tell these men came to work, not to chat. Amos gave them a rundown of the land, their sleeping quarters, and where they could let their horses out. Then I got the lay of their skill sets and prowess with a gun, and I divvied up some shifts for them based on where I could use them the most out here.

Once everyone knew their role, we brought them up to the house, and Helena and Lucy handed out enough pork and buttered veggies for twice as many mouths. How in the world Helena had managed it all with so little warning was beyond me, but once again, I found myself eating one of the best home-cooked meals I'd ever had.

The rest of the evening was a lot of bustle on the property while we tended to horses and got ready for the night. Aside from Russel deciding he wanted to bunk with Delgado's men from now on, everything was handled with little issue.

Between all of us, we had over forty loaded guns ready to fire at a moment's notice. Including the LeMat I'd started carrying every night. We had eyes watching in every direction now, and no one stood a chance of reaching the house or the stables without us knowing about it.

Trouble was, that wouldn't stop them scouting the place out. This was a point Amos and I couldn't quite decide on.

It had been clear after Frank's murder that the original six had learned enough about the ranch to find the one weak point in their perimeter. This allowed them to sneak in undetected, and to flee quickly once they'd finished what they came to do.

Three of those men were still alive, so they and Sellick would already know the lay of the ranch.

The question was whether they'd use the same inlet or try and surprise us from another direction.

Then there was also the question of whether their anger would drive them to launch a full-on raid, or take a stealthier approach.

For now, without knowing which way they'd ride in from, we kept the patrol pushed out toward the perimeter of the main pastures, the lane, and the gap to the north. Then I dispersed the men among those areas, in a fashion that would allow us plenty of defense in either a raid or a covert situation.

At dusk, I set out for the first watch with four of Delgado's men. Amos would take another four out next, and then Mateo and the remaining two men would keep an eye on things for the last few hours before daybreak. In my experience, an attack was least likely during those hours, so we figured three would be plenty.

My part of the patrol took me beyond the house, past the red barn, and along the wooden fence that ran toward the northwest from there. North of this spot, no fencing or barbed wire closed the ranch in, primarily because of how mountainous the land became up there. This was the area the six desperados had used to their advantage.

The fenceline I patrolled ran along the edge of the draft horses' pasture, too, and I met at the far corner with one of Delgado's men, who remained where he sat on his horse with his eyes trained to the ranchland beyond. Then I'd turn and walk back the way I'd come.

I chose to ride Flint for my watches now since Birdy was officially done taking orders from me, and the old mare didn't make any complaints when I gave her a pat and pulled the stallion out of the pasture instead. He rode well and didn't give me any trouble about the extra work. Then when it came time to turn in, he stayed near the stables instead of rejoining the herd, like he'd suddenly decided he belonged in a separate caste.

"I might need to see the Sanduskys about buying you off 'em," I said as I patted his flank. "You know much about bounty hunting?"

The dappled stallion brushed past me without even a nicker of acknowledgment.

"That'll take some getting used to," I decided as I turned for the bunkhouse.

I woke the next morning to find all had stayed calm during the night. Everyone was well-rested, too, now that we had enough men for three patrols, and morale was good.

I even figured I had some time to head to Pinos Altos for a bandolier to carry extra ammunition, but I didn't even get to saddling up the stallion.

"Your presence has been requested," Lucy informed me when she found me out in the tack room.

"What for?" I asked.

She sent me a wry smile. "That prospective buyer is coming by this morning. And Lena wants you there for the discussions."

CHAPTER 23

The house was silent as Lucy and I sat side by side at the dining table waiting for Helena.

The singer drummed her fingertips hard on the wood in front of her, and I could see a small muscle in her jaw tensing every now and then as she ground her teeth.

Russel and Honey were off under the watchful eyes of Amos, Abel, and Mateo. This meant the three of us would have the freedom to discuss things in full without worrying about how the children might take it.

At the moment, though, I was more concerned with how Lucy would conduct herself.

"You ought to go easy on that table, it didn't do anything wrong," I muttered at last.

Lucy's fingers stopped their drumming. Then she shoved her chair away from the table and paced around like a penned-in shepherd. Her boots struck the wooden floorboards with sharp, purposeful steps, but soon, the light padding of Helena's footsteps came down the stairs.

I shot to my feet as the lady of the ranch entered the room in her best.

This dress must have been one of the 'pretty things' Lucy had bought for her the day we went to Pinos Altos, when she'd complained of Helena's lack of modern mourning clothes. The laciness looked like the sort of thing the singer would fawn over, but the style suited Helena very well.

It was a deep, dark purple gown with black lace trimmings and a few little ribbons here and there, and together with the confident look on her face, it made Helena look like a rich estate heiress. But the soft look in the woman's blue eyes betrayed how much experience she had in the world, and the somber color suited her approach to life lately. All her motherly goodness and faithfulness shone clear as day on her beautiful face, too, and she held herself like only a woman of true quality would.

I could recall plenty of women I'd seen in dresses as elegant as this one, but not one came to mind who wore it so well.

"Is it alright?" Helena asked as her smile faltered, and I realized I'd plumb forgotten to speak.

Lucy laughed as she saw the look on my face, and she brushed past me before I could work out a reply.

"Lena, you look so beautiful," the singer preened as she spun the other woman around. Then she promptly sobered. "Not that this buyer deserves such finery as this. I wouldn't have bought such elegant mourning attire had I known you'd be wearing it for some greedy little… Well. Never mind."

"Thank you, Lucy." Helena smiled. "It really is a lovely gown. I feel like this color suits my mind much better than black did. I don't think even Frank could object to it. I've never seen anything like it. It must be the fanciest thing I've ever owned."

Lucy couldn't help glowing. "The moment I saw it, I just had to see you in it, and the alterations did wonders, I think. You've always been so good with a needle, though."

"Oh, it was a quick fix," Helena said. "No trouble at all, although I do worry the occasion may not call for all this…"

She looked my way again as she spoke, and I promptly woke back up.

"Pardon my manners," I said at once. "You look very nice, Helena. Truly."

Her cheeks were bright pink now, but I was glad my relapse in manners had at least helped her to feel more confident in her attire. She patted her skirts a bit to make sure everything was properly set, but then she straightened up and looked around at the pair of us.

"Are we all ready?" she asked.

"No." Lucy pursed her lips. "But… if this is what you'd like to do, then I'll be here with you for it."

"I'm ready," I assured her. "Although I'm not quite sure what it is you'd like me to do."

"Just be here with us?" she said with a hopeful look. "I know I don't have the right to ask--"

"You do," I cut in.

"Yes, he's on my payroll now, he has to be here if I say so," Lucy added.

"That isn't quite how that works," I said, "but regardless of the pay, Helena, you've allowed me a comfortable place here, and I promised you I'd be of service wherever I could."

"That is true," Helena agreed with a smile. "I suppose that's why I wanted you here. You've done so much for us and the ranch, and you do my husband justice. Every moment, I feel how grateful he is that you're here looking after us, and I know that I wouldn't feel half so sure of myself in all this if it wasn't for you. But you've kept on reminding me of the important things, and it's made it easier for me to get back up after…"

She trailed off as her throat tightened, and I nodded in understanding.

"Well, I'm sure Lucy has told you plenty of times, but you've done very well," I told her. "Speaking with this buyer ought to help ease your mind, too. It'll be good to get an understanding of the sort of person he is, and whether it'd be a good thing to let him settle down here."

"I agree." Helena gave Lucy a brief glance. "It's best to look at the options before making any kind of decision on anything."

"Would you two stop being on the same side?" Lucy huffed. "That ain't fair."

"No one is on any side," Helena laughed lightly. "I am only pointing out that being rash and allowing your emotions to get the better of you is not always advisable."

"Particularly in matters of so much importance," I agreed.

"I don't like either of you right now," Lucy announced and went back to pacing.

Helena and I shared a private smile, but we made sure to adjust our features by the time Lucy stormed back this way.

"This is just a simple thing," Helena said, mostly to herself, it seemed. "I informed the lawyer that I was not decided at all, and that I only wanted to meet the man and hear about his offer from his own mouth."

"Should be a quick visit," I added as I realized Lucy was too upset to speak at present.

A rare occurrence, to be sure.

"Hmm," she managed.

It was just as well, because the sound of approaching hoofs drew my attention to the lane.

Helena and I walked over to the window, but Lucy paced closer and closer to the opposite wall, as if she could keep the man from arriving simply by refusing to see him there.

The lone rider bounced up and down in a lazy sort of fashion, but I could excuse this on account of the long ride he'd taken to reach us. He wore a rumpled duster to keep the sun at bay, even while his hat sat pushed back on his head, and he looked side to side all the way up the lane. He paused just once to look at the new stables, but then shook his head and continued.

I stole a glance at the woman beside me.

Helena's apprehension was clear on her face, but she

looked more prepared to conduct this meeting than she had with that Louisiana man.

She'd certainly gotten her feet under her since then.

The pair of us watched as the man finally dismounted, and he hollered to one of Delgado's men who happened to be passing. Then he pushed his reins into the other's hand and trudged up toward the house without looking back.

"He don't seem too kind," I muttered under my breath.

"Good," Lucy said. "Maybe Russel will shoot him on his way to the house."

"Lucy!" Helena scolded, but when we looked over, the singer only cocked an eyebrow and kept on pacing.

Meanwhile, Helena went to the door, and I followed but stayed a few paces back while she turned the knob and greeted her guest.

"Welcome to the Black Spur," she said like a proper hostess. "Please, come on in and make yourself comfortable."

"Bartholomew Wickett, ma'am." The man tipped his hat.

"Mrs. Helena Sandusky," she said with a warm smile.

"It's a pleasure," he returned.

Then he brushed past and entered the house, and he looked around himself with the discerning eye of a man already fixed on owning a place. He paid Helena no mind after that and even brought himself over into the next two rooms without a word.

Lucy bristled as she watched him help himself to her brother's home.

Even Helena looked a bit put out, so I made a point of joining the stranger in the cozy reading area he'd ended up in.

There were two worn-out chairs side by side with a little table between them, and a short bookshelf in the corner held more volumes than it looked fit for. Not only were the shelves full, but precarious piles of books teetered on the top, along with a couple more near the base of one of the chairs.

Helena and her husband must have passed many peaceful

evenings in here together, and the idea painted such a pretty picture in my mind that suddenly, I wasn't feeling very hospitable toward the stranger.

I cleared my throat to make sure he hadn't missed my arrival.

"Not bad," he told me with a shrug. "Bit tight quarters, but it'll suit."

I smiled, but it didn't reach my eyes. "Quite a large house for the area. Only one with two stories that I've seen for many miles."

"It'll suit," was all he said.

I could tell by his accent that he was from back east, and while this didn't normally rub me the wrong way, it did now. His beard was also straggly and unkempt, and he'd yet to remove his hat.

"We can discuss all the finer points in the dining area," I said and gestured back the way he'd come.

"There's quite a few more ranch hands out there than I was told to expect," he said as he continued looking around. "I was under the impression the widow was struggling with only a small number of workers and more good stock than she could manage."

"Some of the men outside are here for only a short while," I said as I eyed the man.

I found it strange that he'd heard it in that light. Most people around here respected the Sanduskys enough that I doubted many would paint things in such a way. It certainly did a disservice to Helena, but I figured the man's lawyer must have inferred all he wanted to from his previous visit.

The man took his time looking around for another moment or so before deciding to accept the invitation and return to the dining room.

My smile was nowhere to be seen by the time I'd herded him back toward the women.

Still, Helena put on her kindest smile for him and offered

a chair. Lucy chose to stay standing with her arms crossed and a disapproving look on her pretty face, but I placed myself kitty-corner to the man, with Helena across from him at the head of the table.

"I won't need all those men, but any who can prove they're worth their salt, I might consider," Mr. Wickett said without preamble.

Helena blinked. "Alright. Thank you for coming to speak with me today, Mr. Wickett. I've been looking forward to meeting you. Can I offer you anything to drink?"

"I'm just fine," he said. "My lawyer assured me you had some real nice land up here, and it does indeed look nice enough. The price will have to be adjusted, though, on account of them old fences out there."

Helena was about to respond, but the man turned to me before she had a chance.

"The women will be ready to vacate the home promptly, I assume?" he asked.

Behind him, Lucy turned an irate shade of red, and I glanced around a bit pointedly.

"You'll have to ask the ladies," I said. "I only work here."

"What kinda work you do?" he asked instead. "I'm hoping to save me some inconvenience and keep as many workers as I find suitable. You might make the cut, depending."

"Oh, he's on my payroll," Lucy spoke for the first time, and her tone was cold and detached. "He does all the killin' around here."

Mr. Wickett turned a concerned glance in her direction. "Killing?"

"That's right." She smiled.

"Mr. Wickett," Helena said in an attempt to keep things cordial. "Your lawyer mentioned you had some nice ideas for the land. May I ask what you have in mind?"

"Well, the stables will have to be sorted out," he said with a heavy sigh, as if the work already vexed him. "Much larger than what I need, really."

"Oh," Helena said. "I thought you were interested in keeping the horses and–"

"Yeah, I'll take them," he said with a wave of his hand. "From what I hear, they'll fetch a very fine price. Should make up for the purchase of the place. But I don't keep such large herds as this. I move horses real quick, see. I figure with the reputation of this particular ranch, those sales will go even quicker, so I don't need so much room for storing so many. Especially if the men you've got can get them riding real nice real fast, that's all that matters. If not, I'll hire some who can."

"I see." Helena's sweetness had worn out, but she kept up her manners all the same. "And you intend to keep the name, then? On the gate?"

"Oh, certainly, don't you worry, it'll be the Black Spur Ranch for many, many years to come," he said. "Might even keep the branding, since it's established well out here."

"I don't believe the branding is included in the purchase," I said without a second thought. It was a knee-jerk response, but I couldn't seem to ignore how very little I liked this man.

"Anything can be bought," he said without concern. "We'll sort that out by the time of the sale. For now—"

"I'm sorry," Helena interrupted in a firm tone. "I'm afraid there may be some misunderstanding. You see, I invited you here merely to hear your plans for our home. Whether or not the Black Spur is to be sold at all is still to be decided."

The man eyed her with a gruffer look than I expected.

"No, that ain't right," he informed her. "I was told the place was as good as sold."

Helena kept her composure, and I was impressed to see her handling herself so calmly. Lucy sure wasn't. The singer's green eyes darted frantically between Mr. Wickett, me, and Helena.

"I'm not sure where you got that impression, Mr. Wick-ett," Helena said. "At present, I am only considering the idea."

"Considering?" His glower deepened. "You mean you brung me all the way up here in this heat for no reason?"

"I invited you here because your lawyer said you were quite eager and interested," she replied. "I thought it po-lite to hear—"

"Polite," he snorted and shook his head. "This here is any-thing but, ma'am. Now, I understand you're in mourning and struggling to keep this ranch afloat, but that don't excuse—"

"Pardon me, but I don't believe I gave your lawyer any such impression?" Helena looked at me with a hint of ner-vousness now. "The ranch is getting along just fine. I'm sorry to disappoint you at all, but I merely wanted to speak with you and—"

"Ma'am, if I wanted to merely speak with a woman, I'd go to the dance hall," he informed her. "Much less hassle for a higher reward."

I sat forward as his tone sent a spark of anger through me.

"No need to be impolite," I told him. "The woman is sim-ply telling you that you've been misinformed. That isn't her doing, it's the fault of whoever—"

"Misinformed my eye," he snapped and slammed his hand on the table.

The women both jumped, but I didn't bat an eye.

"Now, I wouldn't have even bothered coming up, but I have it on good authority from George Sellick himself that this ranch is as good as sold," the man insisted. "I shouldn't have to state the sort of standing the Sellicks have in Silver City, either. What they say goes."

Helena was pale now and seemed unable to speak. Lucy stared at me with eyes wider than the sun, but I just held the man's gaze as my hand shifted to rest on the gun at my hip.

"George Sellick sent you?" I asked.

CHAPTER 24

"Of course he sent me," Mr. Wickett said with some salt. "You think I'd come all the way up here without any assurance? I spoke with the man just a few days ago, and he said there was no hope for the place, and that the widow had given up on it. Supposed to be available real cheap, too."

"Cheap?" Lucy hissed.

"How much?" Helena asked, only I hardly recognized the voice. I'd been looking straight at the woman when she spoke, though, and there was no denying the hard, icy tone had come from the lady of the ranch.

"Lawyer says it's worth about thirty thousand dollars," the man said and pointed a finger at her. "But I'll pay twenty-seven thousand for it, not a penny more. That's a real good deal for you as well, given the sad circumstances."

"Get out." Helena's eyes were ice now, too.

"Excuse you," he snarled. "You know, you're just about the most unpleasant chit I've ever met. You should be appreciative of the folks trying to help you out, especially after the violence of all that's happened here—"

"You think I need your measly twenty-seven thousand dollars?" she asked, and her expression was a punishing one. "Why, I could spit in that pasture out there and get more than that in a week. This is the Black Spur Ranch, Mr. Wickett, and I'm not some struggling widow looking for help from the likes of you. I'm the owner of the best horse ranch in the territory, and to be blunt, I'd never let a man as ornery as you run this place into the ground, no matter the price."

Lucy looked ready to burst with pride, and I was right there with her.

Our guest looked like he'd swallowed a prickly pear. He stuttered a bit and sent me an affronted look, like I ought to rein the woman in, but I'd never been more content to let a lady have her say.

I simply remained where I was with my palm on my gun, and our guest looked positively livid as he read the message on my face.

"Well, I've never..." he growled as he shoved himself free of the chair and made to leave.

Helena breezed after him, and she looked like an angel of fury on his coattails all the way to the door.

"Next time I see George, I'm gonna make sure he knows you lot are a bunch of crazed, overspirited, unchecked gyps with too much rope. That's what you are."

"That's just fine," Helena slid. "And while you're at it, tell that George Sellick that the Sanduskys will never, ever sell this ranch. So whatever vendetta he's got, he's gonna have to man up and carry on without taking away absolutely everything I have left of my husband."

With that, she slammed the door shut.

I could hear the ornery rancher cursing us the whole way back to his horse, which the Delgado man seemed to have abandoned and left to graze in the front yard.

"Lena," Lucy croaked, and we turned just as the singer burst into tears. "You're... you're s-so beautiful when you're mad! I love you so much!"

"I love you, too," Helena said with an amused smile.

Lucy was a blubbering mess after that, and Helena

propped the woman up while she went on and on about how proud she was of her sister-in-law.

I was proud of both of them. I could tell it had taken every scrap of Lucy's self-control to let Helena have her say on this one, and it took Helena all the will of God to sit through that so-called 'guest's' poor comportment.

"Helena, I must say, you did well," I told her. "I'm impressed you managed to maintain your composure as long as you did. I was just about ready to throw the man out of your house myself by the end of it."

"Yes, well." Helena pursed her lips. "Unpleasant though he may be, I'm more upset with George Sellick. The nerve of that man, sending Mr. Wickett here under those pretenses, and knowing full well how horrible all this has been for the family."

"It's disgusting," Lucy seethed through her tears. "He's rubbing salt in the wound, that's what he's doing. He's trying to be as cruel as he can be, and for what?"

"Revenge," Helena said as her eyes met mine. "Cold-hearted, misguided revenge."

She'd only shared the same with Lucy that I'd shared with her, but both women understood the importance of secrecy here.

Lucy glowered. "Misguided is putting it lightly..."

"Part of me hopes Mr. Wickett does see that Sellick again and tells him what I said," the strawberry-blonde woman murmured as she made her way to the window in time to see the last of Mr. Wickett's horse leaving the lane.

I nodded in agreement. "He'd be awful mad if he did, but unfortunately, I think we might just be the next folks who see George Sellick's face. And plenty more with him, if my hunch is correct."

"Let them come." Helena glanced my way. "We're ready, ain't we?"

"Sure are," I replied. "The first patrol last night went off without a hitch, and the few areas we decided are left too open will be covered well this evening."

"What will we do if something does happen?" Helena asked, and she wore the same no-nonsense look she always did when it came time to get to the real work of a thing. "The children and I and Lucy shouldn't stay in the house, I don't think."

"I agree, it's not safe," I said. "If trouble comes, we'll hopefully have enough warning to get y'all to the bunkhouse before things really kick off."

"That is nice and far from the main living quarters," Helena agreed.

"And it's entirely dark over that side of the property at night," Lucy put in. "Even if we're still making our way there, it's unlikely anyone will see us."

"Make sure they don't hear you, either," I said. "Keep Honey nice and quiet, and no matter what happens, don't come out here trying to help. Hole up there and stand your ground."

"That's a promise I can make," Lucy snorted. "I've never held a gun in my life, much less ran in front of a bunch of them while they're goin' off."

"You've never had anyone even explain the basics of shooting?" I asked.

"No." Lucy shook her head a little nervously. "I suppose that's not so smart, huh? I would've learned, but Frank always said I was too shaky for guns."

"It's true," Helena told me. "She's apt to flinching, and needless to say, the jump of a gun alone is probably enough to startle her too much, nevermind the noise."

"But Lena can shoot!" Lucy added. "She's real mean with a scattergun."

"I know enough," the blonde woman conceded. "And Russel will be with us, too."

"I'll make sure at least one of Delgado's men stays in a

spot where he can assist if anything goes awry out there, too," I said. "But you should be plenty safe with the pair of you armed and all of us out to keep the attackers busy."

"My, I dislike the idea of such violence on our land," Helena said with a little shiver.

"Our land." Lucy smiled from ear to ear. "As it should be."

Helena smiled as well. "As it will be for many years to come."

"You could always find a more... suitable buyer," Lucy said with no conviction.

"No," she replied. "All of this has helped me to see how very little I'd like to let others live in my home. Frank built this place for us, and there's no price anyone could place on this ranch that would feel suitable."

"I'm so relieved!" the singer laughed. "Deep down, I knew you'd listen to Jesse's good judgment on this, but I must admit, I was worried there for a moment."

"Jesse's good judgment?" Helena put her hands on her slim waist.

"Yes," Lucy said with a curt nod. "He's been right all along, hasn't he? At least you listened up in time, though."

There was plenty that could be said to this, but Helena didn't seem able to find the words. She simply sighed, looked my way, and let a full-bellied laugh escape.

I left the women to their merriment after that and set out to join the ranch hands. The morning was getting along now, and Delgado's men had taken to work on the ranch as if they were being paid to do it.

Granted, Delgado insisted on covering any pay I was intending to give them for their help, so in a way, I supposed they were.

I finally found the ranch hands in the stables settling the two broodmares who were due to give birth any day now. Honey and Russel were in charge of keeping Bonita happy in her stall while Mateo and Abel tended to a young mare named Sweet One who'd be having her first foal.

"Cálmate, Dulce, estoy aquí contigo," I heard Mateo murmur as soft as a lover might.

I quietly came over to the furthest stall and found the young ranch hand gently stroking the mare's swollen belly, while Abel rubbed his thumbs in small circles at the base of her long neck. She was a gorgeous chestnut-and-white pinto of some kind, with blue eyes and a touch of red to her mane, and she leaned into the caring touch of the Spanish ranch hands.

"Is she getting ready?" I asked in a low tone as I joined Amos outside the stall door.

"Seems like it," the black man said. "I don't like the timing much."

"Well, it's just more good news, ain't it?" I said with a grin.

Amos' head whipped toward me, and my smile widened.

"Seems Helena's come to a decision," I told him and the others. "She's keeping the ranch."

The celebration that broke out among the ranch hands was a strained and silent one. Well, eventually. At first, Amos whooped and moved to throw his hat, but a rapid-fire scolding from Abel and Mateo caused him to rein it in a bit.

I snickered at the pair of men, who murmured extra soft to their charge to make up for it.

Amos did a much quieter jig instead, and Russel joined in from his spot in the other birthing stall. The pair even danced in a circle at the same time, and when they were done, they pumped their fists into the air.

"That's right," Amos laughed. "Get that kick extra high, we're celebrating. Gotta make sure the dust gets all the way up to your hat."

Russel bit his tongue and doubled down, and Amos and I gave him some applause when he managed a real clean heel-click.

"You hear that, Dulce?" Mateo sighed with his cheek

against the mare's belly. "You are bringing us very good luck here today. All of this is because of you."

"Not quite," Amos snorted.

"Shhhh," Mateo whispered softly, but his eyes shot daggers at the black man.

I worked extra hard to keep the amusement off my face, but it was a quick loss. Something about the tender attention the Spaniards paid to the mares during this time just brought a chuckle out of me, especially the way Mateo doted on them with sweet words and compliments all the while.

"Is that the secret to the Sandusky stock, then?" I muttered and nudged Amos.

He grinned. "Sure is. I'm more of a 'let 'em out to walk and check on 'em later,' kinda fella, but Frank always let these two have their way, so…"

"Because he understood that happy women bring us their very best, no?" Mateo crooned in Sweet One's ear. "Yes, you need your brothers here at your side, and we will not abandon you for anything. Tell us what you need, and you will have it."

Amos and I exchanged broad smiles, but then the broodmare nickered, and there was pain in the sound.

"She will not hold off much longer," Mateo said with a glance at Amos.

The black man nodded. "We'll do all we can for her. Here's praying we pass another quiet night out here."

Abel said something in Spanish, but Amos shook his head in disagreement.

"I don't want to risk it," he said. "That foal the mountain lion got a couple weeks back was enough of a loss. If trouble does come, and them horses in the pasture startle, I don't want no babies caught up in the mess."

"It would be best to keep as many as we can out of the fields," I agreed. "The fewer horses they can reach, the better."

"We got the locks set on the doors this morning, so as

long as there ain't no fires, they should be safe in here," Amos said. "Although I would appreciate it if we could draw any gunfire as far from here as we can if it comes to that. Bonita over there always gives us some stock that fetches a top price. I don't want anything happening to her. We bred her with our best Morgan, too, so that foal will be some very fine work indeed."

"All of our best girls must stay safe," Mateo clarified with a look at the other unoccupied stalls.

They'd be full again by this evening, but I'd accounted for all of this in my planning.

"They'll be alright," I assured him. "I considered the stables when I assigned the men their posts. They know where I want everyone's attention should trouble show up."

"What about my Birdy?" Honey asked with an anxious look.

"Oh, Birdy's very good with this sort of thing," I told her. "She knows better than anyone out there how to keep safe."

Honey's bottom lip quivered. "But I promised."

Amos immediately corrected the issue.

"Birdy's got a stall in here, don't you worry, Honey," he said. "Ain't that right, Abel?"

The Spanish man smiled and nodded.

"Yes, we just haven't found time to line it with silk yet," Mateo put in. "But she will have the very best stall, of course."

"Okay!" Honey said and bounced a bit with excitement.

"We'll keep you safe here, too, Dulce," Mateo crooned. "No bad men will hurt your stables tonight. You can count on Mateo."

Bonita let out a long, impertinent whinny from her own birthing stall, and the young ranch hand peeked his head over the wall to smile at her.

"Sí, mi cariño, I will protect you, too," he chuckled. "Forever, I will lay down my life for you. But Dulce needs me now, or I would be at your side."

Russel snorted and rolled his eyes at the flirtatious Spaniard, and Honey giggled into her hands.

"No laughing," Mateo scolded the pair. "Bonita is very sensitive at this time. She needs to hear how beautiful she is, no?"

"She needs to hurry up and get that baby out of her," Amos sighed. "Should've dropped days ago."

"She is making sure all is perfect first," Mateo said. "Do not rush mi cariño."

"Your cariño's been biting me every time I so much as look at her," Amos snorted.

"Because you do not understand women," the young ranch hand informed him. "Go. Leave us to our work. You are making Dulce unhappy."

Amos silently raised his brow before bumping me with his elbow and gesturing toward the door.

We left them to it and returned to the lane.

"Did Mrs. Helena mention any other buyers she wanted to meet with?" he asked as soon as we were alone.

"Lucy put the idea forward, but Helena's set on staying," I said. "The circumstances of the sale lit a fire under her, I'd say."

I explained the disturbing discovery of how Mr. Wickett came to hear about the ranch from George Sellick's own mouth, and Amos looked as furious as Lucy and Helena had been.

He let out a few of the most colorful curses I'd heard as of late, but then he shook his head.

"The cruelty of folks sure wears on the mind after a while," he sighed. "I've known plenty of it, but not so much out here. Ever since I met Frank and got my standing here, folks always have a good word for me. Hard to imagine someone up and deciding the Sanduskys should suffer like this."

"A grudge is a tricky thing," I said. "Takes a man of strong spirit to shake it, but in my experience, it spurs even the weakest man toward the meanest streak with ease."

"That is true," he agreed as he eyed the distant ridges of the pastures. "But I couldn't forgive myself if something happened to the family. Frank never should have died like that, but Helena and the family?"

He shook his head, and I felt at once how heavy a weight he was carrying on his shoulders.

"They've always treated me like I was their own family," he said. "I couldn't live with myself if I let anything happen to them."

"Neither could I," I admitted. "So we won't. No matter what Sellick sends our way, those kids and those two women will come out of it alive. That's a vow I'm willing to make."

Amos turned to face me, and he held out a hand to shake on it. I returned the gesture, and the pair of us came to a silent pact then and there.

Both of us were prepared to make any sacrifice needed to see this one through.

Here was hoping we made it to the other side.

The rest of the day was filled with preparations, some shooting practice, and checking the fence lines over and over. Nothing could be done about the open stretch to the northwest of the house except to set our sharpest eyes over there, but we also let the draft horses out to graze in the large pasture that stretched north for a ways on that side.

Amos agreed to leave them there all night from now on.

They had the heaviest hoof falls and the loudest bays, so if anything was amiss far out beyond the house, we'd hear them stirring ahead of time.

I ended up borrowing a bandolier off one of Delgado's men, and I packed fifty rounds of .44s for my Winchester into the slots. Then I readied all three of my Remingtons, pulled out my old cross-chest double-holster and fitted her up, and made sure my Schofield and LeMat were both ready to go on my hip holsters. The third Remington would be holstered to my thigh, which I rarely relied on, but since I'd be mounted during my watch tonight, I didn't mind.

The whole time I worked to prepare my weapons, a calm, warm breeze rustled its way through the quiet bunkhouse, and if it weren't for the anticipation building inside me, I'd have said it was one of the finest days we could ask for.

Normally, I took great joy in the beauty of the ranchlands, but a knot at the back of my mind refused to ease into the calm of the day. Even the cheerful breeze and the sunny cactus flowers unsettled my mind.

Delgado's men were in the same predicament.

The men tended to tasks with the focus and rhythm of skilled ranch workers, but all the while, their eyes scanned the surrounding hills like trained soldiers. Not one man passed the house or the stables without glancing at the shadows near the walls, and they each kept at least one firearm within reach at all times.

It was a restless sort of calm before the storm.

By sunset, Sweet One had birthed a healthy filly. The women and children came over to join in admiring the newest addition to the Sandusky herd, and they swooned over the little foal almost as much as Mateo.

The family laughed with the ranch hands over the different names they could choose, and in the end, they settled on Sweet Chile, due to her stark red mane.

Abel wouldn't allow us to linger for too long. According to him, the broodmare needed her space now, and he shooed every last one of us out with the air of a grouchy old lady.

Meanwhile, the sky had gone a bloody red.

The clouds seemed to drip across the mountains in all their fiery hues, and I stopped to admire the view with Helena and Lucy on either side of me, and Honey and Russel just ahead.

The world seemed aglow with all the colors known to

man, and the spectacular display cast the lands of the Black Spur in their best light. The horses that would stay out tonight pranced in the fields, playing some sort of nip-and-run game, and smoke rose from the fire near the bunkhouse, where Delgado's men had begun cooking up their supper.

The smoke lingered over the pastures, and it called to mind the haze we'd been in after the stables had gone up in flames.

"What's that they say about red skies?" Lucy asked uneasily.

"That's for sailors," Helena replied.

"All the same…" The singer shuddered and wrapped her arms around herself. "I think I'll head in."

"I'll stay out with Mr. Callahan and the boys," Russel decided.

"You most certainly will not," his mother said.

"But trouble's afoot, Mama! A man's got to have his wits about him and not be caught up with bedtime and nonsense when murderers are a comin'."

"Where in the world did you hear that?" Lucy giggled.

"From my own mind," Russel said proudly.

"No, Jesse gets the bad men for us," Honey told her brother.

"That's right," Helena agreed.

"Yeah, but I'll get them, too," the boy said.

Lucy smirked. "How you gonna shoot anyone when you're busy washing behind your ears?"

Russel lunged and tried to pull one of Lucy's auburn ringlets, but the woman was faster than that. She carried on teasing the boy all the way up to the house, and I watched the little family go. Honey skipped along with her hand clinging to her mother's, and Russel let his lanky limbs swing without a care while he and Lucy chided one another. Their voices faded as they mounted the steps and went inside, but Lucy paused and looked back at me from the open door.

There was no merriment or playfulness on her pretty face now. I'd seldom seen her so serious since we came to an understanding between us, but her green eyes were wide with worry tonight, and her painted lips parted ever so slightly as she drew a deep breath.

She seemed so small standing there, and despite her lavish hair and perfectly-tailored ensemble, she looked like no more than a girl staring out at the wild world from the safety of her family home.

Warmth spread through my chest as I felt how much she was relying on me. The only reason she could carry on laughing and keeping the children in good spirits was because I'd taken up the work of defending them.

All of them.

I nodded to her, and the woman returned the gesture before finally closing the door.

I remained in the lane for a few minutes longer. My eyes trailed over the house and garden, and beyond them to the corral, the barn, and the trees. I eyed the little spot where Russel and his father used to shoot into the woods that sprawled north from the back of the barn, and then I let my gaze drift to the wooden cross off to the right.

About thirty yards away, in the open land between the distant bunkhouse and the edge of the north woods, was where Frank Sandusky had been laid to rest.

Abel had carved a cross about four feet high and burned a nice pattern down the edges and around the epitaph. In the center, it read:

Frank M. Sandusky
Born 1845 — Died 1880
Good man. Loving husband & father.

It was simple, but it was all that mattered in the end.

They'd secured the cross at the head of Frank's grave, and from where I stood, in the glowing red of the sunset, it looked like the horseman had the best spot on the property. From there, a person could admire the fruits of his labor in all directions for years to come, and truly understand how much a man could build for himself and his family from nothing but hills and horses.

I drew a steadying breath as I gave the surrounding hills another once-over.

Not a soul was in sight, but darkness would be coming on fast.

Delgado's men were nearly ready when I joined them. They'd left enough food for me and the ranch hands, and they'd begun laying out their guns for the night. Some had double-barrel shotguns, or lever-action repeaters, and one man even had a set of mean-looking throwing knives, along with a foreign repeater rifle that Delgado must have acquired for him.

Amos was among the shooters, and just like me, he didn't look ready to turn in for the night.

He got his two Peacemakers and his Henry rifle loaded, and he checked his saddlebag three times to be sure he had plenty of extra ammunition. Then he practiced his draw over and over while darkness settled, and I gathered with the first watch.

"You gonna drag those two out here soon?" I asked Amos as I jutted my chin toward the stables. "They need to be rested up."

"I'll get 'em now," he assured me. "They're just fussing over those mares."

I nodded, hitched my boot in the stirrup, and got up in the saddle. Then I led my four shooters out toward the lane, and we were just about to break apart and head to our posts when lantern light appeared beneath the distant gate.

Two riders were galloping toward us like bats outta Hell, and I immediately recognized the Painted horses from Brimbley's homestead.

CHAPTER 25

"Amos!" I hollered over my shoulder. "The neighbors from the south!"

The black man came running as the four other patrols gathered closer on their horses.

The Brimbley boys reined their mounts in as they met us, and their faces looked young and stunned in the swinging lantern light. They couldn't have been more than seventeen years old, but their father hadn't undersold them.

They'd ridden like lightning to get up here.

"Riders," one of the brothers panted. "Squatters. Torches."

"What you tryna say, boy?" Amos asked.

"We saw smoke to the southeast of us," the other brother said in a steadier tone. "It was just after sundown. We rode that way, and there was a band of men camping near the edge of our land."

"They were starting to pack up," the other boy put in. "Lots of guns, and they were drinkin' and cursin'... Lighting torches."

"How many?" I asked.

"I counted thirty," the second brother said.

Amos looked my way. "They got us by quite a few."

"That's alright," I replied. "We've just been given the upper hand. Boys, how far off do you think they are from where we stand?"

"A few miles," one of them answered. "No more."

I nodded. "Thank you for your help. Now, get on home, and stay armed just in case. Tell your daddy the Black Spur owes your family for this."

"Yes, sir!" The two boys beamed in unison.

Then they turned their Paints, spurred them on, and took off like a shot down the dark lane.

I turned to the others. "Get the rest of your men from the bunkhouse. Amos, send Mateo and Abel out here and then get on up to the house and warn Helena. The family can stay put for now, but make sure she knows we've got an army of thirty coming our way."

Amos took off without a word, and two of Delgado's men rode for the bunkhouse to bring the rest of their comrades out.

"That's a lot of riders," one of the two who remained beside me muttered. He was a clean-shaven man named Hugh, and he held himself like a General despite being only twenty-three years old. "Sounds like this Sellick aims to wipe the place out."

"Sure does," I gritted out. "If he's brought that many, he's gonna aim for that stable and the house the most. He'll want them leveled and hope to kill everyone inside. We've gotta keep them as far from both as we can, without letting anyone make for that bunkhouse, either."

"Sure you don't want us to ride south and head them off before they can reach us?" Hugh asked.

I shook my head. "If we stay here, the ranch is safest. We leave no chance of missing them. Out there, they could take any track, pass us, surround us, anything. And we're in unknown land and outnumbered down there. As much as I'd like to spring an attack on them, there's just too many things that could go wrong."

"He's right," the other man grunted.

"We'll stay, and we'll use this time to make sure we have every advantage possible," I decided.

A couple minutes later, I stood in the light of the large oil lantern outside the stable door. The ranch hands and all of Delgado's men surrounded me, along with Helena and Russel.

"With thirty men coming, I suspect George Sellick himself is among them," I said. "Along with the other three killers: Tommy and Bill Masters, and Boone Slim. Not one of those four men will be leaving this property alive tonight, so keep a sharp eye out for anyone trying to flee."

"Any ideas what they look like?" Hugh asked.

"I have a hunch I've seen Sellick," I replied. "Big man, bit of a gut. He looked real blistered and red when I saw him, and drunk. He's a bleary-eyed sort, with a bulbous nose. The others I've only got some description on. The three missing killers all had longer beards, two with long black hair, one with no hair at all. The one with no hair is missing most of his teeth. One of the black-haired guys also has a triangular scar on one cheek."

"I wonder where he dug up the other men he's bringing," Mateo muttered.

"That distillery, most likely," I said. "The men he hired to kill Mr. Sandusky all worked there with him, so I reckon he has a strong enough standing among them. Whether any of them can shoot worth a damn, I couldn't say."

The men around me grumbled among themselves about this. Then Helena spoke up.

"You said the Brimbley boys mentioned torches," she put in. "You think he's fixing to start more fires?"

"Could be," I allowed. "They certainly could keep coming straight up from the south, torches blazing, and make to raid us from the lane, too. Light everything they can as they go…

But if they suspect or know we've got the place covered, then they won't put themselves in such an easy spot as that."

"Shoot, they come riding up the lane all loud like that, I'm just gonna prop my gun on a post and 'bap!' 'bap!'" Russel mimed shooting his Peacemaker. "Just pick 'em off one by one as they go by. Easy."

"Precisely," I snorted. "And Sellick was a soldier, so I don't think he'd make a choice like that."

"They'll probably come from the north, then," Amos said.

I nodded. "We've got the draft horses to the northwest of us, and we'll still hope that gives us some warning if they ride in the way they did last time. The longer it takes them, the more likely it is they're heading that way. For now, though, I want two riders in both of the front pastures with eyes to the south, just in case."

"Yes, sir," a few men agreed.

"You'll be our first line of defense on that side, so shoot 'em hard and fast where it really hurts," I said. "Buy us as much time as you can. But if the shooting starts to the north, bring us relief quick as you can."

"The gates that let out into the lane are closed, but not locked," Amos told them, and they nodded their thanks.

"Now, we know we're outnumbered, so our best chance is using every structure we can for our own cover," I continued. "Keep these outlaws from using them for cover instead."

"With four in the front pasture, you've still got ten of us," Amos said. "Put us where you want us."

"Eleven of us," Russel cut in with a stubborn glower. "I'm shootin', too."

"You're guarding your family," I told him. "You and your mother are in charge of protecting everyone in the bunkhouse. And while you're there, do everything you can not to draw any attention."

"Yeah, fine," Russel grumbled, but Helena gave me a diligent nod.

"No one will know we're there," she promised.

"You'll have one of Delgado's men not far away," I told her before turning back to the others. "The stable has become a bigger priority with so many raiders on their way. I want four men to take each outer corner. Abel, you're one of them, keep to the back. I trust you to make the right decision for the horses in there."

Abel nodded firmly.

I knew keeping him close to lantern light would give him the best advantage with his eyesight, but I also trusted him to make the right call if there was nothing to be done and we needed to release the broodmares and their foals out into the pasture out back.

I hoped it wouldn't come to that. These incoming men aimed to destroy this ranch, and their last attempt already proved that included the herd. If all went to plan, our own shooters wouldn't give them the chance to get that far, but I wouldn't take any risks.

Sellick was a seasoned army man, and while I didn't know his rank, I did know he was out for blood and vengeance.

There was no telling what he'd try in order to see his means accomplished.

"Let's also have two men staked at opposite ends of the house," I continued, "and one man up in the loft of the barn. Keep your muzzle aimed out that top window and toward the northwest until we know what we're dealing with, but mind your aim. I'll take my regular post along that northwest fence, and Bert will keep his spot on the far corner, too. Us and those draft horses will be our first line if they come from the north."

The men all nodded in understanding, and it was decided that Hugh would take the spot in the hayloft, since he was our best long-range shooter. Amos wanted to guard the bunkhouse, but Helena insisted he was too good a shot to sit all the way out there. Instead, we sent one of the younger men from Delgado's group, who was a much sharper shot than Mateo and was used to working long nights in the dark.

Mateo would be one of the men near the house so he'd have a clear view all around and be able to steady his aim with a little more warning over there. Amos would be in the southern pasture on horseback.

Once everything was decided, Amos and the boy who'd be guarding the bunkhouse started getting the family settled out there for the night. Then the rest of us broke apart and prepared ourselves for the long wait.

I started at my place near the corral behind the barn. From here I could see the woods that started to my right and sprawled to the northeast, but I could also watch over the northwest, where the Sanduskys' open ranchlands rose and fell beneath the moonless sky.

The woods turned craggy and jagged not far into them, and they were where most of our wolves prowled out of. They sprawled all the way up into the mountains, but they were also difficult terrain to manage in the saddle, let alone on foot in the middle of the night.

We had very little to concern ourselves with from that side.

I turned my mount west, and we began scouting along the wooden fence. When I came to the furthest corner, I waited with Bert there for a moment, but all seemed calm over in the draft horses' pasture.

They were in the larger, barbed wire pass to the west of us, the one that stretched north for a ways as well.

I could just barely make out the solid wall of thick, muscled draft horses lolling in the field. There were seventeen in all, and the biggest among them stood twenty hands high at the withers. They must've weighed at least thirteen hundred pounds apiece, and the slightest upset among them would give us warning that something was amiss on their end of the property.

For now, they grazed in peace, with their massive hoofs crushing whole shrubs with ease.

I turned back the way I'd come, and hours passed like that. The night grew cold, and the moon refused to rise. The men rested in the dirt and against walls where they could, and those who rode traded spots to give their backends a break from the saddle.

A couple disturbances came along in the first few hours. One was a pack of wolves who must've followed the smell of the new birth. They lit out of there as soon as they caught on that there was no getting near the scent. Then a mountain lion prowled down from the peaks and straight through the draft horses' pasture, but it didn't stop. It slunk by and carried on heading south, and the horses only spared it a few whinnies.

My eyes darted toward the south every few passes along the fence, but no torchlight shone in the distance. No pounding hooves approached, and around about two in the morning, I decided Sellick and his men must be making their way north in order to circle in from the gap ahead of me.

Still, we kept two men down in the front pastures, while the other two got on foot and took up posts in the barn instead.

Then another two hours passed, and a sliver of moon chose to rise at last.

I'd gotten down and stretched my legs several times by now, but never for too long. My eyes burned with the need to sleep, but my mind wasn't groggy. I was currently halfway to Bert, and I was just figuring I'd take another break once I reached him, but then a sharp snort sounded from the dark.

The noise came from up ahead of me, but not quite where Bert had been all evening.

I reined the dappled stallion in and strained my ear. No other sounds came for just about a full minute, so I nudged him onward.

A few paces later, a whinny sounded far out in the field.

"Bert," I hissed. "Bert!"

The man didn't answer.

I turned Flint around and trotted back toward the barn. As soon as I could make out the barrel of Hugh's rifle up in the loft, I waved my arm and signaled toward the northwest.

Hugh stuck his arm out the window, and I trusted him to spread the word from there.

I needed to go see where Bert had gone off to.

The sliver of moonlight did next to nothing for me out here, and my palms prickled with sweat despite the chill in the air as I trotted along the fenceline. I had my Schofield in my right hand, and I squinted out at the pitch-black landscape all around. Then I slowed my mount as I neared the corner of the first pasture.

I could almost make out the shape of Bert's horse, and the man was up in the saddle. He had his back to me, with his eyes cast out toward the draft horses' pasture.

"Bert," I hissed again as I came to his side. "You hear something, too?"

"I do." He nodded but didn't pull his eyes from the darkness ahead of us. "Not sure yet... I could've sworn..."

"Could've sworn what?" I asked and cocked the hammer on my pistol.

Bert kept staring straight ahead with his lips parted as he tried his best to make anything out in the heavy darkness. Then he shook his head a bit.

"The horses headed thataway," he whispered at last and pointed toward the ridges beyond us. "They been making their way over there real slow for about an hour, but then I thought I heard a jangling... like a spur or..."

He trailed off as the strange sound came again.

It was less of a jangle to my ears, and more of a twang.

Then the sudden baying of angry horses split the silence, and my heart rate kicked up the moment I placed the odd sound.

"Barbed wire," I breathed. "That's the sound of cuttin' wires... They're gonna drive the horses straight--"

The crack of at least five pistols broke through the whinnies.

Seconds later, the mass of draft horses came galloping straight out of the darkness, and with a line of riders shooting behind them, they showed no sign of stopping.

"Son of a bitch!" Bert growled and wrenched his mount around.

I was right there with him.

"Get back to the lane!" I ordered. "Drive them south or they'll crush half our men!"

We were hopefully still hidden from the view of the incoming raiders, but it wouldn't matter much in a moment.

Because the draft horses crashed straight through the first line of wooden fencing, which meant we'd have a full stampede running straight through our defenses any second now.

CHAPTER 26

Bert and I were the only two men on horses this side of the property. Amos and the other rider we had to the south would no doubt already be hauling to our aid, but we needed the draft horses to veer south and hopefully scatter down the lane.

Otherwise, they'd end up blasting their way through the barnyard, the house, everywhere we had shooters stationed.

Then there were the raiders to contend with.

At least, the ones we were able to see.

I counted only fifteen men riding in behind the draft horses, and they whooped, yelled, and cackled as they shot round after round toward the stampede. I had half a mind to rein in Flint and gun down as many as I could from here, but that'd pretty much seal my fate for the night.

The moment the raiders knew me and Bert were running along with them, they'd only have to overwhelm us with gunfire, and that'd be that.

Chancing a shot now would also betray my location to the missing raiders-- the fifteen other men we knew must be coming, but were nowhere to be found thus far.

No, the patrol needed us alive if we were going to do anything about the thousand-pound beasts coming their way.

As of right now, they couldn't do a darn thing to help us, other than Hugh.

The sharpshooter had already cracked off two shots, and one had struck the chest of an incoming raider while the second caught enough of another to make him howl in pain.

"Head the horses off at the corner and start firing!" I told Bert as we galloped toward the corral. "Scare them toward the south and try and push as many as you can away from the house and the barn."

"Yes, sir," Bert growled as we neared the corner.

"Soon as we get them out of there, our men can open fire more easily," I said as I chanced a glance toward the raiders.

We were running almost in line with them, but I couldn't make out their features.

A few flashes of gunfire showed me their sneers here and there, and I thought I saw the ugly mug of the blistered man from the distillery among them, but I couldn't be sure.

That meant George Sellick himself might be over there, possibly with the final three killers, but there was no time to be sure.

The draft horses finally crashed through the last line of fencing, and chaos erupted in the night.

Bert and I opened fire into the dirt as we wrenched our mounts around the fence corner. The five closest draft horses reared up and crashed into one another, but when they saw me and Bert driving our mounts headlong toward them with guns flashing, they made to flee toward the lane.

Meanwhile, the shooters behind the stampede sprawled out the moment they'd forced the herd free, and half of them made straight for the stables while the other half barreled toward the house.

They continued to cackle and shoot wildly as they rode all over the lane and yard, but my patrol had been warned they were coming.

Our men at the stables opened fire on the incoming

attackers, and two men in the barn were firing where they could while horses barreled past the open doors. The pigs inside squealed in protest, but I could hardly hear them over the thundering of enormous hooves.

"Go on, get!" I roared as Bert and I kept pushing the startled herd south, but there was too much chaos now.

Another couple of draft horses joined the group we'd managed to redirect, but then a rogue mare that must've stood eighteen hands high reared up and kicked Bert's mount square in the shoulder.

Bert yelled as he was thrown to the dirt, and about one second later, I came to understand where Flint got his name.

I'd never been so mad at a horse in my life.

Bert's horse slammed into my own, and Flint bucked himself sky-high.

For a few moments, I was soaring above a churning of horses and sparking barrels. Then I came flailing back down toward the dirt.

I landed with a crunch of my knee and a blast from my Schofield, but luckily the bullet plunged itself into the ground. I wheezed a bit as I scrambled to my feet and took in my surroundings.

Flint was gone, along with my Winchester, and there were still too many draft horses loose. They galloped between the structures and smashed into fence posts, walls, and other horses as they went, and the flash of muzzles surrounded them on all sides.

Our men had officially opened fire from every post.

Three bodies were already on the ground ahead of me. Judging by their ratty overalls, they belonged to Sellick's group, but I still couldn't see where the last of his men were.

I jumped backward just as another draft horse catapulted past me, and then I whipped around to find Bert.

He was groaning in the dirt about ten feet away.

"Bert!" I hollered and skidded to my knees at his side. "Bert, get up!"

The man nodded and leaned hard on me as I worked to get him on his feet, and my eyes darted around the dim ground for his gun. Finally, I saw it only a couple feet ahead of us.

"There!" I said. "Get your gun and get to the barn! I'll—"

My words were silenced by the cackle of an incoming rider and the deafening blast of a shotgun behind us.

Warmth splattered the side of my face and neck as Bert went limp in my hold, and I dropped straight to the ground with him.

The second shotgun blast whooshed over me.

I rolled to the side as the incoming hooves almost trampled me, and I caught sight of a bald, bearded raider's toothless smile. He'd already swapped his shotgun for a revolver, and the barrel was leveled down at me.

No sooner had I clocked him as one of Frank's murderers, than I pulled the trigger on my Schofield.

The bullet tore straight through his open, cackling mouth and out the back of his bald head.

I didn't bother waiting around to watch him fall from his mount. I rolled again and grabbed for Bert, but I could already feel he was gone. His head had been blasted open from behind before we'd even reached his gun.

I cursed as I wiped his blood from the side of my face. Then I closed his eyes, grabbed his gun, and took off for the house. I'd shot Bert's full cylinder by the time I made it to the far corner and took cover around the side, and I still knew I had Hugh to thank for most of that.

He'd picked off another of Sellick's men who'd noticed me and tried twice to take me out, but now Hugh was working on helping the men at the stables from his spot in the barn loft.

It looked like several raiders were attempting to shoot up the new structure, and three had gotten torches lit, but our own men had pushed them back a ways. This meant they'd been forced to leave the cover of the stables a bit, but Amos and my final shooter from the southern pastures finally fought their way through the herd to help them out.

They were all locked in a game of cat and mouse now, while the raiders toyed with the guards from the shadows, and the guards attempted to draw the fire-wielders away from the stables.

Amos looked like Wrath itself as he and his mustang galloped headlong toward a man with a lit torch. The black man had his shooting arm extended straight ahead, and he sent a bullet through the heart of the firestarter with ease. Then he circled back, trampled the fallen torch, and shot another raider down in a matter of seconds.

I grinned a little at the ranch hand's natural talent, but then I saw a raider in his blind spot and put him down fast. He crashed to the ground just as the rider nearest to him whipped his mount around and shot blindly in my direction.

In the dim lantern light from the stables, I saw the same blistered, ugly mug I remembered from the distillery.

I moved to fire again, but he was already turned and galloping into the shadows beyond the stables.

I checked the cylinder on my Schofield and found two rounds remaining. Between the two Remingtons strapped to my ribs, the one on my thigh, and the Lemat on my hip, I had twenty-seven more rounds, even without my Winchester or saddlebag on me. Plus my one shotgun blast in the LeMat.

I tried real quick to locate Flint, but he was lost among the enormous draft horses and the cover of night.

That was alright. I'd done more with less.

What I really needed was to settle this down fast.

The raiders had clearly stumbled across the draft horses and decided to use them to their advantage, but at least they'd done their job and given us enough warning.

Now, they were risking our lives.

I eyed the shadowy woods as I realized that might be our best chance at clearing them out of here if they wouldn't be forced toward the lane. If we could drive them toward the cover of the woods, they'd hopefully keep on running to safety and leave us to finish the raiders off. Their hooves were certainly big enough to manage the difficult terrain.

That would also give me time to hunt down Sellick and be sure the final two murderers were wiped out.

I fired off a shot at a passing raider, and as he gurgled and plunged toward the ground, I crouched and ran along the side of the house.

The first of my men I met with was Mateo.

He was hunkered down near the garden with wide, scared eyes, and his Winchester was clutched in his hand.

"We've gotta get these horses into the woods," I told him.

"Russel is gone," he replied.

I stared at his bulging eyes as the words slowly sank in.

"What?" I managed.

"The man you sent to the bunkhouse," Mateo said and fired at a passing raider. He missed, but not by much. "He came running over just before the horses reached us. Russel is missing. Helena is terrified."

I clenched my jaw so hard, my hearing twinged out.

"I'll find him," I growled. "For now, we need those horses out of here."

"Sí, sí, but how?" he yelled. "They will trample us all soon!"

"We just need–"

A resounding crack brought both our heads turning toward the barn just in time to see a draft stallion slam into the corner of the structure.

He took out a good chunk of wall and the corner beam with ease, but the pain of the collision seemed to send him on a rampage. Even as the barn groaned, he kept on barreling straight through it and out the open door on the other side, but the damage had been done.

The upper loft collapsed toward the corner, and I saw Hugh jump from the window with his rifle in hand just in time.

I took out a fleeing raider behind him as two more of our shooters bolted from the cover of the barn. A few squealing pigs took off after them, and the groan of splintering wood sent dust billowing into the sky.

"Dios mío," Mateo breathed.

The barn was mostly standing. A quarter of it had folded down on itself, but the backside was still holding, and none of our men had been harmed.

"Get them into the woods!" I told Mateo, and I wrenched my bandolier over my head and thrust it into his arms. "There's fifty extra rounds. Holler if you see Russel."

Then I holstered my spent Schofield, tore a Remmington from beside my ribs, and ran at a crouch toward the back of the house.

I hollered for the man back there to turn his attention to the horses as well. Between the three of us, we managed to push two more draft horses toward the trees with just a few well-placed shots, and the men who'd fled from the barn caught on to our plan.

They joined and sent another enormous beast headed that way, but that's when I saw the flash of a muzzle in the trees.

I did a double take as I thought the continuous gunfire around me must have confused my vision. But with a little squinting, I saw someone scrambling along the ground. He grabbed the rifle he must've dropped when the draft horses came toward him.

For a brief second, I thought it was Russel, but the boy was much lankier than that.

No, that had been a grown man with a beard in those trees.

What was he doing there?

My heart just about dropped right through me as I saw a second man duck back behind a trunk.

"They came in from both sides," I realized.

This second troop must have finally gotten into position when we started pushing horses their way.

I sent a silent, grateful prayer up that we'd happened to decide on sending them that way, as stupid as the decision was in that terrain, or else we'd have been completely blindsided.

Without another thought, I checked the final four rounds in my Remington and leveled the barrel toward the trees.

"They're in the woods!" I hollered to the men closest to me. "The other raiders came in from the woods! Open fire!"

Everything was gun smoke, bullets, and screams after that.

Our shooters turned their sights to the darkened woods, and the men therein returned fire. Wood blasted free from the barn, the corral fence, and even the trees themselves. Then a couple flashes of genuine fire started up, but the men attempting to light torches were quickly gunned down.

I rushed to the side of the house to take better cover, but the fifteen hidden men were relentless. They were spreading out every chance they got, and some seemed to have snuck around our sides already.

They rained bullets on us without pause, and one of Delgado's men let out a scream of pain to my left.

I managed to get over to him in time to give him cover fire, and I glanced over my shoulder real quick to see a chunk of flesh hanging loose from his thigh. He hadn't collapsed, though. He seethed through clenched teeth for a moment or two as he reloaded his rifle. Then he jacked the lever, sent me a nod, and kept on shooting.

Once I was sure he'd be able to handle himself, I ducked down, bolted back toward the front of the house, and took out a rogue raider who'd hidden in the dark pasture across the lane.

How he'd managed to get in there, I wasn't sure, but this was bad.

There was no way he'd gotten all the way over there from

the woods. Which meant we'd lost track of at least one of the initial raiders.

Not to mention, Russel Sandusky.

"One thing at a time," I told myself as I scanned my surroundings.

Most of the raiders' horses were running around without their riders by now, so more could've hidden themselves as well.

My mind immediately went to the bunkhouse that lurked in the shadows far beyond the fight, but not a single spark of gunfire flashed in that direction.

A quick look around showed me that three of the men guarding the stables had been drawn away by the arrival of the fifteen raiders. I didn't see Abel anywhere, but it looked as though he hadn't needed to release the horses from inside.

I was relieved at first, but we needed more defenses over there.

No sooner had the thought come to mind than a man ran from the darkness between the house and the stables.

The flickering of flames had already started up in his hands somehow, but he'd thrown whatever he held before I could blink.

Then I registered the bottle of sloshing liquid, the rag stuffed down the neck, and the flames burning at the top.

CHAPTER 27

The raw, killing calm of battle settled over me as I raised my revolver and tracked the arc of the liquor bottle through the air.

I had one shot remaining in my Remington, and I pulled the trigger before the bottle could reach the stables.

An explosion of fire burst in midair as my bullet struck true. Flames rained down into the lane, along with whatever liquor had been in there, and more fires caught wherever it splattered down. Luckily, it was all rocks and dirt below, nothing that would truly catch, but I had bigger things to worry about.

The man who'd thrown the flaming bottle whipped around and shot without pause.

In the flickering fire, I registered his blistered, drunken, cold-blooded face just as pain lanced through my hip.

His second bullet missed me by inches as I threw myself behind the cover of the house again, but the blistered man was my primary target now.

I knew the crack of a Colt .44 anywhere.

He was a Union man, and with honed reflexes and killer aim.

George Sellick himself was a matter of yards away from me, and he wasn't alone.

Some other raider had been hissing at him from the dark before he threw the bottle, and the pair of them argued back and forth now as I swapped my spent Remington out for my second.

The pain in my hip was teetering in and out of my notice, and I chose to let my war mind take over and drown out any last hint of it. Then I gritted my teeth and forced myself back up on my feet.

I'd only been down maybe ten seconds, but Sellick had hidden himself well in the meantime.

I fired on two raiders I spotted beyond the garden. Then a rifle cracked from near the shadows of the stables, and Sellick cried out.

Abel's face appeared just long enough for him to adjust his aim, and he pulled the trigger again, but Sellick and his buddy returned fire instantly.

A chunk of timber blasted off the corner of the stables, but at least Abel had ducked back to safety in time.

He'd also enraged the bluebelly. Even with horses still darting around relentlessly, Sellick fired his last three rounds toward Abel in quick succession.

The third struck the large oil lantern above the breezeway door.

I pivoted out of my hiding spot and fired on Sellick just as flames erupted above the entrance.

The Union man's left arm was already drenched with blood thanks to Abel, and he kept it cradled tight against him, but my bullet still found his elbow.

Spit flew from his mouth as he screamed in pain and crashed into the shadowy garden for cover. His companion's rifle flashed a second later, and I lunged aside right as a draft horse cut between us. The horse barely scraped by without a bullet, but there was no time for me to return fire after that.

The two men had vanished by the time the horse galloped off.

Meanwhile, the flames had caught on the stable doors.

They lapped their orange tongues across the wood like ravenous wolves, and the pealing cries of the broodmares echoed from inside. It struck me hard that I could recognize Birdy's call among them, and fury washed through me.

Shouts rose up from Delgado's men as several of them bolted for the structure. I barely registered the pain in my hip as I took off with them.

Every step felt too slow while the fire spread in waves over the large doors, and no sooner had I reached the stables than a bucket was shoved into my hands.

Abel had already gotten the pump going, and three other men were grabbing buckets.

"Another over here!" a man yelled, and I threw my bucketful on the door ahead of him.

Two more quickly followed from behind my shoulder, and smoke hissed over us as we doused the area completely. I blindly grabbed for another bucket and made sure nothing else would catch there before I moved to grab another, but then Mateo caught my elbow.

"Go, we have it!" he yelled.

I looked around to see the men did indeed seem to have the fire under control already, and even Birdy had settled inside.

That meant I could get back to Sellick.

My hip was throbbing in earnest as I stumbled out of the smoke and squinted through the darkness.

The gunfire between the house and the woods had lessened, but it was still going on and on with no sign of stopping. Most of the loose horses had corralled themselves to the outskirts of the mayhem, and no other fires had started up.

The barn still looked ready to cave in on one side, but

more importantly, two men were crouched and sprinting toward it from the shadows of the garden.

"Sellick," I growled and forced my legs into a run.

I crested the hill just in time for Sellick's companion to catch sight of me over his shoulder. He whipped around and fired his rifle, and the dirt to my right blasted apart as I returned the shot. My own bullet struck the barn directly above the bearded raider's head, and George tore the rifle from the man's hands to fire on me himself.

His drunken shots struck the garden fence, the edge of the house, and the grass between my boots before I managed to get myself to cover.

A grin hitched on my lips as I caught my breath, and not just because Sellick was panicked and shooting worse and worse. I wouldn't put it past him to be twice as deadly in this state if he really set his mind to it, especially after seeing the look on his face a few times now.

That man looked mean enough to steal the coins off a dead man's eyes.

No, I grinned because I knew without a doubt that the long-haired, black-bearded companion whose rifle George had just stolen was one of the six murderers I'd been after.

My job just got that much easier.

Sellick fired two more times in my general direction, but then a wash of bullets flew between us. Five loud screams ripped through the night as our shooters doubled down on a group who'd tried to press forward to the house. I shot down two of their front men, swapped out my Remington for my third, and took down another man before two black and brown draft horses tore across the stretch of grass between me and the trees.

Finally, I chanced a peek toward the barn, and I found Sellick scrambling to grab the reins of a passing stock horse one of his men must've rode in on. He missed his chance and ended up dodging a volley of shotgun blasts instead, and he lost hold of his companion's rifle to boot.

The companion in question was currently sneaking into the shadowy entrance of the barn.

I narrowed my eyes, raised my gun, and fired.

The bearded murderer jolted as my bullet blasted through his shoulder. Then a second tore through his chest, and the man keeled over without a sound.

Sellick stepped right on his corpse as he lunged into the cover of the half-collapsed barn.

I moved to follow but got cut off by three of Delgado's men. One of them was bleeding from a large wound in his arm, and the other two were dragging him around the side of the house for shelter. A line of bullets ate up the dirt at their heels, and my eyes followed the trail so I could take out two men with repeating rifles.

The moment the group passed to safety, I checked my path and darted forward. Then I ducked into the barn, slid between two fallen beams, and silently pressed my back to the wall.

George's grating breaths echoed through the dusty air, so he hadn't fled just yet. I could hear him fumbling to reload his Army Model now.

He'd have six shots when he was done.

I only had my LeMat left.

I holstered my last spent Remington as quietly as I could manage and carefully swapped it for my LeMat. I considered waiting for a second shotgun blast somewhere outside to cover the cocking of my hammer, but I wanted this over and done with.

Now.

I cocked the hammer, and Sellick's haggard breaths went silent.

I let him stew in the notion that he wasn't alone in here, and then I finally spoke.

"Did you think it'd be that easy?" I asked.

A cylinder clacked into place, and a hammer cocked hastily before a bullet struck the wall above my head.

He had sharper skills than I'd like, but I didn't move a muscle.

A few more screams rose up outside, and a death wail split the night before a renewed hail of bullets broke out.

I used the noise to move myself over to the opposite end of the hay pile. I nearly tripped over a dead man I found there who must've gotten crushed when the barn collapsed. He wasn't one of our own, so I paid him no mind as I listened for the heavy breathing of my target.

"Who are you?" Sellick demanded in a slurring roar.

"You know who I am," I said.

The man must've reeled around. I heard him lose his balance, and an errant bullet was sent through the roof of the barn. Sellick swore and fired again, and this time, he managed to blast the corner off the nearest bale to me.

I ground my teeth and crouched a little lower.

"Yeah, I know who you are," the man drawled in a lazy sorta way. "You're that killer they thought they'd hire to keep me away."

He fired twice more at the same bale of hay, but I managed to shift backward and twisted under a nearby beam. Then I came up along the other wall, and I fired toward Sellick's side of the barn.

He screamed and fired blind, and I dove aside into the pigpen. I managed to get up over the siding while Sellick stumbled behind the hay pile for cover, and I sent two more bullets in his direction.

It sounded like he dropped lower just in time, but he still groaned and cursed several times.

"You done wasting bullets?" I asked.

I knew he had to be out, so I silently shifted past the pigpen and ducked behind a heap of roofing. From here, I could see Sellick's boot. He was sitting on the ground behind the hay bales, and judging by the blood all down his leg, I'd struck him somewhere above the knee already.

I took aim at his boot and sent a bullet through the ball of his foot.

The man screamed and rolled, but then a rifle cracked, and I felt a blast of air as a bullet whipped past my hat.

I rolled aside, and Sellick's drunken snickers filled the barn.

"Oh, I'm nowhere near done," he slurred and shuffled himself to his feet.

I immediately realized he must've found a gun on the dead man who'd been crushed back there. What kind of rifle it was, and how many rounds he had left to him, I had no idea.

This wasn't ideal.

The gunfire outside was dying down at least.

I shifted to the side and fought the urge to wince in pain as I spoke. "Your numbers are dwindling out there…"

Sellick snarled, but didn't reply. He was shuffling around now and dragging his bum leg and foot along with him.

"What do you think you're going to do as one man against all of us?" I continued and glanced through a gap in the rubble. "You can't possibly kill us all."

"The hell with all of you," the man snarled.

I fired the moment I zeroed in on his voice, but he returned a shot a split second later. I ducked lower to the ground as a chunk of barn roof scattered over my head. Then I silently turned and rose to my feet behind a diagonal beam.

"Y'all can live or die for all I care," Sellick snarled, and his slurring words seemed to drip with venom all of a sudden.

The notion sent an uneasy sensation across the back of my neck.

"But there's no way in Hell I'm letting even a scrap of this ranch survive," he said. "Not after what happened in Lawrence."

CHAPTER 28

A sudden chill trickled along every one of my limbs.

I'd heard about what happened out in Lawrence, Kansas. All of us had, and no one was proud who had half a heart.

The trouble between Missouri and Kansas had been building for some time by the time the war began. Lawrence especially held a prominent place among the strife, on account of its Free State-minded inhabitants.

That day in Lawrence, it had been one of the guerrilla groups who came down on them. Some Missouri boys numbering around four hundred and riding under the orders of a graybacked general. They'd rode into the sleeping town near dawn, just like Sellick, and by nightfall, death and destruction was all that remained.

Fires, looting, you name it, those guerillas let it loose on Lawrence. They'd targeted the black folks and the leaders of the Union-based troops there, but it was primarily civilians they killed.

Word had it, they murdered over a hundred unarmed men and boys of the Union that day. Just rode in en masse and left blood and smoke behind. One telling I'd heard said it was just shy of two hundred who were left for dead, while the survivors hid out in fields, rivers, and cellars to escape the terrors.

The notion put a sharp, bitter taste in my mouth.

There was war, and there was massacre, and what happened in Lawrence, Kansas was a cold-blooded slaughter if ever I heard one.

What survivors there were would never be the same, that much we all knew.

"Every one of them Johnny Rebs who led that raid had the same damn branding on them horses," George sneered, and it sounded like spittle flew from his mouth. "I saw each of 'em going by. I'd remember that branding anywhere."

He fired real quick before he'd even finished speaking, and the beam I was behind splintered just an inch above my head.

I ducked and slid silently back into the corner, and Sellick started ambling around the barn without a care. I could see the barrel of his rifle propped on his shoulder, and despite how much I disliked a careless, drunken shooter, I was relieved he was feeling so cocky.

That'd give me my opening.

"Then I come down to Silver City..." George drawled. "And there's Charles, up on the same filthy, graybacked mount, and offering me one just like it. Said it was the best stock money could buy... Traitor stock."

"The Sanduskys sold to both Union and Confederate soldiers," I said. "They were a neutral party, they didn't have any hand in–"

"They're traitors!" he screamed and pulled the trigger.

His bullet blasted through the wall that ran into mine, and I shifted to bring myself back around to the hay.

"They're traitors to this country, and they will die for the blood on their hands!" he bellowed drunkenly. "They will die the same burning, screaming deaths of everyone back in Lawrence, and I will raze this land the moment their ashes scatter across it! Every last one of them... Especially those kids he's got. No man who kills so many gets to keep their kids."

"Sandusky didn't kill anyone," I growled as Russel's young face came into my mind.

No. Not my mind. He was right in front of me.

My eyes darted back to the shadows over Sellick's corner of the barn, and there in the half-collapsed loft was Russel Sandusky. His young face was set in a grim expression beneath the brim of his father's hat, and he didn't move a muscle. The barrel of his Peacemaker was extended ever so slightly over the ledge of the loft, but he wasn't aiming at anyone.

He was watching the pair of us prowl around below, and hearing every hateful word that dripped from the mouth of the man who'd ordered his father's murder.

I hoped to God he didn't make a move and let this drunken, heartless man catch sight of him. He was a good shot, but Sellick was ruthless and fast.

The boy certainly wasn't ready for the likes of him.

"He was just a rancher supplying warhorses in this country's time of need," I said and kept Sellick's focus on my side of the barn. "Like so many others who saw what we needed out there and provided where they could."

"The hell you say!" he roared and jacked the lever on his rifle to send three bullets straight my way, one after the other.

I scrambled, jumped, and made it to the opposite corner without a scrape, and I managed to send a bullet back his way before my injured hip twinged. Then I staggered and slammed into the wall of the barn, but to my surprise, Sellick didn't fire toward the commotion.

He must've only had one or two shots left.

I was down to four, plus my one 18 gauge, although at this point, I'd much prefer to use just the one shotgun round on this drunken bluebelly and call it a day.

Killers like this required patience, though.

I slid silently along the wall until I came across Sellick's trail of blood. He'd lost plenty due to the four bullet holes in his arm and leg. It was a wonder he was still standing, let alone coming so close to hitting his target, but this all boded well for me.

As soon as I settled myself around the other side of the man, I risked a glance up into the loft. The nose of Russel's gun had vanished, along with his face.

It was time to end this.

I let the gunshots out in the yard fade from my notice as nothing but the rush of my own blood filled my ears. Then I drew a steadying breath as I looked around me and got a quick lay of any obstacles.

"You're just as bad as them," Sellick slurred as he knocked something over in passing. A bucket, by the sound of it. "Defending traitors and taking the lives of innocent men who only—"

"Ride with murderers?" I pulled the trigger.

I struck the wall just ahead of him on purpose to make him turn around. By the time he stumbled and raised his rifle in my direction, I'd already moved three feet to the left.

"Some of them who are murderers themselves?" I continued and fired again.

This time, I struck the pen just beside Sellick's elbow, and he whipped around, but didn't fire. His bleary eyes blazed with a deranged sort of fury as he tried to locate me in the dark remains of the barn.

By now, I was five feet further from where I'd been.

"No, I don't kill the innocent," I said real low. "And I don't defend traitors."

He still wouldn't shoot. He only had one bullet left, and while he'd turned my way, he couldn't see me behind an upturned trough.

"You just think you're squeaky clean, don'tcha?" he spat and readjusted his grip a few times. "You think you're a savior. A blessing on this earth... even while you spill the blood of the men who won this country. The blood of men who earned the right to root out every last one of you rebel scum and set you straight or wipe you out. Whichever comes first…"

I grinned as I finished silently stepping behind the hay pile one last time.

I'd made it all the way on the opposite side of him while he was carrying on, but I wouldn't shoot him in the back. I wanted to look this evil son of a gun in the eye when I finally scrubbed him from this earth.

"No… I don't think so much of myself," I said, and the man wrenched himself around to squint toward my shadows. "I'm just good at what I do."

"And what is that?" He jacked the lever on his rifle as he ducked behind a stall wall.

I took three steps around the hay bales.

"I'm a hunter," I said with a smile the man would never see.

From here, only my silhouette would be revealed against the glow of the hay.

But it was irresistible. Just as Sellick pivoted out of cover and turned his gun in my direction, I flicked the lever on my hammer down and pulled the trigger.

The blast of the LeMat's 18 gauge striking Sellick's forehead from only five feet away caused the top half of his skull to burst open. Tissue and shards of bone splattered all around as his stolen rifle dropped to the barn floor, and the bluebelly plummeted forward with a hard thud a few seconds later.

I slowly lowered my LeMat.

My hearing settled as my pulse quieted at last. Outside, horses whinnied in protest, and a few shots fired, but there were no more screams in the yard. The hollering of men further off, probably trying to flee deeper into the woods, was all I heard aside from the groaning and wheezing of injured men.

I walked forward and grabbed Sellick's shoulder. The blood from his shot-up arm squelched in my grip as I heaved him over onto his back, and I nodded at what I found there.

He was blasted open from the eyebrows up, but he looked like the same George Sellick, so there'd be no issues identifying him.

I stood up and holstered my LeMat.

"You can come on down," I said to the silent barn.

The floorboards in the loft creaked, and Russel slid along the broken beams to carefully lower himself to the floor beside me. He was covered in dust and had his Martini-Henry slung over his back. His Peacemaker was clutched in his hand, and he looked down at the bloody remains of George Sellick.

He didn't say a word, so I finally spoke.

"You didn't shoot him," I said as I eyed the young boy. "I thought you would, when I first saw you up there."

Russel shrugged. "Thought I would, too. But then he tried to kill you those few times, and I figured you deserved to put him down for that. Not me."

I considered the strange expression on his face.

"Bet you've never heard anyone talk quite like that," I said. "There was a lot of hate in that man."

Russel shrugged but didn't meet my eye.

"There's nothing wrong with hearing how bad a person is, and knowing you don't want nothing to do with them," I continued. "It's happened to me plenty of times."

"Really?" Russel looked up at me from under his father's hat. "With the men you hunt?"

"That's right." I nodded. "That feeling you got, that's your mind knowing it'd rather survive than not. That's smart. Truth be told, it takes a certain kinda stupid to look evil in the face and decide you'd like to poke at it. I happen to be that certain kinda stupid."

Russel snickered at this, and I smiled as he straightened up a bit.

"I'm not scared of much, but I was scared of him," he admitted. "The way he moved and talked... He had wicked-sharp aim, even when he was blinded by anger and drink. My Pa always said not to shoot mad or drunk. That you can't trust your aim or your trigger finger. But that man seemed like he could..."

"He could," I agreed. "That's why I tell you staying quiet up there and not giving him the chance to find you was smart. Especially because you knew I was there with you."

Russel smirked a little. "You looked kinda scary, too. Like a mountain lion stalking out in the hills. You moved real quiet and steady, and you looked real calm and unbothered about it. I've never seen a man disappear like that in the shadows."

"Yeah, well," I chuckled. "That's why I figure it's alright to be my stupid self sometimes. I might poke at evil, but I do it as carefully as I can. Now, there's a whole other kind of stupid that you'll probably be hearing about real soon from your mother... That I can't help you with."

"I was careful!" he scoffed at once, as if I was his mother scolding him already.

I held my hands up. "I'm not the one you've got to convince of that. I'm only saying, you had orders, and you went just about as against them as you could have."

"Guess that's why I'm a rancher, not a soldier," Russel sighed. "I don't take orders too well, I much prefer making my own way in things."

"I've noticed," I chuckled.

Russel grew a bit serious as he looked up at me. "I couldn't stand by, Mr. Callahan. Y'all were out here risking your lives for my family's land. For my land, one of these days. I ain't worthy of none of it, though, if I'm not brave enough to fight for it, am I?"

This wasn't really a question. That's what struck me the most.

Russel wasn't asking if I understood him, he was telling

me outright how he saw it, and I couldn't argue with his way of seeing things. He was a smart young man, but also a brave one, and I admired him for the strength of character he'd shown out here tonight.

"You're not wrong," I told him. "But if you want to live long enough to inherit all this land, I suggest you choose more carefully when to disappear from your mama. Word has it, she's a good shot, too."

"That is true..." Russel said with a sober nod. "Although, I did my fair share out here. I killed a whole–"

A volley of gunshots suddenly picked up.

I rushed outside without even thinking of the pain in my hip, but my leg was stiffening up now. I had to force it to keep going as I bolted through the yard and toward the side of the house.

I found three men grabbing a fourth, who was bloody and collapsed into their arms.

"I didn't see him," he hissed through clenched teeth.

Beyond the injured man, three more of Delgado's men were firing into the darkness, but then they stopped and listened.

"What happened?" I demanded.

"Some bastard fled that way," one of them muttered and gestured to the grassy stretch beside the woods. "Lost him, though."

"I didn't see him," the bloody man on the ground groaned. "The gunfire stopped, and I came to see if it was safe."

I looked down, and my stomach dropped as I realized this was the same shooter I'd sent out to the bunkhouse to guard the family.

My eyes darted toward the darkness again, and there in the field, not far from where the bunkhouse was barely visible beneath the tall pines, I saw a spark catch on a torch.

"The ladies," I gasped and shoved through the men in front of me.

The first hints of dawn glowed beyond the mountains ahead of me as I ran into the open stretch between the house and the flaming torch. I could hear men running behind me, but I didn't slow down long enough to look. I just tore past the large wooden cross of Frank Sandusky's grave and kept on running no matter how much my hip protested.

The escaped outlaw was stumbling toward the bunkhouse still. He was close enough that I could see the wooden siding in the glow of his torch, and I tore my LeMat from my holster. It only had two shots left, but I only had to make it another two dozen or so feet before I could trust my aim to strike true.

A shot cracked off then, and the torch fell.

My heart thumped like a war drum in my ears as I kept on running, but as lantern light suddenly glowed in the doorway, I slowed to a wincing hobble.

The five shooters on my heels came to a pounding stop with me. Then we all stared at the sight ahead.

In the dim light, we could see Helena's face and the barrel of her scattergun across her chest.

I couldn't help but grin.

CHAPTER 29

Smoke streamed from the muzzle of the woman's gun as she glared down at the lump of man who'd made it not twelve feet from the door. The disdain she had for him was clear, but there wasn't a single hint of fear on her beautiful face. Only the resolve of a woman who knows she's done what needed doing.

"I've got it from here," I said to the men around me.

They nodded in agreement and quickly headed back to help with the injured.

The torch had almost fizzled out by the time I limped over. I scraped my boot through the last embers and eyed Helena's quarry.

'Lump of man' was surprisingly accurate.

At such a close range, Helena's scattergun had turned the outlaw's chest into butcher meat. He was in enough of a state to turn even my stomach, but I managed to hold my own on account of the face above the carnage.

He bore a scraggly black beard and long black hair, and he had a jagged, triangular scar on his left cheek.

The very last of Mr. Sandusky's killers was finally put down.

I looked toward the bunkhouse.

Helena's eyes shone with worry as she watched me limp

out of the dull blue dawn. I imagined that the blood all down my leg, splattered on half my head, and also covering my left hand wasn't too reassuring, so I sent her a careless grin to try and ease her mind.

Then I gestured at the butchered outlaw over my shoulder.

"I was just about to get that for you," I said. "Guess you beat me to it."

Helena smiled, but before she could speak, Lucy gasped and shoved past her.

"Jesse!" she wailed as she lifted her skirts, lunged into the grass, and threw herself into my arms.

I couldn't have stifled my groan of pain for anything. Still, I did a decent job of staying on my feet while the singer squeezed me tight enough to realign a few sore spots in my spine.

Lucy gasped all over again as she realized I, and now she, was covered in blood.

"Jesse, what happened?" Her hands fluttered all over me. "Are you shot? You're bleeding!"

"Lucy, give him room," Helena said gently as she came over.

Honey quickly hurried out the door after her, and she had tears all down her face when she reached me. I didn't trust myself to crouch down without collapsing at this point, but I removed my hat and plunked it on her head to try and put a smile on her face.

"I'm alright," I assured them all. "The last of the raiders have been taken care of as well, so I'd say everything is pretty well settled out here."

"Settled my eye." Lucy propped her hands on her hips. "This ain't all raider blood you're wearing, I can see it running right out of you! Look!"

I glanced down at my hip, but then I decided it was probably better I didn't get a good look at it.

"I'll be fine," I said. "I think I've got a bullet in my hip, that's all."

"THAT'S ALL?" Lucy blurted out. "Jesse Callahan, you brave and noble idiot!"

I burst out laughing at that, and Honey giggled with me, but the frantic singer was worked up now.

"Sit down!" she insisted. "Or stay standing? Right? Lena, he's shot, what do we do? Oh, Russel! Jesse, Russel's missing, and we've been beside ourselves–"

"He's by the barn," I cut in. "He's alright, don't worry. Not a scrape on him, but he's been up to quite a lot tonight."

"Oh, thank the Lord," Helena sighed and clutched Honey's little shoulders. "I should've known he'd sneak off like that, but I thought with so much going on, he'd be smart enough to know it just was not the time to go against his mother."

Lucy snorted. "Are we talking about the same Russel?"

"He felt it was his duty to fight beside us, since we were all out there defending his family's land and whatnot," I explained. "He did well, too, but I'll certainly leave it up to you to decide how to proceed with this one…"

Helena nodded with resignation, but I could tell she was struggling to muster up any real anger about it. Her son was alive and safe, and her family and ranch had survived.

All her prayers had been answered.

"Let's get you to the house," she said as she looped her arm around my waist. "Lucy, get his other side, will you? Honey, you stay right next to Mama, okay?"

"Don't lose my hat," I told the little girl. "I can't do my job without it."

Honey nodded diligently.

"Yes, that's what matters most in times like this," Lucy said sarcastically as she settled herself under my free arm. "You wouldn't be half so intimidating to the men you hunt without the proper hat."

"That is the secret," I agreed through clenched teeth, and we started off.

The two women braced me up all the way to the house.

Sunrise was fully upon us by the time they let me down on the porch steps with Honey, and then Helena hurried inside to fetch her medical kit. Lucy made sure I was comfortable before going to help with the other injured men, and Honey planted a little kiss on my cheek to thank me for 'getting rid of all the bad men.'

"You're very welcome," I chuckled. "Wasn't half so hard as I thought it was gonna be, don't you worry."

She returned my smile with one twice as big, and the pair of us sat happily together as Mateo and Abel made their way toward us.

The pair made a big show of applauding when they saw me. Neither appeared to have taken a single scrape, and they smiled with the kind of tired pride I liked to see on their hardworking faces.

Of course, all around them, blood and bodies lay in the dirt, the grass, and behind just about every corner, but Delgado's men were all alive and accounted for. Aside from Bert. Five others were badly injured, but Hugh had already ridden for the doctor in Pinos Altos while I was out at the bunkhouse.

I'd call that a win, given the circumstances. Without a doubt.

"The hero of the day!" Mateo sang with one of his big, toothy smiles as he reached the porch. Then he gestured to all the blood. "I would worry for you, but you are smiling, and Honey is happy, so I know all is well. This is just how Jesse looks after a hard day's work, yes?"

Honey giggled and nodded so hard, my hat flipped into her lap.

"Oh, certainly," I snickered. "I oftentimes find myself marinating in blood and unable to stand. Does a body good."

Mateo laughed, and I joined in his amusement, but then I glanced at Abel.

"I owe you for helping out with that situation near the

stables, too," I told him. "Those men you shot at turned out to be Sellick and one of those Masters boys."

Abel's weathered face pinched into a smile, and he shook his Spencer rifle high above his head.

"You're a heck of a shot when you need to be," I agreed with a chuckle.

"Yes, he will be bragging like this for a long time," his brother sighed.

I snorted. "Where's Amos?"

"Cleaning up in the woods," Mateo replied. "He was the first to finally find an opening, of course. He knows that land well. You should have seen it. He looked like a fierce warrior leading the men in there. He ended things quickly after that. I shot some very bad men myself, but I admit, he shot more. He finished the last of them out there with some of Delgado's men."

"Of course he did." I smiled.

"But you caught up with Sellick?" the young ranch hand asked eagerly, and I assured him I'd taken care of the bluebelly, but that we'd discuss the details of it later.

For now, I wanted to sit and watch the first streaks of sunlight burst over the Black Spur Ranch.

There'd be plenty of cleanup, but I'd learned long ago to enjoy the blessed calm after so much violence, and I intended to do just that.

Of course, that was until a screeching bay broke out in the stables.

"Bonita! It's time!" Mateo gasped, turned on his heel, and took off with his legs pumping high and hard. "I am coming, mi cariño! Mateo is here! I will not abandon you for anything!"

Honey squealed with delight at the prospect of the new foal, but Abel looked plumb worn out on the day already.

The older Spaniard sighed and looked up at the sky, and he muttered something I didn't understand too well, but I caught 'big show' and 'princess' in there somewhere. Then he held out his hand for a very giddy Honey to take, and the duo left to help the bossy broodmare through her birth.

A healthy, purebred Morgan colt was born within the hour, and Honey named him Jesse. By then, the sun had fully risen, the doctor had arrived, and Russel finally mustered up the courage to face his family.

I had to admire the audacity of the kid.

He came whistling his way around the house and toward the porch while I waited with Lucy for my turn with the doctor. He behaved like it was any other day, and the pretty singer chucked half a loaf of bread at the young boy as soon as he was in range.

"What in the world were you thinking?" she yelled. "Shootin' up outlaws is no kind of work for a young boy!"

"Hey, I got 'em, didn't I?" Russel shot back. "Four of those fools. I got 'em real good from up in the hayloft, so I'd say it most certainly is the kind of work for--"

"Russel Sandusky!" His mama burst from the front door. "You killed four men?!"

"No, I defended my home from four no-good trespassers," Russel calmly replied. "And I was real careful about it, too."

He then went on to explain every shot and all the care he took before pulling the trigger each time based on where everyone was located, whether horses might get injured, and even if he thought the breeze might disrupt his aim. He spoke with the kind of attention to minute detail that only a twelve-year-old is capable of recalling, and his mama's eyes started to dance with amusement, despite her initial concern.

"Well," she huffed once Russel finally stopped to draw a breath. "That does sound like you were safe and responsible about things. Just…"

Her throat closed up as her eyes suddenly brimmed with tears. She came down the steps and pulled the young boy tightly against her, and she buried her lips in his unruly hair.

"Don't grow up too fast, alright?" I heard her mumble.

Russel looked annoyed and wriggled out of her arms.

"I've been grown for years, Mama," he scoffed. "And this here is serious business, protecting a ranch. Ain't it, Mr. Callahan?"

Helena sighed in exasperation and swiped her eyes. "Go tend to something, will you?"

"The bodies?" Russel nearly exploded with excitement. "I can help drag 'em all–"

"No, the horses!" his mother snapped. "Tend to the horses and just… Horses only, you understand?"

Russel groaned, but Lucy shot him a haughty smile as she got up and started prodding him toward the pastures. I didn't doubt she'd be watching over his shoulder for quite a while after what he'd done.

Poor kid.

"Lord, that boy just might be my greatest test," Helena said and dropped down onto the step beside me.

"He did well," I said gently. "He showed real skill, and more importantly, good judgment. You should be proud."

"I am," she whispered, and when she looked my way, her big blue eyes were swimming with tears again. "He's my baby, though. It's hard watching our babies grow up so fast in such a harsh place."

I nodded. "But it's a gift to be able to watch them do so."

My voice came out gruffer than I'd intended, but I cleared my throat hard.

Helena studied my blank expression for a long moment.

"It is." She blinked rapidly and looked away. "It truly is a blessing. And I am proud of him. And you. This whole mess has been so violent, and you had no reason to stay and handle things here for us, but you—"

"I had plenty of reason," I assured her in a firm tone. I had to grit my teeth to shift around so I could look at her properly, but then I held her gaze. "I want you to know what happened to your husband was unjust and unprovoked. He was a good and honest man who provided what he could for his country when the time came to do so. It's no one's place but God's to judge him, and the way I see it, George Sellick and those six men robbed the lot of you of years and years of well-earned happiness. I promise I had every reason to stay and see that proper justice was delivered."

Tears streamed silently down Helena's cheeks as she managed a small nod. Then I opened my arm to her, and she scooted closer to lay her cheek against my shoulder.

I held her quietly as the weight of the last several weeks gave way to the beginnings of peace, and neither of us moved for quite some time. I think we could both feel how nice things were going to be at the ranch from here on out, but I was also struck by the ease with which we naturally comforted one another, like we'd been acquainted much longer than was the case.

That was how things tended to go, though, when danger arrived and blood started spilling. Decorum and polite tendencies naturally gave way to good old-fashioned understanding and connection among folks.

And as I sat there– bloody, tired, and leaning on a good and beautiful woman– I decided I hadn't been so content in a long, long time. I was hundreds of miles from my true home, but against the odds, I'd enjoyed a little slice of something like it out here in the last few weeks.

Helena and I stayed there in comfortable silence as we watched the men gathering up discarded weapons, and the last of the horses being led into their pastures, including Flint.

That'd have to be my next task.

I narrowed my eyes at the gray-dappled stallion. He'd kept my tack and supplies safe all night, but I didn't reckon he was the right replacement for Birdy after all. He was certainly the highest quality mount I'd ever had the pleasure of riding, but in my line of work, I needed more than that. Luckily, I knew some ranchers who'd be able to help me out.

Finally, the doctor came up the steps. Then the good woman beside me held my arm and bore all my sweating and groaning through the painful process of digging a bullet three inches deep out of my hip.

I was just about ready to pass out by the time they laid me out somewhere soft and cool. Gentle hands caressed my face, and a cold, damp cloth was pressed to my sweaty forehead. I heard Honey whispering somewhere close by about how much better I did than Bonita, but then Lucy's skirts shuffled her out the door, and the room grew silent.

A heavy, merciful sleep was just about to fall over me when I heard Deputy Wallace's voice somewhere in the house. His spurs clinked their way toward me a moment later.

"Mr. Callahan?" he whispered rather loudly.

I managed to pinch an eye open. "I'm off-duty."

"Don't I know it," the deputy laughed and came closer. His eyes bulged at the bandaging around my pelvis, and he removed his hat as if he was standing beside my deathbed.

"It's not as bad as it looks," I sighed. "What can I do for you, Deputy?"

"I'll be out of your hair in no time, Mr. Callahan," he said hastily. "Just came by to get the details of everything and confirm the deaths. Brought the undertaker, too. Now I'm on my way down to Silver City myself to give Whitehill and Tucker the report on what happened out here. Mr. Robinson and Mrs. Sandusky explained it all to me, including how you got that Sellick yourself. Mr. Delgado's men recognized his… uh, face. I just wanted to check if there was anything in particular you'd like to put in about all this?"

"Yeah," I grunted and settled back in to sleep. "Tell Whitehill that Grant County owes me another payment. He'll like that."

The deputy snickered a bit, but agreed to deliver my message.

"You rest up quick now," he said on his way out. "The whole town's waiting…"

I forced my eyes open again. "Waiting? What for?"

"Why, for the killin' hand of the Black Spur, of course!" He flashed a smile. "Don't think just cause we're mountain folks we don't know how to show our gratitude. Miss Rosa's already got the whole town planning a celebration in your honor!"

CHAPTER 30

"Jesse, don't fill up on that breakfast," Lucy scolded me. "They're cooking up a whole feast over at La Casa Dorada."

"Hold on, how come y'all get to call him Jesse and I still gotta call him Mr. Callahan?" Russel demanded from the seat across from me.

"Because that's the respectful way to address gentlemen," his mother said as she put another flapjack on my plate. "Jesse, you eat as much as you want. You're still pale…"

"He's not pale, he's bored," Lucy sighed. "You can't cage a man like him too long, Lena, or they start to fade. Isn't that right, Jesse? He needs that open range and fresh wind on his cheeks."

The pretty singer sent me a glittering smile, and I smirked as I worked on my breakfast.

We'd be leaving the ranch in a couple hours to join the celebration the Vallejos family were throwing in my honor, and while I fully intended to enjoy every delicious bite of their cooking, I wasn't about to miss out on Helena's own fare.

The woman seemed intent on fattening me up, and I had half a mind to let her.

The last week had passed in a blur of repairs and cleanup. Those among Delgado's men who were fit enough stayed for another day after the attack to help out, but the injured were ridden back to Delgado's straight away with the local doctor. He'd been doing all he could for them there.

As far as my hip was concerned, it sure felt better once the doctor had dug the bullet out of it. He hadn't looked too pleased with the state of the wound, but he gave me laudanum for the pain and promised to check back in as regularly as he could.

I'd never quite liked that sort of medicine. I'd only been taking a small nip here and there when I truly couldn't stand the ache, but my lack of compliance made Helena so mad that she'd ended up insisting I stay in the house all week so she could look after me herself. She still let me pass on the laudanum as I saw fit, but she downright refused to yield in any other regard.

I would've preferred staying in the bunkhouse so I could help out where I could, but with the family all intent on seeing me rested and healed up, I'd resigned myself to shuffling back and forth on the porch and watching the ranch hands come and go all day long.

Today, I'd finally be allowed out again.

"But I should get to call him Jesse!" Russel's indignant voice caught my attention as he shot to his feet, even though it only afforded him an extra couple of feet in height. "We've got ourselves an understanding! We're on the level with one another, as men! We been shootin' together, and-and… We saw some things together, too! Right? That's a whole lot more than some flapjacks or bandages–"

"Excuse me?" Lucy gasped. "Russel Sandusky, did I just hear you put yourself above your own mother in this house?"

"I…" Russel shifted his weight, but he wasn't one to back down once he'd committed. "Maybe I am! I'm the man of this here house now, and–"

"Ha!" Lucy narrowed her eyes on the young boy, and her smile twisted into a mischievous grin. "You think you could do a better job of running this ranch already? Standing just three feet high and weighing no more than a sheep?"

"I weigh plenty more!" Russel's ears turned bright pink. "And I'm not three feet! I could do a mighty fine job runnin' this ranch!"

"Hmm... are you sure about that?" Lucy popped a small, round tomato in her mouth and chewed real slow as she held the young boy's gaze. "Because to my eyes... your mama's still a better shot than you are."

I rolled my lips to keep a smile from breaking across my face. She'd gotten the boy where it really hurt.

Russel was red all over now.

"Yeah, well, she- she–" He gulped in some air. "She's had longer to practice, and you don't know nothin' about it!"

With that, the boy stormed out of the room, and his feet smacked every wooden stair all the way to the second floor.

Lucy giggled, and Helena rolled her eyes, but she couldn't help laughing a little.

"You ought to stop teasing him," she said halfheartedly.

"Absolutely not," Lucy sighed and buttered her bread. "Boy's got a head bigger than anyone I know now that he's 'defended his land from no-good outlaws.' And his daddy didn't raise him to put himself above anyone in this family."

"True." Helena smiled sadly.

"He'll settle," I said. "Some boys gotta get real stubborn real young if they're gonna grow up knowing how to be patient with headstrong fools."

"Do you speak from experience?" Lucy cocked her head to the side.

"Not personally," I chuckled. "Just knew plenty of boys like him growing up."

"Hmm." The singer narrowed her eyes as if to challenge the truth of this, but then she returned to her meal. "Well, he better behave at the party today. I stopped in there yesterday, and Rosa says just about everyone is fixing to be there. Which means I'll of course be looking my very best, do not fret."

"I would expect nothing less," Helena said with a smile. "Can I get you more to eat, Jesse?"

"No, I'm full to bursting," I assured her.

"And how's your hip?" She chewed on her lower lip a bit. "Still too achy to sit for long?"

"It pinches a bit," I admitted. "But it'll be fine. Just need to get up and moving is all."

"So soon?" Lucy's green eyes looked worried.

"I meant today at the celebration," I said.

"Oh… good," she laughed. "I thought you meant you were moving on already. I was gonna say, I haven't even gotten around to paying you yet."

"You haven't?" Helena's blue eyes flared with embarrassment. "Lucy, after all he's done? You should've paid him ages ago–"

"I will," Lucy said a little anxiously. "It's only we're still working out the price."

"No we're not," I chuckled. Then I held out my palm to her and grinned. "In fact, I demand payment. Helena's right, it's long overdue."

"I'm sorry." Lucy glared at me. "I'm afraid I don't have it on me at present."

I cocked an eyebrow. "You're too famous not to carry just one little dollar on you."

"A dollar?" the lady of the ranch gasped.

It was at this time that I realized Lucy had hidden the details of our agreement from her sister-in-law. I would've felt for the singer after being exposed, but the daggers her eyes were shooting my way didn't leave much room for remorse.

After all, she'd shaken on the deal, so done was done, in my eyes.

I couldn't resist snickering at the look on her face.

"Pay him more than that," Helena hissed.

"I'm trying to," Lucy growled back. "He won't let me!"

"That is true," I said.

Helena was mortified at the thought. I could tell she was about to launch into a very logical and well-meaning speech about what was due to me after all that had taken place, but then a twelve-year-old boy with a woman's bustle tied around a stick like a flag entered the room.

I did a double take.

Russel grinned without remorse as he planted the stick on the floor with a loud thump.

"You weren't using this silly fluffy thing, right?" he asked his aunt.

Lucy gasped and shot to her feet. "Russel Sandusky, you give me that bustle back right now! Don't you know to leave a lady's things alone?"

Russel stuck his tongue out and bolted for the door.

"Why you…!" Lucy bolted right after him.

Honey squealed with laughter as she rushed onto the porch, and her mama and I were right behind her once I got to my feet.

The young boy had already cleared one of the wooden fences, and Lucy hitched her skirts way up to her thighs before jumping after him.

My eyebrows shot up at her careless display of her stockings and the little garters that held them up, but I supposed I wasn't surprised. She didn't seem to care that her fancy hair had tumbled loose, either, or that all the household could hear the colorful threats she was promising the young boy.

Russel turned around to taunt her with the bustle again, and Lucy doubled down and put on a burst of speed.

I tried to recall the last time I'd seen a lady dressed so well and running as fast and wild as a loose pup. My mind came up blank.

Mateo and Abel were out in the same pasture gathering

two horses up, and when they saw the pair streaking by, they started hollering for Russel to hurry up.

Abel in particular seemed deeply invested in the boy's fate. He took off his hat and started smacking it on his own thigh like this would hurry the boy along, but I didn't reckon he stood a chance.

His wiry arms were pumping hard as the bustle flew all around on the stick, and Lucy didn't slow down even as they started up the hill ahead of them. The pair disappeared from sight after that, and Helena laughed heartily as she shook her head.

"That boy deserves what he gets for that one," she sighed. "I've told him about ten times to mind his own."

"Is that ten times this week, or today?" I grinned.

"Today," she laughed.

A while later, they came back over the hill. Lucy was perched bareback on the back of a white Tennessee Walker, with her bustle flag proudly propped against her shoulder. She kept her nose high, too, while Russel slumped along behind her mount.

At least they'd returned with enough time to prepare for the party.

It was an affair the entire family was eager about. The ranch hands had all bathed and put on their best, and I joined them in my city vest and the only pair of pants I had left to me at the moment. We hitched two draft horses up to the wagon for this one, but I made sure to give my mules a few of Mateo's carrots to make up for it.

Amos had ridden out to Delgado's the day before and asked to borrow a few men off them as guards, and once they arrived to keep an eye on the place, the family piled into the Sanduskys' biggest wagon.

Amos and Abel rode along with us on horseback while Mateo and I sat in the back of the wagon with Russel, and the ladies took the wagon bench with Honey between them.

The ride through the foothills and up into Pinos Altos was a merry one now that everyone felt safe again. The children laughed and pointed out all the birds they saw along the way, and I taught them the names I'd learned for them during my travels.

The women found all this fascinating, but the kids soon became restless. Mateo and I just did our best to keep them from climbing all over and rumpling their outfits before we arrived.

As soon as we reached the livery, the men and Russel jumped to the ground. They helped the ladies down as well, and I scooted myself to the edge of the wagon before easing my way down to the street.

Lucy immediately looped her arm with mine. She carefully steered me up onto the boardwalk as the others gathered their things to follow.

"You don't have to help me," I told her.

"Hmm?" she asked innocently.

I sighed. "I can walk just fine."

"Who said anything about helping you?" She arched an eyebrow at me. "I happen to look fantastic on your arm, and I did say I'd look my very best, didn't I?"

I chuckled at the shameless little smile she sent to all the other ladies looking our way, especially because I knew without a doubt that the singer was worried about me. She'd been letting Helena tend to me all this time, but at every turn, Lucy had been anxiously fluffing pillows, reheating water for fresh tea, and generally lingering in the background just in case a fly happened to bother me or something.

"Lucy just can't go anywhere without a parade, that's all," Russel said with a big eye roll. "She's too famous for her own good."

"Well, in that case…" I grinned. "We'd best get you inside, Miss Kimber. Your public awaits, and all that."

"That's better," she laughed and tossed her perfect auburn ringlets.

Then she let me pretend to escort her while I hobbled down the thoroughfare and up the steps into the lively celebration already starting up in La Casa Dorada.

"It's him!" a man called over the crowd. "It's Jesse Callahan!"

Cheers broke out, and a swarm of locals surrounded me and the residents of the Black Spur Ranch. Hugs and hellos were exchanged all around, and it eventually took Rosa and both her parents coming over to free us from the entryway.

Rosa seemed to glow all over when she saw me, but she didn't make such a fuss like everyone else. She just calmly put herself between me and the wall of people trying to press themselves closer to my side, and I offered her a grateful smile.

Shasta and Diego Vallejos announced our arrival to the rest of the saloon and welcomed us on behalf of Pinos Altos. They lined the long countertop with a whole spread of colorful foods, and they invited everyone to enjoy themselves as long as they liked.

Then Lucy happily took a spot beside the piano to kick things off. She sang a light and cheerful tune that would never be heard anywhere so fancy as an opera house. She still sang it with her whole heart, though, and I could see in her green eyes how much joy she found in bolstering people up and spreading merriment through song.

Her voice captivated absolutely everyone in the room, and she graciously obliged when the patrons kept requesting songs of the famous woman.

In the meantime, Russel and Honey went off to run all over the place with the other children, and Helena and the ranch hands worked on greeting all of the neighbors.

Rosa kindly snuck me away and walked with me to the bartop.

"I am pleased you came to celebrate with us," she murmured softly. "I was worried when Lucy said you were badly hurt."

"I'm not hurt too bad," I assured her. "And I certainly wouldn't miss a gathering like this, even if you've done far more than was needed."

"Have I?" was all she said, but the lack of concern in her tone got a chuckle out of me.

"The townsfolk seem happier than ever," I said. "I imagine that was your real aim…"

Rosa sent me a private smile as she blushed a little.

"Speaking of aim," she said instead of answering, "You will have to tell me one day what the real account of everything is. I fear there is no one else I can trust to stick to the facts."

"No?" I asked as we reached the counter. "What have I been up to out there?"

"Well… let me see." She smirked as she pulled her long, chocolate-brown hair over her shoulder. "Already, I have heard that you killed all of the raiders yourself with ease."

"Naturally," I replied, and she giggled softly.

"I also heard that you killed none of the raiders, forced them to surrender, but then sent them into the woods to be found by the Apache," she continued.

"No, that's a little grim for my liking," I said with a frown as her mother came over with a fresh beer, a steaming dish of chile con carne, and a side of sopaipillas for me.

"Here you are, Mr. Callahan," Shasta said with a bright smile. "Plenty more is coming, too, so eat up!"

"Thank you kindly, ma'am," I said in earnest.

Rosa rearranged the setting to look just right before turning that same warm smile my way.

"I agree, I find that tale too dark for a man like you," she said. "That is why I choose to believe the most likely story."

"And what is that?"

"That you rode out of the Black Spur entirely alone,

prowled the foothills for days, and one by one, murdered the fifty men closing in on the Black Spur Ranch."

A slow smile spread over my face. "That one. That's how that went."

"I expected so," she said with a small nod.

"Now, the real shame of it is that I didn't have you out there to help me," I said. "I could've used your… expert talents against those forty men."

"Fifty," she corrected.

"Precisely. Those eighty men wouldn't stand a chance against you."

That one got a full laugh out of the mysterious woman.

She threw her head back as the warm, husky laugh drew the attention of every man in the vicinity, and their eyes burned with envy, as if they'd been trying for years to get a laugh like that out of Rosa.

Heck, most of them probably had.

"Well," she said as her amber eyes met mine. "Perhaps I will have to lend a hand the next time you rustle up as much trouble around here…"

She sidled away without another word, and I was left with a wonky smile on my face.

After that, I did all I could to talk with everyone who came my way. Older ladies with their pretty daughters seemed to make up a lot of the guest list, but there were plenty of miners, cowhands, and merchants from the area who came out to shake my hand and hear about the raid.

Luckily, Gilly and Mateo were prepared to wow everyone with their accounts, and I was grateful for their commitment. Their loud, boisterous retellings in the corner of the saloon kept me from having to repeat myself over and over, but the more times they shared the tale, the more people seemed to show up to hear it.

I listened in once in a while to make sure they weren't

getting too colorful with the details, but mostly, I just laughed and enjoyed it.

"You look better already!" Deputy Wallace clapped a hand on my shoulder in greeting.

"Good to see you, Deputy." I turned and tapped my hat. "I feel much better. Got some healing to do, but I'm not too worried about it."

"Good, good," the deputy said. "I've got a couple telegrams here for you from Silver City, but it's nothing too pressing. Just wanted to be sure you got them straight away."

I took the slips and nodded my thanks.

There was a telegram from Sheriff Whitehill, and another from Captain Charles Sellick himself.

The captain certainly seemed determined to live up to his rank. He expressed his deepest apologies and sympathies, and the shame and scorn he felt over his brother's actions were made quite clear. He offered any and all reimbursement Mrs. Sandusky should want, along with just about anything the new widow might need, and he even insisted on sending his personal doctor to tend after all the wounded, particularly myself.

The sheriff's telegram was much less verbose. He merely informed me of the sum of the reward money Grant County owed me for any wanted men among George Sellick's posse.

"That's the full sum, too, for all the wanted, including the new charges," the deputy said as he gestured to the paper I was reading. "The sheriff went over to Delgado's and tried to parse out the reward among the men who helped y'all out, but they wouldn't have any of it. I guess Delgado threw him off his land over it. Not sure what that's about, but fair is fair. Looks like all that bounty is yours... I sure can't think of anyone who deserves it more."

Deputy Wallace shook my hand with a proud look about him before he headed off to talk with Lucy.

I glanced back down at the bounty Delgado had made certain Whitehill paid entirely to me.

Seven hundred and eighty-three dollars.

It wasn't quite my largest bounty to date. The Hobbs brothers still held that honor, unless I lumped Jeb Osiah and Petey McCaw into things. That seemed like cheating, though.

Regardless, it was more than I'd expected. In one fell swoop, I'd made myself a pretty penny on this one, and all in all, I'd be coming out of the Black Mountains a richer man for it.

The notion sent a sprinkling of excitement over me as I briefly wondered where to set my sights next. There'd be banking to do, and plenty of clothes to mend or replace. Not to mention replacing Birdy, deciding what to do with the mules...

I glanced across the gold-clad room of La Casa Dorada, and that anticipation I so regularly eased into right about now suddenly shifted to something else.

Helena was speaking with some neighbors, but her eyes were already on me when I looked her way. She had a soft smile on her lips, and not far away, Lucy giggled with some local girls. Rosa was calmly listening to every word the old-timers at the other end of the counter were saying to her, and all the while, her delicate hands moved deftly to polish the bartop and replace their drinks.

I looked around next at the folks who'd gathered at La Casa Dorada for the celebration.

I recognized the faces of all the Sanduskys' neighbors, Gilly, and some regular rubberneckers from town. There was also the gossiping counter clerk and her Postmaster husband, and scores of other folks who wanted to join in the fun and get a look at the man who brought the Hobbs boys in, ran the rustlers out, and defended the legacy of the greatest horseman in these parts.

I'd be a cold-hearted fool not to feel how nice it'd be to

stay around the area for a while longer. Strictly speaking, nothing too pressing was spurring me on, either.

Before I could think further on it, a big and tall man with a big, sandy-blond beard shuffled into the party, with a few of his best shooters behind him.

I recognized each of the men Delgado had brought along with him as some who'd helped us defend the Black Spur Ranch. The group smacked the dust from their chaps and vests as they eyed the gathering of locals, and Delgado grinned through his cigar smoke when he saw me by the counter. Then he slowly made his way over and stopped a few times to shake a hand or offer a lady a respectful bow of his head.

"Not bad, Killer," he chuckled in that gravelly way of his as he made it to my end of the counter. "Not bad at all."

He reached out a hand, and I shook it in return. His grip was firm and deeply callused, with rough splits in the pads of his fingers that scraped like nettles.

"Heard you got a hitch in your step." He gestured to my hip. "Got a good doctor for it?"

"As a matter of fact, Captain Sellick of Silver City will be sending his private doctor up to take a look at it," I said with a grin.

"Of course he will," the cattleman chortled. "He don't want you coming after him next. You managing alright?"

"Pain's settled down," I assured him. "I just prefer to stay on my feet for now, at least until sitting isn't so unfriendly."

He snorted at that.

"My men had a lot to say about what went down out there," he said as he braced a boot against the brass bar beneath the counter. "Sounds like you had a heck of a mess to take care of."

I chuckled at his particular way of putting it. Then I explained the basic rundown of things from my side, and the cattleman listened carefully to each word.

When I'd finished, Delgado grinned real wide with his cigar still clamped between his teeth.

"Miss Rosa, please bring this man a fresh drink on me," he called down the counter, and the woman smiled as she went to oblige the request. "I can't recall the last time I heard a tale quite like it. I tell you, it's just the sort of thing Frank would've gotten a kick out of hearing."

He drew a deep breath, and I caught the slight rattling sound his lungs gave off. He looked suddenly older as sadness washed over his face, but then Rosa returned with not one, but two fresh juleps.

Delgado smiled at once and thanked the woman graciously before sliding one of the glasses my way. He raised his own.

"To friends," he said. "Old and new."

"To friends."

We drank, and the julep sparked across my tongue with a tang that sure put my hip even further out of mind.

"So, where you headed next, Killer?" Delgado asked.

I shrugged. "I haven't decided just yet. I need to find me a new horse first."

"I think I know a good spot," he deadpanned.

"After that, I suppose I'll see where I'm needed most," I continued. "Same as usual."

"Uh-huh…" He puffed his cigar and sent a rather pointed look past me.

I turned and saw Helena and Lucy were now at the counter, and they were fussing over a heaping plate of food that I had a feeling Rosa was about to bring my way.

"Don't say it," I muttered before Delgado could start in about me finding a wife.

"How many good-looking strangers you think come through here that ain't already married?" he scoffed. "The rest are either scabbed, scrawny, scary, or all three. Now, you wanna talk about doing a duty for your country, well… I'd say the country's in need, boy."

He gestured again toward where Rosa, Lucy, and Helena all spoke in a friendly way among each other.

They were each done up beautifully today, it hadn't escaped my notice. I'd realized earlier this morning that Helena was wearing the deep purple gown with the black lace that had momentarily caused a lapse in my manners the other day. Lucy's bustle was back in place and making her look like the height of sophistication in a crisp white ensemble, especially with her soft auburn hair cascading down the back of her head.

Rosa had clearly spent some of her well-earned bounty money on a new embroidered skirt that was a shade of gold I'd never seen before, and it made her look as warm and inviting as the sun itself.

Together, the three women made up the nicest view in the region, and with all their friends and relations gathered around them, they were the very picture of feminine class and goodness.

I shook my head before I thought any further on all this.

"Then there's that boy's ranch," Delgado continued. "Plenty more trouble could come their way before Frank's son is old enough to take on so much. Someone's got to keep a tight hold on it for him until then. And that someone's got to be ready for anything."

I was about to reply, but then a ruckus struck up down the street.

The cattleman craned his neck to look out the front window, and I followed his gaze.

Three men on horseback were tearing down the main thoroughfare like a dam had broke. Hugh was among them, so it was no surprise that they stopped outside La Casa Dorada, but I furrowed my brow at the frantic way they dismounted and ran for the entrance.

"Delgado!" Hugh called out as he burst through the door.

The cattleman gave a harsh whistle and waved the men

over, and the three riders made straight for us. The others who'd arrived earlier with him also beelined through the crowd and joined in the discussions.

"Is that new blood or old blood on that vest of yours?" Delgado asked Hugh the moment he reached us.

The cattleman was sharp. I hadn't even seen the splatter of red on the man's dark brown vest. A few more drops were scattered on his inner right sleeve as well.

"New," Hugh replied. "A whole outfit came down on the ranch about an hour after you rode out. Must've been about fifty or sixty of them."

"Son of a bitch." Delgado chucked his hat onto the counter. "How many we lose?"

"Looks like about a thousand head were let out and run to the–"

"Not the cattle, damn it, the men," Delgado growled.

Hugh swallowed and nodded in understanding. "Four-teen, sir."

The cattleman nodded real slow as the folks nearest to us got quiet. I raised my brow as I watched the bearded man's expression shift quickly from sadness to irritation.

"See now, this right here..." He snatched his broad-brimmed hat back off the counter. "This is why I don't come into town anymore. This shit right here."

With that, Delgado shoved his hat on his head and stormed toward the door. Hugh and the other riders followed closely on his tail, but the cattleman stopped abruptly at the entrance and turned back.

"You're on my payroll for this one, Killer," he called and pointed in my direction. "I'll see you at the pass bright and early."

All at once, I felt the eyes of half the saloon turn my way.

The answer seemed simple.

"I'll be there," I said with a nod.

"Good..." The cattleman gave a dark chuckle that echoed behind him as he left the saloon with his posse in tow.

I chuckled as well while I finished my julep.

Looked like I'd be sticking around a little longer.

END OF BOOK 1

Made in the USA
Columbia, SC
02 January 2025

50958227R00198